Don Diego Vivar Stepped Briskly into the Big Front Bedroom . . .

"Oh, it *is* you!" Carolina cried. She threw herself into his arms and silenced anything he might have to say with her soft eager lips . . .

His lips left hers and trailed tantalizingly down her white throat, across her smooth bosom, he was loosening the hooks that held her bodice, it was slipping away . . .

He swept her up into his arms, and fell with her onto the big square bed. The moments sped by—delicious golden moments snatched from time. She had lost Kells, but she had him back again! Every breath, every rasp of his skin against her own thrilled her.

"Oh, Kells," she whispered. "I thought—that you were dead."

"Señorita," he said regretfully, "it seems you have mistaken me for somebody else. I am Diego Vivar, late of Castile . . ."

D0684159

by *New*

Valerie Sherwood

"ONE OF THE TOP FIVE MOST WIDELY READ AUTHORS IN THE UNITED STATES TODAY."

—*Winston Salem Sentinel*

Books by Valerie Sherwood

Lovesong
Windsong
Nightsong

Published by POCKET BOOKS

Most Pocket Books are available at special quantity discounts for bulk purchases for sales promotions, premiums or fund raising. Special books or book excerpts can also be created to fit specific needs.

For details write the office of the Vice President of Special Markets, Pocket Books, 1230 Avenue of the Americas, New York, New York 10020.

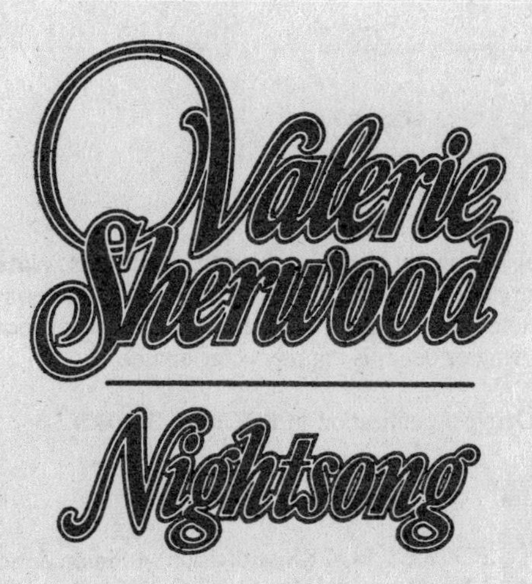

PUBLISHED BY POCKET BOOKS NEW YORK

This novel is a work of fiction. Names, characters, places and incidents are either the product of the author's imagination or are used fictitiously. Any resemblance to actual events or locales or persons, living or dead, is entirely coincidental

Another *Original* publication of POCKET BOOKS

POCKET BOOKS, a division of Simon & Schuster, Inc.
1230 Avenue of the Americas, New York, N.Y. 10020

Copyright © 1986 by Valerie Sherwood
Cover artwork copyright © 1986 Elaine Duillo

All rights reserved, including the right to reproduce this book or portions thereof in any form whatsoever. For information address Pocket Books, 1230 Avenue of the Americas, New York, N.Y. 10020

ISBN: 0-671-49839-8

First Pocket Books printing September, 1986

10 9 8 7 6 5 4 3 2 1

POCKET and colophon are registered trademarks of Simon & Schuster, Inc.

Printed in the U.S.A.

WARNING

Readers are hereby warned not to use any of the cosmetics, unusual food, medications or other treatments referred to herein without first consulting and securing the approval of a medical doctor. These items are included only to enhance the authentic seventeenth-century atmosphere and are in no way recommended for use by anyone.

DEDICATION

In loving memory of Tarbaby—son of Princess, my very first cat—lovely Tarbaby of the gleaming black fur and brilliant green eyes; vivacious Tarbaby, who whirled gracefully high up into the summer air, trying to catch butterflies—always a second too late; Tarbaby, who gave back the challenge of the mocking jays who screeched at him from the tree branches above the grapevines; Tarbaby, who played with me so joyously along the maze I constructed in the deep snows of our garden one winter; Tarbaby, who was always gentle with me and yet kept all the dogs in the neighborhood cowed—to Tarbaby, bright companion of my youth, this book is dedicated.

AUTHOR'S NOTE

In this rousing tale of the exciting 1600's, I bring to you the wild adventures—both amorous and desperate—that now befall that reckless Colonial beauty, Carolina Lightfoot, and her gallant buccaneer lover, Captain Kells.

Their tempestuous story is set in the Golden Era of that Colonial center of trade and fashion, old Port Royal. In reconstructing this interesting seventeenth-century town—and I have been meticulous as to streets, topography, the location of its various forts and shops, etc.—I have employed ancient records and maps and the latest archaeological research, but I have tried as well to recapture and bring to you in vivid life the exuberance, the extravagant gaiety, the rich fashions, indeed the whole glamorous way of life being enjoyed when this fabled port of the West Indies was at its height, its harbor flapping with the sails of many nations, its handsome four-story brick residences and enormous warehouses bursting with the booty of golden galleons, its sandy streets rattling with buccaneer cutlasses. The old port is given to you in all its infamous glory—a jewellike setting for that jewel of the Caribbean, Carolina Lightfoot, the dazzling Silver Wench of the Spanish Main.

Although the characters and events in this story, save for those noted here, are entirely of my own imagination, I have relied heavily upon historical detail. For example, the short wild voyage of that gallant frigate, the H.M.S. *Swan*, did indeed take place, and Hawks's mind-boggling adventure, which seems well nigh incredible, is based upon the actual experience of one Lewis Galdy, Esq., which is carved in stone—indeed Hawks's epitaph is borrowed almost intact from Galdy's headstone in a Port Royal churchyard.

Even Moonbeam the cat's decorous dining, course by course, at the family dining table in Essex to the delight of invited guests, is based upon an actual cat from English history whose devoted owner enjoyed her pet's company so much that she trained the cat in "good table manners" and allowed her to sup with the family.

As to Acting Governor John White, he was indeed acting governor of Jamaica at the time, and an eyewitness account of the Rector of St. Paul's Church, one Dr. Heath, places him on board the ship *Storm Merchant* where my heroine finds him, but whether he continued governing from aboard her I have no idea; indeed I was able to learn nothing about Acting Governor White, save that he drank wormwood wine! So everything concerning him and his family is entirely of my own invention—I hope I have not unduly maligned him.

You will also find in these pages a faithful recording of one of the great catastrophes of the Western World—and I have spared no effort in delving into historical and archaeological research, using eyewitness accounts wherever possible, to bring it to you in all its fantastic panorama. Where fact could not be established, I have of necessity relied upon invention. For example, I was able to find out what the weather had been preceding the event—but not after.

As to "Diego Vivar," both Spanish intelligence and Spanish records were very good in the time period of my novel, and he could easily have met his end in such a place and in such a manner.

When the buccaneers lost their foothold in Jamaica, they really had nowhere to go. Tortuga was unattractive by comparison—and it was French (France and England were engaged in naval warfare at the time). Those buccaneers who were left— and remember that many were at sea at that time—regrouped and headed for the numberless low sandy cays of "The Shallows," which today we call the Bahamas. The town they flocked to was the pirate base of Charles Towne on New Providence Island, which in 1690 had come to be called Nassau. Although the migration of the buccaneers to the Bahamas really marked the end of buccaneering as it was in Morgan's time (Morgan was four years dead when the buccaneers left), the pirates of Nassau (which had become in all probability the wildest town anywhere) continued to roam the Straits of Florida and to haunt the Windward Passage and the Mona Passage. There were several attempts to uproot them, and it is of one of these, a combined attempt of the French and Spanish to subdue these fierce sea rovers, that I write—although I have set the date a little earlier than it actually happened, the better to fit my story.

In the attack herein described, the men—those that could be caught—were promptly slaughtered, the women taken as slaves to Havana. And so it is also of old Havana that I write, in the days when brooding El Morro, standing guard over Havana harbor, was just over a hundred years old, and pirates and buccaneers alike were hanged without mercy and without regret on the Plaza de Armas.

Although the Spanish may not have planned to raid Jamaica in 1692, it was certainly believed that they did plan to raid Jamaica and drive the English from the West Indies in Morgan's time, and it was Governor Modyford who, realizing there was no English fleet to help him, persuaded Morgan to collect the buccaneers and mount a raid on Porto Bello, thus keeping the Spanish occupied with other matters than invasion of their neighbors. Thus, although the timing is a little off, the situation I have described—though imaginative—could well be an accurate one. Spies *were* sent in to assess military might then as now, and could not one of those spies be handsome—and susceptible to a woman as beautiful as Carolina?

Perhaps my family background predisposes me to a special interest in buccaneers—and other valiant patriots who in times past have fought for their country in unorthodox ways. For my maiden name was McNeill. I am the great-great-great-granddaughter of Captain Daniel McNeill of whom young George Washington wrote in a letter (duly preserved and framed in the Library of Congress) from Winchester, Virginia, that Captain Daniel McNeill across the mountain could furnish him with three hundred men (for Dunmore's War). During my Pentagon years, I took pleasure in researching in the Army Library the seafaring efforts of a later Captain Daniel McNeill, privateer, who sailed his own vessel to North Africa to subdue the Barbary pirates on behalf of his country. And it was pleasant to realize, when in residence at Dragon's Lair in Washington, D.C., that but a few short blocks away was the home of Stephen Decatur, one of our country's heroes, who had sailed as a young officer under that same Captain Daniel McNeill. Somehow it brought history close and privateers even closer. And Captain Dan'l, as family tradition calls him, would surely—had he lived in buccaneering times—have been a buccaneer!

As to the buccaneers, those myriad unfortunates who sought exile for political reasons, many of whom—like the hero of my story—had felt the jaws of Spain clamp down upon them and been brushed by the dread fires of the Inquisition, how they must have savored their gains against a nation that had driven them from island to island and tried to sweep the seas clear of them! It was the buccaneers (who by rights should be called "privateers" since they fought no flag but Spain's) who saved the West Indies from Spanish invasion and kept those lovely islands of the British, French and Dutch from becoming mere links in a necklace of Spanish might that girdled the Western Hemisphere!

And ask yourself, without the buccaneers, could we have held *our* coast? How thinly scattered then were our tiny Colonies along the east coast of North America! Had Spain swept the Caribbean clean of opposition, what then?

I say we owe a debt to these buccaneers. A debt that will never be repaid, true, but at least we can honor them in memory. This may well be the last novel I ever write with a buccaneering background—that background I love so well!—so I invite you now to sail with me into the glories of a lost world, to learn its secrets and thrill to its challenges.

Should anyone ask "Who speaks for the buccaneers?" they will assuredly have their answer:

I speak for the buccaneers!

Do you speak of buccaneers?
Oh, remember them with tears,
Those men we hanged 'twixt high tide and the low,
For we owe them all so much,
We, the British, French and Dutch,
Those men that we dishonored and brought low!
For they saved the Indies then
And though they were desperate men,
They'll be recalled wherever trade winds blow,
Their stories sung wherever free men go,
Their ghosts sail out across the sunset's glow. . . .

—Valerie Sherwood

CONTENTS

Nightsong

PROLOGUE
PORT ROYAL, JAMAICA

Spring 1692

In love's fair arms they lie tonight,
Embracing in the pale moonlight,
Convinced no earthly storm could sever
Their bonds of love, drawn taut forever!

Beneath a pale moon that shed its light upon Jamaica's southern coast, a slender curving sandspit cut like a scimitar into the deep dark sapphire of a night-silvered sea. Scattered across that white waste of sand and cut off from the mainland by a gloomy mangrove swamp, evil in the half light, lay the wickedest city in the western world—Port Royal, home port of the buccaneers.

On Queen's Street, a block from the waterfront down Sea Lane, the trade winds blew softly through the open second-floor windows of a handsome brick house and cooled with scented breezes the gleaming bodies of the dark-haired man and the moonlight-blonde woman who tumbled in wild embrace upon the big carved bed.

The lean buccaneer who sprawled there with his lady was accounted the best blade in all the Caribbean. He was the notorious Captain Kells, whose name resounded like a great gong across the Spanish Main. A name the very mention of which caused the captains of

Spanish treasure galleons to blanch or redden angrily according to their natures. The pale moonlight gilded his long muscular legs, his narrow buttocks and broad handsome back, and cast in shadow his hawklike sardonic face just now so intent.

For the lady he clasped so fervently in his arms was the light of his life—and he knew he soon must leave her.

She trembled and sighed against him. A soft moan escaped her lips and his hard face softened as he pressed tender kisses upon her smooth hot cheeks. And from his heart went up a silent prayer to a God he no longer believed in that she would be safe in this wild town in which he must leave her.

She was not, he knew, apt to go unremarked.

For the woman he clasped in his arms, her lissome body silvered by moonlight, her hair a starlit mass spread out upon the pillow, wore the most famous face in all Port Royal. Endless stories were told of her: of her breathtaking beauty (apparent to all and staggering to those who first glimpsed her). Of her wild but aristocratic past (much exaggerated by gossips, who ever choose to believe the worst). Of her tempestuous romantic entanglement with the most dangerous sea rover of all in a port populated by dangerous sea rovers—Captain Kells (all too true!).

Some said he had married her, some said he had not. Others laughingly maintained that he was an insatiable bridegroom and so determined had he been to bind her to him that he had married her again and again: On Tortuga, in Virginia's Tidewater from whence she came, in Essex, in London—even in the Azores. And some of the stories were true.

But true or not, she would ever be the bride of his heart.

All Port Royal envied him her favors. They called her—affectionately, these buccaneers from so many nations—the Silver Wench, and in the moonlight she was more than lustrous, she was magnificent. Her sweet young body (she was only one-and-twenty) fitted sublimely to the sinewy lines of her tall determined lover and they lay locked in ecstasy, oblivious to the wild carouse that as usual was making the nighttime streets of Port Royal horrendous with noise.

Even though the clocks had all chimed midnight, the din of carousing in the rows of taverns had scarcely diminished—indeed, many had roared to greater fervor as men who had come by their gold in mortal combat lightly gambled it away or tossed it to the nearest inviting wench for her favors.

But the singing and the yelling, the clatter of tankards and the rattle of cutlasses, the howls and tinny laughter, came only faintly to the tall brick house on Queen's Street, and the pair who strained upon the big square bed heard it not at all.

Their concentration, sublime in its intensity as they shuddered in ecstasy and then drifted down from the heights, was only upon each other—and on the sudden question the woman with the starlight hair now put to her able lover between their bouts of fiery lovemaking.

"Kells," she said, using the name the buccaneers called him, although in truth he was Rye Evistock of Essex and that was the name he had married her under on shipboard just off the Azores. "You don't really want to leave me, do you?"

Her voice was wistful and the strong arm of the buccaneer, just now lying outflung beneath her as she lay on her back studying the stars, tightened as if to shield her from the world. "I *never* want to leave you," he said in his deep rich voice—and it was the God's truth that he was speaking. "Don't you know that, Christabel?"

He had used the name the buccaneers called her, for to them she was—would always be—Christabel Willing, the Silver Wench of the Caribbean, who had set Tortuga aflame with her caprices and had married at last the Lord Admiral of the Buccaneers—Captain Kells. She smiled that he should call her that but indeed here in Port Royal she had almost forgotten that she had been born Carolina Lightfoot, aristocratic daughter of Virginia's Tidewater country, or that her mother ruled in queenly splendor the great domain of Level Green upon the York River, largest and finest house to be found in all of Colonial Virginia.

"But . . . you *are* going?" she murmured at last.

"I must," he sighed.

"I know you feel you must go but—oh, Kells, please don't." Her voice was wheedling and her slender hands traced a fiery persuasive path down his belly and groin, burrowed enticingly below. "Don't sail away—stay with me."

It was a siren's song—and Kells was not slow to respond to it.

Wakened to passion again, he turned over and drew her slim, yielding body against his own, caressing her tenderly. But he did not answer, although he took her again, driving her to frenzy with his ardor, and let her go at last with yearning.

"This is a terrible place for you to leave me," she murmured sleepily.

His grin was a white flash in the starlight, half seen. "Terrible?" he said humorously. "There is no better house in the town than this one. It is strong and defensible and decorated to your taste. You have servants, the latest Paris gowns, jewels, the city at your feet. Would you trade all that for a meager life at sea, storms that howl in the rigging, mouldly bread, water turned green in the casks, the ever-present danger of meeting the entire might of the Spanish treasure *flota* at one time—or the Vera Cruz squadron—and being blown out of the water?"

"Yes," she said, as definite as he.

"I'd given you credit for better sense," he laughed. And, sounding pleased with himself, he rolled over and was immediately asleep.

The longcase clock in the hall chimed the hour—it was two A.M.

Beside the sleeping figure of the buccaneer, Carolina lay in the starlight, thinking. Her pleas had made no impression on him. This hot night of lovemaking which had left her so breathless had not moved him either.

Unable to sleep, at last she rose restlessly and donned a paper-thin silken shawl from the Orient that had come to this buccaneer port via the pirates of Madagascar. The shawl was of a cool Chinese gold, heavily embroidered in white silk—a pattern of sumptuous twining roses. The long pale silken fringe swished along her slim bare legs as she went and settled herself in the window for coolness and looked out over the moonlit town.

A city of some eight thousand souls met Carolina's somber gaze—and all of them crowded into two thousand buildings that pressed toward the waterfront where the goods of the world streamed in and out. There was no fresh water here, and everything had to be brought in by boat. Yet there were handsome brick residences all about, and big warehouses stretched along the waterfront.

Kells had brought her here from Tortuga when war between England and France had accomplished what the Spanish could not—broken up the Brethren of the Coast. For Tortuga had a French governor, and buccaneers were fiercely loyal to their own countries. So the French buccaneers had stayed on Tortuga, and the English buccaneers had found a new home in Port Royal, where wine and money flowed. Still—she now admitted to herself—she had been happier on Tortuga than she was here. In Tortuga their sprawling white house had been a fortress against all the world, but here in cosmopolitan Port Royal the world reached out to her, mocking her with the life that they could never have back in England, in Essex, where Rye's family still lived. Not Rye—*Kells.* She must remember to think of him as Kells because that was who he was condemned always to be—Captain Kells, the daring Irish buccaneer whom no one had ever guessed was that aristocratic English gentleman, Rye Evistock. *Until I came along,* she thought bitterly.

Indeed it was all her fault. If Rye had never met her, she told herself, his secret would perhaps have been safe. Or if not safe, *dealt with.* But she *had* come along and, she told herself bitterly, ruined everything for him—forever.

Her self-denunciation was interrupted by a shadow that scurried out of the house below and ran, barelegged and with a shawl thrown over her head to make her more part of the darkness, barefoot down the street.

Carolina frowned. That would be fifteen-year-old Gilly, she guessed, slipping out to keep some tryst at a waterfront tavern. Probably with some brawling chance-met buccaneer. There was no question of Gilly's being robbed of her virginity—she had long ago lost that in the wilds of New Providence, which lay to the north—but there was always the danger that Gilly might be pounced upon by one of the pimps who did not know that the girl was under Carolina's—and therefore Captain Kells's—protection. She might be spirited away to one of Port Royal's numerous brothels!

Thinking of what might happen to Gilly brought Carolina's thoughts abruptly back to the day she had first met the girl, the day on which she had received The Letter and made a decision that was to alter her life. For in a strange tortuous way, it was that decision which was sending Kells off buccaneering again. . . .

Indeed the sight of Gilly's flying form racing down the sandy street had brought it all back, and in her mind Carolina was strolling through the town on a late winter day and feeling carefree in the comfortable knowledge that Kells had left the buccaneering trade behind him—forever.

BOOK I

The Silver Wench

I'll sing to you a devil's song
Of danger and of love gone wrong
(And other sins as well!)
And take you through a scented grove
'Mid gold-encrusted treasure trove
Into a lovers' hell!

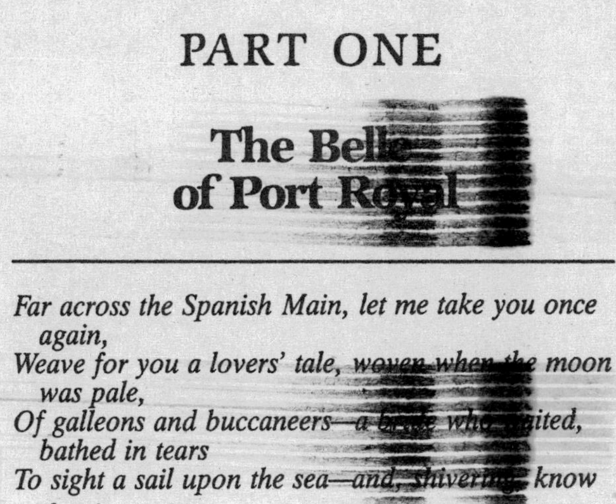

PART ONE

The Belle of Port Royal

Far across the Spanish Main, let me take you once again,
Weave for you a lovers' tale, woven when the moon was pale,
Of galleons and buccaneers—a bride who waited, bathed in tears
To sight a sail upon the sea—and, shivering, know that it was he!

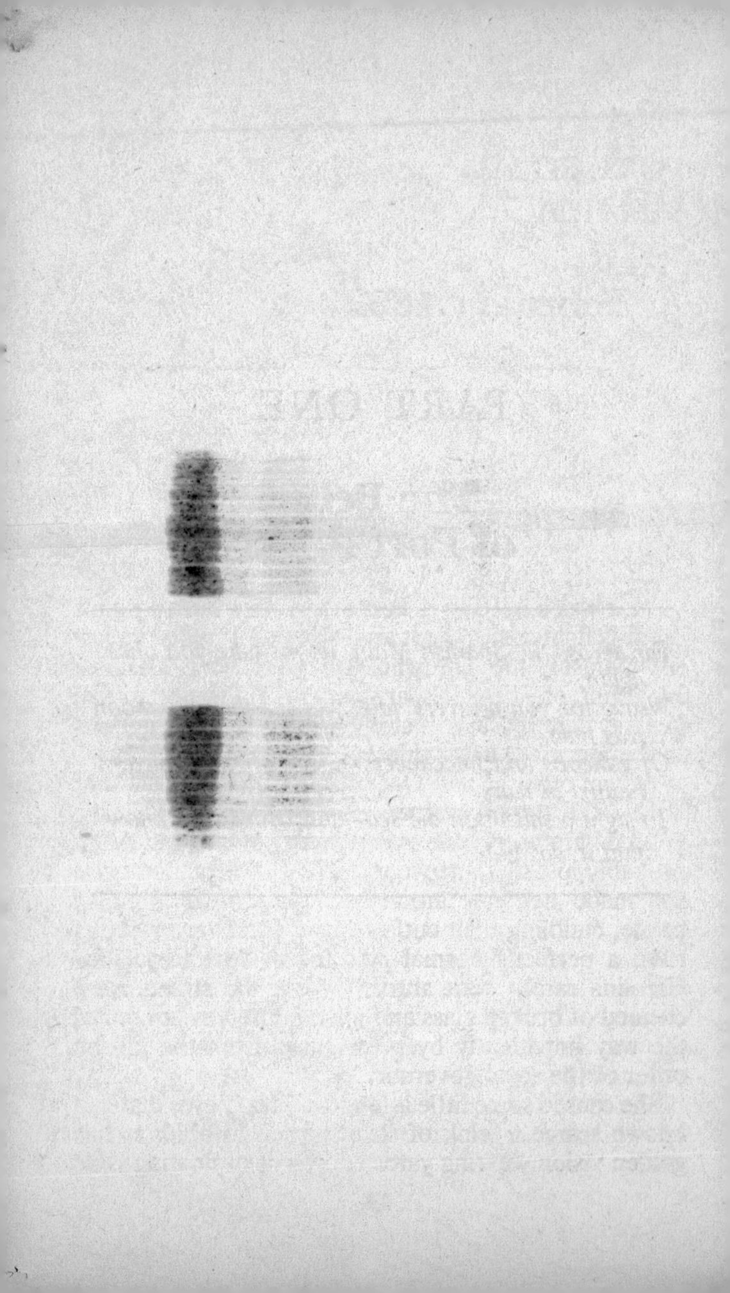

PORT ROYAL,
JAMAICA

February 1692

Chapter 1

It was a hot day in Port Royal. In a butter-yellow dress as light as her heart and swinging a ruffled yellow silk parasol, the girl who had once been Carolina Lightfoot of Virginia's aristocratic Tidewater picked her way daintily down a street littered, as it always was in the morning, with wine bottles and tankards and a variety of other debris. Once she stepped over a pair of boots—the boots' owner was presumably dashing around barefoot—once over a slipper of tangerine satin probably lost by some woman of the streets, and twice she made her way around sodden drunks who lay prone, cuddling their cutlasses and perchance a jug of rum: a perfectly normal morning in Port Royal, for Carolina rarely went abroad before the streets were cleaned of broken glass and human litter, swept out of the way impatiently by press gangs from the jail by order of the royal governor.

She caused some little attention. Bleary eyes that had known scarce a wink of sleep turned to blink at this golden vision wearing yards and yards of floating voile and who swung along jauntily on pale yellow kid slippers—guarded as always by the big taciturn buccaneer called Hawks.

"We should have waited a bit till the streets were cleaned," grunted Hawks. "Ye'll cut your feet on this broken glass." He reached out to steer her around a broken wine bottle whose sticky contents was abuzz with insects.

"Yes, I suppose I should have waited." Carolina tossed back her head with a gesture that swept her thick fair hair away from her neck in the sticky heat. "But it's cooler early, and the market gets so crowded later."

She did not say what she intended to buy at the market and Hawks did not ask. It was not for him to argue with the captain's extravagant lady whether she wanted to buy a fashion doll from Paris or some China tea and spices or a length of Italian silk or French laces. Everything—even shrunken heads from the jungles of South America and fine Bordeaux (when everyone knew England was at war with France)—*everything* found its way sooner or later into Port Royal harbor. The goods of the world changed hands here. Hawks could only hope Carolina would not load him up so heavily he'd have trouble getting his cutlass arm free, for the town was alive with riffraff this morning and he did not care for the way some of them were looking at his lustrous charge.

They had passed from Queen's Street down a narrow street between the tall brick buildings that crowded this city built on sand, and they were just emerging onto High Street on their way to the market when there was a sudden disturbance on Lime Street loud enough to drown out the hawkers' crying out the virtues of their fresh-caught fish and crabs.

As they turned the corner onto High Street they came under the observation of two gentlemen who were observing passersby from the open first-floor window of a tall brick house. The younger and taller of the two had the look of an adventurer about him. He was wiry and well built; his body had a lithe grace that had pleased many women. He had a smooth olive-skinned face, a high forehead, an aquiline nose, black winglike brows and a cleft chin of exceeding firmness. And beneath those winglike brows a pair of narrowed tawny-gold eyes looked haughtily down upon the crowd —for Port Royal not only stayed up late, it got up early. His black hair swung like coarse shining silk against the shoulders of his dark olive coat as he lounged in the windowsill, his back against the green-painted wooden frame, one long leg swinging indolently over the sill. His lazy demeanor was contradicted by the alert look in his tawny eyes as he took in the scene before him, and from time to time he murmured quick questions to the man who hovered behind him and answered in a low urgent voice.

As Carolina, daintily picking up her floating yellow voile skirts to avoid more broken glass, turned the corner, the man in the olive coat straightened slightly.

"Madre de Dios!" he murmured in Spanish under cover of the clamor. "To find a beauty like that—here! These buccaneers do well for themselves indeed!"

"You must remember to speak in English," warned his heavyset friend behind him in a worried voice, "else our lives will pay for it. I will remind you, Ramon, that I do this for you out of old friendship and—"

"I know, I know," chuckled his younger friend, his admiring gaze still fixed on Carolina. "And I will remind you, John, to call me 'Raymond' and not 'Ramon' and to remember that for the moment I am *French*—a renegade, perhaps, but still French." He was about to ask John who the golden vision was when distant shouts and running feet erupted from Lime Street into High Street. A cart piled high with oranges was knocked over and the oranges cascaded into the street, rolling along the gutters like bowling balls. Several people tripped over the oranges and went down beside the overturned cart. And the reason for all this commotion—a ginger-haired girl of perhaps fifteen summers running as if for her life—darted through the turmoil, collided with Hawks, and with an anguished squawk ricocheted to the ground directly in front of Carolina.

As she fell, the girl's plain brown kirtle tumbled upward, revealing a startlingly handsome red silk petticoat and a white chemise edged with lace ruffles, in sharp contrast to her dirty bare feet and sun-bronzed ankles.

From the crowd, stumbling through the rolling oranges, panted a blowzy woman in magenta satin whom Carolina recognized as one of the well-known madams of the town (indeed, it was said the governor himself patronized her establishment at times), and right behind her a fierce-looking bawd in stained pink silk who roared, "After her, Sadie! Don't let her get away with my chemise and your petticoat!"

Carolina looked down, astounded, into the fallen girl's sharp-featured dirty face and met a pair of woebegone brown eyes.

"Oh, lor', don't let them get me!" wailed the girl, clasping Carolina around the ankles. "They'll have my hide for this!"

The enthusiasm of the girl's desperate assault might have toppled Carolina had not Hawks, with a sudden imprecation, seized his captain's lady by the arm and righted her. He would have removed the girl's grip on Carolina's ankles with his boot save that Carolina stayed him and turned to face the girl's pursuers.

"Before you touch this girl," her voice rang out, "tell me, what is her crime?"

Her crime was fairly obvious—this girl would be one of Port Royal's ever-shifting floating population, a scullery wench, perhaps, who had gone to work in one of the brothels. Not pretty enough to make her way as a prostitute, for competition in that field was hot in Port Royal, she must still have wanted finery—and so she had stolen a chemise and a red petticoat and been caught in the act.

"She's a thief, that one! And me and Tilly both says so!" shrilled the magenta-clad madam, who came to an abrupt stop before Carolina and her frowning bodyguard.

"That she is!" roared the big woman in pink, coming up behind Sadie so suddenly that she bumped into her, almost knocking her down. "Don't let her get away with it, Sadie!" She pushed the madam forward so violently that she stumbled. "Pull the petticoat off the slut's back, and then I'll pull off the chemise!"

Carolina had asked her question only to give herself time to think what to do, and now her decision was swiftly made as the girl who lay on the street beseechingly clutching her ankles burst into tears. "Don't let them strip me on the street, mistress!" she wailed. "Oh, don't—please!"

"I can promise you they won't strip you here on the street," said Carolina with a warning look at the two women, who were now fiercely regarding her, hands on hips. "Tell me," she said sternly. "Did you steal these clothes?"

The girl stopped crying abruptly. Her eyes widened. Then she gulped, "It was because they was beating me—both of them. With a stick!" She regarded Carolina in rising panic. "I only wanted to get even!" she wailed.

Carolina, who always fed lost dogs and cats, and who had more compassion for human strays than could be found anywhere else on this island, gave her a look of sympathy. This pathetic waif had no home, no family—Carolina didn't have to ask; it was readily apparent.

Naught but the clothes on her back, and those were about to be ripped from her body.

She turned to the two women. "I am taking this girl home with me," she said flatly. "The clothing will be returned to you within the hour."

"We'll have it now!" screeched the woman in stained pink, who was advancing menacingly on Carolina.

Hawks looked dismayed. Interfering in a fight between women never worked out for a man, but he must defend the captain's lady at all costs.

"Well, John," chuckled the man who lounged in the window. "I see I am about to rescue a lady!"

Ignoring his friend's clutching arm, and his desperate, "Wait, Ramon, that woman is—" he dropped catlike to the street below and reached the quarreling group in a single bound, sending a bystander staggering as he did so.

And before Hawks could even bellow "Get back!" and push Carolina and her unlikely charge behind him, a rich masculine voice came from behind Carolina.

"No one will be stripped in the street," was his level pronouncement. "*I* stand to defend this lady."

Carolina swung about—to the disappointed grumbling of the ogling crowd that had gathered about, hoping for a melee—and met the tawny gaze of a stranger. A tall dark-haired stranger in dusky olive who moved with assurance and had a naked blade swinging negligently in his hand.

Faced by glowering Hawks and this new, more deadly menace, the two bawds fell back, muttering.

"The clothes'll be sent to you, Sadie," Hawks told the angry madam with relief. "I'll see to it myself."

Carolina ignored the pair. She was regarding the stranger in some wonder. He was extraordinarily handsome, she saw, as dark as any Spaniard, but there was no mark of the don about his casual clothes, and his English was flawless.

"I do not believe I know you, sir," she said slowly. "But I am most grateful to you nonetheless."

The stranger made her a sweeping bow. "Raymond du Monde, at your service, mademoiselle."

Carolina acknowledged his greeting graciously and extended her slender hand. The stranger bore it to his lips, met her gaze with laughter in his eyes as he kissed it—and held it a shade too long.

It was a shade too long for Hawks, too. Just as Carolina was about to give the stranger her name, Hawks broke in.

"Captain Kells'll be grateful to you," muttered Hawks. He spoke with feeling for he knew in his heart that he could not have raised his cutlass against a woman, and it would have been hard holding off two of them. And what would the Captain have said had he returned to find his lady scratched and bruised and with perhaps tufts of her beautiful blonde hair torn out?

The stranger caught that remark and for a moment there was a new gleam in his tawny eyes. "Captain Kells?" he asked in a slightly altered tone.

Carolina was used to having men's expressions alter at the mention of her buccaneer husband, but she winced when a voice from the crowd remarked audibly, "Gor', don't he know he's talkin' to the Silver Wench?"

The gaze of the handsome stranger upon her was steady. She noticed the little V-shaped scar at the corner of his mouth, the cleft chin, the dark line of jaw scraped clean with a razor. "Silver Wench?" he murmured. "You will forgive me, mademoiselle, but I am new to Jamaica."

"I have been called that," she admitted stiffly.

He seemed to reflect. "Ah, I recollect now. Then you must be—"

"Wife to Captain Kells," put in Hawks before Carolina could reply. He moved uneasily, wishing Carolina would take the young wench—who had by now scrambled to her feet although she was still keeping close to Carolina for protection—and get them gone from here. The dark stranger was looking at Carolina in a most admiring although slightly inquisitive way. He had sheathed his sword and was smiling at her—and there was something in his smile that put Hawks in mind of a black panther from Africa that he had once seen break free of its bonds aboard a ship. There had been no subduing the panther once it was bent on freedom; it had killed three men before it was brought down—and there was something in the stranger's olive-skinned face that reminded Hawks of that panther. "We'd best go home, mistress," he muttered.

But Carolina was not listening. She was smiling into the stranger's face. "I think you have just saved me from a very nasty encounter, Monsieur du Monde," she said steadily. "My husband is away up the Cobre, but he will be back tonight, and I know he would wish to thank you himself. We would be honored to have your presence at dinner tonight."

Beside her Hawks choked. The Captain had been away on some business up the Cobre River all week and he was indeed expected home tonight. But what would he think about his lady inviting a perfect stranger—and one chance-met on the street at that—to break bread with them on his first evening home?

The stranger was gallant. His dark face flushed a little darker. "I will be honored," he declared.

"Good," said Carolina breezily. "We dine at seven. Our house is on Queen's Street. Anyone in Port Royal can tell you where."

That was certainly true! Everyone in Port Royal at one time or another had had the house of the famous buccaneer and his almost equally famous lady pointed out to him. Even this stranger who had been in town only since yesterday evening had had it pointed out to him. His eyes glinted.

"I will be there, madame," he promised with another deep bow.

"Should we not be getting on to the market?" wondered Hawks uneasily.

"No, we'll go home first and get—what's your name?" she asked the girl.

"Gilly," supplied the girl promptly. "I've—got no last name, rightly," she added, mumbling.

Nothing Gilly might have said could have been better calculated to gain Carolina's sympathy. She herself—had not Fielding Lightfoot chosen to overlook his wife's indiscretion—would not have had "a last name, rightly." But he had, and so she was Carolina Lightfoot instead of Carolina Randolph, as she might have been if her mother Letitia had been able to marry her cousin Sandy. But Sandy had a mad wife and could not divorce her. It had all led to such terrible trouble. . . .

Looking at dirty, underfed Gilly, Carolina felt she might, under other circumstances, have been looking at herself.

"Never you mind," she said comfortingly. "Do you have a place to stay?"

"No," mumbled Gilly.

"Well, you do now." Carolina's voice was brisk. "I'll take you home and get you settled. The market can wait." She turned to Hawks and as she did so her gaze passed over the two angry women, thwarted of their prey. "After all, I'll want to get the"—there was the faintest insulting pause—*"ladies'* clothes back to them as soon as possible."

There was an angry sniff from the madam and a squawk from the bawd beside her, but they made no move to follow as Hawks, hiding a grin, turned to accompany Carolina back the way she had come.

Raymond du Monde watched their progress, smiling, until they had turned the corner off High Street. Then, ignoring the door, he put his hands on the green windowsill and hauled himself up to where his friend John, gone several shades paler, was waiting.

He vaulted into the room.

"How could you so call attention to yourself, Ramon?" John cried reproachfully. He hastened to close the shutters behind his friend.

" 'Raymond,' if you please," Ramon said absently. He brushed off his cuffs fastidiously as if the dust of the street might have contaminated them.

"I was about to tell you that woman was Kells's wife when you threw yourself into the street!"

"The Silver Wench? Ah, yes, I should have known that it could be none other." Ramon drew a deep sigh. "These clothes I am wearing do not appeal to me, John. Do you think a better suit could be procured for me on short notice in the town?"

John stared at him, aghast.

"Surely you do not actually intend to dine at his house?" he cried. "I heard you say it, but I thought you were making a pleasantry with no intent to do it!"

Ramon's soft laughter held a wicked note. "Indeed, John, wild horses could not deter me from dining with the lady!"

"But you heard her! Her husband is expected back tonight. *Kells himself!* I'll remind you that 'tis said Kells personally spied out Porto Bello before he raided it—"

"As I am spying out Port Royal," interrupted Ramon with a grin.

"And I'll remind you also that *you* were in Porto Bello just before that raid!"

"I left—some have said providentially." Ramon's thin lips twisted. Although his head was cool, his manner was flippant. "Had I stayed but a day later, John, I would have met this infamous Captain Kells too soon! As it is, I will be glad to meet the fellow at last!"

"Yes, yes, you are sure your sword could have turned the tide," said John Daimler in an agonized voice. "But although you assuredly did not see *him,* Ramon, you are overlooking the fact that Kells may have seen *you* there! After all, you were in command of one of the forts there just before the raid."

Ramon shrugged. "True, there is always that chance."

"And if he does recognize you, there in his dining room, have you considered the probable consequences?" pursued Daimler.

"I will meet them when they come—*if* they come," was the indifferent response.

"And you would take such a risk on the off chance a wench will favor you—and a buccaneer's wench at that?" John Daimler's temper exploded at last.

The straight black brows that faced him drew together; the narrow jaw seemed to square a trifle. "I know that we were boys together, John, and played together in the courtyards of Toledo," he said silkily, "but do not presume too much on old friendship. Where the ladies are concerned, I accept advice from no one!"

"Madre de Dios!" thundered John. "You will get us both killed!"

"You go back to your Spanish beginnings, Juan," chided Ramon, his good humor restored. "Please do remember—as you have been reminding me ever since I arrived here last night—that as of today I am French and you are English. And now, since it is a most beautiful day, I find myself ready to go to see the forts. I am anxious to assess their strength and"—he grinned with a flash of white teeth—"their vulnerability!" He beamed at Daimler. "Be of good heart, John. Remember, if I succeed in subduing this cursed island, I may well be made governor of Jamaica. And if I am, John, you shall assuredly become my lieutenant governor!" He slapped his old friend on the back.

John Daimler shook his sandy head and mopped a brow dampened from more than the tropical heat that was even now spreading over this city built on sand. It was true that he had been promised much if this mad venture succeeded, but at the moment he wished with all his heart that it had never been begun, that he had left what Ramon chose to call his "Spanish beginnings" buried as they had been these many years. His Spanish mother had died long ago in Toledo, his Spanish relatives had never really accepted him—indeed had scorned him after her death. They had been glad enough to pack him off to England when his English father, long estranged from his mother, had died and left him a small shop in Bristol. And John Daimler had come away to the West Indies, believing that change of location would change his life. In England, with his strong Spanish accent (since lost), he had not been well accepted; but in brash new Port Royal he had hoped to forget his divided heritage and choose the one that had given him a start in the mercantile world—he could be all English.

And then this devil out of Havana, this boyhood friend from an almost forgotten past, had ferreted him out: Ramon del Mundo, scion of one of Spain's most aristocratic houses. And John Daimler, grandson on his mother's side of Juan Mendoza for whom he had been named, had gone along, for he had a good trade here with the English, and in this buccaneer port that would have gone out the window had they guessed him to be even half Spanish. Or so he had believed at first. Now that he was in the plot, he was not so sure. He regretted every moment. He wished fervently that he had told Ramon del Mundo to go to the Devil and let rumors be spread as they would.

Rumors could be denied. This harboring of a Spanish spy fresh from Havana—even overnight—could not.

And it could bring him a length of hemp around his neck.

"Did you see her eyes, John?" His friend was addressing him.

"Yes," admitted John Daimler in a resigned voice. "I saw them."

"Amazing eyes. They flash silver in the sunlight. Did you notice?"

"No," croaked John. "But I will take your word for it. Have you not a wife in Spain?" he burst out.

The face that whirled toward him was carved in granite and John Daimler felt called upon to add, "Someone who would regret this folly which may well cost you your life?"

The cold face relaxed. "As a matter of fact I have not, John," was the careless answer. "But even if I had, I would be hard pressed. . . . Did you notice her hair, John?"

Daimler gulped and nodded.

"Pure sunlight—but at night it would be pure moonlight. Have you never imagined such a sweep of hair across your pillow, John?"

John Daimler admitted he had, but he doubted that Ramon heard him. Ramon was still musing.

"And her skin, John—like very silk. And the way she walked, light and proud and carefree. Women at the Spanish Court do not walk that way, John, they do not stride free. They mince, they float . . . it is very attractive—but I prefer this. Did you not take note of the way she walks, John?"

"I think it is time I take you to view the forts," said John sternly. "There are three of them: Fort James, Fort Carlisle, and Morgan's Line. You will be well advised to take note of their defenses."

Ramon del Mundo sighed. "You are right, John. And after I have checked out their defenses, I will do a bit of shopping in the town. For a suit to grace a lady's table at dinner."

John Daimler groaned.

"Promise me," he pleaded, "that you will not dress in the Spanish style, Ramon? You look Spanish enough as it is!"

"Oh, as to that . . ." Ramon del Mundo airily tweaked an imaginary mustache; he had shaved off his own in anticipation of this venture. "We will have to see what is available, will we not?"

Meanwhile, Carolina was heading toward Queen's Street with Gilly in tow.

At Hawks's laconic, "The cap'n may not like having you invite that strange Frenchie to dinner on his first night back," she turned and gave him a withering look. "And here comes that other Frenchie," he muttered under his breath.

Carolina swung about to see that Louis Deauville, the Huguenot gentleman who had taken rooms recently in the house across the street from them, was approaching, twirling an ivory walking stick.

Louis Deauville had come upon the town like an avalanche, burying the scruples of most of the ladies of Port Royal with his *savoir-faire,* his wicked gaze that seemed to strip away the satins and the laces, exposing the tingling flesh beneath. Hardly a feminine breast that did not beat a trifle faster when Louis Deauville entered the room, scarce a lady to be found who did not beam at the sight of his tall, lounging figure, or treasure one of his gracefully worded compliments—tailored, each was sure, to her particular charms. And his boudoir tales, whispered into feminine ears, were so marvelously risqué and yet so gallant that they were repeated and tittered over behind waving fans—though seldom murmured into husbands' less appreciative ears. It was the lighthearted opinion of the ladies of Port Royal's elite that the fascinating Monsieur Deauville was a nobleman traveling in disguise (a rumor perhaps inspired by his own lips), that he was a man of vast wealth back in France (for was he not everywhere running up bills?), a beau of the Parisian *haut monde*—and that he had slept with every desirable woman in Paris!

He presented, therefore, an alluring challenge.

Carolina did not believe Louis Deauville was a nobleman in disguise. She thought he had been more likely a dancing master or a fencing master back in France—certainly that would explain his nimbleness and wiry strength. She had little doubt that he had bedded every pretty lady who was willing to go to bed with him, but she was inclined to doubt that his conquests included the French king's mistresses (as he claimed) or the beauties of the French Court. She thought him a charming rogue and was wary of him.

But the story that had reached her third-hand over tea with the wife of a rich merchant in a handsome residence on Broad Street had intrigued her indeed. It seemed that Monsieur Deauville had spent a brief time in London. While there he had unhesitatingly hurled himself in front of a runaway carriage and when he had gotten the horses to stop, he had been promptly embraced by the carriage's sole—and trembling—occupant, a striking lady in a peacock-blue gown. She had taken him home with her, regaling him along the way with the story of how she, a former headmistress, had turned her fashionable school into an even more fashionable gaming house.

At that point Carolina had sat up straighter. *Jenny Chesterton!* she had thought in amazement. For she herself had attended Mistress Chesterton's School for Young Ladies in London and knew that when scandal had broken over her pretty ears, young Mistress Chesterton had quickly converted her fashionable school into a gaming house.

"Do go on," Carolina had urged her hostess.

"Well, there was not much more," her hostess had told her with a shrug. "Save that he claimed he had an affair with a beautiful former charge of the lady, who was in residence at the gaming house." Her lips twitched. "I am not sure that I believe it, but it is a delightful story."

Save that he had an affair with—! Carolina had set down her cup with a slight clatter. *Could the affair have been with Reba, her former roommate? Reba who had since caused her so much trouble? Reba had certainly been "in residence" at Jenny Chesterton's gaming house for a time!*

That had been on Thursday, and she had been dying to ask Monsieur Deauville about it ever since.

Now, as he approached, walking jauntily and twirling his cane, she eyed him speculatively. She would indeed love to question him. . . . But now, with Gilly in tow, was not the time.

"Perhaps I should invite Monsieur Deauville to dinner as well," she murmured irrepressibly to Hawks. "'Tis said there's safety in numbers, Hawks!"

Beside her, Hawks had no inclination to reply. He watched with deep disapproval as the Frenchman greeted Carolina effusively. It had not escaped Hawks's attention that Carolina seldom left her front door but that their new French neighbor, a dandy who this morning dangled a single earring and was resplendent in a suit of popinjay-green, managed to stroll along after. He wondered if that was how they managed things in France, getting on with married women, and his dark frown deepened.

"'Tis good to see you, Monsieur Deauville," Carolina was saying. "But I am surprised that you are still here. I thought you said you were on your way to America?"

In point of fact, Monsieur Deauville had but recently

fled from America with an angry husband thundering on his trail, but he had chosen to claim that he was but lately from Marseilles, a place where, as it happened, he had been born.

"I linger here because of"—his hazel eyes lingered on her bosom, rising and falling in the heat—"the climate, madame. So delightfully—warm." He looked as if he were growing warm himself as his gaze roamed over Carolina's dainty young breasts.

"Ah, yes, well, we must not detain you, Monsieur Deauville," Carolina said hastily, observing the direction of his gaze. "I have a new serving girl to get settled in my household today." She jogged Gilly with her arm and Gilly turned with a start from her rapt consideration of Monsieur Deauville's purse, hovering so temptingly near—why, she could be off with it like *that!* As easy as snapping her fingers!

"Come along, Gilly," said Carolina, and Gilly gave up the purse with a sigh and trudged along beside her new mistress.

Carolina hurried on toward home, and Hawks muttered, "I don't like the way that Frenchie looks at you!"

Carolina privately agreed that Monsieur Deauville had a way of stripping her with his eyes, but she was still irked with Hawks for suggesting that Kells would be displeased by her choice of dinner guests.

"I am sure Monsieur Deauville has at least a wife and six children back in France," she declared airily. "You misjudge him, Hawks. He is a harmless flirt."

Hawks snorted, and spent the rest of the walk home listening to Gilly fabricate tales of her life in Bristol where, according to her version, she had been badly treated at home, cast out to live in rags, unfairly jailed, and had lost a lover to the gibbet—her sorrows seemed never to end until, at their front door, she found herself out of breath.

"She'll steal your ear bobs, this one," Hawks said sourly, nodding toward Gilly as he held the door for Carolina.

Gilly turned and made a face at him.

"Oh, nonsense, Hawks," Carolina said reprovingly. "The girl's in trouble. She'll be glad of a place to stay. Won't you, Gilly?"

"Oh, yes, mistress," Gilly said quickly. *Too quickly,* thought Hawks. And with too much of a smirk. Gilly caught his thoughts from his disapproving look and stuck out her tongue at him the moment Carolina's back was turned.

Carolina went through the door into the cool interior of the front hall, unaware of how Gilly's sharp brown eyes gleamed as she stared about her at the handsome furnishings. Carolina had taken in a waif today—and not for the first time; most of her servants had been picked up from the gutter.

And now—this pitiful half-fledged girl. Smiling down on Gilly's ginger head, she had the ennobling feeling that she had done the Right Thing.

Chapter 2

Before Carolina had taken three steps down the hall, one of the servants, a girl named Betts, hurried forward to tell her that a message had just been received from "the master." Captain Kells would not be coming home tonight; indeed he might be detained up the Cobre River for as long as a week.

Carolina felt briefly annoyed; had she known Kells was not coming home tonight she certainly would have postponed her dinner invitation to Monsieur du Monde.

But her impetuous dinner invitation was forgotten when the same serving girl—a child of the London docks, her face scarred by her misadventures, a girl whom Carolina had rescued and who adored her beyond measure—handed her a letter and said solemnly, "'Twas delivered by Captain Trollope of the *Hopemont,* mistress, who said he had it by Captain Carleton of the *Bombay,* who told him he could not recall who it was gave it to him."

"Never mind, Betts," Carolina said dryly, snatching up the letter. "I can *guess* who it was gave it to him!"

For her sister Virginia always clung to the forlorn hope that even though the authorities had come and searched Rye's father's house, that the present whereabouts of the notorious Captain Kells had escaped them.

Carolina sighed—how like Virgie to believe that!

But the letter was to her a breath of home. She paused only to give Betts, who was frowning a little as she stared down at Gilly, instructions to remove Gilly's petticoat and chemise and turn them over to Hawks, who would dispose of them.

Betts looked amazed at such orders from her mistress.

"If I give her underclothes to Hawks, what's the girl to wear?" she blurted. "Just her dress against her skin?"

"Just see that she has a bath," said Carolina, who was impatient to read her letter. "And a dressing gown. I'll find her some proper attire as soon as I've read this." She waved the letter. "Gilly, go with Betts. She'll take care of you."

Gilly fixed Betts with a belligerent eye. "I'm hungry," she announced sullenly.

"Of course you are," said Carolina. "Betts will get you something to eat. Go along with you now."

Gilly flounced away arrogantly after a doubtful Betts, and Carolina went into the cool, airy high-ceilinged living room to read her precious letter.

And that letter, which had reached her so circuitously, took her mind from everything else.

It was indeed from her sister Virginia, written from Essex—and since Virginia, worried that the authorities would trace her letters to Carolina, wrote so seldom, its arrival was an event.

"I should have penned this letter sooner," Virginia

began apologetically, *"but I am kept busy with Andrew's literary projects—he has just begun a new translation of Virgil!"*

Studious, bookish Andrew! Carolina's face broke into a smile. He and Virginia were so well suited.

But the next lines made her catch her breath.

"I am afraid I have sad news for Rye," wrote Virginia. *"His older brother Giles died last week. He drank himself to death at last—just as we had predicted. And the end was terrible—he screamed and saw demons and clawed at the sheets. I could not face it. I ran away although I know I should have nursed him, but Andrew said I was right for I must keep a happy face for my little one. And we may have another death soon, for although Rye's father is still alive, he gasps for every breath—indeed I do not see how he holds on at all."*

Carolina expelled a deep breath. For a moment the hand holding the letter dropped to her lap and she looked out through the window at the brilliant blue sky over Jamaica.

Kells's brother Giles was dead. And his father soon would be.

They had discussed what was happening far away in Essex, Kells and she—and Carolina had not been happy with his conclusions.

Rye Evistock was elderly Lord Gayle's third son. But his wastrel eldest brother Darvent was dead, shot last year in a brawl over a wager in a Colchester tavern. They had been aware that Rye's brother Giles, next in line for the title, was slowly drinking himself to death and might well precede his father to the grave.

And in that event, when old Lord Gayle died, Rye Evistock, who was next in line—not Andrew, the youngest son, but Rye, whom the world knew as Captain Kells—would inherit the title and the family estate in Essex.

He would become a viscount, he would be Lord

Gayle—not just plain Rye Evistock. And once he became Lord Gayle, would that not help him win his pardon from the King? Carolina had asked anxiously.

The man who called himself Kells had given her a wistful look and rumpled her fair hair with tender fingers.

"You must not look forward to that, Carolina," he had sighed. "For in the event that I were to inherit the lands and the title, as matters stand now everything would most likely be seized by the Crown. Indeed I've been toying with the idea of renouncing all claim and letting the title and the estate pass on to Andrew."

Virginia's husband! Her brother-in-law would wear Rye's rightful title—her sister would become Lady Gayle instead of her!

And now this letter, telling her that Giles had drunk his life away. . . .

And now Rye would renounce all claim and they would sink a little farther into their island prison.

Carolina clenched the letter with a grip that crumpled the paper. She would not tell him yet! He had borne his two older brothers a measure of ill will, believing that between them they had wasted the family holdings and broken his father's heart—still it would grieve him to learn of Giles's death and his face would grow grim, his jaw stonier as he resolved to give up his heritage.

She smoothed out the parchment and began reading again. She read and reread it, devouring every word. Dear Virgie, happily married at last to Rye's brother Andrew and living in his father's house in Essex—it had been over a year since Carolina had heard from her.

"I am expecting my second child in late summer," Virginia's letter confided. *"Andrew is hoping it will be a girl since we already have a fine boy. But I will be pleased enough if—whatever the baby turns out to be—it is as robust as little Andrew, who is playing at my feet*

and tugging at my skirts as I write this. We are all well here in Essex and Andrew plans to take me down to London if there is a Frost Fair. We will have our names printed on a card on a printing press set right onto the ice of the frozen Thames!"

Carolina frowned as the letter dipped into other problems, back home in the Tidewater: *"I have been home to the Tidewater only once since you left. Things are very bad there—financially, I mean. Tobacco prices are low, no one has any money—and I really think that this time Father will lose Level Green. Oh, he should not have built that huge house, he must have known he could never pay for it! Mother and he continue extravagantly, however. Their horses and carriages are the finest, Mother met me wearing an exact replica of a Paris fashion doll she had received but recently, and Father was just as splendid in a new rose satin suit trimmed in gold braid and a great new periwig that cost a fortune—he hasn't paid for either of them yet, I'll warrant! But they are getting along better now in other ways. They didn't have a single spat all the time I was there—which must be something of a record for them, they've always quarreled so much!"* (Here Carolina smiled, for the pitched battles between Letitia and Fielding Lightfoot had caused local wags to nickname their first home "Bedlam." Their quarrels were legendary, the subject of constant gossip in Williamsburg and Yorktown. Her expression tightened again as Virgie's flowing scrawl mentioned their older sister Pennsylvania:

"No one has heard from Penny—not a word since Emmett came back from Philadelphia. No one at home speaks of her now. Everyone is sure she must be dead—after all, it has been seven years since she ran away with Emmett to the Marriage Trees! And if Emmett knew where she was and was just too stubborn to tell, we will never find out from him because he drowned last summer while fishing. He was wearing big

boots at the time, and before he could get them off they filled with water and he was dragged under. By the time anyone could get to him he was dead. It made me shiver, remembering what a dolt we all thought him and not nearly good enough for Penny, and now—if she is still alive—she is a widow and doesn't even know it. Even Della and Flo have stopped romanticizing about Penny and imagining her running away somewhere to become an actress. They are quite grown up now—it made me feel old to see our little sisters beginning to talk about boys and betrothals. Some of their older friends are already spoken for, can you believe that?"

There was more, for it was a long rambling letter—the kind Virginia usually wrote, on those rare occasions when she wrote at all—but these were the parts Carolina read over and over. Virginia's words brought back to her pictures of their older sister, tall statuesque Penny with her vivid red hair and her impatience and her swift, wicked smile and husky voice and ready laughter. Penny had been Fielding's favorite, Carolina remembered wistfully. Indeed, Penny had been everyone's favorite, including hers! They were right to miss her at Level Green. For the thousandth time she tried to imagine what had happened to Penny and could envision nothing good.

But that other reference, the one about losing Level Green, worried her, and she tossed aside the letter and began to walk restlessly about. Fielding had certainly not needed the largest house in Virginia—but he had built it anyway! He had squandered his inheritance, which could have kept him forever, on that one big wonderful impossible project—and her mother had been so proud of it! Ruefully she remembered how Letitia and Fielding had quarreled over where the furniture was to go when they had first moved in—and then had run up flocks of new bills trying to fill the multitude of rooms. It would break her mother's heart to lose the house—and it would kill Fielding, too. And even though Fielding was not her real father—although he *had* tacitly claimed Carolina as his all these years—even though he had never loved her, she still felt a kind of responsibility to him, for after all, he had not cast her out, not even when her impending marriage to a buccaneer had made her a scandal in the Tidewater.

She was aroused from her perusal of the letter by sounds of warfare coming from the kitchen. Carolina dropped the letter and ran toward the noise, which culminated in a loud howl as she reached the kitchen door.

The sight which greeted her gaze was a comic one. In the low-ceilinged kitchen, Cook stood before the hearth glaring, with arms akimbo. In the center of the floor Betts was trying to push Gilly's thin body down into a metal tub. Gilly's ginger hair fairly stood on end; she was spitting like a cat and she screamed her defiance. As Carolina reached the door, Gilly slammed her big wet sponge into Betts's face, sending the taller girl back against the sturdy wooden table on which reposed a couple of lobsters and a large earthenware bowl of beaten biscuit dough.

"What on earth is the matter?" demanded Carolina.

"This water's too cold," wailed Gilly. "It shocks my tender skin, it does!"

Carolina would have replied tartly that they all bathed in the tepid water, for constant heating of large amounts of water for baths made the house unbearably hot and damp—but just at that moment she caught sight of a huge bruise on Gilly's wet, bare shoulder.

"How did you get that, Gilly?" she asked gently.

"Get what?" Gilly looked alarmed.

"That bruise on your shoulder."

"Oh, *that?*" Gilly was about to shrug, but she saw the concern in Carolina's face and decided to make the most of it. "They was beating me just before I run away," she declared dramatically. "Those women who were chasing me when you saved me."

Cook sniffed and Betts, who was trying to wash the soap from her eyes in a basin, muttered something that sounded like "Ha!"

Carolina gave them both a reproving look. "Well, I'm glad I found you in time, Gilly, but we all use lukewarm water here. I'm sure you'll get used to it."

Gilly looked glum. In point of fact, the bruise had come from a rough cuff from her current lover and had been delivered when he had found Gilly picking his pockets. She decided she had not made her point well enough. "They treated me powerful mean," she added.

"Yes, well, no one will beat you here, Gilly. When you've finished bathing, wrap yourself in a towel and come up to my room. I'll see what I can find for you to wear." She turned to Betts. "Did Hawks take the petticoat and chemise back?"

Betts, who was just drying her wet face, nodded. "He left a little while ago." She forbore saying that the petticoat had almost had to be dragged off Gilly, who insisted she "fancied" it. "He said he wouldn't be back for a while," she added.

Carolina recalled that Hawks had a predilection for brothels. She expected him to be gone half the night. She didn't say so. Instead she turned to Cook.

"I've invited a guest for dinner," she said. "Lobster will be fine, and green turtle soup. I see you're making biscuits, and do you think you could manage a great tart?"

"I think so," said Cook, her good humor restored.

"Good," smiled Carolina. "Your dinners are always wonderful."

"I'll see what else I can manage," grunted Cook. She was one of Carolina's "finds" herself. She had spent her life working in hot kitchens, driven to desperation by bad-tempered housekeepers, and Carolina's easy way with her servants always melted her. "Maybe a bit of conch, maybe a bite of fish," she muttered.

"Gilly could wear Nell's things," suggested Betts. "She's about Nell's size."

"You're right," said Carolina. "I'd forgotten Nell didn't take her work clothes with her. What a good suggestion, Betts!"

Betts glowed.

"Who's Nell?" Gilly asked suspiciously.

Betts answered before Carolina could. "Nell was a fool," she said bluntly. "She had the best job in this house she'd ever had in her life—easy hours and easy work. And she chucked it all away for a trader who'll drop her in the next port he goes to."

"Nell only took her best gown with her," sighed Carolina. "She was under the impression she'd never do housework again."

"And you say she left her *work* clothes here?" asked Gilly sharply. She felt very disappointed. The red silk petticoat and lacy chemise had made her feel like a *lady*. And here she was being proffered *work clothes!*

"Yes. Dark blue linen. Very neat. Indeed you can serve supper in those clothes tonight—you *have* served tables at some time, haven't you, Gilly?"

"Oh, yes," was the eager response. "I worked in a tavern in Bristol and again in an inn. I serve very elegant," she added with a toss of her ginger curls.

Carolina hid a smile as she left. That smile might have wavered a bit had she guessed the reason for it: Gilly was hoping to make a good impression on the dark stranger who had stepped forward with bared blade to defend her in the street. Her dancing thoughts blithely ignored the obvious: that it was Carolina's beauty that had brought out that flashing blade.

Carolina dressed for dinner with her usual easy elegance. She wore a jade-green gown that brought out sudden flashing green lights in her amazing silver eyes.

The gown had three-quarter sleeves and a figure-hugging bodice that swept out into rustling jade-green silks over a lime silk petticoat. Emerald earrings flashed from her ears, and a single emerald on a golden chain found its way to the cleavage between her high rounded breasts.

She had finished combing her hair and piling it into the tall sweep fashion now demanded, when she paused and put down her silver comb and studied herself in the mirror. A slight frown creased her smooth white forehead.

The dress *was* cut a trifle low for dining alone with a stranger. Its jade-green color seemed to highlight spectacularly the pearly skin of her bosom, the tops of her breasts. She supposed she should change it. . . .

But then, practically *all* her dresses were low-cut. Kells liked them that way. It amused him to show her off, his flamboyant lady, and let all Port Royal envy him!

Carolina shrugged. This dinner after all was only a courtesy gesture. Did it really matter what the strange Frenchman thought?

Monsieur du Monde was punctual. He arrived even as Carolina was finishing her toilette. She gave a last pat to her hair and would have swept down the stairs but at the last moment she hesitated, ran back and extricated from the bottom of a huge locked chest a little silver-encrusted box of teakwood. She opened it and stood staring down at the contents winking up at her against the box's dark red velvet interior. Before her—worth a king's ransom—lay the diamond and ruby necklace the buccaneers of the *Sea Wolf* had voted as her "share" when she had maneuvered them out of a delicate situation—at least it seemed at the time that she had done so. She lifted it, letting the huge stones run through her hands caressingly. On an impulse she decided to wear it, for she had been thinking hard ever since she came home and this, she knew, might be the last occasion it would ever grace her neck.

She removed the emeralds from her ears and substituted gold earrings—whatever she wore in her ears would be eclipsed by the barbaric beauty of the huge pigeon's-blood rubies with their frosting of heavy gold and diamonds.

That necklace, she told herself critically, would not only cover a large part of her bosom but surely distract the average man from thoughts of lust to thoughts of avarice! Smiling at that, she swept downstairs in her rustling froth of light skirts to greet her dinner guest.

Betts had let him into the living room and he rose quickly at her approach and swept her the deepest of bows—but not before his gaze had focused on that fortune in gold and diamonds and rubies that blazed about her neck.

The de Lorca necklace, by God! he was thinking. For surely it could be none other. He had heard stories that the Wench had it, had gotten it under peculiar circumstances which had been hushed up by the Duke. That it had been a ransom for the Duke of Lorca was the official story, but there were other tastier ones the gossips told. Looking at those fabulous stones, Raymond du Monde was ready to believe them all!

Du Monde himself was a peacock this night. He was attired in violet silk, cut in the elegant French style (he had been hard put to find this suit and get it altered at short notice, but a scattering of coins had accomplished it). The Mechlin at his throat was a white froth set, unfortunately, with a dull pink stone of little value that he had borrowed from John Daimler. Still, his lilac silk stockings flashed from his well-turned calves in the candlelight, his strong thighs were encased in violet silk trousers and a burst of gold braid on his wide-cuffed coat completed his glittering appearance.

"I am sorry, but my husband has not yet returned

from the Cobre," she explained. "I have had a message from him that he will not reach us in time for dinner"—Best not to let this handsome and rather dangerous-looking stranger know that the master of the house would be gone for another week!—"but perhaps you will join me in a glass of wine before dinner?"

Raymond du Monde tried to look suitably disappointed at the absence of her husband—and failed. He accepted the wine she poured but he could hardly keep his eyes from the necklace—or the frosty tops of her round breasts so cunningly displayed in her simply cut green gown. *Madre de Dios,* what a woman she was! She had a breathtaking, almost virginal loveliness despite the amused challenge of her gaze. But the necklace—oh, surely it must be a copy. In this weak light, who could tell? He could not help questioning her.

"I believe that is a famous necklace you are wearing?" he murmured as he sipped wine that gleamed less red than her rubies.

"Yes, it is the de Lorca necklace," she told him with composure. "The diamonds are from Tibet, the rubies of course are from India. You will note their slightly uneven Oriental cut."

He had noticed. He sipped his wine. "But is not the de Lorca necklace a famous Spanish treasure, owned by some great house in Spain?"

Her smile flashed. "The Duke of Lorca once owned it. It was a gift to me of the buccaneers, for a small service I was able to do them."

His golden eyes widened. It gave him a new view of the buccaneers, that they could afford to make a gift like this one! "It must have been a very great service indeed," he murmured.

Her slim white shoulders moved expressively and the necklace glittered. "Well, it was thought at the time that I might have won them all a king's pardon—but as it turned out, I did not." Her lips twisted bitterly.

"Ah, I see." He did not quite see, and he wished he dared to press further and get her version of the famous story of how the de Lorca necklace had changed hands in the Azores, but he dared not. This, after all, was a buccaneer port and he a Spaniard. "Then you are saying that under English law you are still—?" He sought for the polite way to say it.

"'Outside the law' is the phrase you are seeking, I believe," she said with composure. "And yes, it is quite true. We cannot return to England, and we stay here on suffrance. Jamaica is still protected by the buccaneers and my husband is—unofficially, of course—Lord Admiral of the Buccaneers."

Raymond du Monde had good reason to know it!

"I have met the Duchess of Lorca once," he said tentatively.

"Really?" The delicate hand that was twirling the stem of a crystal goblet came to a full stop. "Where is she now?"

"No one knows. It seems she has gone into seclusion." Did he note a gleam in the silver eyes opposite him? If so, the lady was making no comment.

"Shall we go in to dinner?" She had noticed that his glass was empty.

He rose from one of the comfortable cane-seated chairs and proffered her his arm.

Thus in gallant fashion they swept into the large dining room where Carolina frequently gave dinner parties for as many as twenty guests. Upon the long table was a bewildering array of silver, and a dozen candles in wall sconces lit up the room. There was a huge centerpiece of fruit and exotic tropical flowers, and the windows were open to the velvet darkness and the night air that streamed in from the sea.

"Faith, I'm surprised you have your windows open with so much plate about!" he could not help remarking, for he personally considered this city a den of thieves.

She gave him a mocking look. "Few would care to steal from Captain Kells," she assured him. "He is known to bring speedy justice to wrongdoers."

A new view of buccaneering, surely!

"But we have a treat for you," she added. "We will be served tonight by the young girl you saved from harm on the street today." She nodded as the door to the pantry opened and Gilly came in.

This was an entirely new and more subdued Gilly. She wore a plain gown of indigo-blue and with it a white apron and a flowing white linen collar. Her riotous ginger hair had been combed severely back by Betts and was topped by a white ruffled mobcap. She had been transformed, it seemed, from street urchin into neat little serving girl—but her eyes betrayed her. They nearly started from her head at the sight of Carolina's necklace and she tripped and almost lost the silver tray of soup bowls she was carrying.

"This is Gilly, whom you saved," said Carolina. "I thought you might not recognize her."

The Spaniard's gaze passed over Gilly without interest. Turning to smirk at him, Gilly caught that indifference and flushed. In other circumstances she would have stuck out her tongue at him but under Carolina's watchful eye she knew she must behave. Her gaze went back to the necklace and she set the silver soup bowls down with a clatter.

"It is green turtle soup," explained Carolina, lifting her spoon. She smiled at him. "If you are but recently from France, you may not be familiar with it. It is a specialty of my cook's."

Raymond du Monde sampled his soup and pronounced it delicious.

"As you can see, I have taken Gilly into my household as a maidservant," said Carolina when the girl had left the room. "She has been badly treated by life—she will get better treatment here."

A soft heart then. . . . Somehow the Spaniard had not expected this in a buccaneer's lady.

"I have indeed had green turtle soup before," he said. "But none so delicious."

Carolina smiled. "Cook will be pleased."

She was studying her dinner guest as she spoke. "I have never been to France," she said. "Is it very beautiful?"

He shrugged. "I am from Marseilles, a crowded dirty port city." It was his Spanish distaste for the French that was speaking.

Her winglike brows lifted. Plainspoken for a Frenchman! Those of her acquaintance had usually beat about the bush when speaking to a lady.

Yet despite his French name, despite his claim to be from Marseilles, and for all the French foppishness of his dress, there was something about this Monsieur du Monde . . . something *Spanish*. And she who had lived on Tortuga and seen and talked to so many Spanish prisoners there awaiting ransom or working out their ransom, had sensed that about him. After all, Spain had many dashing cavaliers—and some would consider it great sport to pay an impudent incognito call on Tortuga and dine in the home of the Lord Admiral of the Buccaneers!

Idly, she tried him on it, wondering if she could catch him out. As he bit into his lobster, she asked in Spanish, "Are you staying here long?"

Perhaps it was his concentration on the lobster, perhaps the dazzling effect this beautiful woman was having on him, but Raymond du Monde, before he could think, answered in Spanish, "Until tomorrow only."

He looked up as the words left his mouth and saw her smiling at him. Like the adventurer he was, he came instantly alert—and mounted his attack. "You speak amazingly good Spanish," he complimented her.

"So," she said dryly, "do you, monsieur—or should I say *señor?*"

The words hung on the empty air, pervading the sudden silence as Gilly, who had just come into the room, carrying a big platter of beaten biscuits, paused, round-eyed, and stared at Monsieur du Monde, whom the lady of the house had just indirectly accused of being Spanish.

But the dinner guest proved equal to the occasion. He flashed a smile at his hostess. "One picks up a smattering of all languages at New Providence," he admitted engagingly. "Your own proficiency, I would imagine, came from Tortuga?"

Behind him Gilly gasped. New Providence had no buccaneer port like Port Royal, with a royal governor and a bustling trading center—only a pirate port with lean-to shacks set up on the sand. Desperate tales were told of New Providence. And Gilly knew they were all too true—*she* had come here from New Providence.

Carolina was still smiling but her eyes narrowed. His answer had satisfied her, for it suited the man who spoke. He *could* be a pirate—and perhaps a renegade Spaniard to boot. Oddly she found herself regretting that he was not a buccaneer, for buccaneers were privateers really, patriotic men who would never attack ships of their own flag or those of their country's friends. Buccaneers fought only Spain.

"So you are from New Providence?" she murmured. "Recently, I mean?"

He shrugged an affirmation. "One must be from somewhere, I suppose."

"I have often wondered about the place. What is it like there?"

She was challenging him, he thought. There was a good mind behind that winsome smile, those flashing silver eyes. "It is a hellhole," he said bluntly. "There are words that would describe the place in French—but they are not for a lady's ears."

"That bad?" she mocked him.

"Worse," he said with feeling, for he had heard evil stories about New Providence—stories that would truly offend a lady's ears.

"Still I am told there are some colorful people there." She sensed his withdrawal but refused to let go of the subject. "Rouge, for example?"

He guessed she was testing him, and under his lace collar he began to sweat. Who could guess what this elegant lady might know of New Providence or its denizens? But Rouge, at least he had heard of. She was famous far and wide. "What do you wish to know of her?" he asked cautiously.

Gilly had set down the platter of biscuits and now she paused in the door and watched him brightly.

"Oh, I don't know," Carolina said vaguely. "What she is like, I suppose. Accounts of her differ so."

If that was true, he had a chance! "An Amazon," he declared flatly.

"I am told she wields a cutlass like a man."

"Not so well," he said indifferently. "She has scars where"—he grinned—"they don't show. Shall I tell you about them?" His face lit up with a wicked smile. He would fling back the elegant lady's challenge!

"Never mind," said Carolina hastily. "I just wondered—is she very beautiful? I have heard rumors."

"She does not hold a candle to *your* loveliness," he declared gallantly. "In fact, I found Rouge quite plain!"

With a satisfied expression, Gilly closed the door and retired into the pantry.

"Come now, I did not ask for a comparison!" laughed Carolina, tossing her head beneath that hot gaze. "But I have been told that Rouge is a queen among the pirates, that her hair is like flame, that she has many lovers, that she wears men's clothes—and I wondered what she really looked like."

"Ah, she wears men's clothes," he agreed airily, feeling that was a safe admission. "But she has no air, no style as *you* do, my lady."

Carolina, hard-pressed on this subject of her beauty, changed the subject, and Gilly, who had had her ear pressed to a crack of the pantry door, strolled back to the kitchen looking smug and insulted Cook, who warned her, cleaver raised, that if she didn't hold her tongue she'd chop it off.

Unaware of the altercation in the kitchen, Carolina called softly to the cat who, fed in the kitchen by Cook, who adored her, now strolled lazily into the dining room through the pantry door that Gilly had left carefully ajar.

"This is Moonbeam," she told her guest, reaching down affectionately to pet Moonbeam's pale shining fur. The cat mewed softly in answer and began to purr.

Ramon del Mundo looked politely down at the cat. He saw a striking white Persian cat with broad paws and an enormous plumelike tail, who rubbed against Carolina's skirts and looked up at her adoringly with big green eyes.

"A handsome animal," he observed. "And well named."

Carolina smiled. "It was Kells who named her." She remembered the day Kells had brought the cat home to her, a half-grown kitten and most distrustful. A failed ship's cat was Moonbeam. She had detested the sea so much—meowing and clinging to anything that she could with desperate claws—that the crew had at first named her "Landlubber," then got rid of her in disgust.

Carolina, who shared with the kitten a preference for keeping her feet dry, sympathized with Moonbeam's dislike of slippery decks strewn with salt spray. "It must have been terrible for her, having to lick the sea salt from her long fur all the time," she had said, cuddling the kitten. "What shall we name her?" Kells's voice had softened and he had run a gentle hand across Carolina's hair. "I thought we'd name her Moonbeam for she has a pale shimmer—like your hair." Now, dining with this new-met stranger, Carolina's face grew dreamy as she remembered—and the glow that lit her eyes as she thought of how Kells had said that made her something to behold.

Across from her, the Spaniard-pretending-to-be-a-Frenchman caught his breath at the sight and from the depths of him he envied her lawless buccaneer lover.

Chapter 3

In the long dining room Carolina was studying Raymond du Monde's dark face, his mobile mouth, his expressive features. And especially his eyes, wicked and flaring golden in the candlelight. Eyes that commanded, mocked, eyes that could hold one pinned by their gleam. . . .

Outside, in the distance, the wild Port Royal night was just beginning. From somewhere came the homing cry of a bird and a snatch of raucous drunken song and laughter. In the eerie jungle of mangrove swamp that lay between sandspit Port Royal and mainland Jamaica, the stalking night had begun, and little creatures scurried through the dark to safety. In the jungles up the Cobre the parrots squawked sleepily and the planters sat on their porches and slapped at mosquitoes—and gave up and went inside.

But here in the elegance of her long dining room Carolina studied her dinner guest, and wondered about him, for she was inwardly sure he was not what he seemed. About her white neck the fabulous necklace glimmered like blood against snow. They might have been anywhere in Europe and not in lawless Port Royal.

Moonbeam had sunk luxuriously down by Carolina's feet, purring. Absently Carolina rubbed the fur just behind Moonbeam's pointy ear with her toe, and Moonbeam's purr grew louder.

The man across from her was smiling.

"I am told you loosed a jaguar once," he observed, skillfully spearing a bit of lobster. It was but one of the many stories he had heard about her, for he had been asking discreet questions about town all afternoon and had learned that people were eager to share what they knew about the glamorous Silver Wench.

It was then she knew where she had seen eyes like his before. They were the eyes of a cat, a big dangerous cat.

She shrugged. "Many stories are told of me—some of them are even true."

He was delighted with her answer. "But about the jaguar," he urged. "Tell me about that."

She remembered the jaguar all too well. The big cat had been brought in by sea, captured somewhere in the wilds of Mexico. And captured along with the galleon that was to bear her to Havana. Carolina had first seen the proud lustrous animal exhibited on the deck of a buccaneer sloop that had sailed into Port Royal harbor. Seen it tied and helpless but roaring its defiance at its captors.

"A female," a young buccaneer had told her casually. "The Spaniards said they caught her trying to protect her cubs."

"What of the cubs?" she had asked.

"Escaped," was the prompt reply. "They shot at them but the jungle was dense and they got away. But they were young and they probably died without their mother. She might have killed someone had not a lucky shot felled her."

The signs of that "lucky shot" were there, a long gash where the shot had grazed the skull, cut through a ribbon of fur and stunned the big cat, who had then been taken alive.

"So they ran off her cubs, left them to die, and took her away to sea?" Carolina's voice had been unsteady.

"Yes. Is she not a beauty? Our captain thinks to sell her to a man in the town who holds dog fights and cock fights. Think of the sport we will have when we put her in a walled enclosure and loose the dogs on her?"

Carolina had not wanted to think about that. She demanded to see the captain immediately.

"How much," she had asked him peremptorily, "for the jaguar?"

Surprised, he had named the price he hoped to get in town. "But I might get more," he had said with a frown.

"I will pay you twice what you ask," she said. "In gold. If you will sail me up the Cobre where I will release her."

"*Release* her?" The captain was obviously taken aback.

"Yes." The word was spoken crisply. "Release her."

The captain of the sloop had gnawed at his lip and thought about that. Finally he had agreed.

Kells had been gone, on the other side of the island. It was Hawks, a darkly disapproving Hawks, who had accompanied Carolina on that journey up the Cobre. She had made friends with the big cat on the way—after a fashion. At least she had sensed a kind of wild understanding, a kinship in those lamplike golden eyes.

And when at last she had chosen a place to release the jaguar, she had insisted on doing it herself. Hawks had nearly exploded at her insistence.

"She will turn on you, Hawks," Carolina had insisted. "But she will not turn on me. I am sure of it."

Hawks was considerably less sure. He had turned menacingly to the men about him, who had watched with fascination as Carolina, the knife in her hand flashing in the moonlight, had advanced upon the dangerous animal.

"If anyone so much as breathes, I'll have his ears for it," Hawks had growled. And to Carolina he had said, "At least have a pistol in your other hand—in case she does turn on you after all!"

"All right." Impatiently Carolina had taken the pistol Hawks proffered.

About her the men watched tensely. Hands crept toward cutlasses—and pistols.

"Stand well back, Hawks," Carolina instructed. "I think we're near enough to shore that she can leap over. I don't know if she can swim."

There was sweat on Hawks's brow now. He was cursing silently—and praying, too, although he would never have admitted it.

The big cat had been positioned half over the ship's rail. Swiftly, with her razor-sharp knife, Carolina had slashed the bonds that held the animal, and leaped back.

But she need not have worried. The jaguar had no thought for those on the sloop. In a single fluid bound the big cat gained the shore, disappearing into the dark wall of green jungle, black and silver in the moonlight, that almost scraped the sloop's hull.

But behind Carolina, as the cat leaped, a shot had rung out.

Carolina had swung around and without thought instinctively fired at the man who held a smoking pistol. With a look of disbelief on his face he had crumpled to the deck.

It had been a very tense moment. Hawks always

sweated when he recounted it. "There I was on the deck with a whole crew of armed men," he had said with feeling. "And the captain's lady chooses to shoot one of them!"

The man had lived. Carolina, shooting as she whirled, had dealt him only a flesh wound.

"Why did you do it?" she had asked in an anguished voice as she stood over him while he held on to his bloody shoulder. "Why did you try to kill her?"

He hadn't known really. A lovely wild thing just released—his instinct had been to kill it. And brag about it later. But along with the pain, he had felt shamefaced as he looked up at the Silver Wench bending over him.

"Do you think he hit the jaguar, Hawks?" Carolina had demanded.

Hawks had shaken his head. "No, the shot went wild. The sloop lurched as the cat went over."

She had insisted on staying where they were, anchored until dawn. A quick search had revealed no bloody trail on shore, but there were the imprints of big pads on the marshy earth.

"I promise you," Carolina had told them all with flashing eyes, "that if anybody hunts that animal down —or if any of you so much as tell where we dropped her off—that I will ask Kells for your heads for it!"

They had shuffled their feet and looked at each other uneasily. The Silver Wench was always more than one bargained for—but she had shot one of them. And now was threatening the rest.

It was Hawks who had saved the day.

"Captain Kells will take it kindly that you have done this favor for his lady," he had rumbled. "And now we'd best get us back and leave the cat to fend for herself. I'll be buying the whisky when we get back to Port Royal. Meantime you should look to that shoulder, Roy."

"I shot you. *I'll* bind up the wound," Carolina had told Roy bluntly.

She never, Hawks remarked later, said she was sorry she had shot him. Indeed he was sure she was not! But she did not wish to see a fellow human suffer. A strange contradiction, was the Wench.

And now her dinner guest was asking her, "Is it true you loosed the jaguar yourself?"

"Yes," she sighed. "It is true. I have done many reckless things."

There was admiration in his narrow gaze. *What a woman!* he was thinking. *So wild and free. What had this buccaneer ever done to deserve her?*

"I am told your husband was away at the time. What did he say when he heard?"

"Oh, Kells was furious," she admitted frankly. "He made me promise that I would never again sail up the Cobre without him. Or have dealings with jaguars."

He chuckled. "I can well imagine." But then he grew serious again, studying her lovely delicate features in the candlelight, the slim white hand that held a stemmed wineglass. "But I cannot help but wonder . . . why did you do it?" he asked softly.

Across the handsome table her silver eyes flashed. "Because she was beautiful and brave—and she was only protecting her own when she was caught. I could not let her die for it. And sometimes," her voice grew dreamy, "I think of her out there, stalking the blue hills, padding the jungle floor by moonlight. I think of her looking out to sea and wondering if her cubs are safe."

"Perhaps they are," he said softly. And there was an answering light in his golden eyes as he spoke.

"I like to think it," she said and took a quick sip of wine. Her voice was husky. "I like to think that she has found a mate worthy of her and that she will bear other cubs and they will love her."

And across the table in this buccaneer's house, across a forest of silver captured from Spanish galleons, a man who considered himself the enemy of everything she loved lost his heart to her. All his life Don Ramon del Mundo had taken his women lightly, almost mockingly. Women, he had believed, were for pleasure. Except the one he would one day marry, of course—she must have an enormous dowry to bring back to life his depleted estates in Spain. Now, looking at this buccaneer's beauty in her low-cut jade gown, he knew what it was to dream.

"This Kells is a lucky man," he murmured.

The sudden sincerity of his voice struck her. She looked up abruptly and caught the hot light in his tawny eyes.

"Perhaps not so lucky," she said bitterly. For was it not really all her fault, this predicament Kells now found himself in? Life had stretched forward so brilliantly for them—for a while. Kells had sought and received his pardon for buccaneering, they had planned a big wedding.

But then Kells had been the victim of a devilish plot. In England a peer of the realm—seeking to disguise his own villainies—had impersonated Kells and sunk several English ships. And once again made Rye Evistock an outlaw.

And so it was as Captain Kells that her proud lover had gone to sea again. He had caught the culprit, of course—off the Azores. But when the culprit had turned out to be the Marquess of Saltenham, who was her best friend Reba's betrothed, Carolina had pleaded with Kells to save him—and he had. Much to her present regret.

For Reba's termagant mother had mustered up paid witnesses to swear that Robin Tyrell, Marquess of Saltenham, had not even been near the ocean, much less guilty of the maraudings in question. And Rye

Evistock and his lady had gone back to Tortuga once again to resume their false identities of Captain Kells and his Silver Wench, Christabel Willing.

On Tortuga it had somehow been possible to forget —most of the time—the life they should have had. But here in Port Royal it was not. Every day brought with it fresh reminders. For although Kells and his lady had been welcomed by the governor here—a governor who chose to wink at the presence of buccaneers in his domain since they were a stout defense against the Spanish in nearby Cuba—Port Royal was a cosmopolitan city. English gentry came here fresh from London. Landed island gentry came down the Cobre River or sailed from other parts of the island to attend parties at the governor's house in Port Royal.

Kells and his lady attended those, too, but there was always a certain sadness in their eyes when they returned home after one of them. For such evenings brought sharply back to them all that they had lost.

Although they had never actually spoken of it—not in words—there was tacit agreement between them not to bring a child into the world while they lived under the shadow of the sword here in Port Royal. Kells, she knew, did not want to rear his sons to be buccaneers or his daughters to marry buccaneers—and what other fate could there be for the children of such as they? It was not the price on his head in Spain which disturbed him, she knew—even though, now, that price had gone up to fifty thousand pieces of eight—it was the charge of piracy that hung over his head in England, a charge that would forever bar him from holding his rightful place in the land of his birth.

They lived on the governor's sufferance here in Port Royal. But Acting Governor White would soon be replaced, and a new governor might be less friendly. It seemed they were always to live beneath the shadow of the sword.

And so they made do as best they could. They entertained buccaneers and tradesmen of the better sort, and they were frequent guests of the governor. But it was not the life they would have chosen for themselves, and they both knew it.

Carolina wrested herself back to the present. "I am surprised the friends of the man you shot did not turn on you," her dinner guest was saying.

They were back to the jaguar. . . .

She shrugged. "I suppose they might have, had it not been for Hawks. He guards me, and he is very resolute."

"Yes," he laughed. "I have seen him."

"And then," she mused, "there is my husband's reputation. Kells is—formidable." Her voice was wistful. She was wishing he did not *have* to be so formidable, that he could settle into the life of the English country gentleman he was cut out to be. "But then," she changed the subject gracefully, "these are old stories about my various follies. Tell me about yourself, Monsieur du Monde. You must have had many notable adventures—your very name means 'man of the world.'"

Indeed it meant that in Spanish as well as in French! Ramon del Mundo's golden eyes kindled. She wanted stories, did she? Well, he would tell her stories!

And so for the rest of the evening, that sworn enemy of all things English, a man who had come to Jamaica to plan an invasion, to spy out Port Royal and learn the weak chinks in the armor of its defenses, kept up a running stream of stories that made Carolina laugh.

None of them were true, of course. Like himself in his present guise, they were a sham.

A sham meant to impress a lady.

And all the while his mind was fiercely conjuring up what it would be like to have her with him in bed, to feel that silken body turn toward him, to see that lovely face regard him with trusting eyes in the moonlight, to touch those soft lips that would be slightly parted as she melted into his arms with a sweet sigh of surrender. His temples throbbed as he imagined himself making love to her, as he felt her turn and moan in his arms—and tremble with an ardor that he would incite in her. And afterward she would whisper as she lay against his chest—"Ramon, Ramon, I never knew it could be like this!"

Yes, brave and beautiful though she was, he would bend her to his will—and she would be glad to be bent.

The worldly Spaniard, whose very name conjured up daring and dashing deeds in the hearts of the mantillaed ladies of New Spain, was falling in love.

He cared not what he said or what she said that magical night—it was enough just to be in the same room with her, to devour her with his eyes. And to imagine. Especially to imagine.

He would be back for this woman one day, he told himself. He would come back at the head of an invading host, he would wrest her from her buccaneer, *he would make this glorious wench love him!*

"It is too bad you are not staying in Port Royal," she told her guest wickedly at parting. "For you could have met our neighbor, Monsieur Deauville, who is lately from France. Perhaps you know him already—he is from Marseilles, too."

Raymond du Monde assumed a suitably melancholy mien. "A pity indeed," he agreed with a sigh. "I should have been overjoyed to make Monsieur Deauville's acquaintance, but there is no time."

"Ah," she murmured sympathetically, but with mischief flashing in her eyes. "Being from the same city, you would have much to talk about."

"I have been gone from Marseilles a long time," he told her vaguely. "But I spent my youth there."

A misspent youth, she had no doubt! But she smiled

at Monsieur du Monde and let him kiss her hand in parting. "I am sorry Hawks is not here to accompany you home," she told him regretfully. "The streets of Port Royal are dangerous by night."

The streets of Port Royal were dangerous at any time, but her departing cavalier started as if stung. "I will manage to win my way through them," he promised her sternly.

"I am sure you will," she said, hiding her mirth, for if ever she had met a dangerous man, she was sure it was this one. Perhaps not so formidable as Kells but—formidable nonetheless. "I bid you good evening then, Monsieur du Monde," she said demurely. "And wish you well in all your endeavors."

He gave her an odd look as he left—but then, of course, he told himself, she could have no idea what those endeavors might be.

John Daimler looked up as Raymond du Monde entered.

"Well, Ramon," he growled. He had been imbibing large amounts of wine as he worried about his reckless—and unwanted—guest, and his voice was roughened by it. "And how did your dinner with Captain Kells go?"

"Oh, Kells was not yet back from the Cobre so I dined with his delightful lady," was the airy response. "She has no peer among women, Juan—none at all."

"She's a clever wench to boot," agreed his host sourly. "I hope you were close-mouthed, else she might have found you out!"

"I was discreet. Besides, who could doubt me? Do I not make a fine Frenchman, Juan, rigged out in these French silks?"

John Daimler snorted. All the wine he had drunk had made him bolder. "I hope the Silver Wench has not got such a hold on you as to make you stay in this place, for it's death that's staring us in the face if you do. His lady may not discover you for what you are, but Kells will ferret you out in five minutes!"

"Oh, surely he is not so great an adversary as that! Dangerous I will admit but—"

"Oh, deliver me from your banter!" Daimler slammed his heavy tankard down with a force that rocked the oaken table. "Do ye go tonight or don't ye?"

"I go tonight, John," sighed Ramon. "And I will leave you these French clothes to sell and thus help provide for the men I'll be sending you."

"The men you'll—?" John stopped to stare.

"Yes, a month from now—two months at the latest—a pinnace will be arriving from Havana. You'll know her—she'll be the same one I arrived in and will leave in, this night. And she'll bear armed men."

John fell back; his face lost color. "You're planning to attack Port Royal *from a pinnace?*"

His guest sighed. "You didn't let me finish, John. My plan has not yet been approved by Spain—but it will be, never fear. I will send my pinnace with a small advance guard—fifteen men, no more. They will all be hand-picked. And I'll be arriving in force to lead them, John, with a fleet of warships behind me. This early group will look like Englishmen, talk like Englishmen, they'll make friends at the forts—that way they won't be noticed when they slip in and cause havoc during the attack."

"And my part in all this?"

"Only to find them housing, John. And pass on to them any messages I manage to send."

John Daimler was staring at the shadow of a hanging iron chandelier suspended from the ceiling. The shadow suddenly looked to him like a noose. Indeed he could feel the hemp around his suddenly perspiring neck at this moment. With big spatulate fingers he loosened a collar grown suddenly too tight, and jumped as a cheerful Ramon clapped him on the back.

"Don't look so glum, John. 'Tis a lieutenant governorship you can look forward to!"

More likely a gibbet, thought John. But he was in it now—too late to back out. This Spanish devil would find a way to wreck him if he did. "Aye, I've that to look forward to," he echoed in a hollow voice.

Carolina, who had only been exchanging friendly banter as she bade her departing guest good-by, had no idea of the amount of heat she had engendered. Had you asked her, she would have answered frankly that Raymond du Monde was attractive, yes. And that he had a way of looking at a woman with those tawny gold eyes that must have seduced many an unwary maid.

But she, of course, would never be one of those, she would have added airily. Still—it had been an unexpectedly delightful evening. Since Kells chose to be on what seemed to be one of his interminable trips up the Cobre River of late, at least she had had good company!

She tripped lightly up the stairs in her jade gown, and once in her own room viewed a flushed, rather excited face in the beveled mirror. That reflection brought her up short. Had she looked so to the Frenchman? she asked herself uneasily. Like an excited young girl? Her color rose at the thought. And this necklace that glimmered so barbarically around her neck, she really should not have worn it—it was flaunting their wealth. True, Raymond the Frenchman had been well-dressed this evening, but many a man had a good suit of clothes and no prospects. All in all, she felt rather ashamed of herself to have made such a display.

She removed the necklace, went to the huge trunk with the curved top, and opened it. Rummaging down, she slipped aside the trunk's false bottom, swiftly opened the teak and silver box, and dropped the necklace inside to rest on its dark red velvet interior. A moment later and the trunk's false bottom had slid back into place. Resting on that false bottom was an identical teakwood and silver box, and inside that box was what appeared to the casual glance to be a duplicate necklace. It had been made for the Duchess of Lorca, and now Carolina owned them both—the fake and the original.

And she kept them one atop the other with the trunk's false bottom in between just in case someone managed to penetrate the house and find the necklace. A thief would not want to be burdened with this enormous heavy trunk—he would snatch the silver-encrusted box containing the first necklace he came to—and he would depart with the wrong necklace. The original would be safe below.

She heard a sound at the door and saw that Gilly had opened it and stood watching her with those avid brown eyes.

Carolina frowned. "You must learn to knock before opening doors, Gilly."

Gilly looked dismayed. "I only asked Cook if I couldn't come up and help you get undressed—all those hooks and things." In point of fact, Cook had thrown a wooden spoon at Gilly and told her to get out of the kitchen; if she stayed there'd be nothing but broken crockery since she'd already dropped a bowl and managed to demolish two plates, but Gilly saw no need to mention that.

Carolina relented. "All right, Gilly," she sighed. "You can come in and unhook me although usually Betts does that."

Gilly flashed her a bright insincere smile, and moved forward with alacrity. Had Carolina been looking into the mirror she would have seen Gilly's face, alight with avarice, staring first at the back of Carolina's white neck, now devoid of the necklace, and then at the big curved-top trunk that she had seen closing as she entered.

It would be easy, Gilly was thinking. *Easy.* . . . Jarvis, her lover, had told her it would be easy, and she had not believed him. Now she knew that she could pull it off, all by herself. Jarvis was impatient, but now that she thought about it, there was no hurry. She would bide her time, she would become a trusted servant, and in her own time she would pick a quarrel and leave the house with the necklace—and someone else would take the blame, for she would be far away. She would be smart this time—not like that time in Bristol when she'd stolen the gold and jet mourning ring and gotten herself thrown in jail and then been transported for her pains. If the ship hadn't foundered and her papers been lost, she'd be slaving away as a bondservant at this very moment! As it was, she was but one of a handful rescued from the sea—and none of the others knew about her. She'd made up a story and it had been believed. After that she'd drifted.

But now she saw her future clear. She could buy herself a golden world—with the necklace. Just the gold links would take her any place she wanted to go. And the rubies and diamonds, why, they could buy her a new life! And why should Jarvis share in that future? Oh, she needed time to think, to plan.

"You should have thanked our French guest for saving you today." Carolina tossed the words over her shoulder.

Gilly paused in her unhooking. "He may be French," she said scornfully, "but he's lying if he says he comes here from New Providence! I'd have remembered him!"

Carolina turned slowly around. "*You* came here from New Providence?" she said in an altered voice.

Too late, Gilly realized her error. "I was shipwrecked," she said hastily. "I come from Bristol, like I told you."

Those silver eyes were contemplating her now, seeing her more clearly. "Were you there long, Gilly?" Carolina asked almost casually.

"Not so long," mumbled Gilly. Carolina's scrutiny made her nervous. "I thought to do you a good turn by telling you he ain't what he said he was," she defended.

"And so you may have. . . ." murmured Carolina, asking herself why a man would claim to be from New Providence when he was not. New Providence was the sinkhole of the western world. Surely there was no credit to be gained by claiming acquaintance with such a place!

Encouraged by Carolina's words, Gilly rushed on, determined to ingratiate herself. "And he didn't describe Rouge right either. Rouge ain't no—whatever he said."

"Amazon," said Carolina absently. "It means a warrior woman."

"Well, I don't know as I would call Rouge that either," said Gilly in an injured voice. "It's true she's tall and she wears men's clothes, and I've heard tell she could fight with a cutlass, but I never seen her do it. Rouge is *beautiful!*" she burst out. "She has more red hair than I ever seen and when her eyes flash, there's not a man on New Providence that doesn't turn to look at her!"

"Indeed?" Carolina's brows elevated at such heat from Gilly. "And what is Rouge to you, Gilly?"

"Nothin'," mumbled Gilly. "But," her voice flared up, "Rouge was good to me. When Ace and Blackboots wanted to throw dice for me, Rouge said she'd have Fletch kill the pair of them if they didn't let me alone."

"I see." Carolina gave her new serving girl an odd look. "It would seem that you are perpetually being saved, Gilly. First by the famous Rouge and now by the Silver Wench." Her voice held a scathing note. "But that hardly explains how you got to Port Royal, does it?"

Gilly swallowed. She hadn't realized Carolina would ask her that.

"You came here on some pirate ship out to survey the local shipping, out to watch the merchantmen who came here to trade with the buccaneers and catch up with them later after they'd left with their goods, didn't you?" asked Carolina in a hard voice. *"Didn't you?"*

Gilly was looking at her in panic. "Yes, I did," she cried. "But I run away—leastways I *tried* to run away, and they caught me and put me in Sadie's house. She dressed me up in Tilly's petticoat and her own chemise and said it was enough for me to wear, I'd look juicier to her clientele!" She began to sniffle. "And I managed to get my dress back and put it on over the top of them, and I jumped out the window onto a cart and slid off the cart, and I was running away with them chasing me when I tripped and fell—and that's when I looked up and saw *you!"*

It wasn't true, of course. Jarvis had indeed taken her to Sadie's brothel, and while there she had idly filched the chemise and petticoat. She had been dancing around the front room, showing off. Jarvis had come in at that moment, muttering excitedly that the Silver Wench in a yellow dress had left her house and was strolling toward High Street. Gilly had hurried outside and Sadie and Tilly, noting their clothes disappearing with her, had given chase. Whereupon Gilly had thrown herself down at Carolina's feet.

But to Carolina, Gilly's story was believable. Terrible things happened in this part of the world, worse yet in New Providence. It was entirely possible that Gilly had been spirited here to wear away her youth in a brothel, and had run from the place in terror.

"I'm sorry, Gilly," she said in a softer voice. "It was just that when you mentioned New Providence . . ."

"I know," Gilly said quickly. "It's an evil place. I never been anywhere so evil." Her curiosity got the better of her. "Have *you* ever been there?" she asked.

"No, thank God." Carolina shuddered. She turned as Betts knocked softly and entered. Betts gave Gilly an affronted look. "Never mind, Betts, I'm all unhooked," Carolina told the girl. "Find Gilly a place to sleep, won't you? I think Nell's old room would be best."

Betts started to protest because Nell's old cubbyhole of a room lay directly between hers and Cook's, and she didn't relish having Gilly as a neighbor! But the mistress seemed bent on favoring the street girl, even though she and Cook had both recognized Gilly for a bad one at first sight!

Gilly was smirking as Betts led her away.

Chapter 4

Carolina's mind as she undressed for bed was not upon the handsome stranger who had devoured her with his eyes at dinner—nor even with her adventurous husband who was gone up the Cobre so unexplicably often of late: her mind was on Level Green and the world she had known in Virginia's Tidewater country. She sat long at her dressing table combing her long fair hair, but her troubled eyes did not see her beautiful reflection in the lovely beveled French mirror Kells had bought for her when they had first moved here: she saw instead her mother's reckless face, and the dark blue eyes seemed to hold a restless appeal.

She had run away from the Tidewater angry at them all, but now they were in trouble. Deep trouble. And Virgie had written to her, she guessed, in the hope that she would help them out. She could of course ask Kells to send them money; he was very rich, and he would do it if she asked him. But—Kells had no reason to love her family; they had near got him killed the last time he was there.

No, if she did this thing she must do it herself. With her own resources.

Moodily she went over and took out the diamond and ruby necklace the buccaneers had once awarded her. It was really the only thing she owned that Kells had *not* given her. She toyed with it wistfully, for the de Lorca necklace meant something to her. In a way it was a symbol of love regained when she had thought all was lost.

With a sigh she put it away in its usual hiding place. It was worth a fortune; if she sent the necklace to her mother at Level Green the Lightfoots would have money to burn. They could pay off Fielding's debts, they could give handsome dowries to their younger daughters, they could live their extravagant life forever.

She slept restlessly and dreamed that from somewhere a great voice was saying: *You can have the man or the necklace—you cannot have them both!* And the Cobre River was in flood and she was on a crazily built raft, floating down the river and hanging on for dear life. And suddenly, on one side of the raft, in the water just ahead, she saw Kells—and he looked dead, with his dark hair floating in the riotous water. And on the other side of the raft just ahead she saw a hand reach up holding the de Lorca necklace, its rubies sparkling like splashes of blood, its diamonds catching the light brilliantly. She heard herself give an anguished cry and snatch at Kells's dark hair, trying desperately to drag him onto the raft. And about her at that moment she seemed to hear the Devil's laughter, and her head jerked about and she saw the hand with the necklace disappear beneath the foaming water.

She woke with a scream and found that her fingers were twisted not in Kells's heavy shining dark hair but in the lace of her chemise, and that she had ripped the delicate fabric. She lay there, shaking, still under the spell of her terrible dream. And then she tried to laugh at herself for there was no question of her ever having to choose between Kells and the necklace, nor was she ever apt to raft down the Cobre.

She got up restlessly and walked to the window to let the trade winds dry her hot face, damp in the heat. Outside the velvet night was sparkling with stars. She heard a bawdy song and looked out to see Hawks come down the street with a rolling gait and an unsteady walk. He had doubtless been visiting a brothel, possibly Sadie's place, for Hawks—dour fellow that he was—loved the wenches. He was obviously very drunk and he fell against the door downstairs and banged for admittance.

Carolina sighed and threw on a light robe, then went down and unbarred the door to let him in. Hawks looked abashed to see her.

"I'm sorry," he said in a slurred voice. "I'd expected Cook to let me in."

"Cook sleeps like the dead," said Carolina, and for a moment wished *she* did, instead of dreaming terrifying dreams. "No matter, I was awake. And I feel safer now that you are back in the house, Hawks."

He gave her a wide drunken smile and tried to bow. The gesture almost toppled him over on his face. "I promised the cap'n I'd protect you and protect you I will!" he said with a loud hiccup.

"I know you will, Hawks," laughed Carolina. "But I'm hoping that we'll neither of us be put to the test this night! Good night, Hawks."

She turned and went back upstairs and to her surprise met Gilly, just coming down from the attic where the servants had their cubbyhole rooms.

"What are you doing up, Gilly?" asked Carolina in surprise. "Couldn't you sleep?"

Gilly started guiltily at sight of Carolina. Actually, she had been about to dart into Carolina's room while Carolina was downstairs talking to Hawks. "Why, I"—suddenly she could not think of a good lie—"I heard voices and I wondered if there was trouble," she said weakly.

Carolina felt ashamed of what she had been thinking. She had wondered uneasily if Gilly had crept down to spy out the house, and now the girl, flustered, seemed to have been worried about her. "Come down to the kitchen, Gilly," she said in a warm voice, "and we'll have a bite to eat. You can tell me more about New Providence," she added kindly. "It must have been terrible for you there."

"Oh, yes—just terrible," Gilly agreed hastily.

"And you can tell me more about Rouge—that woman fascinates me. Tell me, how did she get her name?"

"I asked her once and she said it was her red hair—a French pirate named her that."

"If she'd been a brunette, I suppose he'd have christened her Noire or if a blonde he'd have called her Blanche!" laughed Carolina, trying to set Gilly at her ease as they went downstairs.

But although Gilly ate heartily, her answers were not very responsive. She had hoped to have a quick look at the trunk in Carolina's room while her mistress was downstairs, but she had missed her chance.

She ate glumly and Carolina put it down to the sharpness of her voice that had told the girl she didn't quite trust her.

The next morning after breakfast she again put on her yellow dress, added a sweeping straw hat to shield her fair complexion from the hot tropical sun, and again ventured out into the town. Hawks disapproved of these ventures; he would have preferred to keep her safe inside the house, and besides he had a pounding hangover, but he accompanied her without comment, slouching along with his hand ever near his big cutlass.

Carolina glanced curiously about her as they passed the place where the stranger had vaulted from a window to her side, but she saw no familiar faces. Indeed, John Daimler, relieved that the pinnace with his dangerous guest had departed the night before, had closed his shutters, shut up the house and taken himself off to visit a friend who lived past Portland Pitch to the east—a friend whom he hoped might be willing to take in the Spaniards when they arrived, and thus get them off his hands.

He had been attractive, had Raymond du Monde, thought Carolina, glancing curiously up at the closed shutters of Daimler's house, and he had given her an interesting evening. She wondered suddenly if he had really gone, and she found herself hoping in an unguarded moment that he had not.

With Hawks shouldering a way for her through the crowd, she made her way down to the market in the heart of High Street. A cart lumbered past, carrying huge turtles to market. Carolina felt sorry for the great sad-looking things, so awkward out of water—but they were the staple of the island diet. Five steady-eyed buccaneers, all armed to the teeth, were carrying a small heavy chest into the goldsmith's shop and the goldsmith was beaming, nodding his head to greet them and rubbing his hands. Seabirds screamed overhead, then streamed on by, spying some garbage being dumped into the harbor. Two sleek, gleaming Maroon women swayed by, each steadying a stalk of bananas on her head. An old man trudged by, barefoot, carrying a huge straw basket of *chochos,* a vegetable much like squash, and nearby an Indian woman with a singsong voice was melodically calling out the virtues of akee, displaying the big red pods with their black seeds and yellowish flesh.

"Don't never eat that before the pod bursts," cautioned Hawks. "It'll poison ye!"

Carolina nodded. She knew that, but Hawks never failed to caution her. She supposed Hawks was trying to make up for one of his rare excesses in getting drunk last night.

A group of traders whisked by for the great market bell had just sounded. Slaves from Africa with gleaming black bodies would soon be auctioned off—for the English had taken over the slave trade from the Dutch, and Port Royal, with its convenient location for ships coming from Africa and its marvelous harbor that could accommodate five hundred great ships, had become the busiest slave mart in the Americas. But it was neither slaves nor the latest merchandise that Carolina had come to view.

She made her way through piled-up stalks of bananas, mountains of oranges and avocados and lemons, rosy gold mangoes and rich green limes, weaving her way through the crowd and the stacks of fruit until she came to another part of the market. Here were native palm leaf fans and delicate flexible straw hats, finely woven leather sandals and belts—a whole array of crafts native to the islands.

Laconic as always, Hawks made his way beside her with his big cutlass never far from his hand, for he knew there was no treasure ashore or afloat that Captain Kells valued as much as he valued this slim girl with the silver-gold hair. He was perplexed when Carolina came to a halt before a display of cheap wooden pattens—for the sand on which the city of Port Royal was built stretched down so deep that no piling had yet reached bottom and there was no mud to speak of. Why would Captain Kells's lady be wanting pattens in a town where there was neither mud nor snow? he wondered. But he made no comment when she carefully selected and bought a pair. Curious as to what she was up to, he accompanied her home.

She stopped before their front door.

"Hawks," she said in a low voice, "I need a favor. Do you think you could hollow out the sole of one of these pattens—and then put the leather back so cleverly that no one would ever know? And "—she hesitated—"do it privately, Hawks. Mention it to no one and let no one see you do it."

Hawks gave her a flashing look of understanding as he took the pattens from her hand. He was always whittling things, and it would be no great job to make a little strongbox of this patten if that was what the captain's lady wished. Quickly he set about it and brought it to her bedroom when it was done.

Carolina thanked him and closed the door. Once alone she opened the trunk and took out of it the fabulous ruby and diamond necklace set in gold and weighed it in her hands. It was very heavy—far heavier than the wood it had replaced. She put the necklace back and went down and asked Hawks quietly to insert a small amount of lead in the other patten. Hawks obliged.

Back in her bedroom she sighed as she wrapped the necklace in a small silk kerchief and slipped it into the thick hollowed-out sole of the patten, then she went down and silently handed the patten to Hawks. She watched as he put it back together so cleverly that no one would guess it had ever been tampered with.

Hawks looked after her speculatively as she left. He was the soul of loyalty and devoted to both Captain Kells and his lady. He assumed that Carolina had set up a small private bank of her own for coins in case, some rainy day, she found herself without funds.

Early that morning Carolina had sent word to Captain Banks, who plied his ship, the *Morning Star,* between the islands of the West Indies and the Virginia coast. Her message said that she knew the captain was sailing tomorrow and she would be pleased if he would do her the honor of dining at the home of Captain Kells tonight before he left.

Captain Banks accepted with alacrity and arrived promptly—for invitations to the home of the Lord Admiral of the Buccaneers were much sought after. Besides, he liked the captain's lady and was one of the few who were privileged to know that she was really Carolina Lightfoot of Virginia's Tidewater. He was dazzled when she received him wearing a diamond and ruby necklace above a vivid green gown—and wished he'd bought that new suit today that he had passed by as much too expensive. He cleared his throat, rose to his full five feet, and beamed his small dancing blue eyes at the captain's lady.

"I've been told Captain Kells is out of the city, and it's sorry I am to miss him," he said sincerely.

"Yes, he's away up the Cobre," sighed Carolina. "Although I can't imagine what's so fascinating up there!"

The little captain chewed on his mustached lip. "There's plantations," he suggested thoughtfully. "Perhaps," he added, eyes twinkling, "you're about to become mistress of a great plantation—like your mother."

Carolina's smile was a little forced. She looked quickly about to see if any of the servants were listening, but the pantry door was tightly shut. She relaxed then—for none of the servants knew her origins and she did not want them to know. "I do not think I would make a very good mistress of a plantation," she admitted honestly. "It requires a certain talent, you know."

Captain Banks had heard tales of her extravagance,

and through Kells himself he knew of Carolina's proclivity for helping the less fortunate, and that her attempts to aid Port Royal's waifs by hiring them and taking them into her house did not always end happily. But he felt a large affection for the kind heart that prompted her to do such things. Now he wagged a pudgy finger at her. "I'm sure 'tis a talent that can be learnt."

Carolina doubted it. She hadn't had much talent for it back at Level Green—she doubted she'd have much talent for it now.

"You'll see," chuckled the stout little captain across from her. "No doubt you'll one day find yourself sailing up the Cobre to your country home!" He leaned forward. "There's rumors of it in the town here."

Carolina sat straighter and tried to hide her astonishment. What she had considered mere banter might have some basis in fact, then? Surprise kept her more silent than usual as she ate the good dinner of gungo pea soup, curried goat, and bammies, which were delicious cakes made with cassava flour—all of which Cook had prepared with her usual finesse.

After dinner Captain Banks rose with a flourish and excused himself, saying he was sorry not to linger after such a wonderful meal but that there were things to be done aboard ship, what with sailing so early the next day, and he'd best get himself aboard right now and attend to them.

Carolina was glad to hear he was going directly to the ship.

"Captain Banks," she said, "I've a favor to ask of you. I know that you sail to Yorktown and from there it is no great distance to Level Green."

"Aye," he said heartily. "I'll be glad to drop by and give them your regards."

"That wasn't quite what I had in mind," admitted Carolina, and he gave her a quizzical look. "I wanted you to deliver a small package there for me." As she spoke she picked up the pair of pattens which had reposed on a nearby chair and folded them carefully into a linen napkin, tied it fast with a length of riband. "I would be pleased if you would deliver this pair of pattens to Mistress Letitia Lightfoot at Level Green and none other," she told him, adding with a smile, "My mother does not approve of me, and would not accept a handsome gift from me, I am sure, but while these are only cheap pattens, still they are the kind she has always wanted and they are so easy to procure here." She laughed and then sighed. "It is hard not to be able to go home, Captain Banks."

The stout little ship captain cleared his throat. He knew the Silver Wench's story and was on her side all the way. "They'll come around at Level Green," he assured her gruffly. "Families most always do. Meantime, the *Morning Star* and me will deliver this package most careful-like to your mother, Mistress Caro—"

"Christabel," she corrected him swiftly. "I always use that name here so as not to shame my mother any more than is necessary, for she shudders to think of me living in a buccaneers' port!"

Captain Banks smiled. She was a good daughter, was Carolina Lightfoot, for all she'd gone off the deep end over a buccaneer!

And watching them through a crack in the pantry door, Gilly, who had witnessed the last part of this scene, sneered to herself. There stood Captain Kells's wife, decked out in a fortune in rubies and diamonds, sending such a small and shabby gift to her mother, who apparently lived in Virginia. Not that *she* would send *anything* to her mother, no matter how rich she got—not even if she knew where her mother was, which she didn't. In jail most likely. But once she was very rich, she planned to send bright red garters to everyone she liked—she would even send a pair to

Rouge in New Providence. Rouge, who would laugh and throw them away, for Rouge went barefoot mostly. Gilly yawned and let the crack of the door close, then went off to badger Cook, for whom she had formed an instant dislike. When *she* had the necklace, she'd buy her a house as big as this one and hire women like Cook and beat them with a stick if they dared to answer back!

Gilly couldn't wait to be wealthy—she wanted to trample the world. She was daydreaming about it and didn't even notice the package when she came in to clear the dishes and heard Carolina asking Hawks to give the good captain escort through the town—"for he's a good friend of ours, Hawks, and I wouldn't want him to get his head broken the night before he sails. See him on board safely, won't you?"

If Hawks was surprised, he did not show it. A little fellow like Captain Banks might well need protection on the nighttime streets of Port Royal. But he *was* surprised to find Carolina lingering about downstairs when he returned.

"Well, did you see him safe aboard, Hawks?"

"Aye, that I did," he said soberly. "And his package with him."

Carolina gave Hawks a winning smile. He was as loyal to her as he had always been to Kells, she thought—more of a jewel than even those rubies that were already on board the *Morning Star,* carried there unwittingly by little Captain Banks.

But the stout captain had given her something to think about. Was Kells really up the Cobre shopping for a plantation? The idea had never occurred to her. She had thought he was upriver on a trading venture—or perhaps finding backers for a buccaneering voyage, for while Kells rarely took the *Sea Wolf* out into the sea lanes these days, he did occasionally send Lars Lindstrom—who was now captain of the *Sea Wolf*'s sister ship, the *Sea Wench*—out, and other members of his little fleet. And all these voyages had to be financed, the ships provisioned, the crews assembled, the loot divided—when there *was* loot, for pickings were thin now. The Spanish had grown warier.

Kells was an administrator now, she thought with a shrug. She doubted he would ever go to sea again—at least as a buccaneer. But did these trips up the Cobre mean that he was going to abandon the sea altogether and become a planter?

She could hardly wait for the week to end to find out!

Chapter 5

Kells came home from the Cobre bronzed and smiling—but his smile did not quite extend to his gray eyes. Carolina sensed a difference in him even as he swept her up into his arms for an exuberant kiss, even as he spun her about so that her wide skirts billowed out.

"Kells," she sighed against his hard chest. "Oh, it's so good to have you back!"

"Is it now?" He put her down and grinned at her, and she was caught as always by how dangerous he looked with his light gray eyes flickering in that darkly tanned face, his dark heavy hair swinging free. "And here I'd thought you might have found other interests while I was gone!"

He's heard about Monsieur du Monde! she thought in dismay—for she had enemies as well as friends in this town, and one of them might well have told him some garbled story about what had happened.

"I'm sure whatever you've heard, it's all wrong!" her guilty conscience prompted her to say.

His hard face softened and she realized what he had said was merely careless banter. "You have brought home another stray?" he guessed humorously.

Carolina flushed a little but she tossed her fair head defiantly. "The poor girl was running down the street in terror with two of those awful women from the brothels pursuing her. I am sure they meant to beat her half to death!"

"But you intervened?"

"Of course I did! She doesn't know her age but she can't be more than fifteen!"

He sighed. "What am I to do with you?" he asked whimsically. "Will you never learn that most of these street strays aren't to be trusted?"

"Well, I'm sure this one is different—and besides, look at Betts, see how well she's turned out! And Cook—well, Cook was never quite a stray, was she? But you'll meet Gilly at dinner and *do* remember not to frown at her when she serves you from the wrong side—I'm having to correct her quite gently for she's under the impression that having worked at a tavern in Bristol, she 'serves very elegant'!"

"I'll try to remember," he promised with mock meekness.

"Come upstairs—I'm sure you'll be glad of a bath after your hot trip down the Cobre. Why didn't you tell me you were buying a plantation up there, Kells?"

His expression, which had been gentle upon her, hardened. "Who told you that?"

"Oh, the gossips seem to know more about us than we know ourselves!" she said airily.

"You've been misinformed," he said, and there was a rippling anger in his voice—or was it something else? She couldn't be sure. "You shouldn't listen to gossip," he added sharply.

She supposed she should not—rumors certainly ripped through Port Royal at hurricane speed. She felt a sense of relief for she had not wished to live up the Cobre, but she was abashed at his tone, reproving her—for what?

"I'll have your bath brought up," she said uncertainly, and started toward the kitchen to tell Betts and Gilly to fetch hot water. "Dinner is almost ready."

"Good," he flung over his shoulder. "We had a bit of trouble on the Cobre, bottom of the damned boat got stove in."

She paused and turned to stare up at his tall muscular figure taking the stairs three at a time. "You could have been killed!" she cried indignantly.

He stopped and grinned briefly at her over the landing. "Not likely," he said. "We were near shore. I threw a rope over an overhanging branch and maneuvered us to the riverbank where we patched her up enough to make Port Royal. But it was cursed hot work and all our food went into the river. I'm starved!"

Thankful that at least they did not have to *live* up that dangerous river and make the trek up and down incessantly, Carolina shook her head in dismay and went off to order up his hot water. Then with a sober face she went upstairs to her own room to dress.

Instinctively she felt that something was wrong, though he had said nothing, and as she dressed for dinner she quickly opened the curved top trunk, which was always kept locked with a key that she wore fastened to the waist of her petticoat, and opened the false bottom. It was a shock to find the box empty—and then she remembered: it was empty because she had sent the necklace to her mother in Virginia to pay off the debts on Level Green.

She felt oddly lost without it, for she wore that necklace whenever she felt insecure, because it was not something Kells had given her, she had won it herself, earned—despite the fact that things had turned out badly after all. The necklace had been truly hers, hers to give. . . . And now—oh, well, she would wear the copy.

"Well, aren't we got up splendidly?" Kells greeted her with a grin when she came downstairs wearing a white gown and the glittering necklace.

"I am dressed in celebration of your return," she defended.

He studied her keenly. "But wearing the copy and not the original. Tell me, have you lost the necklace?"

She started, for she had forgotten that those keen gray eyes of his saw everything, that they could tell paste from real. The fake "diamonds," he claimed, lacked the light-gathering brilliance of the real ones—no one else had ever seemed to notice, but, then, she usually wore the original.

"I sent it to my mother," admitted Carolina. "They were about to lose Level Green and—and I couldn't let it happen, Kells. No matter what they think of us."

"How very noble of you," was his dry comment. "At least it makes my decision easy," he added cryptically.

She frowned at him. "Whatever do you mean?"

"Nothing," he said with a shrug. "Let us go in to dinner." He proffered his arm.

And so they went sailing into the green dining room to feast on the best repast Cook could create. Kells pulled back Carolina's chair and seated her with ceremony. He had changed from the casual leathern breeches and flowing shirt he had worn up the Cobre and was dressed in good civil English clothes again, a dark gray suit, wide-cuffed with silver buttons, a froth of white lace spilling over his fine hands and highlighting the handsome emerald ring he wore, which matched a similar stone in the snowy Mechlin at his throat. Carolina was inescapably tempted to compare the deep green fire of his jewels with the single pink stone Monsieur du Monde had sported. But, then, she told herself, Monsieur du Monde was not the Lord Admiral of the Buccaneers.

The pantry door swung open.

"Kells," said Carolina, looking at him across the forest of silver that graced the frosty white linen cloth, "this is Gilly. She will be serving us tonight."

And Kells's dark head swung about as he turned to gaze upon the young girl who had just entered the room. Gilly stared back at him avidly, her brown eyes bold and sparkling. Indeed she was so fascinated she did not move.

"Gilly," said Carolina with a sigh. "Captain Kells would like his dinner served now."

Gilly gave a start and quickly bobbed a curtsy. She gave the handsome buccaneer captain a brilliant, admiring smile. She made all of her usual mistakes in serving, but Carolina did not chide her. Obviously Gilly was bedazzled just being in the same room with the famous buccaneer.

Kells's gaze upon Gilly was thoughtful as she left the room, and Carolina, afraid he did not like her, said quickly, "Gilly is most amusing. She has spent some time upon New Providence."

"That does not recommend her," he growled.

So she had been right: Kells did not like Gilly! "I mean, she tells interesting stories that entertain me," she explained.

"Most stories about New Providence—if true—would not entertain you," Kells told her bluntly. "They would horrify you."

She watched, nettled, as he finished his conch soup. Perhaps a good dinner would put him in a better mood! She let Gilly clear the soup bowls away and bring in the fish before remarking airily, "Gilly told me she knows Rouge!"

Kells looked up from his fish. "*That* does not recommend her, either."

"Indeed? What do *you* know about Rouge?"

"Very little. I have seen her but once."

"You have actually seen her? This woman everybody talks about? You never told me that! Tell me, what does she look like?"

He grinned at the consternation in her face. "She has horns instead of hair," he said. "And gigantic muscles that bulge when she walks."

"Oh, stop teasing me!" she cried in exasperation. "Gilly insists Rouge is beautiful—and kind. Tell me what she *looks* like!"

"She is indeed very beautiful," he said meditatively, and Carolina felt a bit chilled. "But as for being kind?" He snorted.

"Where did you see her?" she demanded.

"I put in at New Providence once for repairs after a storm. I saw her on the beach, standing there in men's clothes with her red hair streaming down, inciting two fellows to kill each other with cutlasses."

"And did they?" she asked, fascinated.

"No," he sighed. "They staggered away—they were both very drunk—and she pulled out the cutlass she wore at her belt and ran after them, shouting, with the naked blade waving in the air. The argument wandered behind one of the lean-to shacks that dot the beach and I lost interest."

"Do you think anyone was killed?"

He shrugged. "Very possibly. Life is cheap in New Providence."

"And that was the only time you saw Rouge?"

"Yes. This girl, this Gilly"—he dropped his voice—"if you are bent on giving her a new life, I suggest you let me find her employment in one of the taverns."

"Oh, no, Kells, she'd promptly slip back into her old

life—why, she could even end up in one of those brothels on Thames Street."

"Which may be where she came from." He sighed. "Very well, Carolina. I will not cross you in this matter since you are so set upon it, but as I will be away so much and—"

"What? Why will you be away?"

His eyes glinted. "Tell me about Monsieur du Monde," he cut in briskly. "And why I might have heard rumors."

So he had spoken to Hawks and Hawks had told him! "I—Monsieur du Monde sprang forward to rescue Gilly," she said in confusion.

"And you invited him to dinner."

"Well, I had expected *you* to be here," she said in her defense.

He accepted that. "This Monsieur du Monde, what is he like?"

"He said he was from New Providence, but he ain't," supplied Gilly, who had just re-entered the room with a large platter of biscuits. "I'd have seen him there—he ain't the kind could be missed."

"Oh, he couldn't be missed, could he?" Kells turned to Carolina with a grim smile playing around the corners of his mouth. "I am sorry I didn't meet this Monsieur du Monde. Tell me, what did you learn about him?"

"Not very much—"

"All lies," said Gilly dispassionately. "He looked like a liar to me."

"That will be enough, Gilly," said Carolina. "You are not to enter into our conversations when we are at dinner. You have set down that tray. Don't just stand there staring at us, return to the kitchen."

"Yes, *mistress!*" said Gilly, flouncing away.

"And you should be more grateful, Gilly. After all,

Monsieur du Monde saved you from a beating most likely!" Carolina flung after her.

The door closed a little too hard.

"You will not be able to train that one," murmured Kells, shaking his head. "Go on, tell me about this Frenchman."

"I am not sure he is French," she said slowly. "There is something very Spanish about him. And when I shot a question at him in Spanish, he replied instantly in flawless Spanish."

"A Spaniard . . ." he said thoughtfully.

"Oh, well, I don't *know* that, Kells. He claimed to be from Marseilles. Perhaps he is."

"Many men claim to be from Marseilles. A crowded, indifferent, polyglot city—a convenient place to claim to be from, for one could get lost in the crowd there. Didn't you tell me our new neighbor, Louis Deauville, also claims to be from Marseilles?"

"Yes, I did." She flushed for she guessed Hawks had informed Kells of the way Monsieur Deauville, who had come to live across the street from them, always paid court to her, usually erupting from his house the moment Carolina left hers, finding ways to speak to her, seeking her out in the market. She brought the conversation back to Raymond du Monde, considering it safer. "Anyway, I cannot say that he is *not* French. He said he had come from New Providence most recently, that he had only spent his boyhood in Marseilles."

Kells quirked an eyebrow at her. "But you thought he was Spanish?"

"Well, I could have been wrong."

"I doubt it. Your instincts are very good about these things."

"Anyway, he is gone so we need not bother about him. He told me he was leaving the very next day."

"Gone. So soon? Did he say where he was going?"

"I don't remember—no, I don't believe he did."

"And you were not curious enough to ask him?"

"Well, after all, it was not my affair. I only invited him to sup with me because—"

"Because he came to your aid, I know. Still . . . I wonder what he wanted and how he managed so handily to come to your aid?"

"Oh, that's ridiculous!" she burst out. "He couldn't have *planned* it! After all, how could Monsieur du Monde have known that Gilly would run down the street and trip and fall down right in front of me?"

"Yes," he mused. "A fortunate fall, was it not? I wonder how she happened to do that. . . ." He raised his voice. "Gilly, you can come out now. I can see your eyes shining in the crack of the pantry door."

Reluctantly Gilly opened the door. She looked sulky, and Carolina gave her an angry look.

"If you eavesdrop on us, Gilly, I will have to send you away," she said sharply.

Gilly, furious at being caught up in her spying, promptly burst into tears and ran from the room.

Kells's hard gaze followed her flight. "Better find the wench another place," he advised.

"No, I will give her another chance," Carolina said. "But tell me, why would the gossips have it that you were trying to buy a plantation along the Cobre?"

"Because I was."

"But I thought you said—"

"I said I was not in the process of buying one, not that I did not wish to."

"Oh." She spoke the word soundlessly.

"Well, do not look so alarmed. I had thought it would be a simple matter since money is offered to me freely for buccaneering ventures. But oddly enough, I can find no backers for this enterprise. Men are willing to risk fortunes with me in the hope of immediate and dazzling gain, but they are quick to point out that buying land and making it pay is a long road."

"You could do it!" she said hotly, on his side now and quite forgetting that she had been against the project.

"Oh, I am sure of it. But men with money to invest sheer off from it. It would seem that my longevity as a buccaneer is not highly regarded. Oh, it is couched in fine words, but it is explained to me that I must pay cash." He gave her a wry look.

They had finished their dinner now and were sipping the strong ruby-red wine of Portugal—port, named for the town of Oporto from whence it came. Her silver eyes mirrored her astonishment.

"But you have ceased buccaneering. Everyone knows that!"

"No one believes it. Perhaps even I do not." He shook his head tiredly.

"Then ignore them and pay cash!" she exploded. "Forget these other men who only seek to profit on your dangerous work."

There was a rueful look in the gray eyes that looked down upon her tenderly. She looked so lovely there in her white gown with her breast heaving with indignation—so innocent, so untouched. And the effect somehow heightened by the barbarity of that opulent necklace, glowing like red coals and white fire.

She caught her breath. "Surely there is no lack of money? I mean—"

"All the elegance that you see around you?" His lips twisted in a wry smile. "Ours is an expensive household to keep up."

"But you have so much gold," she protested. "So much—"

"Held safe for me in England, yes, but only I can touch it. And you do not want me to go there."

She sat down suddenly, feeling that her legs would not support her. "No, I do not!" Carolina said faintly.

"And yet, Christabel"—his gaze upon Carolina was wistful—"I must do *something,* else we will have to sell this house."

"Then sell the house!"

"No, I do not propose to do that." His face was stern. "In the first place it would be dangerous. If the feeling is noised abroad that I am slipping downward, there would be those who might be bold enough to try to sell me to the Spaniards for fifty thousand pieces of eight."

She had forgotten that!

"What do you propose to do?" she asked in a small voice.

"I propose," he said, spacing his words, "to resume my profession. The world sees me as a buccaneer—by God, I will be one!"

"Oh, no," she said unhappily. "I couldn't stand it—worrying, wondering where you are, whether you are still alive!"

He gave Carolina a moody look. "You will have to stand it," he said shortly, "if we are to survive." And then he added more kindly, "It is either that or England, Christabel. I must have money—and soon."

And she had sent away the necklace that would have saved him! It was already almost a week away, somewhere on the high seas. . . . She felt overcome by guilt. "Kells," she said, stricken, "I am sorry about the necklace."

He gave a short laugh. "It does not matter." His voice was bitter. "I would have been driven back to buccaneering eventually anyway, I suppose. You made a mistake when you chose to love me, Christabel. Some other man would have brought you a better life—a peaceful home, children, surroundings in which you could hold up your head."

"Oh, no, don't say that!" Impetuously Carolina circled the table and flung herself into his arms. "Don't ever say that! I've never been sorry, Kells, never, not even once!" It was not quite true—there had been moments—but just now, charged with emotion, she *felt* that it was true, and the intensity of her feelings seemed to shudder through her slight frame.

Kells gave her a tender look. She was so reckless, so gallant, his fiery lady. She took every fence at a gallop, she flung her heart over, Devil take the hindmost. . . .

She drew away from him, breathing excitement. "Tomorrow night is the governor's ball. You will speak to the governor. *He* will find you the necessary backing!"

His smile was tender as he swept Carolina's slight figure up in his arms and bent to press a light affectionate kiss upon her parted lips. "What will be will be, Christabel—at least we will have tonight!"

Gilly, who had slipped out of the pantry and was peering from the dining room into the hall, watched him take the steps two at a time and felt a stab of envy.

THE GOVERNOR'S HOUSE
PORT ROYAL, JAMAICA

Spring 1692

Chapter 6

"I wonder what she is like." Carolina was pulling on her gloves as she spoke, despite the sweltering heat that had not dissipated with the night.

"Who?" asked Kells. He was frowning at the carriage that had just drawn up smartly before their front door.

"The governor's cousin, Mistress Grummond. After all, the governor is giving this ball for her," she reminded him. "You must remember to be very gallant and dance with her several times—the governor will like that."

Kells snorted. "He's unlikely to notice—he'll be spending his time wondering why I was such a damn fool as to order up a carriage when we live close by!"

Carolina gave him a reproving look and carefully adjusted her wide skirts before allowing him to hand her into the carriage. Carolina had insisted they would make a much more impressive entrance if they rode up to the governor's house rather than walking to the ball as most of the guests would probably do. "Not to mention the state of our shoes," she had added to cap her argument. "Satin slippers are simply ground up by this sand." She wagged a black satin-clad toe at him.

"No one will be looking at your feet," he assured her as he climbed in beside her, an impressive figure in gun-metal satin, the wide cuffs of his stiffly skirted coat encrusted with silver and an emerald gleaming from the frosty burst of Mechlin at his throat. "They'll be too occupied staring at the rest of you."

Carolina flashed him a winning smile that displayed a double row of even white teeth. "That was what I had in mind," she admitted modestly, looking down with satisfaction at the black and silver creation an excited Betts had helped her into. She had taken the time to pirouette before the mirror and was certain that this was the most dramatic gown she had ever owned. Indeed the dressmaker had done a wonderful job, for the daringly low-cut silver tissue bodice fit her delicately rounded breasts and narrow waist to perfection. The silver tissue sleeves ended at the elbow in an enormous burst of sheer black lace, and the tiny waist was emphasized by the width of the silver tissue skirt. But what made the dress so spectacular was the shepherdess effect given the tight bodice by crisscrossed black satin ribands and the wide black satin insets flowing from the waist, which were shaped like long flower petals sweeping down the wide skirt. Her shining fair hair was swept up with studied casualness in the new higher mode which allowed several shining locks to dangle down carelessly to caress her smooth white shoulder. Betts, who was clever with such things, had set small bursts of brilliants on black satin ribands into her hair so that they outlined and made the most of its daring sweep down to her shoulders. Diamonds glittered from her ears, and across the bare expanse of her white bosom the ruby and diamond necklace wound a fiery trail, for she intended to look opulent tonight!

He laughed, but he cocked an eyebrow at her, for he

was an indulgent husband and paid little heed to how much she spent. Arriving ship captains bringing the world's goods to Jamaica knew—if they were experienced in the Port Royal trade—that the finest fabrics, the most lustrous silks, would find a ready market with Captain Kells's dazzling lady. "You do me credit!"

"I changed it slightly from the Paris fashion doll it was copied from," she told him airily. "This effect of silver petals on the skirt is of my own invention."

His gray eyes glinted. "Our new French neighbor across the street, Monsieur Deauville—who will undoubtedly be attending the ball tonight—will be brokenhearted that you have elected to change the design of the fashion doll he gave you," was his ironic comment.

Carolina was startled. Did he know everything that happened, her tall buccaneer? The horses' hooves continued their muffled clip-clop down the sandy street as she made him a cautious answer.

"When Monsieur Deauville moved in across the street while you were gone, the cart carrying his baggage overturned," she explained. "Hawks and I had just come out of the house on the way to market, and Hawks assisted the men in getting poor Louis's baggage out of the street." She could have bitten her tongue for calling the Frenchman "Louis," but it was too late.

"And so instead of rewarding Hawks, who bent his back to aid him, 'poor Louis' sent *you* a fashion doll," Kells remarked without expression.

Put *that* way it did sound very bad, she thought. "Louis Deauville was merely trying to show his gratitude," she said a trifle crossly.

Kells laughed. "And pay a tribute to beauty at the same time! Well, no matter. I will meet Deauville tonight, I have no doubt."

Carolina had no doubt at all that he would meet

Louis Deauville tonight. The handsome Frenchman had been dogging her footsteps. Indeed he had formed a most disconcerting habit of popping out of his house and bowing deeply and exchanging pleasantries every time she went to market. "Hawks talks too much," she muttered, guessing rightly the source of Kells's information. "Poor Louis is harmless! But he is French and Frenchmen do pursue women!"

"Harmless . . ." murmured her buccaneer thoughtfully, for the town had been flooded with stories of the Frenchman, and in all of them the new arrival had cut quite a figure. "We will see how harmless 'poor Louis' is! Well, it seems we have reached the governor's house after our long journey!" He dropped lightly from the carriage and assisted Carolina down while other satin-clad guests, streaming toward the governor's wide-fronted brick house, turned to stare curiously at the striking pair.

"Get rid of the carriage, Hawks," said Kells, glancing up at the laconic buccaneer, who had volunteered to drive them.

"No, bring it back when the ball ends," Carolina said instantly, for she had already spotted Louis Deauville through the brightly lit door and had no wish to bait Kells by having the attractive Frenchman join them for the walk home. "We will leave in style!"

Kells grunted and Hawks hid a grin as he turned the team about, a maneuver necessitated by the position of the building, which was set at an angle with the street as if to command a view of Fort James on the point.

But Carolina's impressive entrance was destined to be spoiled. Even as they were about to step through the doorway, where the portly little governor in bronze satin was standing next to his wife in apple green and an arrogant young woman in pink silk, there was a howl from the direction of the kitchen followed by such piercing screams that the governor and his wife both broke and ran for the commotion; the woman in pink—who must have been his cousin, Mistress Grummond—trailed distractedly after them, leaving the arriving guests to fend for themselves.

"Someone upset a boiling kettle, I'll be bound," muttered someone at Carolina's elbow.

"Over somebody else from the sound of it," came a cheerful observation from behind her.

And Carolina found herself looking into the smiling face of Louis Deauville, who must, she thought irritably, have deliberately stationed himself with a view of the door, for he bobbed toward her eagerly the moment they entered.

By the time she had introduced the Frenchman to Kells, by the time all the proper pleasantries were exchanged, by the time the panic in the kitchen had been quieted and a doctor summoned for the sobbing servant girl who had accidentally dribbled scalding sauce onto her foot, by the time Acting Governor White and his lady were back in position to receive at the door, Carolina and Kells were deep into the room, the music had struck up, and Louis Deauville had made her an impressive leg and demanded the honor of the first dance.

Kells was conversing with an upriver planter who was urging him to buy the property next to his, a subject which might keep him occupied for the next half hour, so Carolina was pleased enough to glide out upon the floor with the engaging Monsieur Deauville, for she was dying to ask him about his adventures in London.

"I am told you know London well, Monsieur Deauville," she challenged him.

The Frenchman, a marvel this night in fawn satin heavily stitched with orange silk, shook his golden periwig gracefully and admitted to having some small acquaintance with the town.

"And perhaps some acquaintance with its gaming houses as well?" Carolina asked negligently, permitting him to twirl her about so that her wide skirts billowed.

"Indeed yes," was the blithe rejoinder. "What would the so beautiful lady care to know about them?"

The so beautiful lady smiled up at her elegant dancing partner and murmured, "I wonder if you could tell me about a certain gaming house—let me see if I can remember the name. Could it be Mistress Masterson's?" She frowned as if searching her memory.

"I believe you mean Chesterton," he supplied promptly. "Jenny Chesterton's."

"Ah, yes . . ." Carolina's face cleared. "And was she not once a headmistress?" she wondered vaguely.

"Indeed she was!" the Frenchman agreed gaily and promptly led Carolina into a pattern of steps so intricate that she decided he must indeed have been a dancing master back in France. "She maintained a very select school for young ladies, so she told me, until she was discovered *en déshabillé,* I believe I must call it, with one Lord Ormsby."

Carolina chuckled inwardly. *En déshabillé* was a mild way of putting it, for Jenny had been discovered by the mama of one of her young charges, clad in her chemise, in the midst of a wild game of Blind Man's Buff with Lord Ormsby and some of his rowdy friends—all of them caught prancing about, very drunk, in their smallclothes.

She was careful not to betray a personal knowledge of Jenny Chesterton or her establishment. Instead she looked up at Louis Deauville with her large lustrous eyes and said in a wheedling voice, "I am told you have some wonderful tale to tell about the place—something about an English schoolgirl?"

Beneath the power of that silver gaze, Louis Deauville's fawn satin chest expanded. "Ah, she was a pretty piece," he sighed. "A head of wonderful auburn hair, *très merveilleux, très élégant."*

Yes, that would have been Reba—marvelous auburn hair, very elegant!

Carolina's next question was flung out carelessly. "Did you know her well?"

Monsieur Deauville's eyes glittered with amusement. "You wish to know if she was my paramour, *non?* You wish to hear of my amorous adventures, my *affaires de coeur?"*

"Not all of them," chuckled Carolina. "We would find ourselves dancing till dawn!"

Flattered, Monsieur Deauville beamed.

"Just of your *amourette* with her," specified Carolina, giving him a wicked glance. "I am told it is an amusing tale."

At this reference to the affair as a "passing fancy," Louis Deauville drew himself up. "But it was *très sérieux,* madame!" he declared with mock solemnity.

"Well, serious or not, I would be glad to hear you tell of it, Monsieur Deauville," laughed Carolina.

"First I must say that I am not so much the gambler," sighed the Frenchman with a charming shrug. (Carolina doubted that statement but she repressed the merriment it brought to her eyes.) "So when this former schoolmistress bore me away to her abode, this gaming establishment, I did not care to play but merely sipped wine and observed the play until this *jeune fille,* this glowing glowing beauty, this—"

"Auburn-haired girl," murmured Carolina, wishing he would get on with it. "The one with the elegant clothes."

"Ah, yes." His expressive face mirrored an ecstatic memory and he paused to let her expectations mount. "But I did not meet her at once, you understand. She was indisposed." (*Probably sleeping late,* thought Carolina skeptically, remembering Reba's old habits.) "But later, when the patrons had gone, I was about to leave also, but Jenny Chesterton asked me to stay on. She said there was to be a party. And indeed almost at once an English peer, who I learned was Lord Ormsby, arrived with a party of friends. The gentlemen were all very far gone on drink, and most of the ladies as well—do you think this story too risqué, perhaps, for your tender ears, madame?"

"I doubt it," Carolina said tranquilly.

His eyes sparkled. "There was much drinking of good Bordeaux, the evening grew wilder. Someone brought a sheet and the ladies disrobed down to their chemises and paraded behind it with candles behind them while the gentlemen made wagers as to which lady it was who stood revealed in silhouette."

Carolina could envision the scene. They would have pushed back the tables in the main gaming room downstairs—that room she remembered so well as the stiff front reception room of Mistress Chesterton's School for Young Ladies and as a citadel of virtue—and the men, drunk enough to slosh their wineglasses, would have lined up on the gilt chairs, all in a row, to cheer on their favorites as each minced out in a state of undress behind the sheet to pose saucily with the candlelight behind her and only a thin sheet between her and the onlookers.

"There was one young lady whose—er—profile I could not quite recall. She was not, you understand, to be overlooked. She was a shade taller than the others and of a more delightful—er—stance."

Reba always stood proudly, thought Carolina. *And thrust her chest out provocatively.* Ah, yes, Deauville would indeed have noticed *her* enticing silhouette behind the rippling sheet!

"Afterward we all played Blind Man's Buff in our

smallclothes and there were pretty indiscretions all about."

Carolina could well imagine!

"The ladies, I am afraid, got very drunk and the auburn-haired beauty, who seemed not so used to drinking, tripped while dancing and fell upon a wine-glass that had rolled out upon the floor and cut herself on the hip. I carried her upstairs, away from the fray, and washed the cut. It was, you understand, necessary"—his wicked grin flashed—"to remove the young lady's chemise in order to attend her wound properly and—ah," he finished regretfully, "the dance is ending. I regret I cannot say more, madame."

A cut on the hip! And when Carolina had shared a cabin aboard the *Mary Constant* with Reba, she had acquired a small new scar on her hip! Carolina remembered remarking on it and Reba had shrugged and muttered something about broken glass.

And now her irritating dancing partner was regretting that he could not say more!

"Oh, but you *must* say more, Monsieur Deauville!" cried Carolina in a state of near panic lest this elusive Frenchman disappear into the crowd before telling her all there was to know. "I cannot let you escape. You really must dance the next dance with me!"

Deauville's grin deepened. He prided himself on his timing and knew he had caught the attention of the woman in black and silver at last. Now he shook his head chidingly at several young bucks who were just converging upon Carolina. One of them had heard her last remark and was staring open-mouthed at the couple as they glided out upon the floor. The dazzling Silver Wench begging this Frenchie from nowhere to dance with her while she snubbed the cream of Port Royal? His indignation caused him promptly to repeat what he had heard to both of the disappointed young bloods who had joined him. Soon the story of Carolina's beseeching remark was all over the room and heads were turning curiously to eye the handsome pair, who were gazing at each other in such rapt fashion as they trod a measure.

But Carolina was happily unaware of all this furor. She was hanging on Monsieur Deauville's words.

"And *she* was the schoolgirl?" she heard herself saying. "Indeed, Monsieur Deauville, I can scarce credit it!"

Her dancing partner nodded urbanely and executed a difficult turn with aplomb. "The chemise presented no obstacle," he informed her with a bland look.

Carolina almost choked. "And you—?"

"Carried her away to paradise, madame—or so she said! Ah, she was of a vivacity unmatched. Her fervor enveloped me, destroyed me!" He rolled his eyes mischievously toward the ceiling.

Carolina blinked. His meaning was transparently clear. Plainly Reba had not spent *all* her time at Jenny Chesterton's mooning over her lost marquess! Indeed there was obviously much that Reba had not told her!

She let Deauville rave on, describing Reba's eyes ("russet pools"), her skin ("purest silk"), her mouth ("a delicate rosebud"), her hands ("fluttering hands"), her feet ("daintily flying"), but she could not resist giving him a skeptical look for *she* remembered Reba's russet eyes as hard as agates, her rosebud mouth often intoning harsh things, her "fluttering" hands waving imperiously at servants, and her "dainty" feet tapping the floor angrily when her will was not instantly obeyed.

Deauville sighed. "Ah, she was an amazing beauty, this lady. The most glorious I have ever seen save for one—yourself, madame. Indeed you are a jewel of price in that gown!" His hot gaze played over Carolina in her elegant shepherdess gown, and rested lingeringly on her breasts now rising and falling with the exertion of the dance and threatening to break through the delicate silver tissue of her bodice. "I have no doubt you could match her," he added significantly. "Indeed that you could best her, feature for feature."

Sans chemise, no doubt! thought Carolina, hot color rising to her face.

Across the room a tall gentleman in gun-metal satin arrested the wineglass he was just then raising to his lips and regarded them with a narrow gaze.

"Monsieur Deauville—" she began protestingly.

"Ah, call me Louis!" Monsieur Deauville's golden periwigged head bent slightly over hers and his voice deepened. "For you, *ma beauté,* are incomparable!"

It was very pleasant to be told one was beyond compare, whether or not one believed it.

"You must not call me 'your beauty,'" Carolina chided him a little breathlessly—but her eyes were dancing as she said it.

"But, *mon Dieu,* it is of such a truth!" he exclaimed, whirling her about.

"Nevertheless," cautioned Carolina, laughing, "let not my husband hear you say it!"

The Frenchman's voice was tinged with insolence. "Why?" he scoffed. "Is he of such a *dangereux* disposition?"

"He is a dangerous man at all times," she warned him lightly. "But truly I have enjoyed hearing about your English schoolgirl, Monsieur Deauville. I found it all most amusing."

Deauville saw that the dance was ending—he was losing her!

"Ah, but you have not yet heard all, madame," he said regretfully. "The tale she told me about her life and about some blonde friend of hers—*that* was even more amusing."

Blonde friend! Carolina snapped to attention. That "blonde friend" could well be herself! The dance had ended but she was of no mind to let the Frenchman go.

He bowed but she snatched at his arm. "I am dying to hear—no, no, you must not leave me yet, we must have one more dance!"

Delighted that he could hold this dazzling beauty in thrall with tales from a past that was none so glamorous, if the truth be told—and fully aware, as Carolina was not, that all eyes were upon them—Monsieur Deauville swept the lady in silver and black out upon the floor again with a masterful flourish.

Across the room conversation around Kells grew hushed. The lean buccaneer did not move so much as a muscle, but his gray eyes had taken on a very steely expression.

"Monsieur Deauville." Carolina's voice was breathless and for the moment she was alone in the world with her dancing partner. "*What* did she tell you?"

"She told me she was the daughter of a duke but she had changed her name." (*Daughter of a rich merchant and using her own name!* Carolina corrected him mentally.) "She said she was on an escapade, that she had run away from home." (*That at least was true, but did she tell you that she had been living with a scapegrace marquess?* wondered Carolina.)

"Did she tell you where her family seat was?" she asked scathingly.

Deauville frowned. "No, she was rather vague about that," he admitted. "She insisted that she could not tell me because she was escaping from the unwanted attentions of some fellow who wished most ardently to marry her." *(Reba was the one who wanted most ardently to marry!* thought Carolina. *Her marquess wanted to escape, and I was the one who plunged them into matrimony at the last!)*

"Go on," she prodded impatiently.

Deauville was searching his memory, perhaps embroidering now.

"She told me her father had far-flung interests and that she had quarreled with her mother over her blonde friend who had come to visit her."

Carolina missed a step.

"And what was the basis of this quarrel?" she managed in a tight voice.

Deauville was frowning. "I cannot—ah, I remember now." His face cleared. "She said her blonde friend was very wild and had paraded about London by night dressed as a man."

By now Carolina's silver eyes were snapping. It was true enough but it had been only for one night! How *dare* Reba tell this—this total stranger about it! And what else might she have told him? Carolina's face, hidden from view from Deauville as she looked down at her satin toes, was mutinous. Deauville, unaware of this, went obligingly on with his tale.

"She told me that her blonde friend had visited at their country house and had horrified her mother by accepting a quantity of gold for her favors from a gentleman who just then was paying his addresses to *her* and—"

Carolina's head came up. "Oh, how dare she?" she cried indignantly, coming to such an abrupt halt on the dance floor that Deauville almost lost his grip upon her. Across the room her buccaneer saw her abrupt halt. He straightened and strode through the dancers toward her. "Telling lies about me when she knew very well—!" She checked herself for the Frenchman was regarding her dizzily.

"You *knew* this lady?" he demanded in amazement.

Carolina tossed her blonde head. "I knew her very well indeed! We attended Mistress Chesterton's school together—before it became a gaming establishment. I am delighted to know how Reba got the scar on her hip, Monsieur Deauville, and I hope she did you no harm as she has done so many others!"

The lady in question had indeed done him no harm save to spend all his available cash and forget him the moment the money was gone, but Deauville was too astonished to admit it. He stood stock-still amid the milling dancers and stared down at the flushed angry face turned up to his.

A moment later Kells had reached them.

"Has this fellow insulted you?" he demanded.

"No, indeed," said Carolina with energy. "It is Reba Tarbell who has insulted me—or perhaps I should say the Marchioness of Saltenham since that is what she is now called! *This* gentleman was just telling me how she got the small scar on her hip!"

Since Deauville had no idea he had been dallying with a future marchioness and Kells had no idea that Reba had a small scar on her hip—or if she did, how it could possibly matter to Carolina—both men looked down at her, dazed.

Kells recovered first.

"Deauville," he said firmly. "I think I had best finish this dance with my lady. She is upset."

The Frenchman, aware that he was in beyond his depth, nodded gravely and strode through the dancers, frowning as he tried to sort it all out.

Curious looks followed the tall buccaneer captain as he swirled his gorgeous lady about the floor. "Is this why you have been clinging to Deauville, entreating him to keep on dancing with you?" he demanded. "To learn about Reba?"

Carolina nodded angrily. "But I haven't been *entreating* him to dance with me, just entreating him to finish his story! Oh, Kells, Monsieur Deauville had an affair with Reba while she was staying at Jenny Chesterton's—can you imagine? And she told me all the time she had been pining away for Robin Tyrell!"

The straight line of her buccaneer's mouth altered into a twitch of amusement at the corners. "I can see the tale might interest you," he agreed dryly.

"Oh, she is a dreadful liar!" Carolina cried indignantly. "Saying I accepted gold from you for my favors!"

Her buccaneer's cold eyes strayed to the Frenchman watching the dancers silently from the sidelines. "Did Deauville say that?"

"No, he told me Reba said it was 'her blonde friend who came to visit her,' and I told him her story was an out-and-out lie!"

Kells laughed. "So you identified yourself as the 'friend' of the story. Very clever, Christabel!"

Carolina flushed at the critical note in his voice. "And to *think* that I was the one who got her married to Robin! Made her a marchioness!" Indignation heightened her already high color and sharpened her voice. "Oh, how I wish I could undo that!"

"It was not precisely a marriage made in heaven," Kells reminded her. "With that harpy for a mother-in-law, the Marquess of Saltenham must frequently wish himself dead!"

"Oh, if only they would both but cross my path once more!" Carolina ground her pretty teeth.

"You would hoist them to the yardarm, I presume?" He grinned, for it had been pleasant to learn that although Deauville's interest in Carolina was very marked, his lady's interest in the Frenchman had been fleeting.

"Or something very like!" rejoined his lady crushingly. She reminded herself abruptly that she had not come here to discuss old friends or old times but to get financing for Kells's plantation on the Cobre. "I am afraid I have been distracted by Monsieur Deauville's story," she said apologetically. She looked about her, searching the crowd. "Where is the governor?"

"It seems his suit was ruined by the debacle in the kitchen," laughed Kells. "He went upstairs, all splattered, to struggle into another coat, and word has filtered downstairs that in his hurry he split one of the seams of his new one and must needs wait about whilst it is mended—all his others being too gravy-stained to wear! His wife and cousin are greeting the latecomers."

Carolina's good humor was restored. After all, Reba and Robin Tyrell, Marquess of Saltenham, were far away in England. There was small chance she would ever see either one of them again.

Having satisfied himself that Carolina was not being annoyed by some insolent fellow, Kells relinquished her for the next dance to the elderly doctor who had come to attend the injured serving girl and who stayed to dance a measure with the prettiest girl in the room.

"The wench will recover soon enough," the old doctor told Carolina placidly. He snorted. "Faith, 'twill teach her to have more respect for hot pots when she handles them in the future!"

And so it was that Carolina did not meet the guest of honor until some time later—for her beauty and her light step made her a popular dancing partner. Over first one satin shoulder and then another, she saw Kells drinking with the governor, who had come downstairs at last and was mopping his brow. She wondered if Kells was having success in getting the governor's backing—but of course he would! Kells's powerful figure fairly exuded determination—who would *not* want to back him in any venture? Even a plantation up the Cobre! Carolina tossed her head in a manner that set her white-gold curls dancing, and Louis Deauville, now watching her ardently from across the room, thought she looked more ravishing than ever.

Brought up breathless beside a small group which included the arrogant figure of Mistress Grummond, Carolina heard her voice say piercingly, "This climate has near overcome me. I do not see how any of you endure so much heat!"

"We grow used to it," was the mild rejoinder.

"Indeed it has prostrated me," sighed young Mistress Grummond, wielding her fan so energetically that the frizz of curls on her forehead danced. "I have been unable to rise from my bed all week."

Carolina turned to look at the complainer. Slender, dark-haired and of a sallow complexion, Mistress Grummond seemed not to have much in common with her florid cousin, the governor. Nor did her voice contain any of his humor as she added pettishly, "There are two sights in this out-of-the-way place" (Mistress Grummond hailed from York and was impressed by it) "that I have promised myself before I leave, however, no matter how hot the weather!"

"Really, and what is that?" asked a bored voice.

"A sight of the woman they call Rouge and that other one—the Silver Wench."

A sudden embarrassed stillness fell over the gathering and Carolina, who had just had a glass of port placed in her hand by the adoring Monsieur Deauville, filled that silence with a light laugh.

"You will find the two have not much in common," she observed.

"Really?" asked Mistress Grummond avidly. "And why is that? Are they both not pirate's women?"

"No, the Silver Wench prefers buccaneers." Carolina's voice held an undercurrent of laughter. "And you will be better off if you do not meet Rouge, who queens over New Providence." She turned to answer something Monsieur Deauville was asking, leaving someone hastily to explain to Mistress Grummond the difference between pirates and buccaneers.

But she could not help hearing—for Mistress Grummond's voice was both penetrating and loud—the lady's next question: "Who was that woman who entered into our conversation and how does she know so much about it?" And the chuckled answer, "She is the Silver Wench herself."

"What?" cried Mistress Grummond, her sallow face flushing. "You mean my cousin invites her *here?"*

Carolina stiffened. She turned to face the newcomer. "Here and everywhere," she said crisply. "I will remind you that Acting Governor White may rule this island but buccaneers control the sea. And the sea"—she paused for emphasis—*"surrounds* this island."

That flushed face was still looking at her indignantly, but for once Mistress Grummond could think of nothing to say. She turned abruptly and made her way through the crowd.

"I fear the governor's cousin likes neither our climate nor our ways," came a rueful observation.

"I fear the governor's cousin must needs *learn* to like them if she chooses to remain," said Carolina, nettled.

"You forgot to add, *your* beauty rules Port Royal," said Kells, coming up behind her and claiming her for the next dance.

He had obviously heard the entire exchange—and did not care. Why should he worry about what some chit from Yorkshire thought about them?

"Have you spoken to the governor?" she asked as he whirled her about the floor, and he nodded.

"The governor shares the general opinion. He is overextended, he has no ready money, no prospects of any—still, should I choose to go to sea again, he would somehow find the money for a share in the enterprise."

She stared up at him indignantly. "I can't believe he said that! You would make a *wonderful* planter! I have a good mind to speak to him myself!"

His grip tightened on her hand. "You will let the matter drop," he advised her. "I have no wish for the governor to know how straitened matters are for me."

"Well, at least I will plead a headache and leave early!" she flashed.

He shrugged. "As you wish. I find these crushes beastly hot myself. My coat feels stuck to my back."

"Then we will find Governor and Mistress White and bid them both a good night," she declared energetically.

She was still smouldering when they stepped through the front door.

"I thought you were worried about your slippers and must needs wait for Hawks with the carriage," he said, grinning.

"Oh, bother my slippers! We'll walk home!"

Kells swung into an easy gait beside her, but he kept a sharp lookout for thieves and footpads who might be lurking in dark doorways at this time of night and not recognize him for who he was—a dangerous buccaneer despite his fine clothing. Side by side they strolled back across the sandy way beneath the big white stars that lit the velvet night.

"You looked lovely tonight," he told her affectionately when they had gained her bedroom. "And loyal, too." He tilted her chin up with one finger and looked down into her face. "You would have bearded the governor for me."

"I still will!"

"No," he said ruefully. "That die is cast. There is no other place to turn."

But there would have been if she had not been so rash as to send away the necklace!

"You will think of something," she said confidently.

He drew her lovingly into his arms. "You are a citadel of misplaced confidence," he murmured and buried his face in her perfumed hair.

"Wait," she said breathlessly, as his warm hand pressed her bodice downward. "This material is fragile —you will tear it."

"Then by all means let us get it off," he laughed, and expertly helped her with her hooks, then watched her slide the sumptuous black and silver gown from her slim body.

Now clad in her chemise, Carolina helped Kells ease the tight gun-metal coat from his broad shoulders, smiling to see him give a sigh of relief to be rid of it. He caught that smile and swooped her up, carried her to the window. The wind caught her light chemise skirts and blew them back against his muscular thighs as he stood holding her, letting the tropical wind caress them both as he looked out at the velvet Caribbean night.

She looked up at his dark visage, trying to divine what he was thinking, but his expression in starlight was unfathomable and told her nothing. As if aware of the sudden uplifting of her head, he bent his own and rubbed his cheek gently against hers.

"Carolina," he said huskily. "Do not be so upset. We have been through so much, we will conquer this, too."

Carolina pressed her head against his chest that he might not see her tears. He meant so much to her, this stalwart buccaneer, whom the world seemed determined to send back to a life at sea.

And even as they whispered and caressed, even as they forgot the world and slipped into ecstasy, Gilly, who had seized the opportunity to slip out before the house was locked up and who would slip back in again by morning's light, lay wrapped in the arms of her pirate lover in an upstairs room of a waterfront dive on Thames Street—complaining.

"The Silver Wench's *always* got the necklace on,

Jarvis," Gilly was telling him in disgust, even as she wriggled against him, trying to get her legs arranged more comfortably. "I think she *sleeps* with it."

"You'll find a way to get it," Jarvis panted—for at the moment he was absorbed in more pressing matters, with the girl's hot young body crushed against his own.

Jarvis had no idea that Gilly was planning to double-cross him, just as Gilly, who woke with the dawn with her mind still sparkling with rubies and diamonds, had no idea that the necklace she lusted after was but a fake. . . .

Carolina, too, woke with her mind on the necklace. If only she had not sent it away! But it was gone and she must make her plans without it.

Kells had left by the time she awoke—off to see to the outfitting of the *Sea Wolf,* she guessed. The only consolation in that was that it would take him some time—and that would give her maneuvering room.

But how to maneuver? She puzzled about it all morning, giving short answers to everyone, biting her lip and frowning.

"Do you think the mistress is ill?" Betts asked anxiously of Hawks.

Hawks snorted. "Ill?" he scoffed. "She's upset that the cap'n plans to go to sea again—and she'll find a way to stop him, I'll wager!"

But morning turned to afternoon and the hot Caribbean sun beat down mercilessly on the seething city, baking anew its sun-bleached bricks and gilding the great market bell and the sweating greased backs of the blacks who were being auctioned nearby. Ships came and went from the harbor, cargoes were unloaded and hauled over the hot sand—and still Carolina paced about her bedroom.

"Go away, Gilly," she told the girl absently, when Gilly knocked on the door with some trifling message from Cook. "Tell Cook to deal with the matter—I'm thinking."

And thinking with the trunk lid shut and doubtlessly locked! thought Gilly, hard put to conceal her own annoyance.

The shadows had grown long, sending a violet light over the steaming town, when Carolina came at last to her decision. It was a simple one, an unavoidable one—she had known it all along.

And perhaps, she told herself, it was for the best.

But it would take some doing for Kells was sure to resist.

So that night she dressed with seductive care. The light lawn gown she wore, palest pink over a deeper pink chemise, was just short of a chemise itself. Its delicate lace foamed airily over her elbows; it was cut so low that her white shoulders gleamed and her breasts were in danger of popping out of the deep square neckline. Her petticoat too was barely there, of thinnest silk of an even deeper pink, so that her whole body appeared to be blushing. This was no night for barbaric ruby necklaces. She wore around her neck a delicate chain of glittering gold with a teardrop diamond glistening between her breasts. Her ear bobs, too, were tiny diamonds, flashing like raindrops, and her moonlight hair was caught up with pale pink ribands.

She could have been a wood nymph or a water sprite with her gray eyes silver in the violet light of the swift tropical dusk—and she was so lovely that Kells, coming in hot, tired and hungry, was arrested by the sight of her standing there on the stairs to greet him as he entered.

"You look more ready for bed than dining," he murmured humorously, not wishing her to know how just the sight of her could heat up his blood and weaken his firmest resolve.

Carolina gave an airy shrug that rippled her delightful breasts, already so near to coming out of the pretty gown.

"'Tis a hot night," she murmured archly.

"And likely to grow hotter, I see!" he laughed, taking the stairs toward her two at a time.

Carolina fled before him like a songbird blown by the wind and reached their bedroom door just ahead of him.

It was fortunate for Gilly on the second floor that she had heard Kells enter and had had time to flee, because she had seized the opportunity to slip into Carolina's bedroom the moment Carolina had left it, and had run to the curved-top trunk. "The first time I've found it unlocked!" she would later wail to Jarvis. "And wouldn't you know they *both* came running into the bedroom and almost caught me—and then Cook scolded me for being gone and I had to stay downstairs and help *her* till they went to bed!" she added, aggrieved.

"There'll be other times," Jarvis assured her, draining his tankard and running his hand up her skirts.

But although Carolina, intent on her plans for the evening, failed to witness Gilly's sudden departure, Kells's keen eyes caught a flash of indigo skirts disappearing down the hall. It brought to him sharply how precious was the woman he was leaving in dangerous Port Royal—and how vulnerable.

"I'll have a strong lock put on that door tomorrow," he told her. "You're to keep it locked and wear the key while I'm gone."

"Oh, Kells!" she protested impatiently. "The house is secure enough with Hawks standing guard!"

"There will be more than Hawks standing guard," he assured her. "I intend to station three other men here to help him. Your door needs no lock while I am here to protect you, but once word is spread about that I am gone—"

"You think I will be kidnapped and held for ransom?" Her upturned laughing face challenged him.

He frowned down at her. Did she but know it, his enemies could make him deliver himself to Spain by just such a tactic—but to say so would only frighten her, just as his real reason for the lock was to forestall someone slipping into the house past that new serving wench Gilly, for example, and be waiting to overpower Carolina in her bedchamber. "Promise me you will keep this door locked," he insisted. "Both when you are in the room and when you are gone from it."

"But someone could come in by the window," she mocked him. "After all, it is only the second floor!"

"Tomorrow, twin balconies will be constructed at these windows—and there will be a solid iron grillwork that no man can penetrate without making enough noise to awaken the dead."

"And suppose there is a fire? What then? Am I to burn to death because I am so well locked in?"

"I have thought of that," he said. "The floors of these small balconies which will jut out over the street will be of wood. I will leave an axe beneath your bed and in case you wake to find the house blazing, you may chop your way to freedom in seconds and drop into Hawks's arms below—if he has not already raised a ladder and started chopping at the balcony himself."

She stared at him in open-mouthed amazement.

"But it is no matter," she declared. "I mean, it is all unnecessary."

"Necessary to my peace of mind," he said grimly, divesting himself of his sweaty shirt as he spoke. "And thus no small matter to me."

She shrugged and called for his bath, then watched him take it. She soaped his back for him—running her fingers lightly down his back and up into his shoulder-length dark hair—then stepped back with a light laugh when he shook his head, sending droplets of water flying about, some of them landing on her. And when he was done and rose dripping from the tub, sun-bronzed and gleaming, she bubbled with laughter as she helped towel him dry.

"What are you so happy about?" he wondered, for this sudden lightness of spirit made him uneasy.

She tossed the towel away and surveyed his naked form, smiling. "I am happy because I have come to a great decision—the only decision."

He watched her warily. "And what decision is that?"

She came toward him like a blown leaf and embraced him as he stood there.

"I have written to my mother—the letter is on my desk." She nodded in the direction of her small slanted boxlike writing desk, which sat upon a table nearby. "Fielding will have paid off his debts with the necklace, his creditors will all feel secure—now he can borrow again and send us the money, which you can pay back at your leisure. Meantime you will have enough to buy yourself a plantation on the Cobre!"

Kells stared down at her thoughtfully. Carolina was beaming up at him, very pleased with herself to have worked out such a pleasant solution to their problems. Borrow from Fielding? It was a possibility, he supposed. But he remembered how willing Fielding had been to believe ill of him, how eager to turn him over to the authorities on slight evidence without verifying whether that evidence was true or false. He remembered that Carolina was not really Fielding's daughter and that Fielding had always resented her. Even if Fielding did—reluctantly—accede to Carolina's request and ship the money over the sea from the Tidewater, there was no guarantee it would ever reach Port Royal. Pirates, the weather, the Spanish—all presented an ever-present menace.

And there were other problems as well. Indeed he would need to divert some of the money meant for the "venture" into fortifying this house for her protection—but it was best for Carolina not to know that. He could not afford to wait. Especially on something so uncertain as Fielding Lightfoot's whim.

"No, Carolina, it will not work. It would take time and we are too near the edge. Is this the letter?" He strode toward the little writing desk, picked up the piece of parchment that lay atop it, and glanced down, scanning it.

Carolina watched as he tore it in half.

"You will not let me help you," she said sulkily.

"You will help me best by listening to reason. What is done is done. You have made a grand gesture, one that pleased you. Be content with it."

"But you—"

"I will arrange my own salvation," he said crisply. "As I always have."

Carolina turned on her heel and ran down the stairs.

She was silent and pensive all through dinner, although Kells did his best to cheer her. And when they went upstairs to their bedchamber she clung to him with all the fervor of the lost.

"Christabel, Christabel," he murmured, using the name the world called her. And then with a sigh, "What am I to do with you?"

You could stay with me! she thought, but this was no time for quarreling. Not with his arms about her, not with her body burrowing against his own, not with their legs intertwined, their breath hot on each other's cheek . . . no, these moments were for forgetfulness, when she could dream that he would stay by her side, that they would never be separated.

A dream that seemed real enough while their love-making lasted, but a dream that disappeared, vanished with the heat of the moment. Reality came back as they drifted hazily down into the afterglow.

"Kells," she said, troubled. "You don't really want to leave me, do you?"

Her voice was wistful and the strong arm of her buccaneer, just now lying outflung beneath her as she lay on her back studying the stars through their window, tightened about her as if to shield her from the world.

"I *never* want to leave you," he said in his deep rich voice. "Don't you know that, Christabel?"

He did not *want* to leave her. But he would.

"But . . . you *are* going?" she murmured at last.

"I must," he sighed, and wished again that there had been no Marquess of Saltenham with his masquerades, no Reba with her wily mother, no deep intrigues to ensnare him. What cruel fate had decreed that he and Carolina must never enjoy their heritage, must live forever exiled in wild foreign places?

"I know you feel you must go," Carolina said wistfully. "But—oh, Kells." Her voice held a wild entreaty and her slender fingers traced a fiery persuasive path down his belly and groin, burrowed enticingly below. "Don't sail away, don't go—stay with me!"

It was a siren's song—and Kells was not slow to respond to it.

Wakened to passion again, he turned over and drew her slim yielding body against his own, caressed her tenderly. But he chose not to answer her impulsive plea. Instead he took her again, driving her to frenzy with his ardor, and let her go at last with yearning.

But she had not prevailed. All her efforts had moved him not one whit.

Carolina lay wide-eyed in the dark, listening to the even sound of his breathing.

Her plan had failed. She would have to devise another.

Chapter 7

The hammering was maddening. From dawn to dusk it went on unceasingly, day after day, until the whole house was fitted with iron grillwork. "A fort," Hawks called it, chuckling.

Carolina could see nothing to crow about. "A great waste of money you say we do not have!" she told Kells crossly.

"But will have soon," he promised her with a flash of white teeth. "Spain still sails the seas!"

"Kells." She tried to remonstrate with him. "You have a pardon for buccaneering. If you go back to it now, you will have to get yourself a pardon all over again."

The gray eyes across from her grew murky. "You seem to forget," he said silkily, "that the Marquess of Saltenham's masquerade made me a pirate in the eyes of the king—I *have* no pardon nor am likely to get one!"

Yes, and that was her fault, too! If her friend Reba

had not been so in love with the marquess, if Carolina had not schemed to get them married, then Robin's confession that he had impersonated Kells in piratical ventures against English ships would have gone unchallenged. But Carolina had begged Kells not to take the marquess's life, and Kells had granted her request—so that Robin could marry Reba. And Reba's mother had set up false witnesses to claim Robin's confession was made under duress.

"I suppose you are right," she said wistfully. "And it is something you must lay at my door."

"I lay nothing at your door," he said quickly, and his big hand closed warmly over her own. "It is not your fault you have a kind heart."

She looked at him guiltily, for Robin Tyrell, the Marquess of Saltenham, had been—ever so briefly—her lover. She had thought herself deserted by Kells at the time, of course. Still . . .

"Will those workmen never be through hammering?" she cried, eager to change the subject.

"Everything will be finished before the end of the week," her buccaneer promised her.

In fact, the work was finished on Wednesday and all Port Royal was agog at the "strengthening" of Captain Kells's house—a true fortress, they muttered, what with its little captain's walk on the top where one could view incoming ships.

And at breakfast on Thursday he told her he would be sailing with the tide on Saturday morning.

"But you can't!" she cried, startled. "You haven't had time to careen and provision the ship."

"Lars has already careened her," he said. "I'd promised him he could take her out. But now he'll captain the *Sea Wench* and I'll take out the *Sea Wolf*—we'll sail together."

At least that was some comfort—he would not be alone out there; he'd have another ship to back him up.

"I wish you'd take your whole fleet!" she muttered.

"And scare all the galleons back to port?" he teased. "No, 'tis better this way. Two fleet ships, a quick thrust or two and—back to Port Royal. You'll like that, won't you?"

Her answering smile was wan, for well she knew that voyages—however short they were intended to be—could end up lasting for months. And all the time she would not know whether he was alive or dead. . . .

She was thoughtful through breakfast, realizing bitterly that she had been drifting along day by day, clinging to the hope that some miracle would save them: the governor would decide to lend Kells the money after all; or some departing landowner on the Cobre would urge Kells to take over his plantation on a promise to pay later; or in England Robin Tyrell would have a change of heart and confess all to the authorities, and Kells would be free to return to Essex.

None of those things had happened, of course.

And now Kells had announced that he was leaving—the day after tomorrow!

As she watched him quit the house and swing out into the sunshine, taking long strides down the sandy street, Carolina's delicate jaw hardened. Her buccaneer had left her but one alternative—and she would take it.

When Kells returned for dinner he was greeted by a laughing, excited Carolina wearing a white apron, her long hair bound up in a linen square.

"Housekeeping?" he asked, bemused—for keeping house was not one of Carolina's favorite pursuits. She preferred leaving that to the servants.

"Oh, wait till you see!" She seized him by the hand and ran ahead of him up the stairway, then flung open her bedroom door dramatically.

Kells stopped short. Before him, filled with clutter, Carolina's big curved-top trunk stood open. It formed the center of a huge array of half-packed boxes and small chests. Women's clothing was scattered about the bed. Shoes and boots lay in piles upon the floor. Gloves, parasols, fans, scarves—a wild confusion.

"I know it looks impossible, but I will be ready by Saturday morning!" she promised him gaily.

"Ready for what?" he asked warily.

"Why, to sail with you, of course." Her radiant smile ignored his gathering frown. "Can't you see, this is a golden opportunity for me to visit my family in Virginia? Oh, Kells, you would not deny me passage when you could so easily drop me off in the York and be gone before any pursuit could find you?"

Outside the doorway Gilly hovered. Kells shut the door behind him.

"Carolina," he said slowly, "I would sail you to hell if you desired it—and you know it. But it is not to the Tidewater that you wish to sail. Once aboard the *Sea Wolf* you will find some compelling reason why you cannot be left in Virginia, why you must continue the voyage with me."

Carolina's telltale flush spoke volumes.

"Oh, Kells," she entreated, taking an impulsive step toward him that brought her up flush against the hard muscles of his chest. She looked up wistfully into the sun-bronzed face above her. "Of course that is what I will do! And you should not deny me this. All I want is to go with you." Her luminous silver-gray eyes pleaded with him to understand. "Kells—fate has been unkind to us. It has robbed us of our birthright, of the life we might have shared. But we can have a life together in spite of all the devils of hell—we'll have it aboard the *Sea Wolf.*"

"No, Carolina, we will not." Her loveliness, her femininity, her pleading stance were all hard to withstand, but he managed it with an effort. Gently he put her away from him and looked down deep into her eyes. "You cannot accompany me on this voyage. You must wait for me here."

She took a step back and crunched a fan beneath her heel. Her lovely face was mutinous. "Why? *Why* must I wait here? Other captains take *their* wives with them. Why can you not take me?"

"Perhaps those other captains can stand the thought of seeing their women blasted from the deck, having a broken mast fall on them and crush them, watching them drown in a sinking ship or blown to pieces in battle—I cannot," he said briefly. "There is no use arguing, Carolina. This is one concession I will not make to you."

Her teeth caught in her soft lower lip and her eyes were dangerous. "Will you not?" she asked softly. "Oh, but I think you will!"

"Let us not discuss it now," he said impatiently. "Let us sit down to dinner in a civilized manner and not be at each other's throat over the ridiculous notion of your going to sea on a buccaneering venture!"

Carolina subsided, but her eyes remained dangerously bright all through dinner. She gave short answers to his best quips. And by the time dinner was over, that consuming fear she felt that he might be killed on the voyage and never return to her had made her voice waspish.

"I am going to bed!" she announced, rising.

"Good," he said, laying down his napkin and rising, too. "I will accompany you. Hawks can wake me early in the morning in good time to complete the provisioning of the ship."

Leaving! That was all he thought about! Filled with indignation, Carolina ran up the stairs ahead of him, flung open the door of her bedroom, kicked aside some half-filled boxes whose contents scattered before her, and walked over them to her dressing table where she busied herself with taking the ribands out of her hair.

All too aware of his lady's dangerous mood, Kells stood with arms folded amid the clutter and watched Carolina without speaking.

Suddenly she turned from her dressing table and her silver eyes flashed. "You *should* take me with you!"

"No," he said wearily. "We have been over all that before. I will not take you into battle, Christabel."

"Then do not go!" she cried passionately. "*Why* must you go to sea again? In heaven's name, why?"

He ran raking fingers through his dark hair. He was finding it hard to be patient with her but he managed to keep his voice even. "Because"—he spaced his words —"as I told you before, we can no longer afford our style of living *unless I go to sea!* This house, your clothes, your jewels—"

"I do not care about them!" She tore off the glittering necklace she wore about her neck and hurled it to the floor. She was almost in tears. "Indeed I do not want them if that is what having them means!"

He sighed. "There is an alternative, of course. I have money in England."

"No!"

"I repeat," he said sternly, "I have plenty of money in England, but I must go there for it myself—the goldsmiths will release it to no one else. I have told you that—and yet you are equally against my setting foot on English soil."

"Oh, you know why! The authorities are lying in wait for you there. You would be taken—killed! Reba's mother and the Marquess of Saltenham have seen to that!"

"Very possibly true," he agreed ironically. "Still I would chance it if you were not so set against it. So for your sweet sake I will allow my newer enemies in England to live a space longer while I sail out and take what I need from my old enemies—the galleons of Spain."

And perhaps die from it!

Seared by that thought, she sprang up and ran to him, threw her arms passionately around his neck and clung to him—all penitence. At least temporarily. And although her responses to his masculine caresses that night had all the fire any man could desire, there was a certain reservation in her heart against him.

"This is a terrible place for you to leave me," she muttered resentfully when at last he drew away from her tingling body.

About to turn over in bed, he turned toward her instead. His grin was a white flash in the starlight, half seen. "Terrible?" he said humorously. "There is no better house in the town than this one. It is strong and defensible and decorated to your taste. You have servants, the latest Paris gowns, jewels, the city at your feet. Would you trade all that for a meager life at sea, storms that howl in the rigging, mouldy bread, water turned green in the casks, the ever-present danger of meeting the entire might of the Spanish treasure *flota* at one time—or the Vera Cruz squadron—and being blown out of the water?"

"Yes," she said, as definite as he.

"I'd given you credit for better sense," he laughed. And, sounding pleased with himself, rolled over and was immediately asleep.

In the hall the longcase marquetry clock chimed the hour—it was two A.M.

Beside the sleeping figure of her buccaneer, Carolina lay wakeful in the starlight, thinking. The nighttime sounds of Port Royal roistering were muted to her ears as she pondered her problem. Her pleas had made no impression at all on Kells—she might as well have saved her breath. This hot night of lovemaking which had left her so breathless had not moved him either.

Unable to sleep, at last she rose restlessly and donned a paper-thin silken shawl from the Orient that had come to this buccaneer port via the pirates of Madagascar. The shawl was of a cool Chinese gold heavily embroidered in white silk—a pattern of sumptuous roses. The long pale fringe swished along her bare legs as she went and settled herself in the window for coolness and looked out through the new grillwork over the moonlit town.

She sat there brooding, letting the trade winds cool her hot cheeks—and started as a shadow scuttled out of the house below her and ran, barelegged and with a shawl thrown over her head to make her more a part of the darkness, barefoot down the street.

Carolina frowned as she recognized the flying form. That would be fifteen-year-old Gilly, she guessed, slipping out to keep a tryst at some waterfront tavern—probably with some brawling chance-met buccaneer. Not all the locks nor all the grillwork had been sufficient to keep Gilly in!

Carolina sighed. Nothing was secure—not one's house, not one's life, and certainly not one's future!

Kells had said he would sail day after tomorrow and he would sail—she knew him well enough to know that.

And without him, Port Royal would have nothing at all, she told herself. No life, no charm . . .

Below her, parties of drunken buccaneers were even now streaming down Queen's Street toward King's Lane or Sea Lane, lurching against each other with cutlasses clashing, bawling drunken songs, pinching the wenches who staggered along beside them, laughing at their squeals and giggles, making the night hideous with all the sounds of what was called the most wicked city in the western world.

Wicked? The town over which Carolina's somber glance passed was a town of contrasts. In a city unequaled for godlessness in this godless part of the world, Port Royal's skyline was yet dominated by a handsome church that reared its bell tower up into the sky. And the people who thronged this busiest of New World ports by day, if not by night, were proud of their church and considered the present church bell too small—they planned shortly to send to England for a new and larger one.

Well defended the town was, too, she admitted grudgingly, her gaze passing thoughtfully from Fort James on her left to Fort Carlisle on her right—and besides that, somewhere behind her were Fort Charles and Morgan's Line—for the buccaneers had an unparalleled eye for defense. The three major forts loomed over the shoreline, their brass cannon ever ready to defend the city. She almost wished it was *not* so well defended—then she would have a good reason to insist that Kells take her with him.

Her silver-gray eyes flashed. He *should* take her with him—oh, she would make him do it! She would not be parted from him, left behind in this tiresome buccaneer town!

And since persuasion had not worked, she would try another tack! Her eyes narrowed as she thought about it. Finally, sitting there, she came to a decision, and a wicked smile crossed her delicately chiseled features. Pleased with herself, she tossed away her shawl and padded barefoot back through the clutter to bed.

Kells had but one more day to spend here before the *Sea Wolf* and her sister ship, the *Sea Wench,* sailed.

It would, she promised herself, be a memorable one.

Outside in the handsome hallway the longcase marquetry clock chimed four.

Chapter 8

Carolina slept late, only turning over and mumbling something inarticulate when Kells rose and asked her if she would have breakfast with him. Her slight sleepy shrug that deliciously rippled her pale female body, shimmering in the morning heat, was answer enough. He smiled and went out the door briskly, to breakfast alone.

It was afternoon when Carolina woke, stretched, and called for her bath. She lingered long in it, soaping her pale skin with scented French soap, giving a stream of directions meanwhile to an astonished Betts.

"Yes, that is correct—the gown I wish to wear is in the trunk room down the hall. No, I know I have not worn it for a long time, but it is of scarlet silk trimmed in silver and it has with it a black taffeta petticoat garnished also with silver—oh, you cannot possibly miss it, Betts."

Betts's brows elevated at what seemed to her a remarkably strange choice. Why would her mistress, who had so many delightful new frocks, select an old one? And why would she select a vivid red gown rather than one of the delicate ice-blues and ice-greens which were the captain's favorites? And on his last day in Port Royal, too! As she went off to the trunk room, where so many handsome old clothes were packed away, Betts shook her head in bewilderment. It was indeed strange!

But not strange to Carolina, whose plans today were intricate and not yet really worked out. The dress was red—and when she was misbehaving she always wore red. If possible. Red suited her mood when she was feeling wicked.

The scarlet dress was duly brought and sent downstairs to be pressed while a sullen Gilly—red-eyed from loss of sleep—emptied silver pitcher after silver pitcher of warm water over Carolina to rinse off the soap as she stood in the metal hip bath, looking lovelier than any Venus rising from the foam.

Carolina smiled at sight of the red gown when it was returned looking as fresh as when she had first worn it—on a day Tortuga would never forget! Betts felt uneasy at the sight of that smile. For her mistress was known to be capricious—"a handful" was what the captain sometimes ruefully called her.

Over her naked body, Carolina first put on a nearly transparent black silk chemise with sleeves that spilled a delicate spider web of black lace across her white forearms—that was not entirely fashionable now, but Carolina did not care. Her aim at the moment was to be seductive—hang fashion! Next came a shimmer of sheer black silk hose and black satin slippers with high red heels. Black garters, the rosettes set with brilliants, held the stockings taut. Silently Betts held out the black taffeta petticoat, and Carolina let it rustle sensuously down about her slim hips. It was garnished with silver threads and sprinkled here and there with brilliants.

Next came the startling scarlet silk gown, low-cut enough to cause gasps among onlookers had there been any, and with big elbow-length puffed sleeves that were edged with glittering silver threads.

Ah, she had made trouble once in this dress in Tortuga! she thought with a wicked smile as she tucked up the scarlet silk of her wide skirts into big panniers on each side, and fastened those panniers with brooches of flashing jet. The only thing missing was the scarlet ruffled parasol she had carried with it then and that had been lost somewhere long ago. No matter. She would pile her hair high up in the latest fashion and set in it enough brilliants to attract the eye! And several black velvet ribands, too, just to bring out the white-gold flash of her blonde hair!

It was approaching dusk when Kells came home from last-minute preparations of getting the *Sea Wolf* ready to sail upon the morrow, and that timing suited Carolina exactly. She met him in the wide lower hall and gave him a mocking curtsy as he entered.

He stopped still at sight of her.

"I have not seen that dress for some time," he observed.

So he remembered the stir she had caused when last she wore it! Carolina was perversely pleased.

"It's very pretty. I thought I might as well get it out and wear it," she announced innocently. "Indeed I thought we might go for a walk before dinner," she added. "Since it will most likely be our last walk together for some time." She tried to keep the bitter note out of her voice.

Kells made no comment but he regarded her warily. She thought his lean face wore a sardonic expression. So he had guessed she was in a dangerous mood. . . . Carolina tossed her head—at the moment she did not care!

He suggested they take a turn toward Fort James and stroll past Bradford's Wharf up Fisher's Row, where the breeze from the sea would be cooling, but Carolina hated the sight of the turtle crawls, where the huge lumbering creatures were penned—she never saw them but that she did not feel herself to be as much a prisoner of the island as they!

Still she did not demur.

Up Queen's Street they went toward the wharf. The sun hung low in the sky and its golden light turned Carolina's scarlet dress to sudden flame. From the Foot Passage that led down to Thames Street and the waterfront came a crowd of roisterers who had been imbibing strong rum at Littleton's Tavern. To a man, they lurched to a halt at the nerve-tingling sight of this sumptuous woman strolling by with her hair and gown both seeming ablaze.

"Look, lads, 'tis the Silver Wench," hiccupped someone, bumping into his fellows as he, too, came to a halt.

"I'd rather have *her* than gold," said a young buccaneer prayerfully. He had lurched against a brick wall and looked about to slide dizzily down it to the sandy street.

There was a snigger of laughter at his remark.

"Ye'll not have her, Parks," sang out a voice from the rear. "For the Wench is guarded by Captain Kells!"

The warning was heeded. The group fell back a little and quieted.

Carolina ignored them all although Kells frowned.

"Are you planning to turn up Fisher's Row toward the turtle crawls?" he asked her politely when she hesitated. "And perhaps acquire something for tomorrow's dinner?"

Carolina flashed him an impatient look in the waning light. "You know I cannot abide looking at those poor trapped creatures!"

"And yet I have seen you do justice to green turtle soup," he murmured.

"Yes—well, everyone does," she defended. "After all, it is a staple of the diet here!"

"At sea as well." He turned left on Lime Street and left again, leading her down the High Street toward the great Market Bell and the Exchange.

The roisterers from Littleton's staggered after them, keeping their distance but ogling Carolina. Some of their remarks about her beauty were rough enough to bring a frown to Kells's sun-bronzed face, but he kept his temper.

Carolina had just heard her hips described as "swaying delights that would drive a man mad," and her cheeks had grown a trifle pink.

"We are collecting a crowd," murmured Kells as several others joined the following group. "Was that your intention?"

Carolina shrugged. "I am just out for a little air. And what do you mean, 'collecting a crowd'?"

"I mean," he said in an undertone, "that some of those buckos following us are drunk enough to reach out for you. And that is something I will not permit. Do you want to see bloodshed in the street? Is that your aim?" He was loosening his sword in its scabbard as he spoke.

"Nonsense, that won't happen," Carolina said loftily, choosing to ignore the drunken group that staggered after them.

"Then why did you wear that dress?" he demanded, low.

Carolina took two more flaunting steps before she answered him. When she did her voice was tauntingly casual. "Oh, I had understood that your old friend, Captain O'Rourke, was in town, and I thought this dress might stir old memories should we chance to meet up with him!"

Her remark was the more outrageous because it was in this very dress that she had once asked Shawn to take her away from Tortuga, away from Kells. Shawn had been dazzled by her. They had come near to killing each other over her that day, Kells and his old friend Shawn, and Kells had not forgot it. Beside her, the gray eyes narrowed and began to glitter.

"No, Shawn is not in town," he said crisply. "He is rumored to be in Madagascar. You have been misinformed, Christabel."

"Really?" She shrugged an indifferent shoulder. "No matter, we shall have our walk anyway." *And inflame others,* her mocking tone implied.

Blithely Carolina ignored the sudden stiffening of the man beside her. She *did* take note of his lengthening stride.

"You are walking too fast for me," she complained. "I cannot keep up."

"Indeed?" His voice held a tinge of bitterness. "I would have thought few men could keep up with *you.*"

Carolina's silver eyes began to flash resentfully. So he was going to take that attitude, was he? That she was in the wrong? Perversely she ignored the fact that she very obviously *was* in the wrong and like as not to cause a riot, garbed as she was in her present attire. It took a brave man to walk beside her through the gathering dusk of Port Royal.

But at the moment she could feel only tingling malice toward the tall man who strode beside her. She would make him *afraid* to leave her here!

But this boisterous group did not fit her plans. It must be someone more. . . .

Suddenly her lips curved into a wicked smile. There just ahead, strolling toward them with a slightly swaggering gait, was exactly what she was looking for: their neighbor, Louis Deauville, whom Kells insisted was a renegade from his native country, seeking refuge here against being imprisoned for his debts in France.

"Monsieur Deauville." Happily, Carolina greeted the Frenchman's exaggerated bow. "How nice to see you walking out this evening. You must tell me, is that coat you are wearing the latest thing from France?"

"You must be suffocating in it, Deauville," Kells observed unsmilingly.

Beneath Carolina's obvious approval, Louis Deauville's yellow brocade chest expanded beneath its thick crust of gold embroidery. "I was fortunate to find it here in the town," he said.

"The buccaneers' market is a good one," remarked Kells.

Carolina ignored the implication. "It is too bad there are no fashion dolls for men," she said gaily. "I can rarely persuade my husband here to buy himself a new suit. But those cuffs are a miracle! Perhaps you will be good enough to let me borrow your coat so that my husband's tailor may copy those cuffs in gray and silver while my husband is gone?"

"Ah, I was not aware the gentleman was leaving?" Deauville glanced speculatively at Kells.

"My plans are uncertain," murmured Kells, looking down on Carolina's bright head with obvious displeasure. Around them their drunken followers stood about, shifting their feet and mumbling to each other.

Louis Deauville smiled ingratiatingly upon Carolina. "My entire wardrobe is at your disposal at any time," he said with a slight bow that rippled the golden curls of his periwig. "As am I!"

"I shall see that you make good that remark, Monsieur Deauville," Carolina said recklessly.

"And your lady will need an escort to the governor's ball while you are gone." Louis Deauville turned again to Kells. "I understand another one is planned while his visiting cousin is here."

Kells's teeth ground slightly. "If my lady attends the governor's next ball in my absence, she will attend it alone, Deauville. Consider it sufficient if she does you the honor of a dance."

"Oh, I should hope for somewhat more than that. . . ." The Frenchman's caressing gaze passed over Carolina.

"Indeed you shall come to dinner next Wednesday merely for having so handsomely offered to escort me," declared Carolina.

Kells frowned down at her. This obvious coquetry—and with a man he did not trust—infuriated him.

"Deauville," he said, "my lady is overtired. She does not wish me to leave her—you understand?"

"Indeed, I understand very well," purred the Frenchman. *"Mon Dieu,* a beautiful lady must have an airing from time to time. I will be the good neighbor while you are gone, Capitaine, and keep your lady from getting lonesome."

Carolina was laughing inwardly. It was going better than she had hoped. She could almost feel Kells's irritation boiling up in him. If only she could make him jealous enough. . . .

"We will talk about it all next week, Monsieur Deauville," she said with a slanted look.

The Frenchman looked delighted—too delighted, Kells thought. "You will understand, Deauville, that my lady implies much more than she means," he said sternly. "It is a bad habit of hers," he added with a frown at Carolina.

Deauville returned him a catlike smile. "What a lady means is always open to interpretation," he responded suavely.

"She invites you to dinner as thanks for sending her the fashion doll from Paris—it was very good of you."

"Oh, I will be much more good," chuckled Deauville. "I will keep your wife entertained while you are gone!"

It was too much. Kells had a sudden instinct to seize Deauville by the lace at his throat and shake some decorum into him and then to turn this wild wench at his side over his knee and pound some sense into her as well.

"You will not *entertain* my wife while I am gone," he said evenly.

"Indeed?" The Frenchman did not lack for valor. "But while the cat is away, Capitaine, what may not the little mice do?" His tone was insolent, for he liked not the way this tall fellow was scowling at him. He had sent men to their graves for less! For in France Deauville was accounted a swordsman and a dangerous one. His lace-cuffed hand was creeping toward his rapier even as he spoke.

Carolina did not catch the gesture.

"While those two fight," came a chilling mutter from someone who had joined the drunken group behind her—a mutter that sent sudden shivers down Carolina's spine as she heard it, "we could spirit the girl away."

But Kells had caught that remark, too.

"Deauville," he said between his teeth, "you and I may have our differences and I will give you satisfaction at any time you may desire—but this is neither the time nor the place."

"Indeed, I see what you mean," the Frenchman declared amicably, flashing a set of white teeth in Carolina's direction.

And now, thought Carolina, *this wicked-looking Frenchman would blandly agree that they must not leave a lady unattended in the wilds of the Port Royal night, they would all stroll home together and on the way he and Kells would become the best of friends—and all her plans to make Kells jealous would have come to naught!*

She spoke quickly. Before she had time to think, her voice rang out. "I accept your invitation to squire me to the governor's ball, Monsieur Deauville."

Kells swung around. "You will not!"

Deauville chuckled and swept Carolina a magnificent bow—so deep his golden curls almost brushed the sandy street. "I stand in readiness to escort you, *ma beauté!*"

"Back off, Deauville." Kells's voice had gone crisp. "I have already told you that my wife will not accompany you."

Deauville was determined not to appear irresolute in the lady's eyes. He frowned upon the buccaneer. "Capitaine, that decision is madame's alone," was his insolent reply, and with the words he stepped backward and slid his long rapier from its scabbard.

Carolina realized she had carried the game too far. She had never intended to provoke a fight—she had only wanted to arouse flaming jealousy in her lean buccaneer. Panic surged over her.

"Kells," she cried. "I—"

But her voice was lost in Deauville's fierce, *"En garde!"* and Kells's swift, "Get behind me, Christabel," as he drew his own basket-hilted blade from its scabbard.

There was a roar from the drunken sailors of "Give the lads room to fight!" Men shoved each other back to form a rough circle around the combatants. The pack who had been following Carolina had by now forgotten all about her, for they were faced with the new and enjoyable spectacle of a fight between Kells and this insolent Frenchman, who looked wiry enough to be a swordsman himself.

Ordinarily, Carolina knew, men about to duel removed their constricting coats and their boots and fought barefoot and shirted on the sand. But this affray had blown up suddenly and neither man was in a mood to pause and doff his boots. In England, in such a case, a challenger would have flung down his glove before his opponent or lightly slapped his face to begin hostilities; in England an appointed hour would have been set, preferably dawn; in England there would have been seconds and rules and decorum. Here in Port Royal there were no rules. Here two lean and formidable men circled each other warily in the fast-falling tropical night. They moved catlike, seeking opportunity, their long swords snaking out restively, each man testing his opponent's will.

Then the Frenchman lunged, the blades clashed, both men sprang back—and Carolina quivered. She had been a fool to provoke this—it could end in tragedy.

It was darker now. Torches had been brought, and the long blades glimmered gold by their light. Lunge and parry, lunge and parry—though their fighting styles differed, they seemed evenly matched. The Frenchman had flair—his sword flashed dramatically and he cried *"Voila!"* with each thrust. Kells had a deadly accuracy—he fought silently, moving with tireless grace. The torchlight gleamed on their sweating faces. Carolina could see how intent they were, how neither gaze wavered from the other.

By now, running feet were coming from all directions as word spread that Captain Kells was fighting a Frenchman over the Wench. Men were of no mind to miss the battle, for Kells's fame as the best blade in the Caribbean was legendary. There was jostling all around, and Carolina felt herself being thrust back against a door.

To her dismay she saw that they were attracting a large crowd, and as the eager onlookers from the rear surged forward against those in the front, one tipsy sailor lost his footing and fell toward the combatants, lurching awkwardly against Kells's back. He was immediately seized by his friends and roughly whisked away, but Kells's slight stagger when the fellow catapulted into him had cost him something. In that moment Deauville's sharp blade had pierced his sleeve and grazed the flesh beneath.

"Oh-ho, I have pinked you!" crowed the dancing Frenchman, drawing back a blade that was red on the tip, and Carolina moaned.

"Not deep enough," growled his opponent, ignoring the little trickle of blood that dripped down his sleeve to stain the basket hilt of his sword. "You will have to do better."

Carolina was near to fainting. "Oh, stop, stop!" The words burst from her. "I *promise* I will not go to the ball with *anyone!*"

"Ah, but you will," caroled the Frenchman, delighted that he had managed to draw first blood. "You will go with *me.* I, Louis Deauville, insist upon it!"

The words were not out of his mouth before Kells lunged forward in silent fury. Carolina's hands were clenched as the two male bodies almost crashed together. The swords clashed with a ringing sound that brought a hoarse roar from the throats of the rapt onlookers. Carolina wanted to cover her eyes with her hands but she could not. Her terrified gaze was riveted on the fighting pair. She saw them stagger apart—she could not tell if either was hurt. And now they were lunging again, they were dancing to the side, the pace of the battle had become lightning-fast—they were here, there, everywhere, so that the crowd was giving way before them. Oh, God, one of the sailors, intent on the spectacle before him, had let a bottle drop from his careless fingers. It was rolling forward under Kells's feet. Kells had slipped on it, he was falling, Deauville was rushing in—indeed he had a mind to kill his man and make all Port Royal echo to his name. A single thrust would do it!

Chapter 9

A wild scream was welling up from Carolina's throat—but it was never uttered. It was choked off by a huge hand that snaked around her and slammed down over most of her face, quenching all sound. The door behind her opened, she was jerked through it and it closed again—almost in a single motion.

So abruptly did it happen that it took Carolina's breath away. Her mind was awhirl. . . . The blood pounded in her head. In that moment she did not know whether Kells was alive or dead. All she could hear was the wild roaring of the crowd outside, the rattle of cutlasses. But she herself was helpless in the grip of a huge arm that dragged her inside and kept her pinioned with her back forced against the barrel chest of the man who had seized her.

Over his rough hand, she could see that they were in a small low-ceilinged room. She guessed she must have been pulled into one of the small houses occupied by prostitutes that dotted this part of the street. The room itself was dingy and sparsely furnished, containing a wooden table, two benches, a cupboard and an untidy bed from which the room's only other occupant, a florid-faced woman with brightly hennaed hair, clad only in a black laced corset, fancy red satin garters and high-heeled shoes, now leaped to her feet.

"Gor'!" she cried. "What's this, Trott?"

The man Trott, who had dragged Carolina inside and was having some difficulty holding onto his wildly struggling burden, answered her with a growl. "This here's our fortune, Emmy."

Peering closer at Carolina, Emmy shrank back. " 'Tis the Silver Wench! Captain Kells'll kill us!" Beneath the red ochre smeared upon her cheeks her face paled, and even her big white thighs began to shake, sending the ribands on her red garters dancing.

"No, he won't!" snapped Trott. "Kells is outside fightin' with a Frenchie, and the Frenchie just downed him. Nary a soul saw me pull the Wench in, they's all watchin' the fight. And when they do miss her, they'll think she's run away somewheres. Now where can we hide her, Emmy? Think quick, woman!"

But Emmy had no need to think quick—no opportunity even. Behind them the door burst open, propelled by a booted foot, and Kells himself, blade out and flashing at the end of a long arm, leaped into the room. He looked disheveled and a little trickle of blood ran down his swordarm to soak in red the lace at his wrist, but he seemed otherwise unhurt. The burning gaze of his gray eyes made them look like hot embers in his dark face as he advanced menacingly upon Trott.

He was not dead! He was here, come to her rescue. Relief flooded over Carolina, making her weak. She had never been so glad to see anyone in her life.

"Let her go!" roared Kells.

Trott thrust Carolina away from him as if she were

hot, and she caught at the wooden table to keep from falling. "I was only tryin' to save the Wench from them ruffians out there what had her backed up against the door!" whined Trott, eyeing in terror not only the long sword that flicked at him but the four or five angry-looking buccaneers who had crowded in behind Kells.

"Is that true?" Kells demanded of Carolina.

"No," she gasped, straightening up. "He lies!"

"Let us have 'im, Cap'n," urged one of the buccaneers who had come in behind Kells. "You get your lady home."

Kells's drawl had a rough edge to it. "I think not," he said with deliberation. "This fool has dared to lay hands on my lady, so he is mine. Indeed"—his voice rose so ferociously that it reached outside clearly enough to strike fear into those who might plan to do likewise—"*anyone* who touches this lady—whether I am here to defend her or not—had best make his will before he does so, for I will assuredly seek him out!"

Trott blanched and fell into a crouch, his sweating hand clutching his cutlass.

"But you can take my lady outside, lads," Kells said in a lower but no less deadly tone. He brushed Carolina toward them with a long arm as he spoke. "I'll deal with this fellow in a language he can understand."

With an honor guard formidable enough to have done justice to a queen, Carolina found herself escorted from the room. Outside, the street was lit now with many torches. The wavering light gleamed on curious faces but she could see no sign of Louis Deauville among them. She marveled that his body did not lie sprawled upon the coral sand of the street.

She might have asked but her attention was distracted by the sudden clash of steel from the room she had just quitted, punctuated by a woman's high-pierced frightened shrieks.

"Neat, the way the cap'n came up on one arm and

got the Frenchie, warn't it?" Carolina heard one of her escorts say.

"Aye, he's a swordsman," agreed another admiringly. "The best. 'Tis proud I am to serve under 'im."

There was a general murmur of assent among the buccaneers surrounding Carolina, followed by another violent clash of swords inside and a burst of shrieks that curdled her blood—and then the captain himself came out, wiping his blade upon a kerchief.

He looked thunderous.

Curtly, he took Carolina's arm, nodded his thanks to those who had escorted her outside, and turned his face toward home. Confused and upset by the evening's swift-moving events, which had gone frighteningly far beyond anything she had envisioned, Carolina allowed herself to be swept along home. Beside her strode a silent Kells, who stared straight ahead and did not choose to look at her.

She felt forlorn.

"Your arm is bleeding," she said helplessly. "Are you badly hurt?"

He snorted. "Hardly! Else I would not have been able to swing this blade—'tis a scratch only."

Carolina swallowed. "And—and Monsieur Deauville? Did you—?" She could not bring herself to say "kill him?"

He turned about to look at her then, and she thought his expression murderous. "You need worry no further about Deauville," he told her in a bitter voice. "I only speared him in the leg. Had I thought there was anything between you I'd have aimed a little higher. As it is he'll enjoy a long convalescence before he goes dancing again!"

Carolina closed her eyes for a moment in silent thanks that she had not been the cause of Deauville's death. It had been a close call.

When she opened her eyes again Kells was still

regarding her. It irritated him that she should look so riotously pretty, with her big penitent gray eyes luminous as she looked up at him. So innocent, as if she had not been the cause of so much trouble!

"Kells, I—" she began.

"Be silent," he snapped. "I will have something to say to you later!"

She cast a look back at the little knot of buccaneers who followed them, guessing they had come along to make sure Kells got her home without further trouble.

Once inside the house Kells propelled Carolina upstairs before him with a none too gentle hand placed at the small of her back. On the way they passed a startled Hawks, who stared first at the blood dripping from his captain's wrist, then at the torn sleeve and torn lace at his captain's throat, and finally at the dark anger mirrored on his captain's dark countenance, and abruptly went outside to confer in the street with the buccaneers who had followed, and learn the circumstances of this odd return.

Upstairs Kells flung open the door of her bedchamber and thrust Carolina inside, then closed the door after him with his boot and stood glaring at her.

Carolina swallowed. At the moment she felt to blame for all the ills of the world. "For a horrible moment I thought you were dead. I saw you slip and go down. . . ." Her voice trailed off with a shudder. "And then suddenly I was snatched from behind and dragged into that awful room by that man—what happened to him?"

"What do you think happened to him?" Kells asked imperturbably. "I killed him."

"And the woman?"

"I left her in a fit of hysterics. By now she'll be over that and be picking his pockets and checking his shoes to see if he carried coins in them."

Carolina shuddered again. "He had told the woman

to hide me somewhere—I think he planned to hold me for ransom."

"Ransom . . ." he murmured. It was on the tip of his tongue to say, "More like he would have sold you to the Barbary pirates," but he forbore. This was the dark side of life in Port Royal—that world from which he had tried so hard to shield her. Bawds disappeared—who knew where they went? Spirited aboard slave ships to Africa? White slaves in exchange for black? A blonde beauty such as Carolina would bring a fortune from some sheik or sultan. She would disappear behind harem walls and never be seen again. . . . Best not to tell her of the Barbary pirates—such tales would only give her nightmares. "For ransom—very possibly," he agreed coolly.

"And you would not have had the price to ransom me," she murmured wistfully. "For we are back to buccaneering again."

"I would have *found* the price," he growled, trying to sound indifferent. *Not ransom her?* To get her back he would have done anything: He would have sold this house for the first offer, forced his IOU's at gunpoint upon the moneyed traders who frequented this buccaneer port! And if that were not enough, he would have seized the governor himself and held *him* for ransom! The very thought of the lengths to which he would have gone to bring this maddening wench back to his side made him dizzy. He passed a hand over his face as if to brush away his thoughts. "But you were not held for ransom," he said steadily.

"No, thank heaven." She sighed. "Here, take off your coat. Let me wash your wound and bind it." And when his shirt sleeve was pulled back and the wound washed and bound, she gave him a slanted look through her lashes.

"After tonight I—I am afraid to be left here," she said in what she hoped was a small voice.

His rejoinder was not what she had expected. He snorted. "You are afraid of nothing, Christabel! Do not think you can cozen me by prattling of your fears!"

That he could see through her so readily, angered her. "But you can see how dangerous it is for me here," she burst out. "You *must* take me with you, Kells. Tonight proves it!"

He cast a glance at the ceiling as if looking for strength to stay his anger. "So that is why we went through this exercise tonight?" he ground out. "I have killed one man for you and disabled another, and it was all so that I might become apprised of the dangers of Port Royal?"

"To a woman alone, yes!" Carolina said stubbornly.

"By God, you are not alone!" he shouted. "I leave you in a house that is the next thing to a fort! You will be attended and protected every moment." His gray eyes narrowed. "You will not leave the house except in the company of Hawks and whomever else he selects to accompany you."

"So I am to be a prisoner?" Carolina drew herself up indignantly. "Is that what you are telling me? It is to be Tortuga all over again?"

The tall buccaneer gazed down on his maddening lady with a torment of emotions surging through him. She looked so enchanting—a beauty to melt a man's will. An overwhelming desire to take the wench with him swept over him, leaving him sweating, the lace at his throat too tight. He tugged at it in indecision, although to Carolina his dark countenance seemed carved in granite. *Take her with him? God, he could hardly resist!* Ahead lay long empty nights without her, afloat upon an endless ocean.

He wrenched his mind back to realities.

"What you did tonight was inexcusable," he said sternly.

"I know it was," she admitted wistfully, and swayed

toward him. "But take me with you anyway. Sail me to Virginia, Kells. Sail in by night and row me by longboat to Level Green. Let me wait for you there!" (For once in Virginia she would find some other way to keep him!)

He gazed down at her, troubled. That he might carry her to Virginia and leave her at Level Green with her mother while he sailed against Spain was a tempting thought. Tempting—but fleeting. Too well he remembered how Carolina had helped him escape from there—she had tossed him a sword. Before witnesses. Her beautiful arrogant mother had many enemies and some of them might realize how easily they could ensnare him—just by bringing charges against Carolina for helping a fugitive escape. He would come from hell to rescue her, and they would know it. A trap could be set for him there. . . .

He shook his head to clear it. His ardent desire for this silvery beauty was melting his brain. He must away before the wench teased him into making some mad mistake that could cost her her life. Best to leave now!

There were tears in her hopeful pleading eyes as he pushed her gently away from him. All of his being wanted to take her in his arms, to succumb to her pleas, to kiss those tears away. The wrenching struggle to resist such an action harshened his voice.

"I will spend the night aboard ship," he said curtly and turned swiftly on his heel before his resolve could weaken.

Carolina felt as if she had been slapped. Would he rob her, then, even of this last night with him? Leave her without even a proper good-by? A wave of hot indignation washed over her—and with that wave, words to hurt him sprang to her lips.

"I will not be faithful to you while you are gone!" she flung at his departing back.

He turned then. His iron jaw hardened still further. "You do not mean that."

"I *do* mean it!" she flashed, lifting her chin. "I intend to be *very merry* if you leave me here!"

He took an angry step toward her. She had never seen such a daunting countenance. At any other time she might have quailed before that look—but not tonight. Tonight she was too desperate. She stood her ground.

He came to within a couple of feet of her, stood breathing heavily. For a wild moment she thought he was going to strike her, but he thought better of it.

"You will have all the time in the world for it," he said thickly, "for this may be a long voyage. And who knows, there may be some Spanish wench aboard a galleon who, when she joins us, will be as *merry* as my unfaithful wife!"

Carolina gasped. She lifted her arm to strike him only to find it caught in a viselike grip.

"I'd not try that," he said silkily, and flung her from him to catch for support at the bedpost.

Her slipper struck the door as he was closing it. She could hear his boots clattering down the stairs before she could wrench it open.

She started to follow him—no, he would only nod to Hawks, and Hawks would stop her at the door. It would be degrading to be seen struggling with Hawks in the doorway while her buccaneer strode away from her!

Her gaze fell to the coat he had left behind him. She seized it and ran to the open window.

"You have left your coat!" she called to him as he emerged onto the street. "And I cannot get these big cuffs through the grillwork—you will have to come back!"

He did not even look up but swung away, a tall, determined figure, dim in the fast-gathering dusk.

Carolina threw her other slipper at him and missed. She guessed he was on his way to a nearby tavern where he would pick up his men and be rowed out in a longboat to the waiting *Sea Wolf*.

Carolina almost ran downstairs to plead with Hawks to let her pursue him.

But—to what end? she asked herself hopelessly. Kells would not change; she had never been able to change him. He insisted on supporting her in this grand style—and she herself was an extravagant wench, as he was fond of saying—and she knew as well as he that they were seeing the end of the gold that had seemed so inexhaustible when first they had settled here.

Kells was a buccaneer, and this was spring. He was off to snare the passing galleons that would come to the New World with the spring, bearing—not gold perhaps—but arms, rich fabrics, lace mantillas, Toledo blades, all the lavish items that Spain's wealthy colonies desired and could easily pay for. Items that could be sold for a handsome sum in the market of this buccaneer town of Port Royal.

Kells was a buccaneer and he had gone a'hunting. There was nothing she could do about it.

Carolina flung herself upon the bed in a torrent of tears.

A little later she heard a knock on the door and sprang up breathlessly, dashing the tears from her eyes. Had her threat about being unfaithful worked? Had he changed his mind and returned to fetch her?

But it was only Hawks bidding her to lock her door—Cap'n's orders.

"Oh, bother the captain!" she cried. But she struggled up from the bed and turned the key in the big lock, and then went to stare hopelessly through the new iron grillwork of her island prison at the darkly glittering ocean reaching forever away across the moonpath.

Somewhere among that forest of sails in the harbor was the *Sea Wolf*—and morning would find him winging away from her.

Her head dropped into her hands and she sat there, miserable.

A little later she heard Moonbeam softly scratching at the door and making little indignant sounds at finding it shut against her. Carolina got up and unlocked the door to let the cat in. She picked Moonbeam up and held that purring bundle of fluffy white fur close to her for comfort.

"Oh, Moonbeam," she mourned. "I've said things I never meant. I've driven him away and now I may never see him again. . . ."

And that, she knew, would break her heart.

PART TWO

Catastrophe

At night I hear the rustle of your touch upon my gown
And thrill to feel the rasp of silk as it goes sliding down
And wake to find the moonlight streaming in as bright as day
And find that I was dreaming—for you are far away. . . .

PORT ROYAL, JAMAICA

June 7, 1692

Chapter 10

It was past eleven o'clock, the sun was reaching its zenith, and Port Royal shimmered in the oppressive tropical heat. Carolina, as had become her habit of late, had gathered up her calico skirts and climbed to the captain's walk atop the house. She was carrying Moonbeam in her arms, for the cat had been acting strangely since yesterday—mewing and trying to get under furniture as if hiding from a foe. Carolina had cast a suspicious look at Gilly, who had given her back such an indignant glance that Carolina decided Gilly had not attacked the cat. She had taken Moonbeam to bed with her last night and the cat had promptly scuttled under the bed and refused to come out. She had been lured out this morning by the scent of a succulent piece of fish and when she had finished her halfhearted eating, Carolina had promptly swept her up and carried her up to the captain's walk where Moonbeam seemed even more perturbed. Far from trying to jump out of Carolina's arms so that she could walk daintily along the railing—which was her usual behavior—she seemed to want to burrow under Carolina's arm.

"What's the matter, Moonbeam?" Carolina asked solicitously, stroking the long soft fur of Moonbeam's back. "Are you getting sick? Is that it?"

Moonbeam answered with a sound that might have been a moan.

"I'll get you some fresh milk when we go downstairs," Carolina promised.

She tucked the quivering cat under one arm and shaded her eyes with her other hand. She was staring out to sea, automatically checking the name of every ship in the harbor, even though she knew it was futile—in this dead calm, nothing had moved in or out of the harbor for days except rowboats, a fact greatly bewailed in this busiest port of the West Indies.

Her shining hair was gilded by the brilliant sun, and shafts of sunlight leaped gaily along her full yellow calico skirts that drooped in this windless weather against her slim legs. Slowly she counted the ships in the harbor—a score or more, sails furled, lay at anchor in the glassy waters of the harbor. They were all familiar to her gaze, except for several rowboats and a large strange-looking craft which seemed to have no masts and whose name she could not see, which was being rowed into the harbor by long oars, manned no doubt by long muscular arms. But even though she knew the deadly calm this terrible heat wave had brought, she felt a sharp stab of disappointment. For Carolina's brooding gaze was seeking just one ship, the *Sea Wolf*—and it was not there.

She sighed, took mewing, excited Moonbeam in both arms, petted the small animal in an attempt to quiet her, and rested her arms on the railing of the captain's walk that ran atop the house, letting her chin brush Moonbeam's soft fur. This whole week had been breathless and it was worse than usual inside the house today, but being up here on the roof gave some relief and made her tight bodice and sheer chemise seem to stick to her a little less. Her gaze raked the length of waterfront Thames Street, from Littleton's Tavern where—even as in her own kitchen down below—a beef and turtle stew for the noonday meal was being prepared in a heavy copper pot, past the fish market and Sir Thomas Lynch's wharf down to the careening area where the frigate, H.M.S. *Swan,* lay on its side, helpless as a beached whale. The island's other warship, the H.M.S. *Guernsey,* she knew was out on patrol, for Port Royal was expecting the French from St. Ann's Bay to mount an attack at any time. And past the *Swan,* she could see sturdy Fort Carlisle guarding the harbor.

She turned restlessly and swung her gaze past High Street, where the bell tower of St. Paul's church dominated the skyline, to the stocks and the market bell and the goldsmith's shop. She let her eyes wander restlessly on down this long jagged sandspit that housed some eight thousand souls, to the low mangrove swamp on Gallows Point where pirates were hanged, and on across the clear blue and aqua water to the distant line of aptly named hills, the Blue Mountains, hazy in Jamaica's near noontime heat. From those hills the Cobre River flowed past Spanish Town, and along that river Kells had sought a plantation. She sighed again. Plainly it was not to be. . . .

She remembered with bitter regret the day the *Sea Wolf* and the *Sea Wench* had made their stately way out of the harbor, picking up speed as they ran before the wind. She had had no chance to make up with Kells, for he had not returned home before sailing. That she had sent him away from her in anger had worried Carolina more with each passing day.

But somehow the weeks had fled by, and now it was June. Carolina had refused to attend the governor's ball, given in honor of his departing cousin. *Let her depart and good riddance!* had been her comment, muttered to herself. Louis Deauville had sent her a note, gracefully expressing his regret that due to his wound he would be unable to squire her—just as he had penned her a note regretting his inability to dine with her on Wednesday as invited. Carolina had torn up both notes and sent her own regrets to the governor.

Although Louis Deauville had for a time been laid up with his wounded leg, he had made a remarkably fast recovery. And now that he was up and about, he obviously expected Carolina to invite him again to dinner. But she did not. Even though the handsome Frenchman managed to turn up whenever she strolled abroad—closely guarded by Hawks—even though she still found him witty and droll, even though her tingling sense of guilt that she had encouraged him out of caprice forced her to be polite to him, now that Kells was well and truly gone, she could not find it in her heart to invite Deauville to share her table. Some half-forgotten loyalty of the heart prevented her. It was one thing to dally in Kells's plain sight—and quite another to betray him when his back was turned. Carolina had her own code of flirtation—and it was very strict. It did not allow treachery.

She had had word of Kells only once—and that was by happenstance. The captain of a merchant ship that had come into Port Royal had noised it about that he had sailed by a sea battle somewhere off Trinidad. A ship that looked like the *Sea Wolf* was being attacked by a pair of great golden galleons. The *Sea Wench* had been nowhere in sight. No, he had not stayed to watch the outcome of the battle. He had piled on all the canvas his vessel would carry and taken himself away from there!

Carolina winced when she heard it, for it had not told her whether her valiant buccaneer was alive or dead.

That had been three weeks ago, and Carolina had lived in torment ever since.

She had expected him home by now—she had kept telling herself bravely that Kells was invincible, he could surmount all odds—but she knew it was not so. And last week when a hurricane had roared out of the Caribbean and all but swept Port Royal away, she had listened to the tiles of the roofs blowing off and crashing like thunder against the torn-off debris in the littered street below and shuddered. For *he* was doubtless out somewhere in that storm as well, fighting the seas in a gallant vessel that might have had half her hull already ripped away as a result of Spanish shot. . . . The thought terrified her.

But the hurricane had come and gone and left a littered beach and a massive clean-up job for the city. Port Royal shrugged. It was an island port and used to terrible blows. Now but a week later, with work crews busy, the hanging signs were all up again, broken shutters mended, most of the roof tiles put back, the beach swept clean by the tide—the taverns and hostelries had rid themselves of their broken crockery that had crashed down when the storm had blown the shutters from the windows, and it was business as usual in this bustling buccaneer port.

May had brought floods, then had come the hurricane, and now June had brought this depressing spell in which no wind stirred. The suffocating heat wave had lasted all week and brought forth grim forecasts from some of the older townsfolk, who muttered uneasily that for forty years past, indeed ever since England had taken this island from Spain, every earthquake—and there were tremors almost every year—had been preceded by storms followed by a period of sweltering calm such as they were just now experiencing.

Carolina, a comparatively recent arrival, had paid no attention and had scoffed at the foolish old drunk in a nightshirt who two nights ago had run through the town wild-eyed, crying, "First a storm, and now a calm! Take to your heels! This miserable pesthole is going to sink, mark my words!"

But who would pay any attention to that? So many people—including, indeed, one clergyman's wife—were constantly predicting the destruction of wicked Port Royal for its sins!

There was a sound of breaking glass below and Carolina looked down to see a crowd of swaggering sailors passing by in the street, coming from Sea Lane. One of them had dropped a bottle of rum and its contents ran into the sandy street. As she watched, another of their number lurched into a passing fish cart and a loud argument ensued. Now she watched them swagger on up Queen's Street toward High Street, their rolling gait proclaiming them for what they were. One of them carried a large red and green parrot which squawked incessantly.

Now she saw that Louis Deauville had come out of his house and was gazing about. He looked up and saw her and bowed. Carolina inclined her head to him. She knew he was hoping that she would come down and chat, for he was loitering there aimlessly, but she had no intention of doing that.

It was a pensive face she turned toward the mirror-like shimmer of the glassy sea.

Below her, had she known it, Gilly was taking advantage of her absence to slip into Carolina's bedroom.

The past weeks had been frustrating for Gilly, too—frustrating for two reasons:

For one, Jarvis was pressing her. Idling here in Port Royal, he was growing impatient with his doxy.

For the other, she had lost Carolina's favor.

It had come about the day after Kells had sailed, and

it had come about because all her life Gilly had hated cats. When she had first moved into the house, she had been standing idly in the kitchen, waiting her chance to snatch some of the hot fritters Cook was just taking from the fire, when Moonbeam had wandered in and strolled past Gilly.

Gilly had kicked the cat away from her.

Cook had turned just then and had seen Moonbeam going end over end to rise spitting and upset. "You do that again, Gilly," she warned, "and I'll tell the mistress."

"Cat's got no business in kitchens," mumbled Gilly.

"This one has. She has the run of the whole house. And"—Cook's voice rose—"if *I* see you touch her again, I'll take a stick to you!"

Gilly had beat a speedy retreat, and Moonbeam had avoided her ever since—until the morning after Kells had sailed away on the *Sea Wolf*.

Carolina had been sitting disconsolately at her dressing table, combing her long hair and wishing herself dead, when Moonbeam, dashing up from downstairs, and Gilly, coming down from the attic, had both come to a halt just outside her door. Gilly had just asked, "Are you goin' to the market today?" and Carolina was about to answer her when Moonbeam had come flying up and, seeing Gilly standing there, had stopped short and backed away.

Gilly, concentrating on the cat, had thought herself unobserved, for Carolina's back was to her—but Carolina could see in the mirror how Gilly's expression turned ugly and how, as Moonbeam tried to stand her ground—for the cat knew she had every right to enter Carolina's bedroom and jump on her mistress's lap—Gilly drew back her foot to kick her.

"Gilly!" The face Carolina swung to confront Gilly held an expression Gilly had not seen before, and her level tone held a cold warning. "If you kick that cat, I will personally tear those clothes from your back and set you out in the street."

Gilly drew back. "I wasn't about to—" she began to protest.

"You were, don't deny it!" snapped Carolina. Her eyes narrowed. "I may have been wrong about you, Gilly. Perhaps you aren't worth saving. But just so you don't take revenge on Moonbeam when my back is turned, let me tell you if anything happens to that cat, if I find her hurt or limping or cowering somewhere, I will have you whipped and returned to those women whose clothes you stole." She studied Gilly who was shuffling her feet and looking scared. "Do we understand each other, Gilly?"

Gilly mumbled something which might have been "yes."

"In the future," added Carolina, "you will assist Cook in the kitchen, unless Betts asks you to help her. You will no longer need to spend so much time on the second floor. Come here, Moonbeam."

Moonbeam darted past Gilly and jumped onto Carolina's lap while Gilly retreated in stony fury. Gave herself airs, did this buccaneer's woman! she was thinking. And all this commotion over a worthless cat! The next time she saw Moonbeam in the kitchen and when Cook's back was turned, Gilly picked up a heavy pot, intending to hurl it at the cat and then claim she'd dropped it, but the sudden memory of Carolina's warning deterred her: *"If I find her hurt . . ."* Gilly had no desire to be returned to Sadie's brothel where she'd stolen the clothes—those ugly bawds would have her hide, they would!

Reluctantly she had put down the pot, and Moonbeam glided warily past her to look expectantly up at Cook, who laughed and gave the cat a morsel.

With a scornful look at the two of them, Gilly had flounced away.

She had, she told herself, needed time to think. For weeks now Jarvis had been after her to "get the necklace and be done with it." Indeed that had been his refrain every time she had managed to slip away to see him—and that wasn't easy now. She had to pretend a headache or a stomachache and slink away to her own room before the house was locked up, then scuttle downstairs and get outside somehow, and, to avoid suspicion, she had to time her return so that she would appear to have wandered outdoors just after the doors were unlocked "to get a breath of fresh air after such awful pains all night long!" If the two sturdy buccaneers who, along with Hawks, guarded the place, knew about Gilly's nocturnal wanderings, they kept that knowledge to themselves. After all, to their minds she was but a saucy slip of a girl with a predatory smile, kept off-limits to them by a vigilant Hawks, who saw in Gilly dangers that the soft-hearted Carolina had not perceived.

Gilly kept putting Jarvis off, insisting that the house was "too strict guarded" for her to get the necklace. In reality she was searching for some sailor who would take her off the island with no knowledge of the necklace. So she told Jarvis, "I'm locked in nights so tight I can't get out often like I used to. You'll be seeing less of me until I can get my hands on the necklace."

Jarvis had growled because having Gilly in his bed was something he had grown used to on New Providence. "If 'tis too hard for ye, give it up and we'll get us back to Nassau."

Gilly remembered all too well the helter-skelter life of New Providence Island. "Just be patient—I'll think of something," she told Jarvis hastily.

But two nights ago, slipping out, Gilly had strolled the waterfront and found the sailor of her dreams. Jack was young, fresh-faced, just off the sloop *Prudence,* and eager to believe anything Gilly told him. After one night of tossing on damp sheets in a waterfront dive, he would have done anything for her. It was easy for Gilly to talk Jack into persuading his captain to take her with him when he left "as soon as this cursed calm breaks and we get a wind," for she had promised to marry him on shipboard and sail with him back to the far-off Yankee port of Boston, where he promised her he'd leave the sea and help his brother till their little farm until he could build Gilly a house of her own.

Gilly had given Jack a hypocritical smile. Boston wasn't where she wanted to go but at least it was far away, and once there she could break enough gold off the necklace to pay for passage to England. And once in London she'd sell the stones and forget she ever knew "trash" like Jarvis and the ardent young sailor who at that moment would have given his life for her. She'd become a "lady"!

But she *must* get the necklace before the wind came up, before the *Prudence* sailed! She had been watching for her chance all morning long. And now at last, with Carolina gone to the captain's walk above, she had it!

"Where is Gilly?" Cook wailed as Betts came into the kitchen. "She's supposed to be helping me!"

Betts shrugged. "She was carrying out the slops last I saw and not making a very good job of it."

"Sit you down here, Betts." Cook wiped the moisture from her perspiring brow and waved a long iron spoon at a wooden bench. Betts sat down. "We got to have a talk with the mistress about Gilly. She's always whining she's sick and running off to her room and we don't see hide nor hair of her until the next morning when she comes in from outside, looking bleary-eyed. Half the time she claims she passed me on her way out, that I was wool-gathering and didn't see her—and you know that ain't true!"

"I think Gilly's slipping out to meet someone," said

Betts, who had had the same experience with Gilly. "Leastways, she moons around like she's in love."

Cook snorted. "In love? *Gilly?* Not likely! To her kind one man is as good as another, so long as they gives her trinkets!"

Betts thought that might be so. "What's that cooking?" she asked Cook, sniffing the savoury odor that came from the big copper pot that hung from a chain in the fireplace.

"Hawksbill and loggerhead stew," replied Cook, going back to stir desultorily the contents of the steaming pot. "With some bits of beef thrown in."

"Bits" of beef would be right, thought Betts, fanning her hot face with her hand. For she suspected Cook of spiriting away the big cuts of beef that came to the house and selling them surreptitiously down at the market. Turtle, which was plentiful, was their main dish around here. And the mistress was so preoccupied these days she did not seem to notice what she was eating! She gave Cook a resentful look.

"It's too hot in here," she complained, rising. "I've got to get me to some other part of the house before I'm clear melted down!"

"Wait, I'll go with you," said Cook. "We can sit in the dining room. The mistress will be out on the roof, studying the sea for ships this time o' day."

She followed Betts into the comparative coolness of the dining room where the green-painted walls seemed to speak of cool meadows far away.

The two women seated themselves on two of the straight chairs that lined the walls, ready for extra guests.

"D'you think we'll all end up on a plantation up the Cobre?" asked Cook, for like everybody else she had heard garbled gossip about Kells's intentions.

"I don't know." Betts shook her head vigorously.

"But Spanish Town can't be half so hot as here!" She kept on fanning her face.

"Where's Hawks?" demanded Cook. "I haven't laid eyes on him since breakfast and he usually comes into the kitchen for a mid-morning bite o' whatever's cookin'."

"Hawks has gone t'other side of town. Probably to see a woman!" Betts winked.

Cook sighed. She'd had hopes of Hawks for herself—she liked big silent men. Unfortunately Hawks seemed to like slimmer, younger women. Men! She took out her vengeful thoughts on other men. "Those two buccaneers Captain Kells left to guard the place are just sittin' on their haunches outside waitin' to be fed, I'll be bound—don't never occur to either of them to do nothin' to help *us!*"

Betts nodded emphatically. She agreed with Cook that the extra guards were "lazy louts"—especially since neither of them had seemed to notice the new green petticoat she had worn to attract their attention.

They sat together and gossiped in the dining room, glad of the coolness, entirely unaware that instead of "carrying out the slops," Gilly was upstairs slipping into Carolina's bedroom.

Gilly's bright eyes lit upon the curved-top trunk, which Carolina, her thoughts preoccupied with going up to the captain's walk to scan the sea, had carelessly left unlocked.

Overjoyed at being alone in Carolina's bedroom at last, Gilly ran on tiptoe across the floor, flung the trunk open, and began rummaging inside. Beneath the lacy chemises, beneath the scarves and fans and gloves, beneath the petticoats and rosettes and ribands, she found what she was looking for: a silver-encrusted box of teakwood.

She lifted the box out to the light, opened it and pulled out its contents excitedly from the dark red interior of the box. She held the necklace up, marveling at the weight of its gold—for it was the first time she had touched it. Her avid gaze devoured the blood-red brilliance of the rubies, the white glitter of the diamonds. She ran caressing fingers over the necklace and licked her lips. Her breath came shallowly and her heart beat fast.

She sat there staring at it, lost to the world.

This was her future she was holding in her hands—a future that would let her shuck off men like Jarvis and that mewling boy, Jack, so humbly desperate for her favors. *This* would let her sneer at men—as all her life she had longed to do. *This* would let her kick them out of her bed! And more: *This* would buy her a fine town house and a coach and six! And servants! Her eyes glittered. If ever *her* servants forgot *even once* to call her "my lady," she'd stripe their insolent backs with a whip! She'd do it with her own hands and have the satisfaction of hearing them wail! She ran her tongue over her lips, and her brown eyes held an unholy gleam. Transfixed by the wealth she was running through her fingers, she sat there on her haunches. Entranced, spinning daydreams—half-evil, half-wonderful—of what she would do when she sold the necklace.

A sudden noise from down the hall startled her into remembering where she was, and she snapped alert, her head swiveling around to view the door. A quick step coming this way and the cat dashed by. Oh, lor', that meant the mistress was returning from upstairs, for the cat always accompanied Carolina on these journeys, running joyfully ahead of her and circling her skirts, rubbing against her when she arrived at her destination. But the mistress always stayed up on the rooftop longer than this! thought Gilly in consternation. Whatever had possessed her to come running down so soon?

But that quick light step had alerted her to her danger and she cast her eyes about her. She would have run to the big wardrobe and hidden herself in that, but to her mind that was most likely Carolina's goal. She must be coming downstairs to get a hat from the cedar wardrobe's top shelf—a hat to shade her against this devilish tropical sun.

In panic, every nerve quivering, Gilly tried to think of some other place. Under the bed? No, there she could be seen from the door for the light coverlet did not reach to the floor!

On a sudden burst of inspiration, she threw herself into the trunk and cautiously pulled the top down. She gave it a last good tug and huddled inside, still clutching the necklace. She would give Carolina lots of time to clear the room because when she left this trunk and this room, Gilly intended to have the necklace clutched tight in her hand, her hand wrapped in a scarf. She would burst through the front door, claiming she'd cut her hand on Cook's big butcher knife and must reach the doctor before she bled to death—no one would block her way.

So she reasoned as she lay cautiously, half smothered among the chemises. And this time her timing had best be right or she'd be whipped—or hanged. Gilly shivered. And then the necklace—and her dreams of a new life—would be gone from her forever.

The air inside the trunk was growing foul. Still she waited.

In Carolina's slim arms on her high perch above the house, Moonbeam was growing more and more perturbed. Carolina managed to get a better grip on the restless cat and hugged her comfortingly to her breast, murmuring soothing words. She cast one more longing look at the sea, so empty to her gaze for the right ship did not float upon it. Then with a sigh she turned to go back down the narrow stair that led from the rooftop walk.

Abruptly she stopped and turned to give the sea a startled look. That big dismasted ship just now being rowed into the harbor looked suddenly familiar. She leaned forward, squinting into the sun's glare, unable to make out the name, but her heart gave a lurch.

Dismasted . . . part of its hull stove in . . . it still could be the *Sea Wolf!* A glass, she must get a glass to make certain!

Moonbeam was in a state of panic now, her claws digging into Carolina's arm. She put the cat down and Moonbeam raced frantically ahead of her as if being pursued.

Almost afraid to hope, Carolina fled downstairs after her, seeking the glass. Past the longcase clock, past the musket Kells had left in her bedroom and that she had put outside the door—she did not even glance through the open door into her bedroom.

As she searched for Kells's spyglass in the drawing room, she heard Betts arguing with Cook and realized the two of them must have come into the dining room to cool off from the overpowering heat of the kitchen in this sweltering weather.

"*I* don't believe in star gazers," Betts was saying energetically. "And I don't see why *you* do. What an outlandish idea, him saying we'd have an earthquake that would crack the houses apart! Why, all I've ever felt here was a kind of gentle rocking that made the hanging lamps swing!"

"That's because you ain't been here long, Betts. I was here four years ago, and that same prediction was made that we'd have a terrible earthquake and the weather was the same as now—"

"I don't see what it's got to do with the weather!" sniffed Betts.

"That's what I'm telling you, Betts!" Cook's irritation showed in her voice. For forty years now, folks say, we get those earthquakes the same way: first there's a storm and then there's hot muggy weather with nothing moving, same as this—and that's when the earth starts to shake under your feet!"

"You ain't been here forty years," scoffed Betts. "And this town's full of liars."

"I've been here almost five years," exploded Cook. "I was here four years ago when all them houses got shook down—why, the guns were even knocked loose from the gunports on ships in the harbor!"

"That wouldn't never happen in England!" declared Betts, obviously shaken. "I suppose it might in an outlandish island like this one!"

Carolina smiled. She had heard accounts of that quake four years ago, but her mind was not on such unlikely events as earthquakes, which she firmly believed no one could predict. She was tantalized by a certain familiarity in the lines of that ship being rowed into the harbor.

She found the glass, seized a wide-brimmed hat and stuck it on her head. Perhaps it would prevent her from getting sunburned. And that was suddenly important.

Leaving Moonbeam mewing piteously in the front hall and clawing at the door, she hurried back up to view the oncoming ship.

Excitement pounded in her veins as she studied the ship through the glass. It was coming on steadily, the measured beat of the oars carrying it fast across the glassy ocean. It was in the harbor now, and those lines were unmistakable.

Broken and damaged it might be, but one thing was certain: It was the *Sea Wolf.*

Kells had come home!

Chapter 11

"Well, listen to that, would you?" said Cook. She and Betts had retired to the kitchen, and Cook had just bent down to taste the simmering stew when the air was rent by a piteous wail from Moonbeam.

"Do you think Gilly's after her?" demanded Betts.

"Could be—she hates that cat." Cook put down her spoon as Betts went into the dining room to see what ailed Moonbeam. Cook propped the back door open. "Leave it this way," she told the young buccaneer who was sitting on his haunches outside, whittling a piece of whalebone with a sharp knife. "I can't get my breath in here." And she lumbered on through the kitchen to see why the cat's wails still echoed through the downstairs.

"It's all right," said Betts as Cook came through the dining room door. "At least it isn't Gilly. Cat's just sitting there huddled in the corner, meowing, with her fur all standing on end. Do you think she's in heat?"

"Most likely." Cook turned to go back to the kitchen.

"Perhaps—" began Betts, but she never finished her sentence. Her voice was lost in a rumble that seemed to come from everywhere and engulf the earth. She gave a sudden scream as the room lurched sidewise.

Cook, who was caught by the shock while just in the act of turning, lost her footing and staggered painfully against the heavy table in the center of the room. Instead of holding her weight as it would normally have done, it glided away from her, letting her fall heavily to the floor.

The big silver bowls and platters on the sideboard were dancing a jig, the unlit candles of the overhead chandelier fell out upon Cook's prone body as the chandelier swung wildly, and suddenly the big stack of plates which Betts had set a little while ago on the edge of the dining room table slid off with a crash, sending broken blue and white delftware all around the room.

"It's an earthquake!" shrieked Betts, who had staggered against the wall and now ricocheted from it and leaped toward the door.

"Right you are!" gasped Cook and scrambled to her feet.

They both rushed into the hall and through the front door, which would have been jammed by the quake had not the buccaneer who guarded it just opened it as he was passing outward. The shock had thrown him forward on his face into the street, where he was promptly run over by a yowling Moonbeam, who streaked out into the street and took off running toward High Street.

A moment later Cook and Betts nearly ran over him as well.

"It's an earthquake," he gasped, gaining his feet just as Cook's solid form collided with him. And Betts fell to her knees in the street, wringing her hands and praying loudly. Her prayers were punctuated by screams as roof tiles came crashing down and a house up the street collapsed with a thunderous roar.

All over town at that moment, people were praying or running or trying to extricate themselves from whatever had fallen on them. The air was rent by screams and shouts and indignant wails.

Across the street from them came a tremendous pounding as Louis Deauville tried to open his front door which had jammed. In the excitement of overturned carts and falling masonry, nobody noticed him, and finally with a violent kick he catapulted into the street and looked around him wildly, sword drawn.

It was his first earthquake.

Behind the house it was the whittling young buccaneer's last earthquake. He had looked up in alarm at the noise, been thrown sidewise by the shock—and had fallen, impaled upon the sharp knife held stiffly in his hand. The blade had pierced his heart.

In the kitchen the stew pot went over, throwing boiling broth and steaming beef and turtle meat over everything—and sparks and sticks from the fireplace skittered across the stone flooring. In Littleton's Tavern the stew went over, too—only there it scalded three of the kitchen helpers and sent burning brands from the fireplace against the staggering cook, setting the terrified woman's skirts afire.

All across Port Royal at that moment, such scenes were being repeated.

Crouched inside the trunk in Carolina's bedroom, Gilly never guessed it was an earthquake that was rocking the house. First she felt the trunk lurch and then there was a tremendous thump. In panic Gilly tried to raise the lid—and found she could not budge it. Trapped there among fans and chemises and gloves and with the diamond and ruby necklace wrapped around her wrist and tangled in her stubby fingers, she began to wail. The top of the trunk seemed to her to have jammed—*but how could it be jammed so tight she couldn't open it?* She could not know that Carolina's heavy cedar wardrobe had fallen atop the trunk and it would have taken two strong men to remove it. Inside, wailing in terror, it seemed to her that some devil's hand was shaking the trunk.

On the other side of town, Hawks, thrown to the ground by the first violent shock, was almost run over by a careening cart before he could rise. He rolled to the side—and just in time, for a hail of broken masonry and plaster thundered to the ground where he had just stood, burying the cart and its owner. He gave thought to making his way back to see how Carolina and the house were faring, but found his way blocked by buildings that had collapsed into the street. With Port Royal shaking down about his ears he took what he considered the only sensible course: He betook himself to the widest open space in all the town—those fortifications along the sea named for the famous buccaneer Henry Morgan and known as Morgan's Line.

On waterfront Thames Street, in Sadie's bawdy house, Gilly's Jarvis, in bed with a waterfront whore, leaped from the mattress at the first rumble from the hills that grew to a torrent of sound beneath and around them. The whore, spilled from her bed by Jarvis and tumbled end over end by the quake, gave a squeal of fright entirely masked by the howls that rose from the rest of the house.

Sadie's place was tucked in between big warehouses, and as Jarvis, reaching for his drawers, leaped out the window on the sea side, Sadie, thinking to do the same thing, leaned out a nearby window.

Sadie screamed as she saw the beachfront and wharves that Thames Street faced on begin to writhe and buckle, saw long crevasses suddenly open—and it was into one of those crevasses sliced suddenly into Port Royal's sandy face that Jarvis tumbled, head first.

Not only Sadie's scream but many others followed him down.

Jarvis had not made the right move.

Not that it would have mattered. Other crevasses, long rents in what had seemed to be solid earth, were opening up in roughly parallel lines, and Port Royal's foundations were sliding into, falling into the sea.

On either side of Sadie's place big warehouses were the first to collapse, their massive walls cracking, their roofs giving first under the strain of the shifting sand beneath. They and their goods now rumbled into that sand, and Sadie felt her house tugged downward even as the roof fell in. Her wild scream was lost as her head was plunged brutally into the sand, and she was pummeled to death by falling bricks even before she could drown, for the ground now gave way and she and her bawdy house slid into the sea.

In moments, it seemed, Thames Street was no more, and the street just behind it had become waterfront property.

That street, unfortunately, was Queen's Street, where Carolina lived.

Chapter 12

Carolina was perched on top of her house, studying the sea rapturously through Kells's long spyglass, when the first great shock struck Port Royal. Even as she gave a cry of joy when she recognized the *Sea Wolf*'s rakish hull, there was a thunderous rumble from deep within the earth, seeming to come from the Blue Mountains far behind her, and all Port Royal shuddered. The first violent jolt tore the glass from her hand and sent it spinning over the roof. Carolina lost her balance and toppled over to slide along the now slanted captain's walk.

Around her the world seemed to spin about sickeningly. She struck her head as she fell and sat up, dazed and disoriented, to find her house rocking beneath her.

Behind her the white limestone underlying that distant line of blue hills cracked so that the spine of the island was ripped apart and the mountains crumbled, sending down torrents of earth that plummeted into the rivers. A flood of muddy clay was already pouring down the Cobre River like an avalanche—but Port Royal did not know that yet. Port Royal was having troubles of its own.

All about was the rumble of falling masonry. The air was full of shrieks and screams as Carolina stumbled to her feet, clinging to the railing to haul herself upright. The earth was rumbling savagely, the whole town wavered, all the bells were ringing. There were tremendous grinding thumps and crashes everywhere. The market bell plunged heavily to earth.

Before Carolina's horrified eyes, giant cracks appeared in the earth along the waterfront—cracks that heaved and twisted like a boa constrictor swallowing its prey—open, gaping crevasses that swallowed up people and carts and buildings. Screams and howls rent the air, and there was frenzy all about as people poured out of their houses, jumped or tumbled through windows, leaving the less lucky trapped inside under fallen ceilings and scrambled dancing furniture. Most of those the earthquake knocked down in the street struggled up and began to run. Others fell to their knees and prayed.

Now Thames Street was buckling and swaying, the houses cracking and toppling, the great roofs of the warehouses sliding off or crashing down, the goods beneath shifting, sliding. All Port Royal seemed to be dancing and sliding merrily downhill—into the water.

Hard put to keep her grip on the railing of the captain's walk as the very house beneath her shimmied with the vibrations of an earthquake so violent it had all but brought the mountains down, Carolina screamed a warning to someone below who even as she spoke was buried under a falling chimney.

Simultaneously there was an enormous crash as the bell tower of St. Paul's Church crashed down—and a hollow clanging of the fallen bell. From the mountains came a background noise even more ominous—a distant thunder rumbling up from below—and to that

Devil's chorus the entire waterfront convulsed and began to slide into the sea.

Port Royal had been built not on bedrock but on sixty feet of sand. Some of the buildings jutted out on pilings. They went first as their foundations were shaken out from under them. Beneath the heavy buildings, most of them of brick or plaster construction, that unsteady foundation billowed and pitched, broke apart and closed again, pulling the unwary and their goods forever downward to be crushed and broken. The whole city shook and trembled. Although the houses built on pilings in the sand had collapsed first, they were swiftly followed by other buildings. The thick masonry walls of Fort Carlisle and Fort James cracked, and with a deafening roar both forts collapsed into the harbor. Thames Street followed, warehouses and wharves and waterfront dives crashing in upon each other as their foundations gave way . . . tons of sand slithered away from beneath them and tumbled the works of man into the sea.

Carolina, holding on for dear life to her precarious perch atop her house, never heard the muffled screams of Gilly, caught in the dark confines of the curved-top trunk. She never saw Moonbeam streak down the street to disappear around the corner into a cloud of fallen plaster dust.

But from her high vantage point atop her vibrating house, she saw Thames Street shake itself to pieces and, demolished, drop into the sea.

She saw other things as well: Betts on her knees in the sandy street, praying. Cook and one of the burly buccaneers who guarded the place under Hawks's supervision, urging her up "to save herself." Louis Deauville, white-faced and appalled, trying to keep his footing as his house came down behind him, showering him with bricks which miraculously did him no harm save to knock him to his knees. He remained there, crouched and staring at his vanished house and vanished Thames Street, as if it could not be.

Even as she watched, the earth below yawned suddenly and opened up. Carolina was looking down into a long crevasse that zigzagged through the street below her. It opened directly below Betts, who was on her knees, and Cook and the buccaneer, who were urging her to rise—and they all disappeared into its depths. It swallowed up Louis Deauville, too, for the second violent shock that opened it up catapulted him backward into it.

Carolina might have fainted then, but the horrendous noise and the earth's violent waggle kept her too alive to her own danger.

Beneath her the sturdy brick building seemed to slant more violently and at the same time to sink, to lurch downward. The front of the house was breaking forward, and trunks and furniture hurtled through the opening.

Gilly was in one of those trunks, trying to scream through a scarf and a burst of chemise lace that had got sucked into her mouth with her violently indrawn breath as she prepared to scream again. With the forgotten necklace wrapped around her wrist and clutched forgotten in her hand, Gilly, the trunk and the huge cedar wardrobe atop it slid downward across the steeply slanting floor as the building buckled. They crashed into the house wall at a forty-five-degree angle and burst through even as the building disintegrated. The great weight of the wardrobe poked through the collapsing wall, and trunk and wardrobe shot forward through the falling bricks to catapult into the sea.

Around Carolina, on either end of the captain's walk, the chimneys broke, their bricks and mortar scattered into rubble in the street below. But still the roof, though inclined at a crazy angle, held. For Kells—more used to ship-building than house construction—had first had built, while his neighbors scoffed, a wooden framework composed of great timbers that were anchored together as solidly as a box. And those beams and timbers held for a time even while the brick walls around them collapsed away and crashed into the street.

Hers was the last house to fall and so gave Carolina a sight that would be with her always.

Stunned by her descent into the street by trunk—even though her fall had been somewhat broken by a pile of sand—Gilly still pounded and clawed and shrieked unheard. So sturdy that it had survived even this rough treatment, the trunk ricocheted off the slippery sand into the rising sea and so escaped being buried by the falling bricks of the house. End over end it tumbled, terrifying Gilly, who was bumped bruisingly about. It landed in a few feet of water, but its top had been stove in, wedging the lid on so tightly that Gilly could not push it open even though the monstrous wardrobe had been removed.

But the worst was yet to come for Gilly.

A falling pillar shot spearlike through the water, striking the trunk's curved top and shearing it off. And Gilly, breaking free at last, arms flailing as the contents of the trunk rose about her in the water, swirling chemises, scarves and petticoats, seemed about to rise to the surface. But just as her hand—still locked around the necklace like a vise—broke the water and her hair floated free upon the surface, another heavy pillar surged forward to crash against the first—and to imprison Gilly's ankle as it did so.

Gilly struggled and tried to wrest herself free. She was screaming silently in her head as she fought the water in frenzy. But the fallen pillars held her fast, and only her streaming hair and her hand, still tangled in the necklace that had lured her to her death, showed above the water.

That was the sight Carolina saw as the building toppled. And that sight was graven more deeply upon her memory than any other single impression of the earthquake: Gilly's hair rising and streaming from the water, and Gilly's hand holding *her* necklace.

Time seemed to spin out for Carolina then. The swaying, cracking buildings, the awesome rumbles from out of the earth, the rending sound of breaking timbers, the clouds of plaster dust, the screams of the injured and dying—all seemed separate and aloof.

What was hideously real was Gilly—drowning.

It seemed to her in that moment that her terrible dream was coming true—and that the hand in that dream clutching the necklace had been Gilly's.

For Carolina on the roof, the trip down seemed endless for the heavy timbers refused to break as the entire structure settled into the shifting sand. She kept her grip on the railing of the captain's walk and the roof settled down slowly and spilled Carolina out gently upon the ruins of her home.

By the time she reached there, Gilly and the necklace had disappeared, sucked down into the water.

It was Gilly's sudden disappearance—as if she had been snatched away—that galvanized Carolina into action. Suddenly she was scrambling over the roof and she began to run—even as the roof disappeared into the sea behind her.

Trying to escape death in a city that was falling, tier by tier, into the sea, driven on mindlessly by terror like everybody else, she clambered over the fast-sinking rubble and ducked into an alley which would lead her to High Street. Here everything was confusion as people struggled and shouted and whimpered their way from fallen St. Paul's Church and the ruined Market up to Lime Street, which was aswarm with fishmongers from Fisher's Row and terrified people running away from the waterfront.

Up Lime Street Carolina stumbled, with houses collapsing all about, then down Cannon, dodging falling masonry, across Yorke—and she would have crossed Tower Street, too, heading for the sea wall fortifications known as Morgan's Line, for she believed —like Hawks, who had dashed there ahead of her— that she would find there the most open place in this crowded city and therefore less likelihood that she would be crushed by falling masonry.

Many others had had the same idea and there was already a crowd of people huddled in the shadow of the fortifications when she reached Tower Street. Among them she saw Hawks, and she called to him and waved as she ran—it was her undoing, for a rolling brick from a falling building tripped her up and she sprawled headlong into the dusty street.

As she lifted her head she saw that Hawks had seen her. He was trying to make his way through the crowd toward her. But before he could do that the earth opened up suddenly beneath him and the whole close-packed crowd disappeared with what seemed one long piercing human shriek into the yawning crevasse.

A sob rose in Carolina's throat and she scrambled to her feet and would have run forward in an attempt to somehow drag him out before the earth could close in on him like a vise and snuff out his life. But even as she rose, she was confronted by a new menace.

The ocean, forced back by the collapsing land and buildings, had piled itself up into a great wave and was even now pouring over the fortifications.

Carolina looked up dizzily into that wall of water arching toward her. Then she whirled, dazed and terrified, and ran away from that oncoming wave. Choking on clouds of dust from the broken plaster and with no care now for where she was going, she headed blindly into the center of town.

But the water caught up with her before she could

reach it. She was tumbled end over end by it. She choked—and then she was swimming, or trying to, impeded by her wet skirts. Something brushed her arm and she caught at it—it turned out to be a dangling rope. As she clutched it, it was pulled upward, and through the spray she saw that the rope was attached to a sailor's hands and that the sailor was on some kind of a large ship which was wildly riding the wave, carrying her irresistibly over the collapsing housetops of Port Royal.

The flying deck beneath the sailor's feet belonged to the frigate *Swan,* which had been turned over on its side for careening. The ocean, backed up by earth and buildings falling into the sea, had risen into a wave and overwhelmed the ship, lifting it, righting it, and sending it inland to rest upon the rooftops in the center of Port Royal.

Carolina clung to the rope and was pulled aboard by the strange sailor—who saved many lives that day but lost his own when he ventured into an attic where he heard a child crying and was carried downward to a watery death when the house collapsed. Bruised, half drowned, she collapsed upon the deck while the sailor busied himself with pulling others aboard.

"Help me," he called curtly, and Carolina scrambled up to pull on a rope that rescued people clinging to chimneys with their children hanging on to them, lifted people out of boats—for everyone rushed to salvation on this "Noah's Ark" that had suddenly appeared in their midst.

There seemed to be people everywhere in the water —swimming, screaming, shouting, hanging on to things, losing their grip, disappearing. Most of the injured that day drowned so that those pulled aboard were for the most part able-bodied.

Frenzied rescue efforts went on all afternoon, and of each person hauled aboard Carolina tensely asked the same question: *Had they seen Captain Kells?* But none of them had and Carolina's worried gaze, sweeping the sea and the ruined town, found no trace of the *Sea Wolf,* which when last she sighted it was being rowed so valiantly to shore. She never stopped asking but the answer was always the same. No one had seen the captain.

As the frenzied rescue efforts continued, Carolina's mind seemed a dizzy blank. She was called first here, then there, as she went through the motions of helping others.

When the sun sank over Port Royal, the Palisadoes sandspit was a scene of utter desolation. Many ships had been sunk in the harbor. Sturdy Fort James and Fort Carlisle had disappeared. The tall houses were gone—indeed, less than a tenth of the buildings remained standing at all, and most of those were in such ruinous condition that their owners feared to enter them.

Carolina was still working when night fell. Then, like others, she sank to the deck exhausted.

But not to sleep. She stared up at the stars and her tired face mirrored deadly fear. In all the commotion, all the trying to stay alive and save others, she had not been able to find out the one thing most important to her:

Where was Kells? Oh, God, where was Kells?

Chapter 13

The answer to that question was brought to her by Hawks shortly after sunup.

Sleeping fitfully, overshadowed by a sense of doom, Carolina had waked with the dawn and struggled up, stiff and sore from her endeavors and her harsh treatment of the day before. She had staggered to the rail and looked out over an empty landscape of a shattered and drowned city—no, it was not empty at all for there were people and boats already plying their way around or clustered about the drowned rooftops: Householders and divers already at work, trying to recover plate and other valuables from the sunken buildings.

Watching them, it came to her how easily was human endeavor brought to naught. Yesterday at this time there had been a teeming city about her, all life and hubbub. And today . . . today there were groans and yawns about her as others like herself roused to face what the new day might bring.

Her shoulders drooped. Where was Kells? Where

could she find him? Was he alive or dead? No one seemed to have seen him. She did not even know where to begin to look!

As she stood gloomily by the rail, staring unseeing across the waste of desolation before her, she was hailed by a familiar voice and looked down startled to see Hawks. He sat below her in a rowboat, resting on his oars and looking—save for his torn clothing, a jagged cut down one cheek, and two very black eyes—very much as usual.

"Hawks!" she called down to him, amazed. "It can't be you! I saw the earth swallow you up at Morgan's Line!"

"And so it did," he rejoined cheerfully. "But the sea rushed in before the hole could close up and it washed us all out of there. I was one of the few who didn't drown, which is a wonder because I still have this." He patted the cutlass by his side.

"Oh, Hawks!" Carolina was leaning over the rail, so glad to see him alive that she was laughing and crying at the same time. "But what of Kells? Is there any word of him? I saw the *Sea Wolf* being rowed into the harbor just before the earthquake struck but when I looked around this morning I could find no sign of it."

Hawks looked up at her, startled and disturbed. "Are you sure it was the *Sea Wolf?*" he demanded.

"Oh, yes, Hawks, I'm sure. I was studying it through a spyglass when the earthquake knocked the glass from my hand."

Hawks dipped an oar into the water. "I'll see what I can find out," he promised.

"Oh, Hawks—take me with you," she entreated.

He shook his head. "Best I go alone," he said and rowed away.

Waiting for word seemed to Carolina the hardest thing she had ever done in her life. It was two hours before Hawks returned, and she was hanging over the side calling out to him long before he could reach the vessel's hull.

But he didn't answer her anxious questions, which seemed to Carolina ominous. Instead he called up, "Ask them to lower you down on a rope ladder. I been talking to the governor and he's got us a place to stay temporary like."

Careless of her billowing skirts, Carolina climbed down the hastily lowered rope ladder and almost tumbled into the boat. Hawks caught her and there was something reassuring in his strong grip.

"What have you learned?" she asked breathlessly.

Hawks, mindful of eyes and ears on the ship above, said loudly, "Wasn't the *Sea Wolf* you saw—must have been some other ship."

But Carolina, protesting, cried, "It *was,* Hawks, it was!"

When they were out of earshot of the ship Carolina had just departed, Hawks said, "Not so loud, mistress. If the governor hears you're alone, everything swept away, he might not be so eager to see you in furnished quarters."

Alone! The word sank in on Carolina.

"Hawks," she quavered. "Don't beat about the bush—tell me straight out."

"The cap'n's dead," said Hawks on a long drawn-out sigh. And there was sorrow in his eyes and in his voice.

Carolina crumpled to the bottom of the boat, her head in her hands. A long shuddering sigh went through her. After a moment she looked up.

"Where is he, Hawks?" she asked dully. "Can I go to him?"

Hawks, who had loved the captain too, man and boy, was looking out into the far distance, past muddy, scarred, broken Port Royal, across the blue Caribbean, fiercely bright in the morning sun. He was seeing another day, a younger Kells, whose sword had flashed bright in the sun, whose laugh had rung out across the water while the wind sang in the rigging.

"I found one of the *Sea Wolf*'s crew, fellow named Price," he said at last, and his gruff voice sounded almost matter-of-fact. "He was dying but he told me what had happened. It was an unlucky voyage from the first. Off Trinidad they ran into a pair of galleons. The galleons were of a mind to fight, and the *Sea Wolf* blew them both out of the water. But they took some blows themselves and they decided to head back here for repairs. That's when they ran into the *Santo Domingo*. They fought her for three hours and when the sun went down the *Santo Domingo* struck her colors. They took her crew on board—but she wasn't carrying no treasure and she was short-handed because they'd had sickness on board. That's when the hurricane got them. The *Sea Wolf* had been shot up, her masts damaged, and now the whole lot of it got stripped away."

"Yes," cried Carolina, hanging on his words. "I saw it. They were rowing in without their masts—I didn't recognize the ship at first."

"If they'd got here a day later or a day earlier they'd have made it," Hawks said glumly. "But as it was they came right in with the earthquake. The sea picked them up and hurled them into the town same as that ship back there." He jerked his head at the frigate *Swan* which she had just left.

"But why isn't the *Sea Wolf* on top of the houses like the *Swan?*" demanded Carolina.

"Because she was already too bad hurt and she broke up. Everyone drowned—including the cap'n." He cleared his throat, and pointed. "They went down right over there."

Carolina turned to gaze where he was pointing. "It can't be very deep," she said wistfully. "We could send down divers to find him, Hawks." *Or maybe not find him,* she was thinking.

"Wouldn't do no good," he mumbled.

"Yes, it would, Hawks. Then we'd *know.*"

"That's right," he said, suddenly as eager as she. "We *could* send divers down—only what would we pay them with?"

"With promises!" cried Carolina. "Once I get to England, Hawks, I'll have plenty of gold."

"Gold in England won't help," Hawks sighed. "They'll want to be paid now—in coin of the realm."

Carolina had a sudden inspiration. "We'll tell them there's a treasure map on his body, Hawks! That will lure them!"

Hawks gave the captain's lady an admiring look. "We can try it," he agreed. "There's some divers over there."

He rowed them to where some divers were diving into a house, bringing up silver plates for a big bearded fellow clad in a nightshirt, who kept muttering, "Good. Mary will like that."

Hawks leaned over and muttered to Carolina. "He was sick in bed when the quake hit. His whole family's washed away. He's pretending to himself they're still alive. Mary was his wife."

Carolina gave the large gentleman a pitying look. "Could we borrow your divers for a short while?" she asked. "We need them to look for my husband."

"If you have to dive for him, mistress, you won't find him alive," the large gentleman told her gloomily.

"No—of course, I know that. But there was a treasure map on him."

One of the divers looked at her keenly. "Who was your husband?"

His words made Carolina realize how battered and disreputable she looked—no one would recognize the Silver Wench now. Her bright hair was tied back with a piece of rope, her face and arms were bruised. "He was Captain Kells," she said simply and the diver shot a startled look at her and turned to speak to the other one with him. "If the Silver Wench says he's got a treasure map . . ." she heard him say, and his next words were lost to her. But he turned quickly. "We'll dive where you say, mistress." And to the large householder who was looking indignant as he sat astride his roof holding three silver trenchers, he said, "We'll be back soon." Both divers climbed into the rowboat with Hawks and Carolina.

"The wreck's over there, sunk beside that building," said Hawks. "Look." He pointed. "Just to the right of where you see that chimney sticking up." He swayed as one of the aftershocks shook the water.

Carolina also looked at that lone chimney sticking up, and bit her lip. *But he wasn't down there,* she told herself firmly, to still that dull ache in her heart. *He wasn't. No, he was one of the lucky ones like herself. He was looking for her now and he had somehow missed her*—although it escaped her how anyone could miss the frigate *Swan* lying spectacularly on the roofs of the submerged houses in what had once been the center of town. The divers would go down and search the wreck. They would not find him—and that would give her hope.

"My husband is tall," she began. "And dark—"

"I've seen your husband, mistress, many's the time," one of the divers cut in.

The other nodded his wet head and agreed, "Everyone in Port Royal knows Captain Kells."

So they would know him when they saw him. . . . She wasn't sure whether that made her feel better or worse.

She looked about her. There were bodies floating everywhere. She remembered hearing someone say thousands had died.

As if he caught her thought, one of the divers said

conversationally, "The quake ripped up the burying place at Palisadoes and the water tore up the graves and scattered them as was buried."

Carolina felt sick. Hawks turned and gave the speaker a level look, and he fell silent.

They had reached the chimney now, wet pink bricks with water lapping around where smoke should have been coming out. . . . Hands clenched, Carolina sat and watched while the divers went over the side.

The hull was indeed down there, they came back to report—half of it at least.

"Bow or stern?" asked Hawks, who was no diver.

"Stern. We made out the name *Sea Wolf.*"

"Look in the great cabin!" cried Carolina.

"He wouldn't be in there with all that was going on," protested Hawks.

"He might have been."

Hawks shrugged. "Look in the great cabin like she says."

The divers went down again into the murky water. They came up bearing a gold money chain. Hawks snatched it. "Now you'll get paid in gold," he said.

The next dive brought up another money chain.

"Must have been from the dons aboard the *Santo Domingo,*" muttered Hawks, fingering the gold links that could be twisted free and used for money.

"But—did you see anyone?" Carolina asked faintly.

"Not Captain Kells." The first diver, a burly man, turned to Hawks with a frown. "You ought to give *us* one of those chains."

"No, you'll get diver's usual pay," said Hawks.

"We get more'n that today," the other said menacingly. "By rights we should have three-quarters—*we* take all the risk. Besides, there's a sea of mud pourin' down the Cobre and everything down *there*"—he turned a thumb downward to the sunken city—"is still slippin' out to sea. And sinkin'. Soon we won't be able to see nothin' in this ooze. We got to get on to other jobs where there's known valuables—like the goldsmith's over yonder."

"They've already dived on that," Hawks said calmly.

"Yes, but they didn't get it all!"

During this battle of words Carolina noticed that the rowboat had somehow edged a little away from the chimney. She tensed.

"Dive again, please," she pleaded. "See if he's down there."

"Dive again," Hawks commanded harshly.

The two divers exchanged angry looks. One muttered something to the other but they submerged as ordered. When they came up the first diver said sulkily, "He was there all right. But we didn't find no map."

Carolina gave a great heartbroken cry.

"How come you didn't see him sooner?" demanded Hawks. The rowboat was now a few feet farther from the chimney.

"Because a great pile of stuff had fallen on him when the hull broke and the ship went over," was the impatient reply. "Now we've done what we come for. Pay us and let's go."

"Bring him up."

"What?"

"I said *bring him up!*" thundered Hawks.

"Like hell we will! It ain't safe down there—"

As if to confirm that, another of the frequent aftershocks rocked the surface and there was a sudden rumble. The chimney on which the divers sat crumbled, spilling them into the water. They gave a shout and broke toward the boat.

Hawks had seized the oars and was pulling swiftly away. "We'll leave your money with the governor and you can collect it from him," he called. "Diver's pay."

There were angry shouts behind him as the divers tried to swim toward the boat.

Carolina looked up at Hawks through her tears. "If *they* won't dive down and bring him up, Hawks—"

"Nobody will. Too dangerous now with the houses settlin' down and breakin' up."

"But we have two gold money chains! Surely that's enough!"

Hawks shrugged. "Any other day it might be. But not today."

Carolina leaned forward tensely. "But how do I know they haven't made a mistake in that murk? How do I know it's Kells they saw down there?"

"They're all down there," Hawks said softly, and there was sorrow in his voice. "And all dead. Can't do them no good now. But I knew you wouldn't be satisfied till you saw him for yourself. That's why I asked them to pull him up."

Carolina's hands clenched. "I won't believe it!" she cried. "I won't believe he's dead. He's alive, I tell you. He was a fine swimmer. He—" She broke off, staring at Hawks, horrified that she had said *was* and not *is*.

"If he'd been alive he'd've found you afore now," Hawks said solemnly. "Not nothing would have deterred him, not the cap'n." There was admiration in his voice, and regret. Hawks had lost more than a captain—he had lost a friend. "All of them gone. . . ."

And Betts and Cook and Gilly, too—and oh, so many others. Vanished . . .

As if he had had the same thought, Hawks's voice penetrated her gloom. "Buried under the houses," he muttered, pulling hard on the oars as if by strenuous exercise he could dull emotion. "With the sea closed over their heads."

Sunk beneath the sea, fathoms down, trapped in wet green darkness—forever. . . .

Carolina made a little choked protesting sound and Hawks turned a pitying look on her. "You got to be thinking of yourself now, mistress."

Unable to bear the pity in his blue eyes, Carolina swung her attention to the pair of divers, swimming strongly toward the next chimney that stuck up through the water. "We should go back and pick them up, Hawks," she sighed.

"And have them kill us for these money chains? Let them swim to their next job!" Hawks was pulling mightily on the oars as he spoke. "There's no law in this town today, mistress. A man can kill for what he wants, throw his victim in the sea and none be the wiser!" His face was grim. "That fellow back there who'd lost his wife—if that pair of divers bring up enough plate or jewelry, do you think he'll live to see another morning? Why should they share it with him? You heard them—they take all the risks!" He snorted.

Silence fell in the boat.

What he said was true, thought Carolina, dashing the tears from her eyes and looking out over the ruins of the submerged city, afloat with dead bodies. There was treasure in these houses, for Port Royal had been a rich trading town: silver bars, ingots, plate, jewelry, money chains, golden doubloons, pieces of eight. Treasure men thought worth fighting for, dying for.

"Indeed, mistress," said Hawks, who had already thought about it. "I think ye should get ye gone before nightfall. I see there's new ships in the harbor now that the wind's come up and ye should speak to the governor about getting ye on one of them."

"Oh, Hawks," she murmured. "What have I to live for? One place is as good as another."

"Time heals," he said roughly. "And the cap'n wouldn't like it if he thought I let anything happen to you now he's gone."

Dear kind Hawks! And she had given him so much

trouble in times past! With a full heart, Carolina reached over impulsively and gripped his wrist—it was a substitute for a hug.

He gave her a reproachful look as if to say a kindly pat wouldn't swerve him from his plain duty—which was to see that no harm came to the captain's lovely lady. She was a treasure, too, didn't she know it? With her wealth of silver-gold hair and her silver eyes, her silken skin and her sumptuous figure—ah, she was a prize many a man would prefer to all the gold in Spain!

"They're still fighting for the gold today," he ruminated, looking away from her. "But by tonight or tomorrow night they'll already have it all. *Then* they'll be fighting for the women."

And one man with a cutlass could not defend her. . . . Hawks had made his point.

Carolina's back stiffened. She was not going to let Hawks, who had been through so much, die for her.

"We must go find Governor White," she said. "And leave links from the money chain to pay the divers."

They found Governor White aboard the *Storm Merchant,* one of the few ships that had survived the wave. He was harassed on all sides, and his patience was wearing thin. But he accepted the gold links of the money chain that Carolina proffered, and he promised to pay them over to the divers. Instinctively Carolina did not tell him that Kells was dead. It was only just coming to her how great a protector Kells had been—from everything. She let the governor think the divers had been diving on her own house, searching out plate and treasure.

"They are diving on my house now," he said, running a hand over his shaved head, for he had lost his wig in the earthquake. It made him look strange to her eyes. "My wife is broken-hearted, for the house is gone and we have lost everything."

But at least you have her, thought Carolina.

"There will be no rebuilding the town," he sighed. "There is nothing left. Perhaps someday sand will pile up and rebuild the cay which once stood here—and of which we have only a remnant left—but not in my time. Not in my time."

She could sympathize with his despondency for he was an ambitious man who had meant to return home someday—rich.

"Where do you think you will go now?" he asked her. "To that plantation up the Cobre that Kells sought to buy?"

"No," she said. "Not there." She almost burst into tears for if she had not foolishly sent away the necklace, Kells might even now be up the Cobre—safe. Remembering Hawks and the danger her presence placed him in, she straightened. "I have decided it would be best for me to seek passage to England and—and wait for Kells there." She tripped slightly over the words. But it was true in a way, for in her heart she would always wait for him. *Always.* "Can you help me arrange it?"

"I might." He gestured seaward and Carolina saw another ship. "The *Ordeal* has just cast anchor and has a longboat rowing toward us at this moment. Her captain is a friend of mine and he told me the last time he was here that he would make this voyage but one more time from Port Royal to London and then he would retire to his home in Philadelphia and let his son take command of his ship."

"He may have many friends here who will take precedence over me," Carolina said nervously.

Governor White gave her a bleak look. "Captain Simmons will take no one who cannot pay cash, if I am any judge. And few can pay cash when their houses, their fortunes have been swept away—as my own has been," he added bitterly. "But *you* have gold." He studied the money chains she held in her hand. *These buccaneers and their women always seem to have gold,* he was thinking.

Beside Carolina, Hawks moved restlessly.

"Stay here," the acting governor said curtly. "I will see what I can do." He shook his head. "The price of passage anywhere this day is likely to be high!"

"The *Ordeal,*" she muttered. "That's an odd name for a ship!"

"Yes, well, I can tell you where she got the name," he flung over his shoulder. "She was named the *Enterprise* when Captain Simmons first commanded her. She sailed into Port Royal—it was long before my time—when yellow fever had struck the city. And sailed out again, a fever ship. Captain Simmons made his home port of Philadelphia but he was the sole survivor—everybody else aboard had perished. That was when he renamed her the *Ordeal.*"

"That's all this town needs now—fever. Or plague," rumbled a voice nearby.

Heads lifted. What was this about fever? Or plague? There was alarm written on every face.

Now rumors would spread, thought Carolina. *By this afternoon there'd be talk of plague and fever all about the city!*

"Hawks," she muttered impulsively, "come with me to London."

Hawks gave her an uneasy look. "I'd like to go," he said under his breath. "But best not perhaps."

He meant that he was still a wanted man. As Kells had been.

"Hawks," she said in a low voice, "I will send for you. When I have visited the goldsmiths in London, I will see what can be done to arrange a pardon. You will live to see Essex again, I promise you that!"

Hawks swallowed. She would do it if she could, his captain's valiant lady.

"And keep—keep looking for Moonbeam, won't you?" Her voice broke. "She was in my arms just before the earthquake struck. . . ."

She watched him nod solemnly and was about to say more—about hiring other divers when the earth stopped shaking, for the tremors were still continuing in the stricken city, and would be for a long time to come. But she bit back the words. She must get hold of herself—in another moment she would burst into tears.

"I—I need some air, Hawks. It's too crowded here. Come over by the rail. We'll wait for word."

Silently Hawks followed her to the ship's rail.

"Perhaps we should walk about," she said restlessly. "And not just stand here."

Hawks cleared his throat. "Won't do no good to run away," he declared in a compassionate voice.

About to clamber over a coil of rope, Carolina stopped in her tracks. Hawks was right. She *was* trying to run away—from herself, from her memories, trying to escape the thought that Kells was dead. . . .

BOOK II

Rouge

Child of the night wind, daughter of sighs,
Heart full of passion, head in the skies,
Sing me a lovesong sweetened with lust—
Someday all *dreams come to dust!*

ABOARD THE *ORDEAL*

June 1692

Chapter 14

A feeling of unreality still haunted Carolina as, aboard the merchantman *Ordeal,* she sailed out of what was left of Port Royal's harbor. As the ship pulled out into the open ocean she looked not ahead, but wistfully behind her at a watery wasteland.

The tragedy in Port Royal had been of mind-boggling proportions. At least two thousand people had perished; there were bodies floating everywhere. To top the remaining inhabitants' woes, an avalanche of mud had poured down the Cobre River from the broken mountains, inundating the turtle crawls, smothering the loggerheads and hawksbills confined in their wooden-fenced pens, some of whom, with flippers tied as was the custom, had not even had a chance to try to swim. The raging tide of mud had fouled the ruins of the submerged town, already made hideous by floating unburied corpses, and muddied the sea roundabout.

It was an eerie scene Carolina viewed as the *Ordeal* sailed away. A sunken city built on sand—and still sinking. For chimneys and parts of roofs, and the uppermost parts of the masts of ships that had gone down in the holocaust, still remained visible in the muddy waters. Even that fragment of the town the sea had left standing was broken and ruined by the three great tremors that had changed the fortunes of the buccaneers forever.

From Fort James to Fort Carlisle, divers, homeowners and scavengers were busy breaking through those roofs that still peeked out of the water and trying to salvage what they could from the sunken buildings below. In the distance Carolina could watch them crawling and scrambling like busy ants over the broken buildings of what seemed a destroyed Venice. But at its deepest part Port Royal already lay fifty feet deep beneath the sea—and slipping ever downward. Around her the sea was alive with sharks.

Wild rumors had circulated, increasing the hysteria of the survivors: Spanish Town was gone, washed away on a sea of mud, great new crevasses now slashed through the Blue Mountains above them, other parts of the island had fallen into the sea; indeed the entire island was atilt and slowly following Port Royal into the blue depths of the Caribbean!

Carolina had discounted the rumors, heard them dully. For there was an aching background refrain ever roaring through her head, pounding at her temples, making her throat ache: *Kells was gone, Kells was gone. . . .*

And with him, her world.

Governor White had been surprised and chagrined to discover that the Captain Simmons of the *Ordeal* was not the Captain Simmons he had known for several years, but the captain's son. *This* Captain Simmons was young and inexperienced, and his Adam's apple worked a great deal. His father, who had been owner and captain of the *Ordeal*, had died in his sleep two nights earlier and young Simmons had found command thrust upon him. Lacking his father's control over men, Simmons found the job harrowing. The rowdiness of the seamen, the bluff heartiness of the giant first mate as well as his bone-crushing handshake, the reserved wariness of his fellow officers all intimidated him. He brought the *Ordeal* into Port Royal harbor almost empty, for it had been his father's plan to sail fast to Port Royal, pick up goods on the quay cheap for cash and take his son to England on this his first voyage—for young Simmons had been brought up exclusively by his mother and by a maiden aunt who hated the sea. After a time in England, the plan had been to return to their home port of Philadelphia where the old man would retire, leaving his son the ship that had been their livelihood for so many years.

Young Captain Simmons was horrified by what he found in Port Royal harbor.

"Bodies all about!" he had cried. "Floating all around us! And where are the wharves? Half the city seems gone—we're looking at the chimneys and the rooftops!"

Simmons had understated the case for he had never before seen Port Royal. Two-thirds of the town had vanished, and most of the rest wasn't habitable. A sandspit remained.

He had nervously accepted Carolina aboard as a passenger—at three times the going rate. But he had paled at the first rumor of pestilence breaking out in the city.

"Plague!" he had cried, his young voice rising in panic, and ignoring the governor's pleas that he take on more survivors, he had abruptly up-anchored and sailed away.

"Running scared," muttered one of the ship's officers in disgust. "Old Captain Simmons would never ha' done it!"

A red sunset found them beating past Morant Point,

heading for the Windward Passage between the eastern tip of Cuba and the northwest corner of Hispaniola. Sunset found Carolina dining in the captain's cabin and borrowing a needle and thread to mend her torn gown.

"I must apologize for having no women's clothes to give you," said the young captain, eyeing with masculine approval the pretty picture his guest made in her yellow calico gown with bits of her flesh appearing here and there through the rents.

"I suppose I could not expect it since you have no women aboard," sighed Carolina.

"I could lend you some of my own clothing," he suggested diffidently, his boyish face flushing at the thought.

Carolina hesitated. She was no hand with a needle and her dress would be awkwardly mended, she knew. But she was the only woman aboard this ship; word had already circulated among the crew that the celebrated Silver Wench was aboard—she had heard mutterings of it on deck—and it seemed to her that to walk about in trousers would put her on a level with New Providence's notorious Rouge, who wore men's clothing and swung a cutlass.

"No. I do thank you but I will manage to make do with what I have," she said hastily.

"Ah—yes. Would you care for some wormwood wine?"

"No, thank you," said Carolina, who detested absinthe, although it was customarily drunk in Port Royal.

The young captain looked chagrined. He had heard many stories of the Silver Wench—as who had not?—and he had somehow expected someone more flamboyant, more dissolute, than the steady-eyed young woman who faced him across the sturdy oaken table.

"What happened to your husband?" he asked suddenly—for everyone had heard of the famous Captain Kells. "Was he in Port Royal when the earthquake struck?"

"No, he was not," said Carolina. An easy lie—she had already practiced it on the governor, who had probably learned differently from the divers by now. "And since our house was destroyed, I thought it best to return to England and wait until he sends for me."

The young man opposite her fingered his glass and thought about that. The heady thought had just occurred to him that he was captain of this ship and in sole command here—and that this was a very desirable piece of womanflesh seated across from him.

Carolina caught his thought. "My husband is accounted the best blade in the Caribbean," she said carelessly. "Do you fancy the long or the short sword?"

A slight shiver went through her host's thin chest. "I favor neither," he said promptly, and poured himself another glass of wormwood wine. "I am a man of peace." It was what his mother had always abjured him to be—a man of peace. And since he was a thoroughgoing coward, it had seemed excellent advice and he had hewed to it.

"Indeed?" Carolina laughed. "And yet you sail the Windward Passage which as all men know is haunted by pirates from New Providence as well as the ships of the dons! Tell me, how many guns do you carry?"

Captain Simmons's father had been brave to the point of foolhardiness. His stories had terrified his son—especially the one about the fever ship, which was the main reason he had turned tail and sailed precipitously out of Port Royal. It had been frightening enough sailing down the Windward Passage with his father's strong hand to guide him. Now he was sailing back up it on his own—and this buccaneer's wench was jeering at him across his own table.

"You have sailed the Windward Passage?" he asked stiffly.

Carolina nodded. "Tortuga will lie on your starboard side once you have passed Hispaniola. I lived in Tortuga." *Another life it seemed now, far away. . . .*

Captain Simmons took another gulp of wine. "You must tell me about it," he said crossly. "For I have not seen Tortuga, nor am I likely to."

"I am too tired to tell you about it tonight," sighed Carolina, who wished to be alone with her grief. "If I have your leave to retire to my cabin?"

Captain Simmons had been toying with the idea of suggesting that she share *his* cabin but her remarks about her dangerous husband's prowess with the sword had dissuaded him. He rose. "I will see to the arrangements," he muttered and disappeared through the cabin door.

I was right, thought Carolina grimly. *He meant not only to charge me triple the going rate for my voyage to England—he meant to have me in his bed as well!* She decided she disliked the nervous young captain. And realized she must at all costs keep up the fiction that Kells was still alive to protect and avenge her. Plainly her situation on board this vessel hinged on that. Her lip curled. It was little different from being in Port Royal!

Bone-tired, she was glad when the captain returned and escorted her to her cabin. She gave him a wan smile and shut the door in his face, then latched it and tottered to the bunk and threw herself down upon it. She had expected to dissolve in tears but so tired was she that she fell immediately asleep.

Carolina slept—but not peacefully. She tossed and moaned on the bunk, again reliving the earthquake—but with a difference. This time she was reliving, along with her own fate, bits and pieces of what had happened to others.

In her dream she was standing again atop her house when the earth began to shake. Beneath her the brick building seemed to slant more violently and at the same time to sink. The roof was sliding off seaward and as it slid, Carolina saw what waited for her down below and a scream burst from her throat.

Below her in the sandy street a great crevasse had opened up, and house and roof—and Carolina herself—were tumbling into it. The house went in first, almost majestically, along with two surrounding houses. And then the roofs. And then Carolina, clinging futilely to the railing as it buckled.

She went in screaming—and felt the sand close about her like a vise, shutting off her wails, holding her motionless, locked in and suffocating.

The next shock tore open the crevasse and erupted the newly fallen contents into the sea. In her screaming consciousness Carolina felt herself violently jerked upward, the world around her suddenly changed from solid to liquid. She was in the water, she realized desperately, and she almost drowned as she was sucked upward through the roiling water.

She broke the surface gasping and saw in that blinding moment a sight she would never forget. Not all the horrors of Port Royal's fall would ever match that moment.

She was looking at a clawing hand that was just now rising from the water. A hand in which a ruby and diamond necklace was entangled—*her* necklace. And beside the hand a head of streaming ginger hair—*Gilly!* And through a great pounding she seemed to hear Kells's voice, far off, saying, "I had thought to use the necklace as collateral. . . ." and there in the green depths she saw his face, looking up at her accusingly.

She was threshing in the bed now, her whole body turned into one long wild scream. And the pounding was real—it was someone beating on the door.

Bathed in perspiration, Carolina came foggily to herself. She was not in Port Royal, not in the water, she was lying in a bunk in a cabin of the *Ordeal,* and Captain Simmons's resentful voice was bellowing to her through the door, asking her what on earth was the matter?

"I am sorry," she called out in a quivering voice. "I was having a nightmare."

There was a grunt on the other side of the door and the sound of boots stalking away. She supposed the captain was now regretting having taken her aboard.

But somehow her terrifying dream had dispelled the sense of unreality that had dogged her ever since the earthquake. It was all real to her now—real and terrible.

Kells was gone. She was alone. She would always be alone.

There in her lonely cabin she burst into tears. It was like a dam breaking. She could not stop weeping. As the next day passed, she only picked at her food and she stayed in her cabin.

Captain Simmons was perplexed. At the very least he had expected this beauteous lady's company at mealtime and for strolls around the deck. But the *Ordeal* continued to beat its way up the Windward Passage and still the lady did not come out.

Captain Simmons had an answer for that:

He stopped having meals sent to her cabin.

Chapter 15

Driven by gnawing hunger—for after all she was young and strong and in vibrant health—Carolina at last decided to leave her cabin. She would take a turn upon the deck and find out why food had abruptly stopped arriving the day before yesterday. Did this green young captain from Philadelphia think he could starve her into taking her meals with him? She had, after all, paid for her passage—and a handsome price at that!

It was with a glint in her silver eyes that she made determinedly for the door that bright morning. She had dried her tears at last and decided to rejoin the land of the living.

But she had not made the door before the ship gave a lurch and she was sent in surprise against the wall.

Quickly righting herself, Carolina made for the deck where she found a flurry of activity, with sailors scrambling over the rigging and a mountain of canvas billowing above her.

She looked about her. The sun should not be coming from that direction. . . . Why, they were heading northwest—not northeast as they should have been!

The captain hurried by and she hailed him.

"Captain Simmons, why have we changed our course? What is wrong?"

He turned to her, his eyes wild.

"D'ye not see those ships?" he cried, waving his arm in an easterly direction. "They're Spanish!"

Carolina shaded her eyes from the sun and peered in the direction he was pointing. Two very tiny ships seemed to be bobbing on the horizon.

"How can you tell at this distance?" she asked mildly.

In truth Captain Simmons had but fancied he saw a flash of red and gold flying from the mast of one of the ships, but it had translated immediately in his mind into the red and gold flag of Spain.

"'Tis obvious!" he sputtered. "I saw it through my glass."

His beautiful passenger gave him a skeptical look. "They are more likely to be salt ships from Turks Islands coming from that direction," she observed. "And while I have your attention, may I ask why the cabin boy has stopped bringing my meals to my cabin?"

Up until that moment young Captain Simmons had intended only to veer away from a pair of ships that were most likely in these waters to be Spanish, beat his way northwestward away from them, slip through Crooked Island Passage, and turn eastward into the broad Atlantic on his voyage to England. But in his overwrought condition—for he was certain in his panicky heart that they were being pursued by Spanish warships whose one mission in life was to sink his unarmed merchantman—he now came abruptly to a different decision.

"I have changed my mind about voyaging to England," he said testily. "We are setting course for Philadelphia."

"But I have paid passage for England," objected Carolina. "Surely you—"

Captain Simmons regarded this cool island beauty with something akin to hatred. How dare she stand there looking so unconcerned when they might all be blown out of the water if those galleons caught up with them? And to think he had dreamed of her last night, dreamed he was removing that badly mended yellow calico dress from her slim body, dreamed that he was running his eager hands over her silky breasts, pulling off her chemise, kissing her, fondling her—

"Your passage money will be returned to you!" he exploded, giving this buccaneer's woman a look of anger. "When we reach Philadelphia." *Where I will sell this vessel,* he was thinking. *And never sail the treacherous seas again! Lord, but I had narrowly escaped death in Port Royal—if I had but landed a little earlier, my vessel would have been dashed to pieces against the shattered buildings as so many other good ships had been in that cursed harbor!*

Carolina stepped back before the venom in his voice—until she realized that it was motivated by fear. She sighed. After all, what did it matter if she reached England by way of Philadelphia? It would take a little longer, true, but if Captain Simmons returned her passage money she would have enough not only for passage from Philadelphia to England but enough to pay for good accommodations and to buy some decent clothes. She would not arrive in London looking like a beggar wench!

"Very well," she said. "Philadelphia it is. But I have had no breakfast and I have come to inquire if you intend to starve me?"

Before her the frightened young captain seemed to draw himself up. His face grew puffy. "Find the cabin boy and get him to bring you some food," he shouted. "There will be no hot food on board this vessel until we have escaped—*them!"* He flung an arm outward toward the distant pair of ships.

Thinking how much better Kells had managed matters aboard the *Sea Wolf,* Carolina went off to seek the cabin boy, who could find only some cheese and ship's biscuits. She munched them as she watched those tiny ships grow a little closer.

By late afternoon everyone knew that the captain was right: The ships were Spanish.

Carolina expected the *Ordeal* to slip through Crooked Island Passage by night and into the open ocean. But in his panic, sure that the wind did not favor that, the captain drove his ship forward, penetrating ever deeper into that vast chain of islands and cays the buccaneers called "The Shallows," but which others called the Bahamas. With Deadman's Cay to port and Rum Cay to starboard, he was floundering into Exuma Sound. If in desperation he turned west in an effort to reach the Straits of Florida, he could run the ship aground on the Grand Bahama Bank.

By mid morning Carolina had decided that the captain—who was looking bleary-eyed and distraught as he stood beside the helmsman—was in need of advice.

"Had Kells been in your situation," she told him conversationally, "and chosen not to engage, he would have played tag with his pursuers among the islands."

"Exactly what I've been telling you, Cap'n," muttered one of his ship's officers, standing nearby.

Captain Simmons gave them both a grim look. He was fast losing his youth. A gray pallor spread over his face every time he looked past the *Ordeal*'s stern at the steadily gaining galleons which now flashed gold in the sun. "And what would you suggest we do now?" he demanded helplessly of the officer who had spoken.

"*I* would turn hard to starboard past Devil's Point and lose them going round Cat Island," volunteered Carolina, who had not been asked. "I heard Kells say once that he had done that."

They both turned to stare at her.

"Of course," she added cheerfully, "*he* only did it so that he could swing round Cat Island and come up behind them and take them by surprise. *You* will be doing it to gain the open ocean."

"Go away and find something else to do, mistress!" roared the young captain. "Running a ship is men's work."

Carolina shrugged and strolled away. But she noticed that after a hurried conference the ship changed course. Not long after that, the officer who had been there when she had given the captain her advice found her.

"We are all beholden to you, mistress," he said in a low voice. "Young Captain Simmons is too green to be in command of this ship and had his father not died so unexpectedly on the voyage, he would not be. Old Captain Simmons would have followed your advice and struck out for the open ocean. But our young captain is fearful. He has heard tales of the Inquisition—all true, I don't doubt—and he has a terrible dread of falling into the hands of the dons. It is his plan to hug Cat Island's coast and set his course for Eleuthera Island and from there strike out for Philadelphia."

"What do you think of his plan?" she asked.

His answer was a shrug. "I think it will most likely get us all killed, but captain's orders is captain's orders."

Carolina leaned upon the rail after he had left and stared moodily at the pursuing galleons. The sea was a brilliant glittering blue, the sky azure. They were so near land that the air was full of seabirds and landbirds, swooping and crying in flight. Above her the white sails billowed, a mountain of canvas. It seemed incredible that on such a day anything bad could happen. And yet there were those galleons, relentlessly pursuing. . . . If only Captain Simmons could bring himself to steer a bold course. She doubted that he could.

All day they played cat and mouse with the golden galleons along Cat Island's eastern coast. Night found them off the dangerous reefs that fringed Eleuthera's ninety miles of eastern beaches. And there the captain was at last persuaded to strike northward for Philadelphia under cover of darkness. It was an overcast night with no visible stars. The Caribbean night seemed to have closed them in like a dark blanket. There was little wind so they made scant headway, the sails for the most part drooping and flopping. And where would the galleons be tomorrow morning?

Carolina asked herself that question as she made ready for bed. Suppose they were taken by the Spanish? What kind of treatment could they expect?

She tried to take her mind off that. It was not too difficult. Indeed a film of numbness had slid over her mind in the wake of Kells's death. Being captured did not assume the terrible importance it once would have because at the moment she cared little what happened to her.

She would live or she would die—fate would decide.

Meantime she leaned her chin on her hands and sat in gloomy contemplation of all that might have been.

It was better, she decided, to be born lucky than to be born either beautiful or rich. For if you had luck you needed little else.

Neither she nor her two elder sisters had had much luck, she told herself. Look at what had happened to them! Penny, the eldest, for all her beauty and her wild spirit, was lost these many years and probably long dead somewhere in Philadelphia. Virgie had had a tragic life—but she had won through at last to happiness with Kells's brother in Essex; whether Virgie's luck would hold, Carolina, in her present pessimistic mood, would not have cared to wager.

As for herself, whenever she had ended up in the right arms, those arms had been snatched away from her. She had been separated from Kells first by misunderstandings, then by old entanglements and other people's quarrels and chicanery—and now by the sheer chance of his having arrived back in Port Royal at precisely the wrong moment, when a sinking city and a cresting wave had conspired to down his broken ship.

A luckier man would have escaped that.

A luckier woman would have had a chance to say good-by to her lover before he sank beneath the waves.

Carolina's lips twisted bitterly. There was no truth to the cheerful belief that good would triumph over evil, she told herself. Look at Robin Tyrell, Marquess of Saltenham! Look at Reba and Reba's mother! *They* had certainly triumphed and were living no doubt in splendor in England, secure in the knowledge that Robin's crimes had been safely pinned on someone else—Kells.

And now Kells was dead and would never be able to raise his voice against Robin, never retrieve his damaged reputation.

Carolina stared into the dark, her hands clenched, and fervently prayed to God that *she* would someday have the chance to confront the marquess, that *she* would have the chance to bring him down. In Kells's behalf.

A bittersweet vision of Robin Tyrell rose hauntingly in her mind. Dark and attractive, so fleetingly like Kells, Robin had been the dark side of the coin. Memories assailed her, lashed her. Of empty gray eyes, of a dissolute face, of a caressing voice that had called her "dear lady." There had been a time when she had almost believed she could change him.

Now she was older, wiser. Now she knew that people rarely changed—only circumstances.

And Robin and her old schoolmate Reba, the Marquess and Marchioness of Saltenham, were blithely going their way with never a thought for the woe they had left behind them.

Life was unjust.

Carolina threw herself face down upon her bunk, wishing she would smother and never wake, never live to face all the heartache, all the distasteful realities that lay in store.

And lying thus, she fell asleep and dreamed she was a little girl again, back on the Eastern Shore, crying for a lost doll—and for a father who could never love her.

And amid her tears, into that dream on magical boots strode a tall dark Englishman—Kells. Half awake, half asleep, she found herself tossing on her bunk and reliving those wild days on Tortuga, those days when she had by turn loved him and hated him. And in her dream a tall white ship carried them back to the Tidewater and a gala reunion with her mother at Level Green.

Having drifted off to sleep with thoughts of that leisurely world of Virginia's Tidewater that she had lost so long ago, Carolina woke refreshed for the first time in days—and as she went out on deck in a pink dawn that turned the sea momentarily to a misty lavender, she realized that what had wakened her had been the ship's turning sharply about.

The reason for that change of course was glaringly apparent.

Not only were the golden galleons still visible in the distance as they sailed cautiously past the coral reefs that guarded the northeast corner of Eleuthera, but two lean ships flying the French flag were approaching from the open ocean. Captain Simmons had turned tail and was fleeing before them to the west—a course that would inevitably take him down the Northeast Providence Channel.

The young captain had gambled and lost.

It was a black look he gave her when he saw her standing, yellow calico skirts blowing, by the rail. A look that said, *We might have gone round Abaco Island and so reached safety had it not been for your counsel!*

But Carolina, watching the ships approach, had a fatalistic feeling that there were ships everywhere that day on the watch for such as they, and that it would not have mattered whether Green Turtle Cay or even Pensacola Cay, the result would have been exactly the same—a frowning warship bearing down, driving them ever onward.

Like the others aboard she watched glumly as those stout ships herded them down the Northeast Providence Channel, past Spanish Wells, past Hole in the Wall. If they held this course they would wind up at the pirate port of Nassau on New Providence Island.

"What does Captain Simmons intend?" she asked the sailing master when she could get a word with him. "Does he not know that his present course will bring him to New Providence? Why does he not turn hard to starboard and run between Berry Island and Gorda Cay up the Northwest Providence Channel and so reach the Straits of Florida? It is his only chance!"

The sailing master looked hard at this young woman who had studied a buccaneer's charts so well. "I would you were in command of the ship," he muttered, running a distracted hand through his nut-brown hair. "But the captain seems to have lost his resolve. He stands there with his teeth chattering!" He gave his captain's back in the distance a contemptuous look.

"Well, someone must jolt him out of it or we are lost!"

The sailing master gave her a glum look. "I doubt anyone can do it. I wish to God I had never signed on for this voyage!" He was still muttering as he moved on down the deck.

Carolina hesitated but a moment. The captain did not like her, but he must hear her out—all their lives depended on it. For she had little hope for any of them if they reached New Providence.

Squaring her slim shoulders, she marched upon the captain. He stood with his back to her, a beaten dejected figure in crumpled clothes.

"Captain Simmons," she began.

He did not turn. He did not seem to hear her. His head was bowed and he was lost in contemplation of the deck planking.

She opened her mouth to speak again and even as she did the captain's head was jerked upward by a cry from the rigging above and they saw, coming out from behind Sandy Point up the coast of Abaco Island on their right, the masts of a tall ship—and from her masthead she flew the blue and gold lilies of France.

What would Kells have done in such a case? was racing through Carolina's mind.

"Captain Simmons!" she cried. "Turn hard to starboard. Run past that ship. You may yet escape a broadside and reach the Straits of Florida!"

As if in a trance, the young captain stared at the oncoming ship—his only barrier at that point to freedom. Slowly he swung to face the clamor that had arisen behind Carolina for others aboard were of her persuasion.

"It is too late," he said in a hollow voice. "We could never pass her. We would be blown out of the water."

Carolina stared at the beaten captain and in her rage she wanted to burst into tears. How inglorious it would be to go to the bottom without ever firing a shot! Around her the crew was muttering, but they were not likely to mutiny—not in time at least, for they were fast losing their chance as the majestic French vessel moved out into the channel.

Captain Simmons blundered past her as if he could not bear the sight and Carolina watched bitterly as the big warships herded their inoffensive vessel toward New Providence Island and who knew what grim fate.

WELCOME TO NEW PROVIDENCE!

Chapter 16

All day beneath a cloudless sky they had sailed the clear cerulean waters. No shot had rung across the *Ordeal*'s bow. Indeed it was unnecessary. She had struck her colors without being asked to do so and now slunk along, a beaten ship but still intact.

Along with the grim-faced officers, Carolina had remained on deck as the *Ordeal* was herded past reefs of pink coral and over a bottom whose white sand held a brilliance that seemed to highlight the parrot fish and barracuda that held sway in the aquamarine depths. And now their escort had been joined by other ships, silently driving toward New Providence.

No one aboard understood exactly what was happening, why French and Spanish ships were beating together toward Nassau, but Carolina sensed that the jaws of a trap were closing.

And now as the swift tropical darkness fell, they saw ahead of them a line of low, dark green bluffs rising. They had reached New Providence, and the shanty town that was Nassau lay ahead with its protected harbor that could anchor half a thousand pirate vessels while denying access to the deeper draft men of war.

Nature had provided assistance, too. The long sandy spit of Hog Island, dotted with occasional wind-stunted trees, provided a barrier to protect the busy harbor where countless shallow draft ships seemed to be anchored, their white sails turned rose-colored by the setting sun.

At that point a nine-pounder spoke from somewhere along the coast and Captain Simmons in panic gave orders to come about.

It was the wrong maneuver to have made just then. With a jarring lurch the *Ordeal* came to a halt. With the last of the light she had run aground on a sandbar off Hog Island.

Carolina never really understood what happened through the night. There was desultory firing, occasional lights blinking from shore, shouts that came from out of the darkness as great ships glided by. Once in the harbor a powder magazine blew up with a deafening explosion that sent an incandescent array of hot metal and flaming sparks into fiery arcs that hissed back into the black waters. Moonlight glinted on the white surf that boomed off a nearby reef. Carolina had heard that there were two entrances to this harbor—she had no doubt that this determined fleet that had so successfully blocked the *Ordeal*'s escape had blocked them both off.

When morning came, shot pounded around them as desperate pirates tried to run the French and Spanish blockade with their fast, shallow draft vessels. Some of their ships were blown out of the water, some were captured and new crews put aboard to be sent into the harbor to pound the coast. Miraculously the *Ordeal* remained untouched, stuck fast to the sandbar, for the sturdy merchant ship had resisted all efforts to dislodge her.

As the morning advanced, Carolina borrowed a glass from one of the ship's officers and studied the town with curiosity. What she saw was mainly a tent city. Spars had been stuck into the sand with a bit of ragged sail attached to give shade from the brilliant sun. Behind that white sand beach, beyond the pink coral heads and the waving palms, stretched a jungle, and beyond that the coral hills where lookouts undoubtedly kept watch. Carolina wondered if the pirate lookouts had all been drunk yesterday that they had not seen their stately advance and given warning sooner.

The attacking force had gone ashore now and there was fighting on the beach. The nine-pounder in the crumbling fort had been silenced, but there was the popping sound of small-arms fire. She could see men running—and sometimes women with bright skirts flying.

Gilly had been one of those. . . . It was easy to picture the ginger-haired urchin mouthing oaths and jeers as she ran. . . . But Gilly lay deep beneath Port Royal harbor.

Carolina's jaw tightened. This was no time to ponder upon the past, upon what might have been. A longboat was approaching from one of the galleons that had cast anchor nearby, and in the prow was a frowning Spanish officer.

And Carolina, as the only person aboard who could speak Spanish, found herself cast in the role of translator.

Captain José Avila arrived aboard with an armed escort and formally demanded surrender of the ship *Ordeal,* which he termed "an impudent invader of Spain's sovereign seas." He also demanded surrender of Captain Simmons's sword but since Captain Simmons didn't have a sword, he took command of the ship anyway.

"Ask them where they are taking us," squeaked Captain Simmons in an agony of fright.

"He will only say 'disposal will be made of us,'" Carolina reported woodenly.

"Tell him I insist on having another interpreter," cried Captain Simmons.

Carolina turned and gave him a wounded look but she repeated his request faithfully to Captain Avila, who raised his dark brows, snapped his fingers, and muttered something in Spanish to one of the officers who accompanied him. There was a short wait during which Captain Avila instructed Carolina to read him the roster of the ship's company and the ship's manifest.

By the time she had finished that, they had a new translator, a melancholy-faced young man who came on board and snapped tensely to attention. Carolina guessed he was a young officer on his first assignment—perhaps he had been recently a student—and was overwhelmed by suddenly being singled out for duty under the sharp eyes of his commanding officer.

There was a swift exchange of words between Captain Simmons and the go-between. "Tell your superior officer that this ship is *not* an interloper," he said earnestly and there were now beads of sweat glistening on his brow. "We were carrying important cargo to England, there to be delivered to the Spanish ambassador for transshipment to Spain."

He had their full attention now. Everyone, Spaniard and Englishman alike, was hanging on his words.

"And what cargo is this?"

"We carry the Silver Wench of whom you may have heard. She is the woman of Captain Kells, who loves her well. For her sake he will surrender his body to Spain!"

There was a general growl among his men but

Carolina stood transfixed. She turned her accusing gaze on the sweating young captain for a moment, then decided to enter the fray herself.

"It is true I am called the Silver Wench," she told her captor in her very good Castilian Spanish. "And it is true that I will always be Captain Kells's woman!" Her voice rang out. "But—"

"How come you to speak our language with such grace, señorita?" cut in her captor with narrowed eyes.

"I once found a Spanish girl shipwrecked on the Virginia coast. She was the lone survivor of a galleon that foundered in a storm. My father arranged for her return to Spain via the Spanish ambassador in London, but in the months she stayed with us, I learned her language. Later—on Tortuga—I befriended the Spanish prisoners of the buccaneers, bringing them fresh fruit and talking with them—they had few friends there."

The Spanish officer, who up to now had considered Spain had a corner on gallantry, gazed upon the glowing beauty of this admitted buccaneer's woman, and a grudging admiration crept into his dark eyes. Suddenly he swept her a courtly bow.

"You are safe here, señorita," he said. "My men will not molest you." He turned with a frown to Captain Simmons, who had viewed this sudden bowing with alarm. "Tell this quaking captain that my men will now take over his ship for transportation of the prisoners from this pirate stronghold we have just now subdued."

"But we have here the Silver Wench! We offer her in exchange for our freedom!" Captain Simmons cried almost tearfully.

"Tell the young captain that he has a loose tongue," was the scathing rejoinder. "If he allows it to wag any more on this subject, I will have it cut off."

Captain Simmons cringed back and Carolina noted how, as he joined his men, they drew away from him.

She turned to the Spanish officer and gave him a deep curtsy and her brightest smile. "You are a true *caballero* of Spain, *mi capitan.*"

"And you are a dangerous wench," he growled. *But a captivating one,* his smiling eyes added.

Boatloads of women were approaching, Carolina saw, being rowed in longboats by laconic Spanish sailors. She peered past them, looking for other boats —boats containing the hundreds of men who had fought the invasion on shore. "Where are the men?" she wondered.

"Put to the sword," replied the Spanish captain and she looked at him, hardly comprehending. "You took no prisoners?" she demanded.

"Only the women," he said grimly. "Will you do me the honor to be their translator, señorita? For we have found none of them who speak Spanish."

"Yes," Carolina murmured dizzily. *All dead,* she was thinking. Kells had never done anything like that—not when he took Cartagena, not when he took Spanish vessels. He had ransomed them, not killed them!

She was diverted from her thoughts by the first woman clambering aboard—a blowzy woman with broken teeth and the wildest assortment of clothing Carolina had ever seen, topped off with a multicolored bandanna wrapped around her large head.

One by one they came aboard, some laughing, some crying, some making eyes at the men aboard and flirting their skirts invitingly. But the last to arrive was the one who made an impression on Carolina.

She came aboard like a spitting cat and slapped the face of the young officer, who had handled her too familiarly as he helped her over the side, with a crack that snapped his head back.

"Insulting whelp!" she cried. "Watch where you put your hands!"

Captain Avila was watching this byplay with some

amusement. His dark gaze—approving in spite of himself—passed over this splendid bit of womanhood, her magnificent figure only accentuated by the fact that she was wearing men's clothing. A pair of fine upstanding breasts pushed against the white cambric of her torn shirt and through it came delectable glimpses of pale female flesh. Her dark trousers fit rather too snugly and her lower legs were bare—indeed she was barefoot. Her dark blue eyes snapped imperiously and a head of riotous red hair sprang like glowing flame to surround a commandingly beautiful face—and a face accustomed to command.

"This, señorita, is the famous Rouge," the Spanish captain told Carolina humorously.

But Carolina seemed not to hear him. A look of shock had spread over her lovely countenance, and for a moment she seemed to totter.

"Penny," she said faintly. "Dear God, it's really you! *You're* Rouge!"

ON TO HAVANA!

Chapter 17

"*You* are the Silver Wench? *You,* my little sister? I knew that Christabel Willing was the Silver Wench, but I never in my wildest dreams imagined that Christabel Willing was Carolina Lightfoot!" Penny nearly doubled up with laughter.

"Indeed *I* can hardly credit that you are the woman called Rouge," Carolina countered ruefully.

The two women were sitting in Carolina's cabin, which she had hastily offered to share with "Rouge." Penny was lounging lazily back against the bunk with one long leg stretched out, her bare heel resting on the table in a pose her mother would have described sharply as "outrageous," and Carolina was perched on the edge of her chair, studying her beautiful sister, whom the family had so long regarded as "lost."

"Whatever happened to you, Penny? Why didn't we ever hear from you?"

"A great deal happened to me." Penny's brilliant smile flashed. "And do you really think the aristrocratic Lightfoot clan would have welcomed the news that a daughter of theirs was the notorious 'Rouge' of New

Providence? What do you think Mother would have said? Or Father? Or Aunt Pet? Or you, for instance?" she added with a slightly jeering laugh.

"I think we would all have tried to rescue you," Carolina said soberly. "And Kells would certainly have done it."

Those dark blue eyes, so like her reckless mother's, held an amused glimmer. "But suppose I didn't *want* to be rescued?"

"I suppose we'd have done it anyway," sighed Carolina. "Plucked you out bodily and asked you if that was really what you wanted to do with your life!"

"Oh, don't be priggish!" exclaimed Penny. "From anyone else maybe, but I wouldn't expect priggishness from you, Carol!"

Carolina was in a mood to be argumentative. "Well, you must admit New Providence is a terrible place," she said. "Everybody says so."

"Even Kells?"

"Especially Kells."

Penny chuckled. "I never saw him, you know. I was told he'd visited New Providence but at the time I had other fish to fry."

"Yes, he told me. Of course he'd never seen you before so he didn't have any idea you were my sister, but he told me you were inciting two men to kill each other and when they lurched away, you followed them swinging a cutlass!"

"Oh, I probably did," shrugged Penny. "I was just having a tantrum, most like. I doubt I really hurt anybody." She gave Carolina a keen look. "By the way, where *is* Kells?"

"He's dead," said Carolina, feeling a lump rise in her throat. "His ship was just coming into Port Royal when the earthquake struck. The *Sea Wolf* went to the bottom, taking him with it."

"Oh, Carol, I'm so sorry!" exclaimed Penny, and

real compassion lit her dark blue eyes. "I'd heard it was a real love affair—the Silver Wench and her buccaneer."

"It's true, I loved him deeply," said Carolina in a blurry voice. She got hold of herself. If they talked about Kells, she'd be hard put not to burst into tears! "But enough about me, Penny. Tell me all that's happened to you and how you ended up in a godforsaken place like New Providence? All we knew was that you'd run away to the Marriage Trees with Emmett and had got as far as Philadelphia. Were you married in Maryland or in Philadelphia?"

"In Maryland, just over the border. The storm was tearing through the Marriage Trees—a big oak fell and nearly killed us—but we found a minister to perform the ceremony in a house that had a light in it. We woke him up. He was frightened by the storm and wanted to wait till morning but I aimed Father's big dueling pistol at him and he read the words over us in short order!"

"Father missed that pistol but he assumed it was stolen by one of the servants," marveled Carolina. "He never dreamed *you* took it!"

"Yes, well, Emmett had his points but he wasn't the best of protectors. I thought I'd better have a weapon handy in case we met brigands on the road and I had to protect *him.*" Penny's short laugh spoke volumes.

Carolina studied her sister: That long elegant body, that complete self-composure, that relaxed mien of a lounging tigress. It was a face of great beauty she looked into, with a jaw just slightly square and dark blue eyes as reckless as her own. There was something wild and untamed and forever free about Penny with her flashing smile and her luxuriant red hair.

"I never understood why you married Emmett in the first place," she sighed. "Personally, I never could stand him—his eyes were too small and he looked at everyone sort of *calculatingly* as if wondering how he could make them suit his purpose—for all that he was such a dolt!"

"You read him right," murmured Penny. She put her other bare foot on the table, leaned back and folded her strong arms behind her head. Her red hair framed a thoughtful face. "I ran away, of course, because I wanted to be free, mistress of my own fate. But I really think I *married* Emmett to spite my parents because they would have pushed me into a tiresome marriage with some dull-witted fellow who could 'take care of me' sooner or later. . . ." She laughed. "And so I married another dull-witted fellow who was even worse and who expected *me* to take care of *him!*"

Carolina was not surprised. Emmett had, so far as she knew, no saving graces.

"Mother sent to Philadelphia when she found out you were there, and Emmett wasn't hard to find. But all he would say was that you'd quarreled and you'd left him. He never would say what you'd quarreled about."

"I don't doubt it!" Penny's eyes flashed, dark angry sapphires fringed by russet lashes. "Emmett was very sulky. He complained that I was 'too much for him'—in bed, that is. He said I *wore him out!* Can you imagine?" She looked indignant. "Indeed, he said if he had to tumble about all night, he'd be much too tired ever to do any work the next day!"

Carolina could well imagine it; she had always had an instinctive dislike for self-centered Emmett. What she could *not* imagine was Penny's next words.

"But he'd worked it all out," she went on bitterly. "Since I was 'such a hot wench'—to use his phrase—and since I kept him so 'exhausted'—his words again—I could use up my extra energy and keep us both in luxury if I'd just accept the advances of certain gentlemen that he would find for me—and bring home to my bed!"

"Oh, *no!*" wailed Carolina. "I hope you didn't do it, Penny!"

"You're right, I didn't do it!" snapped Penny. "But *that* was what we quarreled about."

"He said you attacked him," remembered Carolina.

"I did," said Penny, aggrieved. "I threw everything in the room at him when he suggested he'd find other men for me—for money." Her smile was grim. "I blacked both his eyes and near broke his nose!"

"No wonder he wouldn't say where you were—he was afraid you'd tell what had happened!"

Penny laughed her throaty laugh. It had a hard sound.

"I don't wonder Emmett didn't care to admit where I was! Oh, we'd quarreled, yes—but for him to seek revenge against me by *selling* me to a sea captain bound for Ireland . . . !"

"Oh, he didn't!" cried Carolina, shocked out of her despondency.

"He did, indeed," affirmed Penny. "Bribed our landlady's two big sons to tie me up and deliver me to him in a sack down at the waterfront! He *told* them that I was a hellion and a harpy and that he was going to send me home to my family and leave me there! Of course, they believed him. And they had no love for me for from time to time I'd rejected both their advances! So one of them throttled me while the other tied me up and gagged me. They thrust me into a hempen sack"—she moved her body restlessly as if she could still feel its coarse roughness against her skin—"and I wasn't let out of that bag until we were four hours out to sea." Her teeth clashed together. "I can tell you that I came out of that bag fighting! And there was this coarse red-bearded giant who said he'd seen me and he'd fancied me and when it turned out Emmett couldn't persuade me to—"

"So this sea captain was one of the 'gentlemen' Emmett intended you to entertain?" gasped Carolina.

"He was indeed—and I'll never forget his coarse red beard that nearly took the skin off my face! He said he had bought me fair and square and he intended for me to keep Emmett's bargain. I gave him a most terrible kick that doubled him up. I had hoped at least to break a few of this scoundrel's bones but he was more durable than that. He rose from the floor with what I would term an ugly expression and reached out lightning fast with one of those cordlike arms of his and knocked me across the room. Knocked me unconscious, he did."

Carolina was leaning forward, hanging on her sister's words. All this from the tall aristocratic beauty who had swept all before her when she danced the stately minuet to a tinkling harpsichord at the Governor's Palace in Williamsburg. She had always thought Penny born to wed at least a governor or a general!

"When I came to, I was tied down in the bunk and he was having his way with me."

"Oh, Penny!" choked Carolina. Her heart ached for her free-spirited sister, brought so low.

"He kept me mostly tied up for three days," remembered Penny grimly. "And on short rations. I was so weak I staggered when finally he let me come up on deck. He said that 'would teach me'—*and it did!*"

"What do you mean, it taught you?" faltered Carolina.

Penny gave her an amused look—on a man that would have been called a *roué*'s look. "Would you believe it, that red-bearded captain made me discover that I truly had a taste for men? I mean, Emmett was nothing—he made me do all the work, it was very tiresome. But Red Beard plunged on me with joy—I refused to cooperate even though he knocked me about. I had begun to believe men were nothing and not worth the effort—having known only Emmett's inept attentions. But now in Red Beard's arms, even though I loathed him, I began to realize that something else existed, some joy I'd never really tasted, never really imagined, something beyond sex"—the dark blue eyes were adventurer's eyes now, boldly questing—"something past what Red Beard knew, past what I knew, something *worth finding*. Yes," she mused, "in Red Beard's arms I discovered I had a taste for men"—she laughed again, ruefully—"just not a taste for *him*."

Carolina's head whirled. "Then Red Beard was the one who brought you to New Providence?"

The red tresses shook a denial. Penny stretched out her long legs and crossed her slim bare ankles.

"What happened to him?" puzzled Carolina.

Penny gave her a lazy smile. "Lost at sea," she said significantly. She stretched her arms above her head and her magnificent breasts rippled. She was like a statue of a reclining Venus lying there stretched out, thought Carolina suddenly—a slightly depraved Venus. "Red Beard had a very handsome first mate. I decided I'd prefer *his* attentions to those of the captain. So I flirted with him—and he fancied me." She gave a wicked little laugh. "And somehow that led to a mutiny. And after some romantic sailing about from port to port, he turned pirate and brought me here to New Providence."

"So you really—" She had been about to say "caused the captain's death?" but Penny caught her thought and interrupted.

"Yes, I objected to being bought and sold like some prize mare! And I objected to being tied up and raped. And being beaten." Penny's beautiful face hardened. "So I had him killed," she said blithely. "After which I felt much better about everything. I felt free. I wasn't free, of course. The first mate made that clear soon enough. He made it clear with his fists." She sighed.

"Oh, Penny, if we'd only known!" Carolina's hands clenched. "We'd have got you out of it!"

"Yes, I dare say you would." There was a jolt and a creaking, scraping sound. "The tide's at the flood—they'll be pulling us off this sandbar. How did your captain ever manage to pile you up on this sandbar, anyway?"

"Inept as Emmett," Carolina said whimsically.

"Do you know where they're taking us?"

"I heard them say Havana."

Penny nodded her red head thoughtfully. "I suppose that's the logical place but I was hoping for somewhere in Europe—Paris, perhaps, or Marseilles. After all, it was a joint attack—French and Spanish. Even Toledo would be a change after life in these islands!"

"Oh, Penny, you couldn't wish us to be taken to Spain! We'd be burned as heretics there!"

"No, I suppose not," laughed Penny. She lifted her head, listening. "The scraping has stopped. We're off the sandbar now. We're getting underway. But you haven't told me anything about the family, yet. How are things at Level Green?"

"Extravagant as ever. Virginia wrote me they were about to go under and I—I did something about it." She told Penny the story of the de Lorca necklace and how she had sent it to her mother to pay Fielding Lightfoot's debts.

Penny rocked with laughter. "You certainly delivered the *coup de grâce* to Father! He scorned you all those years and now it's you who came to save him!"

"I didn't mean it like that." Carolina was vexed. "They needed help—"

"And like a fairy godmother, you waved your wand and took care of all their problems at one stroke! I'd like to have seen this necklace of yours. Or at least the copy you spoke of. What a pity you don't have the copy still—everyone would believe it was the original!"

Carolina thought of the last time she had seen the copy—those blood-red rubies and diamonds that sparkled like tears, clutched in Gilly's dying hand—and shivered. She supposed she would have nightmares forever about the de Lorca necklace, for had she not sent it to the Tidewater, had she offered it to Kells soon enough, they might have been safe up the Cobre River when the earthquake broke apart and inundated Port Royal. She didn't tell Penny that—it was all too fresh and hurtful, that the necklace was, in her mind, tied up with Kells's death.

"Well, it's good to know the Lightfoots are still lording it over the Tidewater," Penny said complacently. "What do you hear from Virgie? Has she landed a man at last?"

Carolina launched into the story of Virginia's early tragedies, ending with, "But everything turned out well for her. She's married now to Kells's brother Andrew and living on the family estate in Essex. She wrote me she is expecting her second child in late summer."

"Little Virgie," murmured Penny. "Married now and soon to have two children tugging at her skirts. And I was still thinking of her as a schoolgirl!"

"We're none of us schoolgirls except Della and Flo," said Carolina with asperity. "And you and I can never go back to what we were."

"Oh, I don't want to go back," Penny said quickly. "I want to go forward and find something better. I'm sure there *is* something better—there must be; it certainly isn't *here!*" She looked about her with some distaste at the cramped confines of their cabin. "Actually I was almost glad that Emmett acted so badly. I mean, it severed all bonds between us, and it ended any thought that I should go back to him because, after all, he *had* gotten up the nerve to elope with me to the Marriage Trees. And anyway, there couldn't be any question of going back to him." She shrugged. "He'd only have sold me again—probably for more money this time!"

"Penny." Carolina took a deep breath for she wasn't sure, in spite of her offhand comments about Emmett, how Penny was going to take this. "Emmett's dead."

"Is he indeed?" Penny said indifferently. "How did he die? Did Father shoot him?"

"No, he drowned. It was last summer. He was fishing and he fell into deep water and his boots filled up and pulled him under before they could save him."

Penny gave another hard little laugh. "How unpleasant for Emmett—and how fitting. To live an unworthy life and die an ignominious death!"

Carolina marveled at how cool Penny was, at how hard she had become. Gone was the impetuous girl—in her place was a woman to reckon with!

As if to rebutt what her sister was thinking, Penny said lightly, "You must remember how relatively innocent I was at the time I knew Emmett. You might say he introduced me to the hard facts of life. I suppose I should be grateful to him and mourn his passing."

Carolina said hastily, "So you lived with this first mate on New Providence?"

"For a while, yes. I enjoyed sleeping with him—when he wasn't drunk and abusive. But he was too possessive, he wouldn't let me branch out. And he was almost as rough as Red Beard. I didn't like having my eyes blacked so I looked around for a way out—and I found it."

"You—found it?" Carolina frowned.

"Yes." Penny gave her a sunny smile. She enjoyed shocking her younger sister, who wore her heart on her sleeve. "I decided no one man could drive him out of port—but two could. So I accepted *matelotage* from the two leading pirates of all New Providence and set up my little homestead in the fanciest shack in Nassau."

"*Matelotage?*" gasped Carolina. "But that's—"

"An old buccaneer custom," smiled Penny. "I see you've heard of it?"

"Heard of it? I nearly blundered into it once—but of course Kells saved me."

"Of course he did," Penny agreed genially. "There was, however, no charming buccaneer around to save *me."*

Carolina was staring at her sister as if she had never seen her before, for this was a new view of Penny, indeed. *Matelotage* was an old buccaneer custom. When two buccaneers wanted the same woman, and the woman was agreeable—or perhaps could not decide between them—they tossed coins for her, and the one who lost the toss married her. The other became the *matelot* and took the husband's place in her bed when the husband was away.

Penny stared back at her coolly. Carolina decided Penny could face anything down.

"Since one or the other of them was usually in port, it gave me a kind of sway there. I must say that I have enjoyed being Queen of New Providence."

So that was the way Penny saw it—Queen of New Providence. And Carolina supposed Penny must have been just that, lording it over these wild men who yearned to possess her. Penny was her sister, she still looked the same—indeed the wild look she now wore had made her even more beautiful—but those words had made Carolina feel she was talking with a stranger. Sisters, but how very different they had turned out to be!

"I am not really sorry to leave Nassau." Penny smiled lazily at Carolina. "I was growing rather tired of it."

"But—your husband, your *matelot!"* blurted out Carolina. "I heard they killed all the men on New Providence."

"Oh, Carson is still at sea and they'll not have killed

Jock." Penny shrugged. "When last I saw Jock, he was running for the jungle and calling to me to come with him. He'll survive."

"I'm surprised you didn't go with him. After all, you could have been killed there on the beach when the attack force landed."

Penny's lazy look from beneath a fringe of russet lashes was expressive. "Carol," she chided, "men don't kill women who look like me—not if they can help it."

Carolina gazed upon her sister. It was probably true.

Penny yawned delicately. "They consider us prizes. I was about to follow Jock into the jungle when I realized that. Then I threw away my cutlass, ripped my shirt open at the front and began combing my hair instead. The battle roiled around me, but no one ever touched me until a French officer came up to where I sat on the sand under the shade of a lean-to and bowed and said in very poor English, 'Mademoiselle, will you be so good to follow me?' And here I am."

Carolina shook her head in amazement. "Penny, there's no one like you—anywhere!"

"That's just as well—all things considered," Penny agreed with her gamine grin. "I wouldn't want too many copies of me around! But I don't see why you should be so surprised that I should want a change. I'm tired of being burned black in the sun—" she gestured with a toast-colored arm. "I'm tired of wearing men's clothes because they're 'practical'! I'm tired of eating pirate dishes like *salmagundi,* full of garlic and pepper! I'm tired of having a cutlass dangling at my hip because I'm afraid I'll be kidnapped and carried off aboard some dirty pirate ship to be doxy to half a hundred men!" She shivered—and then brightened as quickly. "I'd like to go to some new place, wear beautiful clothes, live in a large house, drive out in a coach and six!" Her lazy smile deepened. "Don't look so shocked, Carolina. I was born to be a courtesan."

"Well, where we're going you'll have little chance for all that," Carolina said dryly. "We're more apt to be slaves in Havana."

"Oh, I don't know about that." Penny stretched again and got up restlessly. As she moved, Carolina was again reminded what a beautiful body her sister had, what feline grace. A pair of amused dark blue eyes considered her. "Who knows, I might even end up being the mistress of the Governor of Havana!"

BOOK III

The Beautiful Captive

Like all in the human condition,
Who were never born to win,
We weep for our sins of omission
And all that might have been. . . .

PART ONE

The Spanish Cavalier

His dangerous smile in the morning
Which beams in her bed so bright
Is only matched by the lecherous grin
Which crosses his face by night!

HAVANA, CUBA

Summer 1692

Chapter 18

Chaperoned by lofty galleons whose fore and aft towers gleamed gold in the sun, the *Ordeal* was shepherded through the narrow entrance to Havana's harbor. For the staid old ship it had been a tempestuous journey with its load of prostitutes and bawds from the sands of New Providence. The *Ordeal* was still negotiating the Northwest Providence Channel and had not yet turned south into the Straits of Florida before trouble broke out. Two bawds who had fought over the same man on the beach at Nassau took up the battle again and broke bottles over each other's heads. The scandalized crew of the *Ordeal*—who had by now become mere lackeys of their Spanish masters commanding the ship—had tried to save both contestants, but one of them died of a cracked skull.

That subdued the ladies momentarily, but somewhere between Gun Cay and Riding Rocks some rum was smuggled from the officers' quarters into the large community dormitory the women shared below decks, and they all became royally drunk and burst out upon the deck, some half-dressed and some not dressed at all. In the general uproar it was very hard to restore order, especially since most of the sailors had been long at sea and the sight of a laughing woman, stripped to the waist and waving a bottle, was more than many of them could bear. Heedless of the consequences, many of them had bounded forward, and a wild drunken jig had ensued, with much stamping up and down the deck. Captain Simmons had watched, awed and stricken, as bodies in various stages of undress and passion had piled up in any convenient place—indeed, as his first mate had muttered, you could trip over them.

In their cabin Carolina had been telling Penny all about school in England, about Reba and the Marquess of Saltenham and Reba's mother and all the trouble they had caused, when the commotion outside erupted.

"Do you think it's a mutiny?" Carolina had interrupted her reminiscences to ask alertly.

"No." Laughter sparkled in Penny's dark blue eyes as she helped Carolina barricade the cabin door. "I think it's but another brawling night in Nassau's taverns brought aboard the *Ordeal!*" She smiled at Carolina. "Shall we play a hand of cards, Carol? It will take your mind off things."

To Carolina's astonishment, Penny produced from the folds of her flowing shirt a rather worn deck of cards. It was the last thing Carolina would have expected to see carried by someone in Penny's perilous circumstances, but at the moment, keyed up as she was, she welcomed any diversion. Gratefully she joined Penny at the small wooden table which was practically the cabin's only furniture.

"I met someone in Port Royal who knew you—quite well, I was given to believe," she told her sister soberly as Penny dealt the cards.

"Really? Who? I'll wager he was handsome. And a bounder. Bounders are the only kind of men I seem to care for!" Penny favored her younger sister with a mocking look.

"It wasn't a man. It was a girl named Gilly."

Penny's russet brows elevated. "Oh, yes, I knew Gilly. But"—she studied her sister, frowning now—"I am surprised that *you* did."

"I—rescued her on the street in Port Royal. She was being pursued by two bawds who claimed she had stolen their petticoats."

"No doubt she had!" laughed Penny.

"I took her into my household as a maidservant."

"That was a mistake," murmured Penny, leaning back and studying her cards.

Carolina sighed as she picked hers up. "That was what Kells thought." A shadow of pain passed across her lovely mobile features as she spoke his name, and then was gone. "But I took her in anyway."

"You have too much kindness!" laughed Penny. "I'll wager Gilly stole your ear bobs—and anything else that was handy!"

Carolina gave her sister a troubled look. "*I* thought she worshiped you," she said abruptly. "When a dinner guest said one night that he considered you plain, Gilly smouldered and later leaped to your defense!"

"Did she now?" Penny looked pleased. "Well, she used to follow me around Nassau, begging me to teach her to cheat at cards! It made people wary of me, I can tell you! *I* made the mistake of rescuing her, too, when she first arrived, from a nasty fellow who'd have sold her to anyone with the price—but it did no good." She shrugged. "She took up with another one just as bad."

"She's dead," said Carolina.

Penny looked up. "Oh? One of the bawds knifed her, I suppose?"

"No." Carolina shuddered, remembering how Gilly had died, with her grubby hand rising out of the water clutching imitation gems. She told Penny about it.

Penny did not seem to care. "So she died in the act of stealing your jewels? That should be enough to keep you from mourning her!"

"Perhaps she was restoring them to me—or trying to," Carolina said staunchly. She didn't know why she was defending Gilly, who certainly didn't merit it. She supposed she was rejecting this new casual hardness she found in her sister.

Penny sniffed. "Gilly left Nassau with some bracelets she stole from me—she was seen taking them! Carolina, you're a fool to be so soft-hearted!"

There seemed to be nothing to say to that. Carolina supposed she was. She settled down to playing cards, occasionally starting at some louder than usual howl from the deck.

"I see you haven't lost your skill," she murmured, when Penny beat her easily.

Penny's rich chuckle sounded. "Indeed I have not! Emmett would have been smarter to establish me in a gaming hall rather than sell me!" she added flippantly. "I won rather steadily in New Providence. Unfortunately," she sighed, "I buried my winnings in the sand and there's no chance now of going back for them."

"Oh, Penny," said Carolina wistfully, putting down her cards and staring across the table at this hard but glowing creature who was, astonishingly, her newly discovered older sister. "Do you think you will ever find the right man for you?"

Penny glanced up at the sound of a particularly loud feminine squeal followed by running feet, the sound of a body ricocheting off their cabin door and a string of whisky-slurred masculine curses punctuated by ribald feminine laughter. "Somebody pounced, missed, and is limping away—unsung," she observed. "In answer to your question, Carol—I doubt it. Anyway," she added cynically, "how does anyone know when they've found the right man?"

I knew, thought Carolina sadly, ignoring the hubbub outside as someone bellowed to restore order, followed by a crash which might have been caused by a thrown whisky keg. *Perhaps those were luckier who searched and never found,* she thought, *luckier than those who found only to lose!*

"But if I do find the right man"—Penny's gamine smile flashed—"I promise you I shall know it—instantly!" She cut the cards flashily.

"Penny, he won't stand a chance against you," Carolina assured her warmly.

"I'll wager he won't!" laughed Penny. "Meanwhile, since I can't find the right *one,* I'll make do with whoever appeals to me. Which may run into numbers!"

Penny lifted her head as the sound of a shot rent the air, followed by a jumble of confused shouts. The noise retreated. "I think the dance is over for the evening," she remarked tranquilly. "Buckets of sea water are being sloshed over the drunks to revive them, and the ladies are being dragged back to their quarters to sleep off the evening's festivities."

"You're certainly calm about it! If it wasn't for that stout door, *we'd* have been in it!"

"I'm used to it," was her sister's laconic response. "And much, much worse. Would you like me to describe a rather bad night in Nassau?"

"No, I wouldn't," Carolina said with a shudder. "I'd never realized how protected I was in Tortuga and Port Royal. And now . . ."

Which brought them squarely back to their present predicament.

"I do hope," Carolina told Penny, "that Ramona Valdez is still in Havana—she was to marry the governor there, you know."

"Yes, I had forgotten Ramona," murmured Penny, restlessly dealing another hand. "Do you think she would help us?"

"Of course she would help us! We rescued *her* when she was shipwrecked, didn't we, and returned her to Spain?"

Penny gave her younger sister a whimsical look. "Ramona might not thank us for that—not if the governor she married turned out not to her liking!" She paused. "Do you know anyone else in Havana?"

Carolina laid down her cards. "I don't know," she said. "I did befriend various Spanish prisoners on Tortuga and some of them were later returned to Havana. I don't know if any of them are still there or whether or not they would remember me."

Across the table Penny considered her with a droll expression. "Anyone who ever saw you would remember you, Carol!"

"But maybe in Havana they would not *wish* to remember," pointed out Carolina, frowning.

"There's that possibility, of course." Penny dealt a new hand of cards. "Come on, Carol, concentrate!" she added impatiently. "You're letting me win too easily!"

But with all that the immediate future might hold in store for them, Carolina found it difficult to concentrate on a game of cards.

Penny looked up thoughtfully. "So you really think Ramona would free us?"

"Of course she would!"

Penny shrugged. "People change," she said cryptically.

"Not Ramona—she'd remember how we helped her."

Penny gave her a mocking look. "Or perhaps she'd just remember we were heretics and have us burned at the next *auto-da-fé!*"

Carolina shuddered.

"Come along," Penny said easily. "I didn't mean it!

You'll remember I always had a shocking sense of humor!"

Carolina could not find it in her heart to deny it.

Once again, Penny beat her easily.

The drunken brawl on deck did not continue. The Spanish captain had managed to restore order before they passed Dog Rocks and Deadman's Cays. With half the crew in irons, they had sailed past the Florida Keys into the blue waters of the Gulf of Mexico and at last to the entrance of Havana harbor.

Rising up from the rugged coral rock, the sheer walls of the frowning fortress of El Morro rose up to the east to guard the harbor. Her guns boomed a welcome to the galleons, returning triumphant from their raid. To the west the white city of Havana gleamed in the sun, built of West Indian coral limestone.

To Carolina, this seemed a city of forts, for near El Morro rose another fortress, the Punta, and the town's main square, close to the seawall, was guarded by yet an older fort, La Fuerza, which faced the inner harbor.

The women were—according to their natures—glum or raucous as they disembarked. After the excitement of her first encounter with Penny had worn away, Carolina had slipped back into despondency, grieving for Kells. Not even Penny's best efforts had been able to snap her out of it. But now, resentful that she and her sister should be grouped together with this motley group of bawds, the trash of the western world, who had been cast out upon the sands of New Providence and were now being transported willy-nilly to Havana, she lifted her chin.

They should not see *her* weep! With a dull sense of fatalism—what would be would be!—she sat in the longboat with the others and was rowed to shore across the inner harbor.

Havana went wild that day. The triumphant return of

the galleons—victors, bringing home their spoils—had excited the townsfolk, and they had turned out as if to a fiesta. Gallant *caballeros* with silver jingling on their saddles, elegant señoritas and señoras sitting decorously in their carriages, soldiers from the forts, *mestiza* strumpets, Indian servants with liquid eyes and inscrutable faces, fishermen and fishwives, merchants and their families, harlots from the waterfront brothels calling out encouragement to their kind—they were all there.

Carolina's face went hot at the thought of being marched through that crowd, jeered at and ogled. Worse, being able to speak Spanish, Carolina could understand the bawdy comments directed at her and at flame-haired Penny, who swung rakishly along beside her, barefoot, looking about with apparent unconcern.

Somehow she stumbled through it, head high. Through the Plaza de Armas with its handsome two-story homes and its beautiful cathedral, down a hot street beneath shawl-draped balconies, where young girls leaned over and threw rose leaves down upon the victors, who looked up and waved, grinning salutations.

"They're taking us to the slave market," muttered Penny, beside her. "I can see the bell up ahead. Keep your head high, Carol. This isn't going to be fun!"

As Penny spoke, Carolina cast a hopeless look about her. To be sold as a slave! Somehow—although she had spoken facetiously of it to Penny—she had not expected it to be like this. She had imagined some sort of servitude, from which she would be shortly rescued by Ramona Valdez, for she had clung stubbornly to the hope that Ramona would still be here in Havana. But to be sold! That meant anyone could buy them: some plantation owner deep in the interior, a brothel owner to entertain his patrons, a shipmaster who would carry them out upon the high seas to who knew what terrible fate!

Her gaze swept the cheering throng—and came to rest upon a handsome trio just ahead: an old man, gray-haired, portly and somehow official-looking, who gazed sternly at the crowd from a carriage; and beside him a young girl, who might be his daughter, with a white mantilla spilling from a high-backed tortoiseshell comb over her thick black hair, gleaming almost blue in the sunlight; she was leaning over and speaking with animation to a tall *caballero* who sat astride a nervous horse, controlling the dancing animal with ease, although the horse seemed inclined to go sideways and wanted to rear up.

It was the man that drew Carolina's attention. He was dressed elegantly in black and silver with a burst of frosty Mechlin at his throat and a wide-brimmed hat with a silver band that shaded his hawklike face. In that he was unremarkable, for the dons favored somber garments and he might have been dressed for a ride up into the hills.

But in all else she found him remarkable indeed. A pair of cold gray eyes regarded her steadily from a face bronzed by long hours in the sun—perhaps at the prow of a ship. And indeed he had ceased talking to the young lady beside him and was leaning slightly forward, his gaze intent upon Carolina being herded through the town in her much mended yellow calico. The older man was quick to notice his interest and his stern gaze also swung to Carolina and the tall redhead beside her.

But the *caballero* on the horse, who sat so tall in the saddle, held her gaze. Her lips parted and her breath came shallowly. For that lean hard body was as familiar to her as breathing. Those fine hands, so firm upon the reins of his dancing mount, had caressed her to wild abandon. That dark face, so intent upon her now, was the face she had loved—and thought lost to her:

Kells!

She could not explain it, but it was true. The face she was looking into was *his* face, the face that had lit up her life and now haunted her restless dreams.

He was not dead, he was alive, he was here in Havana, seated upon a big chestnut horse, staring down at her without any visible sign of recognition!

All the emotions that had torn Carolina since the day Port Royal sank, all the pain and worry and guilt and despair fused for a moment with this shock of discovery that the man she had yearned for and grieved for was not dead after all—and she turned pale and wavered for a moment as if she would fall.

Penny had been striding along in the hot sun in apparent disdain. Now she turned in alarm as her sister stumbled and had a swift glimpse of Carolina, deathly pale, staring up at a tall *caballero* in black and silver who watched them from astride a chestnut horse. Conscious of the unfriendly crowd about them, she caught her breath in dismay.

"Oh, for heaven's sake, Carol, don't faint!" she muttered, grasping Carolina's arm and supporting her as her slight body suddenly sagged. "It would be too humiliating!"

Abruptly Carolina got hold of herself. Kells had given no visible sign of recognition but then he was always in control. The very fact that he was here in Havana meant that something was afoot! The divers had lied—they had not seen his body submerged in that drowned cabin. They had lied so that they might swiftly collect their money—or perhaps seize the gold money chains they had brought up from the wreck, and be off to search for loot somewhere else! She and Hawks had both been taken in. The ship she had seen advancing into the harbor when the earthquake struck must not have been the *Sea Wolf* after all!

Her mind raced ahead. What plot could have brought Kells here? Did he plan to take Havana? Why not? He had raided Cartagena and other Spanish towns! Surely this was some bold enterprise like that. How well he had concealed his surprise at seeing her! She was proud of him—but then, when had she not been proud of him? Her heart swelled and of a sudden the harsh sunlight that poured down over Havana was turned before her eyes into drifting gold, the city air with its myriad scents was suddenly the perfumed air of the tropics; the raucous clamor, joyful; the scene before her colorful and gorgeous. Her head lifted and she took a deep thankful breath and flashed a brilliant smile at Penny.

"I'm all right," she said hastily. "Oh, it's too bad we didn't have a chance to comb our hair—mine looks terrible and so does yours!"

"Well, don't overdo it," said Penny in amazement, letting go of her arm. "It's bad enough to be sold but you don't have to look *pleased* about it!"

Carolina laughed. It was a beautiful rippling sound, carefree and young. That laugh reached the ears of the portly gray-haired gentleman in the carriage who happened also to be the Governor of Havana. He gazed upon the pair in amazement. What beauties they were, the statuesque redhead and the slender elegant blonde with her delicious laugh!

Beside him, the fact that the attention of both men had centered upon the two captives being marched to the slave mart was not lost on the governor's daughter.

"Trash!" she hissed.

"Ah, but elegant trash, you will admit, Doña Marina," drawled the tall *caballero* Carolina had identified instantly as Kells.

Governor Corrubedo murmured an assent and Doña Marina spread a look of anger over each of them. She was young and tempestuous and she had no mother to guide her, for Governor Corrubedo's wife had died young and he had not remarried. Her elderly *duena*—her maiden aunt, Doña Merced—could hardly keep up with her and had panted to the governor on several occasions, "You must get her married without delay or she will disgrace you!" But the governor was an indulgent parent and loved his only daughter dearly, allowing Marina a freedom that was unheard of in that day, when Spanish girls of breeding and fortune were kept cloistered behind iron grillwork or sitting in sunny courtyards well guarded by watchful *duenas*.

"Your Excellency. Doña Marina." The tall gentleman on horseback was bowing his good-by as he moved away from them.

"Don Diego took his leave of us very suddenly," said Marina in a spiteful voice as she saw his broad back moving through the crowd away from them.

"Nonsense, *querido mio,*" responded the governor absently. "He doubtless wishes to view the bidding."

"Or perhaps to bid himself!" snapped his daughter.

That thought had occurred to the governor also. Both the blonde and the redhead had been very ripe. Every male eye had followed them as they passed. His gaze passed thoughtfully to Marina. She also was very ripe. Young still—but ripe. Although but fifteen, her figure was lush and her young breasts strained against her tight bodice. She was thinking thoughts of men now, was Marina. The governor sighed. He had hoped to postpone the day but suitors were already arriving at the big spacious house on the Plaza de Armas that he chose to occupy rather than his official residence in the forbidding fortress of La Fuerza.

Some of the suitors who eyed her as she promenaded sedately around the Plaza on Sundays, some of those who were just beginning to serenade her off-key beneath her window, were wealthy, the sons of rich men who could take her across the ocean sea, away to Spain and even the questionable delights of the Spanish Court. Some were the sons of planters with large holdings. But Marina favored none of them.

Marina—and her father forgave her for it since she was young and untried—had a talent for looking in the wrong direction. More specifically, in the direction of the tall gentleman who had just left them—a newcomer to Havana, Don Diego Vivar. And what did they really know about Don Diego? A hero, true, if what was said about him was to be believed. But the voices that labeled him a hero had come from Spain. No one here knew anything about him, about his holdings, his prospects—only that he was a king's favorite sent on a dangerous mission to the New World.

Better far that Marina choose a more suitable mate, the one the governor had already selected for her: Don Ramon del Mundo. *He* had all the proper qualifications. He was young, handsome, wealthy, and reputedly held vast estates in Spain. The governor had been given to understand that Don Ramon had come here only to prove his valor, preferably in some spectacular way. Certainly his foray into the buccaneer stronghold of Port Royal several months ago had been valorous enough, and the governor had encouraged it. If Don Ramon survived such dangerous inclinations, he would seem glamorous to Marina, who was at a romantic and impressionable age.

But Don Ramon had come home only to learn that the King of Spain preferred someone else to execute the plan to invade Jamaica which Don Ramon had so painstakingly built. A Spanish Court favorite was already being groomed for the mission. He would be dropped off directly at Jamaica, somewhere near Port Royal. Meanwhile if Don Ramon would be good enough to assemble a small force to await the stranger's instructions? They could be landed by pinnace and there await the commands of the newcomer sent from Spain.

Don Ramon had been sulking ever since.

And a sulky lover is not a successful lover! The governor had begun to wonder if Don Ramon really had any interest in his daughter at all.

And then abruptly—and in the most romantic of circumstances—Don Diego Vivar had appeared upon the scene. Darkly handsome and with a clouded past, and living in the governor's own house! Small wonder that Marina had become enamored of him! And how could Marina's father be certain such a marriage would be suitable?

The Governor of Cuba frowned. The women had stopped streaming past now. The girls were still throwing flowers from the shawl-fringed balconies, and a general air of fiesta held the old city in thrall. Beside him, Marina fretted.

A sudden thought occurred to him—and Governor Corrubedo was a man who, once a thought occurred to him, would promptly put it into action. He leaned toward his driver and instructed him to push the carriage through the crowd; they would view the slave auction.

But getting there through the crush proved impossible. Disgusted with their slow pace, the governor muttered a few words to his driver, who promptly left the carriage and shouldered his way through the crowd on foot.

The governor had put his plan into operation.

Sheltered by the curved arches and pillars of the arcade—and nearly deafened by the discordant clanging of the market bell—Carolina stood with the other women about to be auctioned off, grateful for the shade. Beside her Penny stood regally, looking slightly down her nose at the surging crowd. The rest milled about, muttering, frowning, giggling and one or two making their hips sway invitingly. But Carolina stood out, for she was standing on tiptoe trying to peer over the crowd—ah, there he was; Kells was approaching on horseback, looking cool and in command.

He would buy her! All was right with her world!

Suddenly she thought of Penny. He must buy Penny, too!

"We are sisters," she cried in ringing Spanish. "We must be sold together."

"What are you shouting about, Carol?" demanded Penny in amazement, for Penny had no facility for picking up languages.

"I am saying that we must be sold together—that we are sisters," said Carolina.

"Well, I doubt they will take our desires into consideration!"

"Someone will," said Carolina confidently. "You'll see." For although she was dying to tell Penny that Kells was here, that he was even now advancing upon them, studying them gravely with his level gray gaze, she dared not. For Kells could only be here in Havana on some desperate mission and she would not give him away for anything!

"You have more confidence in this crowd than I have," Penny was saying as her gaze raked the front row. "I'd say that one over there is a brothel keeper, and those two beside him—God knows what. We'll be lucky if we get through this night, Carol!"

"Oh, I'm sure we'll be bought by someone nice." Carolina felt she could give Penny at least this much encouragement without endangering Kells.

Penny peered down at her younger sister in astonishment. Had she taken leave of her senses? Someone *nice?* They'd be lucky if a whip weren't lain across their backs before the sun went down! Because neither of them were going to submit very easily.

"Well, at least we aren't to be the first ones sold—we'll get to see what happens to the others," she muttered, as a blowzy blonde with broken teeth—got when she stepped in the way of a bottle during a marathon drinking bout in Nassau—was led into the sunlight. "The bidding seems brisk," muttered Penny. "Floss fetched a good price. What was all that talk at the beginning of the auction?"

"Oh, they were talking about how we were being offered as house servants, most of us not being strong enough for work in the fields," Carolina replied cheerfully. She could not resist smiling in Kells's direction. He was looking straight at her with no expression at all upon his strong features.

"Housework, ha!" Penny's tone was scornful. "That fellow who bought Floss is already pinching her bottom—and she's *giggling!*" she added in disgust.

"Yes, well, maybe she thinks she can avoid doing any work at all if she's friendly enough!" Carolina said blithely.

Once again Penny gave her a dazed look. The heat, the strain must have unhinged Carolina's mind, she was thinking. She hoped the same man *would* buy them both—her sister was going to need taking care of!

A frowzy redhead was sold to desultory bidding, and a sulky young girl who looked as though she'd been crying was next. After her came a sultry brunette, and the bidding grew more enthusiastic.

"I think we're next," said Penny, and the crowd parted to let the governor's driver through.

He moved directly to the auctioneer and muttered in his ear. The auctioneer looked startled, but he nodded. He motioned Carolina and Penny to accompany the man, then turned to the crowd.

"Two of the women have been withdrawn from the sale," he announced, and there was a roar of dismay.

"What does it mean?" muttered Penny.

And Carolina, who had glanced quickly at Kells as they were led away and seen a frown cross his face, said anxiously, "I don't know." She turned her head and saw that he was turning his mount around and attempting to follow them. "I think maybe something's gone wrong," she told Penny.

"Stop talking in riddles," said her sister crossly. "*Everything* has gone wrong or we wouldn't be here."

The governor's driver saw a face he knew in the crowd. "Miguel!" He beckoned to the man and they had a low-voiced conversation—too low for Carolina to hear, even though she was straining to try to catch the words. The two women were promptly handed over to the newcomer, a short heavyset individual dressed as a servant. He took them each firmly by the wrist and led them away through a crowd that parted to let them pass and stared after them in curiosity.

"The governor's servant," Carolina heard one of them say, and she froze in fright. Had she been recognized as the Silver Wench? It seemed impossible that she would not be, for so many Spanish prisoners had spent time on Tortuga and then been returned to Havana. Did this mean that she would be imprisoned—and Penny, too, because she had rashly called out that Penny was her sister?

She was somewhat relieved when it was not the portals of one of the forbidding forts, but the portals of a small private house on the Plaza de Armas through which she and Penny were led by their silent guide.

They found themselves in a cool tile-floored hallway, and passed on through a small central courtyard into a rude kitchen. Plainly whoever had built the house had cared more for show and had lavished little thought or money on the back of the house.

Their silent escort called out "Juana," and there was an answering call from the small courtyard at the back, which they could glimpse from the kitchen.

A moment later a big comfortable woman in an apron lumbered in and surveyed the newcomers. Carolina listened closely to their rapid conversation.

"What are they saying?" demanded Penny.

"They are saying that I am to stay here to await Don Diego's pleasure and you—*you* are to go to the governor's house!" Carolina gave her sister a blank look.

"What did I tell you?" Penny grinned impishly, for these better surroundings had restored her sense of humor. "I'll end up the mistress of the governor yet!"

"Oh, Penny!" Carolina was impatient. "How can you make jokes at a time like this?" She turned again, listening to the conversation, for the big woman seemed to be protesting. "She says the governor's house is next door and why should *I* be kept here in an empty house? And the man is saying the house will not be empty"—Carolina's voice quivered—"that the governor has given Don Diego Vivar the house—oh, Penny, the governor has given *me* to Don Diego!"

"Ask if he's handsome," Penny said instantly, and then, "Well, don't just stand there looking so stricken, Carolina. What else are they saying?"

"Oh, nothing. The old woman asked what am I to do here, and the man is saying he does not know, that it is not his business to know, that it is his business only to take orders and that *she* had better do as she is told or the governor will have her beaten! And *she* is saying that the governor is too soft-hearted to beat anyone or he would surely have had *him* beaten long since."

"Well, that's good news," Penny said cheerfully. "I'd certainly prefer a soft-hearted captor! Things are looking up!"

Their escort pointed to a wooden bench and Carolina

sank down. He then seized Penny's wrist and began marching her back the way they had come.

At the entrance to the inner courtyard Penny turned and her impish smile flashed. "Good luck with Don Diego!" she called.

Carolina gave her a black look and said nothing. Don Diego, indeed! Where was Kells?

At precisely that moment the man Havana knew as Don Diego Vivar had managed, through a crowd of people who were now dancing in the street, to overtake the governor's carriage which was heading home.

"Your Excellency. Dona Marina," he greeted them. "Might I inquire what happened to the two women who were withdrawn from the sale?"

"Ah, Don Diego, well might you ask!" He clapped the younger man jovially on the back. "Captain Avila, who commanded one of the galleons in the attack on New Providence, has told me that the pair of them are sisters and that the blonde has rendered some assistance to Spain. I thought it merciful to spare them the humiliation of public sale and of possibly finding harsh masters. The tall redhead I will find a place for in my own household. The blonde shall become your house servant, for I saw you eyeing her!"

The gray eyes gave the portly governor an inscrutable look. "But I am living in *your* house, Your Excellency," he protested. "In what manner—"

"Oh, do not be tedious, Don Diego. I own the small house next door to my own, which has recently become vacant since the Mendoza family left for Spain. It is yours to enjoy until I again find suitable tenants—bachelor quarters, eh?" He slapped Don Diego on the back again. "And you will require more than old Juana to take care of you. True, she will cook your meals, but you will need someone to serve them, someone to tidy up, and make your bed—" *And sleep in it with you.* The inference was clear from the leer on the older man's countenance. "So I have sent the blonde to your new quarters. She now awaits your return."

"Ah," murmured the tall gentleman. "I am indeed beholden." He seemed to struggle with himself. "Your Excellency," he began diffidently, "you have been more than a friend to me. Indeed you have treated me as a son."

"Now, now, my boy, none of that!" was the governor's good-natured response. "Had I had a son, I could only hope that he would be as valorous as you."

"I am in debt to you for everything I possess," continued Don Diego seriously. "This horse, the very clothes on my back. And now this generous offer of a house and servants. I can only say that when my funds arrive from Spain, I will reimburse you twice over."

"No, no," said the governor unhappily, for he had hoped to reduce the gentleman in Marina's eyes, and Don Diego's remarks were undermining that purpose. "We will speak of it later, Don Diego. Go now and investigate your new home. It is the house just to the right of my own—the one the Mendozas just left."

"I know the house," said Don Diego. He smiled rather fondly at them both. "If I may take my leave of you?"

The governor graciously waved him away. His arm had hardly come to rest before a low, furious voice beside him said, "Oh, Father, how could you *do* that? Send Don Diego away from us and give him a bawd to keep him company?"

"I do not know that she is a bawd," the governor said airily. "I know only that she is a buccaneer's woman. Captain Avila said that she had shown kindness to captured Spanish sailors and soldiers on Tortuga."

"I can guess what kind of kindness she showed them!" snapped Marina bitterly.

"Marina." The face her doting father turned to his

child was suddenly stern. "It seems I have been remiss in your upbringing. Henceforth you will show me proper respect and you will *not* question my decisions."

Doña Marina slumped down in her seat and sulked the entire way home. Her father hoped he had done the right thing. He wanted to put some distance between his daughter and Don Diego—at least until inquiries could be made about him in Spain. But he had not wished to incite rebellion.

And that was definitely rebellion he saw glowing in his spoiled fifteen-year-old daughter's eyes.

Carolina meanwhile was having an anxious time of it.

"Who is Don Diego?" she asked Juana.

"A caballero who has been living at the governor's house."

Carolina was bewildered. "Well, then why—"

"I do not understand it any better than you do, señorita. But like Miguel, I take orders. While the governor leased this house to the Mendozas, I cooked for them. Now perhaps I will cook for Don Diego—who knows?" She shrugged and sat down and began to shell a large bowl of beans.

"I think I will look about," Carolina said nervously.

"Look all you like. You will find I have kept the place clean enough! And with hardly anyone to help me!"

Carolina moved into the central courtyard. It was in her mind to escape—but escape to where? Suddenly she remembered Ramona Valdez and she retraced her steps to the kitchen where old Juana looked up.

"Perhaps you could tell me about Doña Ramona?" she asked diffidently. "Where is she?"

Old Juana looked up at her without comprehension.

"The governor's wife," prodded Carolina.

"Ah! *That* Doña Ramona." Juana's puzzled face cleared. "She is long gone. Her husband fell ill and took her back to Spain. That was two governors ago. The one we have now is Governor Corrubedo."

It was a blow to learn that Ramona Valdez would not be here to help her, but, "Does the present governor have a wife?" she asked, thinking of Penny.

Juana nodded. "A wife under the sod," she said. "But he does not remarry. No one understands why."

Thank God for gossipy servants! thought Carolina. "Does he have children, this new governor?"

"One daughter only. You would think the sun rose and set by her slightest word! The governor grants her every wish."

"How old is she?"

"Doña Marina? Perhaps fifteen—I do not know."

And she will give you trouble, Penny, thought Carolina.

She went back to thinking about her own troubles.

"What is Don Diego like?"

"Handsome." Old Juana waved a long string bean at her. "A true caballero. Dashing!"

And she might just as well add *virile, demanding!* thought Carolina glumly. She could see she might well have some trouble with Don Diego. She bit her lip. Across the kitchen, lying on the shelf of a low cupboard, she could see a butcher knife. She eased over toward it under the pretense of scanning the cupboards.

"You keep the kitchen well, Juana," she approved, and old Juana lifted her chin. The woman who was speaking might be dressed in ragged and mended clothes at the moment but she had the face of an angel and a figure to match. Juana little doubted that before the week was out she would be wearing silks and Don Diego would be dancing to her tune.

"I do my best," she said.

Carolina had reached the cupboard now. She turned about and faced Juana. "Can you describe Don Diego?" she challenged.

"Tall. Dark. A soldier's bearing."

Carolina was leaning back on her arms on the

cupboard. Now she cautiously eased one of them back so that she could grasp the knife's wooden hilt. "And women, Juana? Is he fond of women?"

"As fond as most men, I suppose." Juana chuckled suddenly. "It is the governor's daughter who is fond of *him!* Their servants have told me so. They say she tries never to let him out of her sight. And that she becomes very angry whenever Doña Jimena rides by."

"And who may Doña Jimena be?" Carolina had the knife now.

"Doña Jimena is the most beautiful woman in the world," stated Juana. "All Havana throws itself at her feet. I have heard the governor say that men have gone to their death happy just because Doña Jimena Menendez smiled at them!" She gave Carolina a sly look, as if to say, *You will have your work cut out for you!*

"And does Don Diego fancy this Doña Jimena?" Carolina asked idly, moving away from the cupboard with the knife behind her.

"Who does not fancy Doña Jimena?" Juana said, shrugging. "Doña Jimena has the blackest hair, the brightest eyes, the whitest teeth in all of New Spain."

"Is she married?" Carolina was moving away from the cupboard now with the knife concealed in the folds of her yellow calico skirt.

"Oh, yes, she is married." Juana's head nodded. "To the richest man in Havana—Don Carlos Menendez."

"And what does Don Carlos Menendez think of all this?" She must keep Juana's attention so that she would not miss the knife.

"Don Carlos thinks nothing—at least he says nothing. He is too blinded by Doña Jimena's beauty to protest!"

"You are saying that Doña Jimena has many lovers?" Carolina was easing her footsteps toward the door.

"Ah, *si, si!*" Juana was emphatic about that!

"And one of them is Don Diego?" Carolina had

almost reached the palm-shaded inner courtyard as she spoke.

"About that I do not know," old Juana said firmly, and bent to the shelling of her beans. Let the blonde minx find out for herself whether they were lovers! She knew no more, after all, than what the gossipy housemaids next door told her when, shirking their duties, they skipped away from the governor's "palace," as everyone called it, and perched on the benches or wooden table of Juana's kitchen and nibbled her tortillas and giggled over the doings in the governor's household.

Thus edified by back-stairs gossip, Carolina passed on through the courtyard with its tinkling stone fountain and toward the front of the house.

Basically the house had on its first floor only its wide, tiled entrance hall—cool and with only very high grillwork windows to permit air in but to keep out the hot tropical sun—which could serve as a reception room; the large central court, part of which was covered by an open gallery that ran entirely around the courtyard; and the capacious kitchen. Obviously dining was meant to be accomplished in the shade of the palms of the courtyard or in the cool recesses of the gallery behind low stone pillars. The second floor was reached by means of a tiled stairway from the courtyard.

She decided she had best secrete the knife upstairs while she decided what to do—after all, if she stayed in the house tonight with the entrancing Don Diego, whom all the women were after, she well might need to use it!

With that in mind she ran lightly up the stairs and surveyed the two bedrooms—one at the back from which a narrow back stair opened down into the kitchen—and one which occupied the whole front of the house and was reached by means of the tiled unroofed corridor which encircled the inner courtyard.

The Mendozas obviously had taken most of the furnishings with them when they left for all the rooms were sparsely furnished with—in the main—only huge heavy objects difficult to move. There was an enormous cedar wardrobe—empty, for Carolina looked—and a big dark carved square bed in each of the upstairs bedrooms. The Mendozas obviously could not have had a large family. But despite their lack of furnishings, the rooms were airy and pleasant with their white-washed walls and high ceilings. The mattresses were hard but adequate—she glanced at them nervously, remembering that this was Don Diego's lair.

She was still looking for a good place to secrete the knife and had just decided that beneath the mattress at the head of the big bed in the front room was probably the best place when she heard the sound of a booted foot on the stair.

That would be Don Diego!

Carolina froze. He was taking the steps three at a time—there would be no time to hide the knife. She thrust it behind her to be hidden in the folds of her wide skirt. Her heart was pounding.

It seemed to her that he took a long time coming up the stairs. Her heart thudded with each footfall and she clutched the knife with a sense of doom.

She would be polite, she told herself. She would greet this strange Spaniard civilly—oh, God, if only this were not his bedroom!

She steeled herself as the footsteps paused momentarily outside her door—then came on again.

THE HOUSE ON
THE PLAZA DE ARMAS

Chapter 19

Don Diego Vivar stepped briskly into the big front bedroom—and checked himself at sight of Carolina, who, in her excitement, dropped the knife.

It clattered to the floor, and a cool voice as familiar to her as her own said in astonishment, "You will have no need of a weapon this day. *I* will not besiege you!"

"Oh, it *is* you!" she cried. "I was so afraid it would not be!" She threw herself into his arms, and those arms closed about her. She was sobbing against his chest now, that broad familiar chest, and hearing the strong masculine beating of his heart. Between sobs her voice was low and vibrant, choked with emotion. "When I saw you at the market, it was wonderful. I was sure you would buy me, I couldn't wait—" She pulled his face down to hers and silenced anything he might have to say with her soft eager lips. She could feel his response to her, feel the tension in the lean hard body she clutched ecstatically to her own. She could feel his swift response to her kisses, the leisurely delightful exploration of his tongue between her parted lips, the sudden bulge of his masculinity.

His hands were roving over her back now . . . his lips left hers and trailed tantalizingly down her white throat, across her smooth bosom . . . he was loosening the hooks that held her bodice . . . it was slipping away.

Her eyes were closed, and tears of joy sparkled on her long lashes. Her face, which had been so pale at the approach of what she thought was an unknown stranger, was flushed and hot to his touch.

"When they took me away from the sale, I was afraid you would not be able to find me." Her voice was a rushing gasp as she struggled to help him remove her gown. "Oh, do you think we would dare to—here?"

"Why not here?" he said, and she opened her eyes to see that the expression in his gray eyes was as hot as her own.

"Yes—of course." She tried to laugh but her laughter was tremulous, emotion-laden, as she felt her clothing fall away. *"Oh, I have waited so long!* It seems a lifetime!"

"Then you will wait no longer!"

He swept her up in his arms, a naked writhing sprite, tearing at his shirt, covering him with kisses—and fell with her to the big square bed. There were no sheets and the fabric of the mattress was coarse against her bare skin, but Carolina hardly felt it. Had she thought the mattress hard but adequate? Indeed it was wonderful!

It was wonderful because the arms that held her were the *right* arms, the lips that silenced her soft broken murmurs were the *right* lips, the lean body that lay atop her own, giving her such joy, was the body of her buccaneer!

His trousers were open now, he had thrust within her. She thrilled to his touch and her own body, fired with the same heat, took up the rhythm and surged with his, giving him back thrust for thrust in an agony of ecstasy. Away from her sped all the terrors and heartbreak of the past, gone forever in his strong embrace.

The moments sped by—delicious golden moments snatched from time. She had lost him, but she had him back again! Her heart was singing and the joyful exuberance of her lovemaking kept pace with that silent lovesong. Every breath, every rasp of his skin against her own thrilled her. And she who had thought never to love again gave of herself unstintingly and felt an open-hearted joy at her masterful lover's deft way with a wench.

Not even the sea had been able to keep her from him, not earthquakes or tidal waves! *She was back in his arms again!*

But even joy must end sometime and at last, reluctantly, her elegant lover slid away from her and lay beside her, lightly caressing her quivering body, still tingling in the afterglow of passion.

Impulsively Carolina turned over and gathered herself up, resting on her hands just above him. The tips of her soft breasts brushed his lightly furred chest and her bright hair spilled down over his pillow, over his shoulders, in a silken skein as she looked down at him lovingly. For she wanted—no, she *needed* to fill her eyes with him, to reassure herself that this was not all only a lovely dream from which she would soon wake.

"Oh, Kells," she whispered. "I thought—we all thought—that you were dead. Hawks thought so, I thought so! A battered ship that looked like the *Sea Wolf* was being rowed into the harbor just as the earthquake struck, and it was swept ashore and went down among the houses." Her soft hurried voice rushed on. "And Hawks found someone from your crew—he must have been delirious to say what he did—who told him a wild tale about the *Sea Wolf* fighting the *Santo Domingo* and another galleon—and of course we both believed it since he was dying as he told the tale. And I left Hawks in Port Royal and sailed for England, only our ship was caught up in the French and Spanish raid on New Providence and then Penny and I were brought here—and oh, I can't believe it's really you. I've been mourning you for days. I was certain I'd never see you again!"

Impetuously she hugged him.

And was aware suddenly that she was not being hugged back. Indeed she was being put gently away from him as her lover now sat up. He was looking at her warily, and now he rose to his feet, towering over her as he swiftly adjusted his trousers, stuffed his shirt tail back into those trousers.

"Señorita," he said regretfully, "I think you are under a misapprehension."

Carolina, crouched naked upon the square mattress, her hair a tousled halo, looked up at him in bewilderment.

"What—misapprehension?"

"A misapprehension that you know me."

"But I do!"

"When I saw you looking at me on the street a short while ago, I thought I saw a hot light in your eyes. In that"—he shrugged, his gaze lightly raking the lovely young body that had been pressed against his own with such ardor only moments before—"I was not mistaken. And I thought," he went on ruefully, "that it was my masculine charm that had won you to such a gallant display as just now." He sighed. "No woman's arms have ever lured me as yours have today, but it seems you have mistaken me for somebody else."

Carolina stared at him, stunned. She could not be hearing this! It was all a bad dream!

The tall man before her squared his shoulders, and his voice held a regretful note of humor. "It is true that

I was aboard the *Santo Domingo,* but in all else you are mistaken. I am honored to be so warmly greeted, but I have never seen you before in my life."

Life seemed to stop.

Outside a seabird screamed. From the courtyard below came the faint tinkle of the fountain, the sound of palm fronds rustling.

Feeling as if she had suddenly been pushed underwater, Carolina fought to absorb the blow of his words—coming so swiftly, so devastatingly after the wild passion of his lovemaking.

It had to be a joke—some terrible joke that life was playing on her.

"Kells," she pleaded, "don't trifle with me. I nearly went mad with grief when I thought you were dead. I—"

There was a chill in his voice now, a cold light in those gray eyes that had so often looked upon her with such tenderness. *"What did you call me?"*

"I called you 'Kells' for that is who you are," faltered Carolina.

"Kells!" He spoke the name like an oath. "That is the name of the most infamous buccaneer in all the Caribbean, is it not?"

"The most *famous,*" she countered stiffly. "As *you* should certainly know!"

He ran long, raking fingers through his dark hair as he frowned down at her. A variety of emotions fought for mastery on his lean countenance. Then, "What do they call you?" he asked abruptly.

Carolina gave him a look of vast reproach. "Don't you remember?" she asked, wounded.

"I do not," he stated flatly. "Indeed I have never heard your name spoken, señorita—I am sure of it!"

"It is Carolina!" she cried, stung. She leaped up and stood facing him.

"And do you have a last name?" he said inexorably.

She stiffened at that and tossed her head back. As if suddenly aware of her nakedness when *he* was clothed, she reached down for her chemise and struggled into it. Her dress was half over her head before she said bitterly, "Perhaps you also do not recall that before I married you my name was Carolina Lightfoot?"

"Before—?" He was looking at her, thunderstruck.

"Before I married you," she repeated grimly. "A step that I am now beginning to regret!" Her temper was rising and her fingers trembled as she fastened her hooks.

He shook his head as if to clear it. "Señorita," he said formally, "I suppose your lapse is understandable because you have been under some strain—"

A terrible fear was beginning to settle over Carolina, chilling her veins. "I have not been under a strain!" she snapped. "At least not enough to make me lose my mind as you seem to be suggesting! And I can certainly recognize my own husband, no matter how odd the place we happen to meet!"

"Hush," he said, and put his fingers gently to her lips.

She understood then and was horrified at her lapse. The walls had ears! Dear God, had she already compromised his disguise? How could she have been such a fool? He was only *pretending* to be Don Diego, and somewhere—perhaps through a panel in the governor's house that allowed people there to hear what they were saying—enemy ears were listening!

"I'm sorry," she whispered against his fingers.

He was speaking to her now in an even voice, colorless, but driving in every word. "I have no wish to harm you but you must try to take in what I am saying. It seems you may have suffered a loss and for that I am truly sorry. But as God is my witness, I am Diego

Vivar, late of Castile. You are beautiful enough, Señorita Lightfoot, to imprint yourself on a man's memory forever. But you have made no imprint on mine."

"Yes, yes," she said hastily, drawing away from him and looking about her as if to establish where the listeners could be hiding. Her eyes fell upon the big square bed with its hard but adequate mattress. "Where do we sleep?" she asked hopefully, and wondered where the bed linens were.

"*I* sleep here," he said firmly. "And you, Señorita Lightfoot, will find yourself a room at the back of the house. We will cease these childish games of recognition where there is none. Tonight you will share my table and if your manners are good enough, you will be permitted to share it in future. But I accept a lady in my bed only at my own invitation—and *never* in the mistaken assumption that I am somebody else." His lips twisted in a slight grimace that she remembered only too well. "I would be loved for myself alone, dear lady. That is how matters stand with me. But you will call me Don Diego, for that is who I am—Don Diego Vivar of Castile."

The terrible chill she had felt before crept over her once again. Only this time the ice seemed to touch her very heart.

This man looked like Kells, he moved like Kells, he spoke like Kells, he made love like Kells, the very touch of him was Kells to the flesh. *And yet he was not Kells.* He said so. And in a manner that she was forced to believe was the truth.

This was not Kells. This was somebody else. Kells had a double in Spain!

And that double had come to Havana . . . and she had found him . . . made love to him.

Thinking he was Kells.

It had been a long day, a day filled with grief and fear and passionate abandon and too much heat and too little food. And now this wonderful resurrection of her lover had been snatched away from her. The disappointment was sudden and overpowering.

Carolina gave the tall frowning man before her a dizzy accusing look and then her legs seemed to give way like butter.

He reached out a long arm and caught her as she fell.

Chapter 20

When Carolina came to, she was being supported by Don Diego's arm, and water was being dashed in her face by a scandalized Juana, who said disbelievingly, "She *fainted?* But she was fine just a few minutes ago!"

"And fine again," said Don Diego, laying a sputtering Carolina down upon the bare mattress. "I think she is in need of food."

"Dinner will soon be ready," said Juana in a stiff voice that chided, *but not immediately*.

"Bring us some wine, then."

"I will have to go next door to the governor's—"

"I will go myself."

Don Diego rose, and old Juana waited until his boots had clattered down the stairs before she remarked, "Well, you *are* a strange one. You're up, you're down!" She glowered at Carolina, lying there white and exhausted. "Looking all done-in isn't going to get you into his bed!"

Carolina pushed herself up on one elbow. "That will

be enough, Juana," she said with what dignity she could muster—for after all, the servants must not be allowed to get the upper hand, otherwise they would rule you! "I was overcome by the—the excessive heat outside and grew a bit lightheaded, that's all."

No need for Juana to know what had really happened!

Juana gave her a skeptical look. "If you say so."

"And I will see if we cannot get you some help," said Carolina with a bright smile. "This house is too much for you."

Juana lumbered downstairs shaking her head. There was some as wasted no time moving in! She could not wait to tell the serving girls from the governor's house about this—how they would titter! And then one of them would ask archly what was going to happen when this striking new wench with the hair like white metal collided with the governor's daughter and the beautiful and lecherous Doña Jimena! Juana's old face lit up in a grim wrinkled smile. There would be doings worth reporting in this old house soon, she'd warrant!

Don Diego was gone but a short time. He came back bearing a bottle and two wineglasses. Into one of them he splashed some golden liquid.

"A very fine Canary," he told her. "Drink it. It will give you strength."

Carolina took a sip. "I think I would prefer food," she said faintly.

"The governor's servants are bringing us food now," he said. "Listen—you can hear them moving about downstairs. Oh, and the governor sends you this." He gestured with his arm and she realized that he had been carrying, thrown over his arm, a flame-red dress of light voile and a yellow petticoat. "I do not know where he found such bright garments, for his daughter wears only white, but he sends it to you with his compliments and his thanks for having aided the cause of Spain." He looked at her intently. "In what way have you aided the cause of Spain?" he asked curiously.

"I suppose because I used to take fruit to the Spanish captives on Tortuga—and because I befriended a Spanish girl once who was cast away upon our shores in Virginia."

His hard face softened. "So it seems you have a kind heart. . . ."

She gave him a resentful look. How dared he look so like Kells and not be Kells? "I am not so sure," she said wearily.

He grinned. "I will have a bath sent up to you, and if you will be good enough to put on this gown, when you are ready you may come down and sup with me."

Carolina kept on staring at the door after he had left. The resemblance was so striking—*in all ways*—that she still could not believe he was not Kells.

It was one of the governor's servants who brought up her bath—and with it towels and a sponge and scented soap and a new chemise which Carolina looked at doubtfully. It was both wide and short.

"It belonged to the governor's daughter," snickered the serving girl. "We was told to bring it and so we did, but she'll be fit to be tied when she hears!" She snickered again.

Carolina gave her a level look. She was not going to be put on a par with those women who had just been sold in the marketplace!

"That will be all I require, I believe," she said. "Unless perhaps the governor could send us some bed linen? We will need enough for both the front bedroom and the back."

The girl looked affronted. "Yes, your high and mightiness!" she said.

"And please close the door when you go out," Carolina added tranquilly. "Oh, wait—what is your name?"

"Luz," was the sulky response.

"Yes—Luz. And I am Señorita Lightfoot, Luz. Thank you for being so prompt in bringing up my bath. Tell me, the woman who was with me, the one with red hair"—for Carolina could not be sure what name Penny had chosen to use—"how does she fare?"

"I expect you'll see for yourself since she's just now coming up the stairs with your bed linens!" snapped Luz as she flounced through the door.

A moment later Penny burst into the room—a very much changed Penny, for her bright hair was tied back into a pink silk turban and her tight-fitting men's trousers and torn shirt had been replaced by a white bodice of some thin material that was cut surprisingly low for a household that had its roots in strait-laced Spain. It must be the island influence—the hot sun of the tropics must have melted some of the cold Castilian reserve! And encasing Penny's slim hips was a thin black taffeta kirtle that swirled around her bare feet—for no one had as yet provided her with a pair of slippers that fit.

"I have seen Don Diego!" cried Penny. "And you are in luck. He is shockingly attractive."

"Yes—shockingly." Carolina gave her sister a haggard look.

Penny was quick to note that look. Her sapphire eyes narrowed. "I seem to remember that Don Diego was the *caballero* you were staring at when you stumbled as we were being herded toward the market. Don't tell me you fell in love with him at first sight!"

Carolina swallowed.

"Or is it that—?" Sudden enlightenment flooded over Penny's strong features. "Carolina, does he look like someone else?" she asked softly.

"Yes," Carolina admitted miserably. "He reminds me . . ." She broke off, dragging a shaky hand across her eyes.

"Of Kells . . ." murmured Penny. "I remember being told that Kells was tall and dark—and deadly. And certainly Don Diego fits that description!" She studied her younger sister with compassion. "But you can't spend your life grieving, Carol. Don Diego seems quite charming. You must let him make it up to you, patch your life up again. Indeed he has a notable effect on women. Marina, the governor's daughter, leaped to her feet, all smiles and blushes, when Don Diego came dashing in. Obviously she thought he'd come to see *her!* She sat back like a thundercloud and sulked when Don Diego announced you'd been struck down by the heat. The governor rose to the occasion, and you can expect a solid stream of assistance from that quarter. It seems Don Diego rates very high with the governor of this fair city!"

It was on the tip of Carolina's tongue to tell Penny all she knew, but she thought better of it. On shipboard she had been too grief-stricken to talk of Kells and now—she would wait. She would talk at greater length with Don Diego. She still could not rid herself of the forlorn hope that he was really Kells in disguise, and that he would presently find a quiet corner and sweep her up into his arms and explain everything and claim her once again as his own dear love.

"How do you like the governor?" she asked wearily—more to push away her own heartbreaking thoughts than from any real interest. At the moment all she could see before her was one dark uncaring face—Kells's face, disclaiming her.

"I don't know how well I like the governor yet," Penny said meditatively. "But I can tell you one thing, he has a vicious daughter. She left the room like a hurricane and rushed upstairs to her bedchamber and we could hear glass breaking all over the place. She must have swept her dressing table clean!"

"Did she come out again?" asked Carolina, remembering Juana's, *It is the governor's daughter who is fond of* him!

"Yes," said Penny. "When someone went up to report to her that Doña Jimena was riding by—whoever *that* is!"

"Doña Jimena Menendez," murmured Carolina. "Wife to the richest man in Havana." She remembered Juana's, *They say she tries never to let him out of her sight. And that she becomes very angry whenever Doña Jimena rides by.*

"You've picked up a great deal of information in a short time," Penny observed wonderingly.

"Yes, one does sometimes in a strange place." Carolina pushed aside her own problems. "Do you think you are going to be all right over there?" she asked.

"Oh, more than all right," Penny said, "except that I may have to box the governor's daughter's ears. When she came out of her room she was in such a temper that she threw a rose jar at me."

"That was because Doña Jimena was riding by," Carolina said wisely.

"Indeed?" Penny sounded indignant. "Well, whoever Doña Jimena is, she certainly brings out the Devil in the governor's daughter."

As doubtless will I, Carolina thought wryly. *And perhaps with less reason!*

"Anyway, everything you can think of is being sent over: more bed linens, extra towels, dishes, pots and pans, cutlery, pillows, candlesticks, candelabra, candles—I was amazed to see all the things they were bringing. Don't you hear the commotion downstairs? Here, step into your bath before it gets cold! I'll close the door."

"*Why* do you think the governor is doing it?" asked

Carolina, as she slid out of her clothes—torn to rags by her experiences—and slipped gratefully into the warm water.

"Why?" Penny said carelessly. "I'm told that Don Diego is some great hero and that he arrived here nearly dead and was brought back to life in the governor's house. I suppose the governor is proud of his achievement of bringing someone back from the dead."

"Or perhaps," said Carolina carefully, "he thinks that Don Diego might one day marry his daughter."

"That's possible, too," said Penny, stretching her long arms and throwing herself down on the bed. "I'm told he treats him like a son."

"Son-in-law," Carolina said woodenly.

Penny looked at her with bright interest. "Do I detect an interest in Don Diego for yourself? He's certainly gorgeous!"

"Don Diego and I have come to an understanding," she told Penny stiffly. "He will sleep at this end of the hall and I will sleep at the other."

"Oh, but it's such a short distance between!" laughed Penny. "So you told him how things were going to be, did you?"

"No, it was his idea," Carolina said truthfully. She reddened, remembering how she had lain in his arms.

"Indeed?" Penny's russet brows shot up. "Don Diego has fallen in my estimation," she said. "He looked to me to have more blood than that!"

"He has plenty of blood," said Carolina. "I think—it was something I said."

"Oh, and what was that?" demanded Penny.

Carolina, already sudsy, stood up and poured water from a rinsing pitcher over herself before she spoke. "I can't remember," she said dismissively. Penny would hoot with laughter if she knew his decision had come about after Carolina asked, *Where do we sleep?*

"Here, let me help you with that." Penny got up and took the rinsing pitcher away from Carolina and poured water carefully over Carolina's back. "Dinner will be on the table any minute," she reported. "I think you'd better not take too much time with your toilette. We wouldn't want to keep Don Diego waiting!"

Carolina didn't answer. Where Don Diego was concerned, she was very torn. She wanted to see him and yet she dreaded seeing him—it was all very confusing.

"And now, to get you dressed in these," said Penny, lifting up the chemise as Carolina toweled herself dry. "God's teeth, this was made for a dumpy girl!"

"The governor's daughter," said Carolina.

"She isn't exactly dumpy, though."

"Well-rounded," said Carolina.

"Bursting her stays," amended Penny.

They both laughed.

"She's only fifteen," said Carolina. "She still may grow."

"But in which direction?" wondered Penny.

They laughed again. And that laughter made Carolina feel much better. The tension was released. She was skating on very thin ice and must watch her every step, but somehow, despite everything, her world had improved. And it was all because *a man who looked like Kells* had entered it. . . .

"Well, the chemise is too short but who'll see it under the petticoat?" said Penny, stepping back critically from a barefoot Carolina.

"I don't care if the petticoat is too short," Carolina said nervously. "But I *do* hope it isn't too long. I couldn't bear to go around tripping over it."

"You mean you don't sew any better than you did back at Level Green? Well, neither do I—but I've no doubt there'll be expert sempstresses hidden away somewhere in the governor's house!"

But the petticoat turned out to be a shade too short rather than too long. Carolina was very pleased.

"And now the overdress—if it was made for the same woman—should be rather a good fit." As she spoke, Penny was slipping the red voile over Carolina's head.

They both held their breath until the hooks in the back were all fastened. Then:

"It's a fit!" Penny cried, joyfully.

"It feels a little too tight across the bust," complained Carolina.

"Just give it a tug down." Penny seized the bodice and almost ripped the material with her sharp pull but it did lower the neckline considerably and allowed Carolina's soft breasts to round up delightfully above it.

"I wouldn't pull it up into panniers if I were you," advised Penny, walking catlike around her on her bare feet. "That petticoat leaves something to be desired. I mean, it's just plain yellow linen, and yet glimpsed through the folds of red voile as you move—"

"It will look like something aflame," guessed Carolina, whirling about.

"Yes," Penny said, adding gravely, "You look lovely, Carolina." *And woefully distressed,* she might have added. *For all you're putting a brave face on things.* Suddenly she noticed the butcher knife lying on the floor. "Where did that thing come from? It belongs in the kitchen."

"I brought it upstairs when Juana wasn't looking," Carolina said soberly. "I thought I might need it as a weapon. That was—before I met Don Diego," she added. "In fact, I dropped it when I saw him."

Penny blinked at her. "*That* must have been a shock to him," she murmured. "Coming home to find you waiting for him with a knife in your hand!"

"Well—I didn't understand," mumbled Carolina, unwilling to explain.

"Remember to smile when you go downstairs,"

instructed Penny. "We're better off than the lot we came with, you know!"

"Yes." Carolina shuddered. "I hate to think what will happen to some of them tonight."

Penny's russet brows elevated. "*Whatever* happens to them," she said succinctly, "it will be no worse than the things that happened to them *all the time* on New Providence."

Carolina looked up sharply at the inflection in Penny's voice. "You mean—"

"You don't want to hear about the things that happened on New Providence," Penny said softly. Her impish grin flashed. "Not everyone was smart enough to accept *matelotage!*"

A maid came to the door and stuck her head in to announce that dinner was ready.

"What did she say?" sighed Penny. "How I wish I'd paid more attention to learning Spanish when Ramona Valdez lived with us! I can't understand a word that's said in the governor's house!"

"She said it's time to go down to dinner," Carolina explained. "Come with me, Penny, and I'll present you to Don Diego."

Penny shrugged and together the two girls trailed downstairs.

Dusk had fallen—the swift violet dusk of the tropics. The candles had been lit and burned golden in the heavy iron candelabra the governor had sent over. To the man in black and silver who stood with his booted feet wide apart at the foot of the tile stairway, the two girls presented a picture of sharp contrasts: the tall statuesque redhead crisply gowned in black and white, and the daintier blonde in red voile that floated out over her yellow petticoat. She looked like a candle flame, he thought suddenly. Glowing red and yellow below and with a frostier tip—that was her hair, moonlight-fair in this dusky light.

"Ladies," he said, bowing deeply. "I am honored."

Penny beamed at him delightedly. It had been a long time since a man had made such an elegant leg to her.

Carolina swept him her deepest curtsy. "Penny," she said, speaking in English as she had with him all along. "This is my—my protector, Don Diego Vivar. May I present my sister, Señorita Pennsylvania Lightfoot."

"Rouge," said Penny wickedly.

Don Diego looked blank.

"It is just a nickname," Carolina said hastily. "We call her Penny at home."

"Señorita Penny," said Don Diego gravely, "will you not share our repast with us? The governor," he added, scanning the groaning board, "has sent enough, I believe, for ten. It would founder us to eat all that."

"I would like to, sir," Penny said airily. "But I fear I am expected back to dine with the governor." She turned to wink at Carolina, who hoped it was true. "I hope to see you tomorrow."

She left with skirts billowing, and Don Diego pulled back a chair and seated Carolina.

"You look lovely," he said, and sincerity rang in his voice. "Your buccaneer is a lucky man indeed."

"*Was,*" corrected Carolina, looking him squarely in the eye. "*Was* a lucky man."

He studied her as he poured a glass of port wine for her. "And do you wish to publicize the fact that you are now alone?"

"No," Carolina said hastily, deciding to follow his lead on anything that had to do with Kells. "Of course not. I will not speak of it again."

He gave her a contented look from across the table and sipped his port. "I had not thought. Perhaps you would prefer malmsey?"

"You are right," she said. "I *would* prefer it."

"I shall speak to the governor about it tomorrow,"

he said. "His wine cellars seem endless. Tell me," he said curiously, "about your life in Tortuga. Or is it Port Royal?"

"Both," Carolina said promptly. "On Tortuga I was very happy, but I did not know it until I left. In Port Royal I was not at all happy but I tried not to show it."

"And why was this?"

"Because my husband—by the fraud and deceit of others—was forced to continue in the buccaneering life which he had already forsworn."

Across from her the dark brows lifted, and a pair of keen gray eyes sparked with interest. "Indeed? Tell me about it."

"It would take a long time to tell you all, but Kells had received a king's pardon when the Marquess of Saltenham, for his own purposes, impersonated Kells and sank some English ships. Later Kells spared the marquess's life—because I asked it. You see my best friend, Reba Tarbell, was in love with the marquess and I did not want him killed. Her father has scads of money and I knew he could easily buy a pardon for the marquess, but Reba's mother hired false witnesses who swore the marquess was innocent, and Kells found himself once again beyond the law."

"A sad story," he commented. "You have my sympathy."

"I do not want your sympathy, sir," she said frankly. "It is your *understanding* that I desire."

"Indeed? I shall endeavor to see that you have it." He turned his attention to the hot spicy food.

Carolina had thought she was hungry but now she toyed with the food on her plate. There was so much she wanted to know about this man. . . .

"How did you come here?" she asked suddenly.

He shrugged. "By chance. All things are on the knees of the gods, señorita—where we go, what we do there. This Kells, was he so good to you, that you miss him so much?"

Her eyes brimmed suddenly with tears. "He was my life," she said huskily.

"Am I so much like him, then?" he murmured.

"Looking at you is like looking into a mirror and seeing—him," she said.

"Did he speak Spanish too?"

"Fluently. Castilian Spanish. He had spent some time in Spain."

He frowned. "Was he long in Spain?"

"He endured terrible things there," she said shortly. "It made him hate all Spaniards."

"Yes." He sighed. "A man in a green suit strikes us and the next man we see wearing a green suit—we strike him."

"It was a little more complicated than that," she said, stiffening.

"I see. You must defend him at all costs—his vices as well as his virtues. Well, that is loyalty. I am beginning to like you very much, Señorita Lightfoot. You have not only beauty—you have qualities."

"Why did you speak to me in English when first you met me?" she shot at him.

He leaned back, smiling lazily. "But I had been told you were English, señorita. Was I to address you in a language you might not understand?"

"But you heard me speak in Spanish at the slave auction—I called out that Penny and I were sisters and not to be separated."

"Forgive me. The roar of the crowd?" he countered smoothly.

"But you *must* have heard me," said Carolina, vexed. "You were seated on your horse not far away and you were looking straight at me!"

"Ah, you noticed me there." He sounded pleased.

"Of course, I noticed you!" snapped Carolina. "You

made yourself conspicuous by being mounted among a crowd of people on foot!"

"I was preparing to ride up into the hills," he explained. "But I thought better of it when I saw the crowd and then the procession of women being led in. I was puzzled by what was going on."

"I am sure the governor enlightened you!" she said bitterly. "And told you that we were all harlots from New Providence!"

"On the contrary." He leaned forward. "He described you and your sister as 'elegant.'" He smiled upon her. "And he was right!"

"Looking at you," she said, "I would almost believe Kells had a brother I do not know about."

"Perhaps he does," he said gently. "But that brother is assuredly not myself. Tell me," he added in a more curious tone, "did this Kells also dress like me?"

"No," she admitted. "Kells always wore gray. Or almost always. He cared little for clothes."

"Nor I, señorita," he said lightly. "And now you must attempt to do justice to this delicious repast the governor has prepared for us."

Carolina took a bite or two. It gave her strength. She looked up. "Yes, I wondered if you knew just why the governor is doing all this?" she asked frankly. "It seems rather a lot, don't you think?"

His lazy smile deepened. "I think perhaps the governor is more devious than I had imagined. I think he may intend to trick me into folly. . . ."

Carolina stared at him. The man had perception and depth. Again like Kells.

"What folly?"

"With a lady," he said with a caressing look at her. "A lady who flames like a candle."

In spite of herself, Carolina felt the color rise to her cheeks. "And why would he do that?" she inquired stiffly.

"Who knows? Perhaps it has suddenly come to him that he has a young daughter whose head could be turned by an older man."

"His daughter is fifteen and if she grows any plumper she may well burst her stays," Carolina said with asperity. "Her head could be turned by anyone!"

"Ah, you are harsh in your judgment." But his gray eyes were laughing.

"I have not seen her," admitted Carolina. "But it is her chemise I am wearing, and it is both too broad and too short!"

He laughed aloud.

"I am told that she also breaks dishes and whatnot when she is angry."

"You are correct," he said ruefully. "She makes a shambles of her bedroom. All the servants complain of it."

"Does the governor not chide her?"

"Rarely. He is an indulgent parent."

"Then he will allow her to marry whoever turns her head!"

"Not necessarily. A man may indulge his child in everything else, but he may balk at being presented with a son-in-law he considers unworthy of her."

"But *you* are worthy of her!" she blurted, and then looked down, red-faced, at the table.

"How kind of you to say so," he said lightly. "However, we are not speaking of me, of course."

"No, of course not!" She spoke too hurriedly to be believed.

There was a little silence and then Carolina spoke up. "I am told that the governor's daughter is *very* jealous of Doña Jimena Menendez."

"Indeed?" He twirled his glass idly. "And why would that be?"

"I think you know," she accused. "You *must* know." It occurred to her suddenly that she sounded like a jealous woman herself! She fell silent as the dessert was brought in. It was flan, a smooth creamy custard, very rich, and floating in a sauce that tasted of wine.

"I think I must beg your pardon," she said, lifting her spoon without interest. "Looking at your face, I keep forgetting that I do not know you well enough to say things like that."

"You are forgiven," he chuckled. "Indeed it is quite refreshing to hear what is said about one behind one's back."

"Kitchen gossip," she sniffed. "And like as not to be untrue."

"And like as not to be true," he countered.

Around them in the courtyard night had fallen. The fountain splashed in moonlight, as silvery as her pale shining hair. The candlelight picked up dancing gold and orange lights from the sheer red voile of her gown. The trade winds rustled the palms.

"The tropics are delightful, but I think I would prefer a cooler climate," he said, loosening the lace at his throat a little against the heat.

"The climate of Essex?" she suggested.

He shook his head. "Of Castile," he corrected, and his white teeth flashed.

They could almost have been back in their courtyard on Tortuga, she thought dreamily. It was so easy to imagine that this look-alike was really Kells, that he had returned to her in the evening, perhaps from careening one of his ships, and that golden-haired Katje would be coming in shortly to smile a good night to them before she went to bed.

"Mistress Lightfoot." He rose. "Will you stroll with me about the courtyard?"

And that was like Kells, too. She could almost hear him saying it. She rose as if she were in a trance and paced beside him about the stone-floored courtyard.

Suddenly in the shadow of a rustling palm he came to

a halt. He was in shadow, but Carolina stood bathed in brilliant moonlight that made mysterious lights glow like witches' lanterns in her silver eyes. The scent of bougainvillaea and roses and other flowers, pouring riotously over the railing and up the round stone pillars, was almost overpoweringly sweet. A night bird called sleepily.

Carolina waited, breathless.

And then it came—his lips on hers. Lightly brushing. And then more urgent, demanding. His arms went around her. She seemed to flutter in them, and then like the night bird, settled down into those arms as into a nest.

The kiss she gave him was a kiss of yearning.

I will pretend he is Kells, she told herself. *I will pretend. . . .*

His moving lips had pressed her own slightly parted lips wider apart now. His tongue was probing impudently, excitingly, leaving a trail of sweet fire where it touched. He brought her body toward him urgently until she was pressed so tightly to the black and silver of his coat—that coat he had worn, she suspected, to show respect for her, rather than choosing the comfort of just his white cambric shirt—that coat was pressed so tightly against her that its silver buttons bit into her soft flesh.

One of his hands moved downward along her back, tracing delicately her spinal column, and she moved softly against him, surrender and desire in every slightest movement of her lithe young body.

His lips left hers and began a fiery tracery down the white column of her neck, over the pushed-up tops of her breasts, rounded so invitingly by the tight neckline of her voile gown. His tongue had found the cleavage between her breasts and she quivered as its warm wet tip touched her.

A soft desperate moan escaped her.

"Oh, Kells," she whispered. "Kells . . ."

That hard body that held her captive stiffened. Abruptly he drew away from her—and when she would have surged forward, half-fainting with desire, he took her shoulders in his warm hands and held her away from him.

He looked down deep into her eyes but there was a hard note in his voice.

"Mistress Lightfoot," he said. "I want no warmed-over passion. I will not make love to you while you close your eyes and imagine that I am some other man!"

She flung away from him with a sob. "Is it my fault you look so like him?"

"No, nor is it mine," he said grimly. "Well, we may yet know one another better. But in the meantime, Mistress Lightfoot, let us go to bed—you to your bed, I to mine."

He bowed most courteously and led her up the stairs.

Sleep, for the passionate Virginia lass who could almost believe the counterfeit was real, was something she searched for desperately that night—and did not find.

PART TWO

The Dangerous Rival

The songs that they sing about us
May ever be less than true,
But however legend may flout us
My heart belongs to you!

THE HOUSE ON THE PLAZA DE ARMAS HAVANA, CUBA

Summer 1692

Chapter 21

Don Diego was gone when Carolina arose—she was almost glad because her feelings toward him were so mixed. She dressed and wandered downstairs where old Juana—all too aware that Carolina had dined with the master last night—gave her a subservient look.

"Why didn't you call me for breakfast?" asked Carolina.

"I would have," Juana responded honestly. "But Don Diego said you were not to be disturbed." She hesitated. "He also said that I was to accept your commands as *his* commands," she added reluctantly.

So she was to be mistress of the household! Carolina's spirits rose abruptly. She had been, it seemed, slave only for a day! She could only hope that Penny, next door at the governor's house, was faring as well.

"I see you have been furnished with a helper," she told Juana, noting the wide skirts and turban of a young island girl outside, bent over a washtub.

"With two helpers!" Juana declared proudly. Her

broad face broke into a smile. "That one's Nita and the other one's Luz. I just sent Luz on an errand," she added.

Carolina would have preferred not to have Luz, for whom she had formed a slight dislike yesterday, as a servant in her household, but then, she reminded herself, she must count her blessings—yesterday she had been alone and friendless in an enemy city, today she had a house and three servants!

"I think I will stroll about the town after breakfast, Juana," she told the old servant. "And you can be my *duena* and accompany me," she added gaily. "Unless you'd prefer to send Nita?"

"Oh, no, I'll go," Juana said hastily. Not for the world would she have missed this gorgeous wench's first stroll through Havana!

"Wear your Sunday best, Juana," Carolina told the smiling old woman when breakfast was over and the dishes were being carried out by soft-footed Nita, who gave her resplendent new mistress a shy look and bent her head above the crockery plates.

Accordingly, Juana appeared in somber black with her hair pulled back severely. She gasped at sight of Carolina.

Carolina, that day, was not on her best behavior. Her world had been overturned yesterday—more than once. She was in a wicked mood.

"Are you going out—like that?" Juana asked weakly.

Carolina whirled about in her red voile over yellow linen. Those brilliant colors alone, she knew, would mark her as something less than a lady in Havana, where patrician wives and daughters wore black—or white. It was a town of elegant mantillas and rustling dark silks and flashing fans and dark eyes and blue-black hair. Very well, lady she would not be! Instead of piling her hair up—as she would have done in Port

Royal—she had decided to comb it out and wear it down in a glistening white-gold shower over her shoulders and back. It was a spectacular effect she had created with her delicate pink and white skin, her enormous mass of blonde hair floating in the breeze, and the tight red voile bodice and rippling flamelike effect of her red and yellow skirts.

"There is just one thing," she murmured, looking down with a frown at her bare white bosom in her low-cut bodice. "I am sure to be sunburned if I wander about like this. Do you think you could send Nita next door to find me a parasol?"

Juana looked a little dazed, but she promptly called to Nita, who responded with alacrity.

And so it was that a startling sight swept out of the small house on the Plaza de Armas a few minutes later: Carolina like a vision of white and gold and red flame—above her head a black ruffled silk parasol that had once belonged to the governor's wife—and carrying that umbrella, somberly gowned with her eyes bright but her face impassive—old Juana, moving stolidly half a step behind her young mistress.

"Where will we go?" asked Juana, who would have been glad to parade through the whole town and observe the shocked expression in people's eyes as they passed.

Carolina looked ruefully down at her shoes. They had endured an earthquake, a flood, the salt air of the *Ordeal*'s deck, and being marched through Havana's dusty streets—the combination had nearly disintegrated them. "I think we will visit the market, Juana. Perhaps I can find a pair of sandals there."

"What will you use for money?" wondered Juana, doubting this lustrous wench had any.

"I will simply tell them Don Diego will pay," said Carolina with a careless toss of her head.

Juana nodded thoughtfully to herself. Doubtless that would serve!

Their progress down the handsome expanse of the Plaza de Armas was—to Juana, who hoped for drama—somewhat disappointing. One or two gentlemen in wide-brimmed hats, clattering by on horseback, spurs ajingle, turned to stare. A barefoot Franciscan friar in his simple habit of coarse gray sackcloth, with a white cord knotted around the waist, hurried by—averting his eyes, Juana noticed with glee. But as they approached the market the streets grew more crowded. A handsome carriage approached and Juana shook the black parasol slightly over Carolina's head, letting the black silk ruffles shimmer in the sun. She was rewarded by the sight of two elegant ladies, severely gowned in black, who registered shock at the sight of Carolina. Old Juana hid a grin—she had not been so entertained since the governor's cook had pursued Miguel down the street with a knife, screaming that he had taken a mistress!

A group of soldiers from the fort, seeing them, stopped to stare—and were frowned at by a Dominican friar in black mantle, white tunic and white apronlike scapulary, whose way they had blocked.

Carolina swept through them, head high.

"Move along here, you're blocking the path," said a familiar voice in Spanish.

The soldiers moved on with alacrity and Carolina came to an abrupt halt, for in this strange city she had at last stumbled upon someone she knew:

That erstwhile Frenchman she had invited to sup in Port Royal stood before her—indeed it was his commanding voice that had scattered the knot of staring soldiers. But what a difference in his appearance!

Gone was the foppish look that had made him at first sight seem French. Here was a Spaniard born and bred. He was dressed in somber black and he seemed arrow thin. His tawny eyes had a dangerous look, and the wintry gaze he had turned on the soldiery held no slightest vestige of the ready smile she remembered.

This was Don Ramon del Mundo—and he lost a step at sight of her. But he recovered promptly and swaggered forward with a jaunty grin to sweep Carolina the lowest of bows.

"Good morning, beautiful lady," he said in English. "Have you come to take the city?"

"Only the market," laughed Carolina. "So you *are* Spanish! I was sure of it back in Port Royal."

"Your discernment matches your charm," he said easily. "Allow me to introduce myself. I am Don Ramon del Mundo."

"Not Monsieur Raymond du Monde—whose name means, I believe, man of the world?" she teased, reminding him of the last time they met.

"Not French and not du Monde—although the name means much the same thing in Spanish." He fell into step beside her. "Let me escort you to our market, which is most unusual."

"I know," she said dryly. "I narrowly escaped being sold there myself just yesterday!"

He gave her a puzzled look. "Perhaps my English is not so good after all. I do not understand you."

"I was on my way to England when our vessel was waylaid by a Spanish warship. We were escorted willy-nilly to New Providence where a French-Spanish attack swept the beaches clean of pirates. With the men all dead, the 'ladies' of the place were bundled aboard our ship and we were all brought here to Havana to be sold as slaves. And it was done—in the marketplace. Yesterday."

"What?" he cried, aghast.

"You don't keep up with what's happening in Havana?" she asked, slanting a narrow look up at him. "Surely no one could miss yesterday's fiesta?"

"I was up in the hills," he said moodily. "Hunting. All I caught was a touch of fever. It dogs me in this climate." He frowned at her. "You say you narrowly escaped being sold?"

"My sister and I were withdrawn from the sale. She now resides at the governor's palace. I was sent next door to be—housekeeper"—she stumbled over the word—"to Don Diego Vivar."

"Vivar!" Anger flitted briefly over Don Ramon del Mundo's dark countenance and was gone. "I might have known! First he is put in command of my plan to take Jamaica—now he is given my woman!"

Carolina stood straighter. Her silver eyes blazed at him in the tropical heat. "I am *not* your woman!" she cried indignantly.

His somber gaze passed over her. "You would have been," he muttered, "had I been permitted to carry out my plan."

"So you were my guest under false pretenses?" she said resentfully. "You were actually there to spy out the island for an invasion!"

"I offered my sword to a lady in distress," he said imperturbably. "And was invited to sup—nothing more. Surely you could not fault me for that!"

"You would be wasting your time to invade Port Royal now," she told him bitterly. "There is nothing left! The earthquake, the wave swept all before it. The entire town has sunk into the sea."

He shook his head, marveling. Then he looked down with compassion upon her fair head. "That will mean you have lost your house," he murmured. "I am very sorry to hear it."

Her house at that moment seemed the least that she had lost, but Carolina chose not to enlighten him.

"What is your quarrel with Don Diego?" she asked, seeking to change the subject.

"Don Diego seems singularly favored by God," he

muttered. "First, as a king's favorite, he is sent out from Spain to command *my* venture, then the governor takes him up—and now the governor has given him *you*. By the saints, next he will replace me as commander of El Morro!"

She stopped in astonishment on the dusty street and her head swung upward to look at him. "*You* are in command of El Morro?"

"Yes. Is it so difficult to imagine?" He gave a short laugh.

"No, not at all," she said hastily. "It was just that when we sailed in under the guns of El Morro, it seemed such a forbidding place. . . ."

"And you would imagine me in some more lightsome role? Perhaps a dancing master?"

The sarcasm in his tone made her flush. "I did not mean that," she hurried to say. "It is just that to command that fortress on the rock must be very grim."

He shrugged.

She tried a different tack. "What of the men on the *Ordeal?* What has happened to them?"

"They are, all of them, deep in El Morro," he told her moodily.

"Where *you* command. . . ." she murmured.

"Where *I* command," he echoed with a touch of hauteur. He peered down at her suddenly, and his dark brows met in a frown. "Why? Did any of them hurt you? If so, I will punish the culprit!"

Carolina shivered—surely, to be lost in the depths of El Morro was punishment enough even for Captain Simmons, who would have sold her to gain his freedom! "No, no," she said. "Of course not. I just wondered what will happen to them."

The man who strode beside her shrugged again. "The governor will send word to Spain that they have been taken and he will ask what should be done with them. I am afraid it will take some time."

They had reached the market now. It was piled with produce. Indian women from palm-thatched *bohios* sat with expressionless faces behind mountainous stalks of yellow bananas. Blacks and mestizos hawked their wares. They strolled between great piles of oranges and limes and coconuts, stacks of woven baskets, rows of pottery. Bargaining was going on all around them. Old Juana regretted bitterly that Don Ramon and her mistress spoke only English.

"Is there anything you desire to buy?" he asked her courteously.

"I had thought to buy a pair of sandals," admitted Carolina. "My shoes are not much longer for this world!"

Don Ramon cast an appreciative glance down at her dainty feet.

"I will take you to a bootmaker," he decided.

"Oh, but I couldn't let you," protested Carolina. "You see," she confided, a trifle embarrassed, "I left the house without money but I had thought it would be easy enough to explain to a sandal-maker at the market that Don Diego Vivar would come by to pay for an inexpensive pair."

But protests were in vain. Old Juana's eyes were bright as Don Ramon masterfully led his protesting lady to a bootmaker's shop where he personally selected for Carolina a pair of very soft black kidskin shoes with high red heels.

When Carolina suggested that Don Diego would pay for the shoes, Don Ramon waved his hand airily and insisted that *he* would pay for them. He would be back, he told the bootmaker, to do so presently. Meantime he must escort this lady home in her new shoes. The bootmaker, intimidated by Don Ramon's reputation, gave them both a worried look and hastily agreed.

Carolina wondered if Don Ramon really had any money. She thought with compassion that she must get her shoes paid for elsewhere—she would ask Don Diego the next time she saw him.

That was to be sooner than she had imagined for as they were coming out of the bootmaker's shop the governor's carriage clip-clopped by. And sitting in that carriage, being driven about the town, was Don Diego himself—and beside him the governor's daughter, clad all in white with a white mantilla of heavy lace shading her excited face.

If Don Diego felt startled at sight of Carolina, he kept that emotion to himself. His narrowed gaze roved over them both and settled expressionlessly on Carolina as he acknowledged their existence with the slightest of bows.

Beside him the governor's plump daughter leaned out to stare hotly at Carolina—and then turn her accusing gaze on Don Ramon del Mundo, who made her a deep bow. She lifted her chin and turned her head, refusing to acknowledge his greeting.

Irrepressible, Carolina waved gaily at Don Diego and turned about, fair hair flying, to take Don Ramon's gracefully proffered arm. She hoped Don Diego had noticed her high red heels that he would soon be paying for!

"Would you care to see El Morro?" Don Ramon was asking by her side.

"Not today." She flashed him a smile. "But perhaps one day soon? I wonder, could I see the prisoners?"

"It is most irregular," he murmured, smiling down upon her fair hair. "However in your case"—the smile on his dark face deepened—"I think it might be arranged."

"By order of the commandant?" she suggested saucily.

"Something like that. . . ." The crowd swirled round them—two broad-hatted Jesuits in sackcloth, a cimaroon drunk on the local black wine, some leather-clad hunters—but Don Ramon remained immobile, staring down at her. "Would you care to see our waterfront, señorita? Or perhaps I could call you by your first name."

"Yes, do," Carolina said contentedly. "It is Carolina."

"Doña Carolina? A lovely name."

"And I have seen your waterfront."

"But you have not viewed our customs house or La Fuerza, down by the sea wall, from close up."

She shook her head. "Another day perhaps."

"Then perhaps you will share with me a glass of wine?" And when she hesitated, "Oh, have no fear, Doña Carolina, I am not speaking of some filthy cantina on the Xanja Canal—there is a respectable tavern close by that serves an excellent Malaga."

She dimpled at him. "Spanish ladies do not frequent taverns, Don Ramon!"

"Ah, but you are not Spanish," he said caressingly. "And the day is hot. Would you not care to relax beneath cool archways with a tall drink before you attempt the hot walk home in your new high heels?"

Thus reminded of his kindness, she began to laugh. "I would indeed, Don Ramon," she said, inspired by the thought that if she strolled home late, Don Diego would be there to see her escorted home by the commander of El Morro!

Just why was it so important to her to arouse jealousy in Don Diego's broad breast? she now asked herself. *Was it because of his striking resemblance to Kells? Was that what she was doing, assuaging the grief of Kells's loss by imagining Don Diego actually to be Kells?*

She put the thought away from her and hurried along beside Don Ramon, who cut a handsome figure as he escorted her into the dim interior of a nearby tavern where he ordered Malaga for both of them—and wine for old Juana, too, who sat impassively nearby, as if she were in truth a *duena* for a beautiful señorita.

"Perhaps now you will tell me no tall tales about being a Frenchman fresh from New Providence," Carolina suggested with a wicked look at Don Ramon as she sipped her wine. "But tell me the truth about Don Ramon del Mundo!"

Thus encouraged by a beautiful woman, Don Ramon leaned back expansively and his voice rang softly through the coolness of the almost empty tavern. He told her about his homeland—and through his eyes she could see it shining golden in the sun. He told her about his family *estancias,* the beautiful but dilapidated *hacienda,* the tawny pastures with clumps of evergreen oaks surrounded by rooting black pigs. He described rushing streams tumbling by weird rock formations, terraced gardens, and sweeping groves of olive trees with thick gnarled trunks and lovely feathery branches stretching on, it would seem, forever, toward the blue backdrop of the Guadalupe mountains. She saw it as he saw it: a land of sun-bronzed peasants and peaceful herds of cattle and goats, moving through the grassy summer pastures to the sound of tinkling bells.

"A paradise," she murmured and his eyes kindled.

"I have found it so," he said.

"And yet you are here?"

Don Ramon winced. Was he to tell this beautiful clear-eyed girl who sat across from him that he had come to Havana to make the world ring with his valorous deeds—so that he could find himself a rich wife?

Instead he launched into the sad tale of Doña Ana of Austria, daughter of that Don John of Austria who had led the Christians to victory against the Turks in the Battle of Lepanto. Doña Ana had the misfortune to fall in love with the son of Prince Juan of Portugal. Which would have been all right save that Prince Juan of Portugal had two handsome and reckless sons who looked so alike that no one could tell them apart. One son was named Sebastian—and he was by Prince Juan's rightful wife. The other son was named Gabriel Espinosa—and he was by a pastry cook's beautiful daughter. Sebastian, he told her, succeeded to the throne of Portugal.

"And did he marry Doña Ana, then?" wondered Carolina, fascinated by this look-alike tale. "Or was it the pastry cook's grandson she loved?"

"Who knows who she loved?" shrugged Don Ramon. "But it is certain that neither of them married Doña Ana. Against all advice, taking Espinosa with him, Sebastian went off to campaign in Africa—and only one of these two look-alikes returned from that catastrophe. At first everyone believed Sebastian the new king had been killed, but after a time, the one who had returned claimed he was indeed Sebastian and alive after all—he claimed he was so bowed down by his defeat in Africa that he had been ashamed to admit his true identity."

"How confusing!" murmured Carolina, a little curious as to why Don Ramon had told her this story. "Did they ever sort it all out?"

The tall Spaniard gave her a grim smile. "Oh, they sorted it out, all right. Philip II was Doña Ana's uncle and *he* had the man who now claimed to be Sebastian arrested. He was brought to trial and condemned—whereupon Doña Ana threw herself before her uncle, the king, and wept, appealing for mercy for the condemned man. Her appeal was refused and the condemned man—whether king or commoner—was garroted."

"And Doña Ana?"

He grimaced. "Her uncle the king was furious with her, feeling she had disgraced him by fancying a pastry cook's grandson. He locked her in a convent, she was allowed to speak to no one, her privileges of rank were stripped away, and on Fridays she was reduced to bread and water."

Carolina shuddered at Doña Ana's fate, but her mind was on the look-alikes. "Was the truth about Sebastian and his brother ever known?"

"Never. It is one of the great mysteries of my country. Was it a commoner who died or was it a king?"

"And which one did Doña Ana love?" murmured Carolina, as if to herself. *Or,* she asked herself, startled, *did Doña Ana love them both? Was the resemblance so striking—both in appearance and character—that she was unable to separate them in her mind?* The thought brought a sudden staining to her cheeks. "It is hard to imagine that they were so—alike," she said haltingly.

"And yet they were. All who knew them said so. Identical sons of different mothers."

"Perhaps they were really twins—but one of them was spirited away because of trouble over succession to the throne," she suggested.

"Perhaps." Don Ramon gave her a sunny smile. "Perhaps Doña Ana was the only one who knew the truth. Perhaps she loved a king—or perhaps a pastry cook's grandson."

"A pastry cook's grandson who was nevertheless of royal blood—perhaps Doña Ana sympathized with him, a man never able to claim his birthright." She thought of Kells, never able to claim his own birthright, and a trace of bitterness tinged her voice. "Don Ramon"—she shook off those shadows of the past—"it is pleasant to while away the day with you, but I must get me home."

"Of course, Doña Carolina." He rose and gravely offered her his arm.

He is careful not to call me "Señora," thought Carolina. It is because he chooses not to recognize my marriage to Kells! In Port Royal that might have irritated her—here, oddly enough, it did not.

Perhaps because, like tragic Doña Ana, she was suspended in a great confusion of the spirit. She had lost the man she loved—and he had reappeared but from another life, with other memories.

A double, she told herself firmly. *No more than that. Just one of fate's odd prankish tricks: a double.*

She bade Don Ramon good-by at her door and felt his hot lips brush the back of her hand as he made her a most elegant bow and said his good-bys.

"I will take you riding with me," he promised. "Do you like to ride?"

Carolina admitted she did.

"And you have seen but half the city," he added. "I would show you the rest!"

"Later perhaps." His interest in her was more than apparent. Carolina wondered if Don Diego was watching from a window.

But he was still out, presumably entertaining the governor's daughter.

Not till dinner did she face him.

"I have new shoes," she greeted him, twirling about so that her high-heeled slippers showed to advantage.

"So I see," he said sternly. "A gift of Don Ramon del Mundo, one would imagine?"

"Oh, Don Ramon said he would return and pay for them," Carolina said with a shrug, "even though I protested. But I thought you might prefer to pay the bootmaker yourself."

"You are correct," he said crisply, frowning down at her from his great height. "And while you are a guest in my house you will observe certain rules of propriety. I am told that before I arrived in Havana, the governor's daughter smiled upon Don Ramon del Mundo. It would please me to have her smile on him again. You will not stand in the way of it."

Carolina hid a grin. So he found Marina's hot pursuit a bit tiresome—it did not surprise her!

"Don Ramon is an old friend," she said carelessly.

He gave her an astonished look.

"Well, at least I met him before I came here," she amended. "He dined with me in Port Royal."

"He dined with you and your buccaneer?" Don Diego asked in astonishment.

"No, with me alone. Kells was away up the Cobre, seeking to buy a plantation." She studied his face as she spoke, hoping to jog his memory—if indeed he had such a memory—but there was no spark of recognition.

"You are renewing a friendship, then, begun in Port Royal," he said slowly. "I think I begin to understand."

"No, you do *not* understand," she said, her voice sharpened by disappointment. "Don Ramon treats me as a lady, which the rest of Havana does not!"

"Do I not—" he began.

"You bore me to the mattress at first sight!" she flashed.

"I seem to recall that you were more than willing," he drawled.

"You must have known I mistook you for somebody else—you should be ashamed!"

His hard gaze raked over her. "I find it hard to be ashamed of enjoying such a beautiful body," he murmured.

That was what she was to him—a beautiful female body to be enjoyed! Not Carolina Lightfoot, who had loved to distraction a man who was breath of his breath! Carolina felt as if he had struck her a blow.

Blindly she turned and would have fled the dining table but that his voice stopped her.

"You will stay at table throughout the meal, Mistress Lightfoot. I have no wish to dine alone."

Sulkily, Carolina sat back and stared rebelliously down at her plate.

He began to talk then—companionably, as if he had known her always. His lazy voice lulled her as he spoke of the day's doings, how he had spent some time with the governor, how he was being considered to command the inner fortress of La Fuerza in case new orders failed to come from Spain. He was every inch the Spanish gentleman even though out of courtesy he spoke to her in English. She could not fault him.

It is true, she thought, and felt an infinite sadness steal over her. *This man is who he claims to be—Don Diego Vivar, late of Castile.* Her heart bled a little at the thought for her rebellious spirit had never really accepted it.

Had it been like this for Doña Ana? she asked herself suddenly. Had she loved the real thing and accepted the counterfeit? Or had the counterfeit seemed as good as the real?

The glow of candlelight showed pain in her lovely eyes as she tried to reconcile the present with the past.

"Will you not miss Spain?" she asked him wistfully. "Will not Havana seem like exile to you?"

"Odd that you should ask that," he said thoughtfully. "I think that I was cast here by fate, which undoubtedly has some purpose in foiling me of my objective, although I cannot for the life of me imagine just what it is."

"You speak in riddles," she said stiffly.

"Yes, I suppose I do. I was born yesterday, Señorita Lightfoot—although I am indeed Diego Vivar," he hastened to add, remembering her earlier outburst.

"And what does that mean?" she inquired.

"It means that I was on a delicate mission for the King of Spain when the *Santo Domingo,* the galleon on which I was traveling, was blown from the water by buccaneers. I was hurt somehow in the fighting—a head wound." He touched a red scar that came down a shade below his hairline—something she had not noticed before.

"A head wound?" she asked, suddenly intent.

"Yes, it has interfered with my memory."

"You have trouble remembering things?"

He sighed. "Of the present, I remember everything, but of the past I remember nothing. I seem to have been born fully grown here in Havana for I have no memory of how I came here nor where I was before. But of course," he added with a shrug, "much is known of me. The governor has a letter describing me. And those who brought me here were fully satisfied of my identity."

Carolina's heart seemed to miss a beat at this admission, and she looked up at him on a caught breath.

"So," she said slowly, "there *is* something that you had not told me, Don Diego. Your life began, as you say, 'yesterday'—you know only what others have told you—you yourself have no idea who you really are!"

THE GOVERNOR'S PALACE
HAVANA, CUBA

Chapter 22

With her regal carriage and daunting manner, red-haired Penny had established herself overnight as being "in charge" of the governor's great house on the Plaza de Armas. The governor had been so delighted with her that he had supped with her privately that first night (which had so infuriated Marina that she had refused her own dinner and stomped off to bed). Since the governor spoke excellent English, Penny had talked a great deal and charmed him further with her unbridled view of life. This morning as he left for his office in La Fuerza he had told her that henceforth she would sup "with the family," and Penny had been wondering how Marina would take that!

With the governor gone, she had spent the morning intimidating the servants, who had been inclined at first to view her as one of themselves—they must be set straight on *that* point! Hampered by having little command of Spanish, for she had none of Carolina's facility with languages, she was frowning over how to explain what she wanted to one of the serving girls when the front door knocker sounded.

Impulsively she opened it herself and was confronted by a heavyset olive-skinned gentleman in military uniform who blinked at the sight of her, but recovered and said in a surprised tone, "Ah, one of the English ladies!"

Relieved that he should speak to her in English, Penny gave him her most winning smile and said, "Whoever you are, please do come in at once. I am at my wits' end trying to tell the servants what to do, and you can translate for me!"

If he was a trifle dazed to be thus energetically addressed, the military gentleman recovered very well. "Captain Juarez, señorita, at your service!" He swept her a courteous bow.

Pleased both by his respectful mien and by his willingness to serve, Penny swept him into the courtyard and gave half a dozen servants orders—all translated gravely by Captain Juarez.

"Now then," she told him gaily when that was done, "instruct this one—her name is Zita—to bring us something cool to drink. The governor has some fine Malaga. Would you like that?"

Captain Juarez was familiar with the governor's Malaga. He coughed discreetly and asked if the governor was about.

"Oh, no, he just went out. To La Fuerza, I think." Penny led her guest to a grouping of stone seats in the cool shadows of the colonnade, for the heat today was blistering, and even the palm fronds in the courtyard were blinding when the sun struck them. "I am surprised you did not meet him on your way in," she added.

Captain Juarez flushed ever so slightly, a condition that only darkened the weathered olive of his skin. In point of fact he had lurked about across the street until he had seen the portly governor stroll out on his way to his office in La Fuerza. Only when the governor was out of sight had he hurried over to bang the iron knocker of the governor's house. "And Doña Marina?" he asked diffidently. "Is she about?"

Penny, just settling her wide skirts on the stone bench, looked up quickly. From her guest's look of sudden discomfiture, his abrupt loosening of his neckpiece, she guessed shrewdly that he had not come to see the governor at all but to pay a call on the governor's ripe young daughter.

"No, Doña Marina went out much earlier with her *duena,"* she told him carelessly. "I am not sure when she will be back." Her eyes twinkled. "I expect she is riding through the town in some excitement, for last night she was serenaded for the first time below her balcony. The governor fears that now there will be a constant succession of suitors, caterwauling beneath Marina's window every night until he can get her married!"

Captain Juarez gave the magnificent redhead across from him a wounded look. It pained him to hear her speak so lightly of his wonderful Marina, the light of his life! And most especially it pained him to hear that suitors were already serenading young Marina, who, in accordance with Spanish custom, now occupied the front bedroom of the house overlooking the street, so that bedazzled suitors could strum and sing love songs beneath her window and entreat the marriageable young lady above to have mercy and toss down a rose or a lock of her hair. It pained him even more since he was afraid to become one of those caterwauling suitors; the governor had never given him any encouragement and indeed might consider it impudence for him to aspire to Marina's hand, for how could he, living on a captain's pay, support a wife in the grand style to which the governor's daughter was accustomed?

"I had come to inquire about the state of Don Diego's health," he explained, for it alarmed him that he might leave the impression that he had been calling on Marina.

"Don Diego now lives next door," Penny informed him.

"Oh?" In his embarrassment, he had forgotten that.

The Malaga was brought just then, and Captain Juarez quaffed a glass while a pair of sapphire eyes studied him.

"Don Diego's health seems to be excellent. Why should you inquire?" Penny could not resist asking.

"Ah, señorita," smiled Captain Juarez, the wine warming him and loosening his tongue. "I have good reason to inquire for *I* am the man who brought him out of the hell of Port Royal!"

"Indeed?" Penny had heard nothing of this from the governor. She would have something to tell Carolina! She settled herself more comfortably upon the stone bench. "It sounds like a valorous tale. You must tell me about it—so that I can regale Marina with it!"

Marina had already heard it—several times—but Captain Juarez was flattered. Such a tale could scarcely be heard too often.

"But so that you will truly understand, señorita," he explained, "I must go far back."

"Oh, go as far as you like," Penny said carelessly, and poured her guest another glass of wine.

Somewhat dazzled by all this attention, for he was not a man who got along well with women, Captain Juarez leaned forward and began to talk.

Through his eyes she relived his whole mad adventure, which had begun not in Port Royal but in Havana.

He recounted to her the terrible scene when Don Ramon del Mundo had received word from Spain that he would not be leading the expedition to Port Royal which he himself had conceived. Don Ramon's strong face had grown purple, he had sprung forward and seized the King's envoy by the throat, and Captain

Juarez, who had had the misfortune to be present at the time, was certain in his heart that murder would have been done at that moment had he not swiftly intervened and wrested del Mundo away.

"How fortunate you were there!" she said lightly.

Captain Juarez inclined his head in agreement and went on.

Of course he himself, being a military man, could sympathize with Don Ramon del Mundo's plight, for had not Don Ramon worked out a plan of supreme cleverness to seize the buccaneer stronghold of Jamaica, and once Jamaica was subdued, to proceed island by island to boot the English out of the Caribbean? Captain Juarez had been in Don Ramon's confidence and he knew that the entire scheme had been laid before the King's advisors in Spain a year ago. Don Ramon del Mundo had grown understandably impatient—as dashing *caballeros* were wont to do—on hearing nothing from his sovereign after so long a time and had gone to Jamaica himself earlier in the year. They had sailed in as far as Lime Cay and rowed del Mundo ashore by night, then retired to Great Goat Island around the point and picked him up again in darkness by rowboat. Captain Juarez had gone along on this venture but he had had no more than a glimpse of Port Royal by night from the harbor.

Back in Havana, Don Ramon had enthusiastically set about rounding up the party of "advance men" his plan envisioned—and he, Juarez, was to lead them. Don Ramon had been certain that each newly arriving galleon that sailed past frowning El Morro Castle into Havana harbor would bring the word from Spain that would light the torch!

And when word arrived at last it had sent Don Ramon into a passion. Del Mundo's efforts were appreciated, the suave message had said, but more experienced men than he would now take over. Since del Mundo was a gunnery expert, he would be most useful when the golden galleons mounted their assault, and he would not accompany the advance guard as he had hoped, but would wait in Havana for those galleons to arrive—the letter was very definite about that. After Jamaica was taken, his sovereign would no doubt find him some suitable post in the government of the island—nothing was said about the governorship of the island. Meanwhile this Captain Juarez, whom del Mundo had described as being most competent, should go about assembling a few good men—no more than a pinnace could conveniently accommodate—to infiltrate Port Royal as an advance guard. They were to contact del Mundo's friend there, who would arrange for their housing, and they were to familiarize themselves with the town, the location and strength of the forts—and it was important that some of them be able to speak English, as Captain Juarez did.

These men of the advance guard were to attract no attention—only to wait. The letter had been very specific about that. An eminent Castilian gentleman was being sent out from Spain to lead them. This *caballero*'s name was Don Diego Vivar, and both King and Council had every confidence in him. Don Diego was sailing upon the *Santo Domingo* which would take the Windward Passage and pass near Jamaica en route to Panama. Don Diego would be set ashore just off the Jamaican coast in a small boat and would make his way to Port Royal.

The advance guard under Captain Juarez, already there, would recognize him by his boots, which had been crafted to his measure from an old pair left at Don Diego's bootmaker for repair. They had been placed upon the *Santo Domingo* in advance of Don Diego's coming aboard, a gift of the King of Spain. The body of these boots was unremarkable—black, of boiled jack—but their bucket tops were of fine scarlet morocco leather and would bear the initials DV intertwined in gold. These handsome jackboots would serve a twofold purpose: Cleverly sewn into their hardened sides were his orders, not to be opened until his arrival in Port Royal. Second, by their striking color they would attract the attention of the sharp-eyed men who waited for him—and by those intertwined initials DV they could identify him as their leader.

It was at this point that Don Ramon had seized the envoy by the throat.

Captain Juarez could not blame him. It was indeed a devilish disappointment to work so long and hard on a plan and then discover that it was to be carried to fruition by someone else.

But once Port Royal had begun to quake, and its buildings to collapse, Captain Juarez had found himself thinking that Don Ramon must have been born under a lucky star that he had not accompanied the expedition to Jamaica!

Up to now Penny had not been much interested. But now she leaned forward expectantly, for Carolina had not told her many details about the earthquake.

"Tell me about it," she urged. "For I hear it was terrible!"

Captain Juarez accepted some more wine and said indeed it was worse than that. Hearing anguished howls behind him, he had looked back to see a wall of water rushing in upon the town. He had been caught by it, swept on with it, lifted, battered about and half-drowned for all that he was a superb swimmer (he wanted to make sure Marina heard that last!). Finally he had managed to catch on to something solid and had discovered himself clinging to the broken hull of a ship which had been driven by the wave into the town itself. There were pieces of other ships around him—masts, spars, sails—all floating in the water among the chimneys and rooftops along with people screaming desperately for help, grasping at anything that floated or still rose above the water.

Captain Juarez had been in an earthquake once before. He had had no trouble grasping what had happened. This tidal wave had snapped the cables of the ships anchored in the harbor and flung them full tilt into the town. The mass of broken wreckage all about was doubtless from those ships that had been nearest the wharves when the ocean had risen up.

And Carolina had been through all this! thought Penny with a thrill of excitement. Quickly she poured the captain another glass of wine.

Captain Juarez took a deep swallow, drew a deeper breath and told her solemnly that he had looked at the name painted upon the broken hull that rose above him—and almost lost his grip.

Sea Wolf, he had read.

Penny, in the act of raising her own wineglass to her mouth, set it down instead and regarded Captain Juarez with a kind of fascination.

Indignation, it seemed, had given Captain Juarez strength. That he should find himself clinging to the remains of the most notorious ship in the Caribbean had seemed to him an enormous indignity. The flagship of that most infamous of buccaneers—Captain Kells! It was too much. Half-drowned and battered as he was, he had ground his teeth and stolen another look upward.

A man was dangling from the rigging, his boot caught in it. Captain Juarez had ducked as that rigging promptly came down, plunging the man into the water beside him.

At that moment, along with the roar of the water and the sound of things breaking and people calling out, there were ominous creaking, tearing sounds from within the ship he clung to. Captain Juarez recognized those sounds and they spurred him to immediate action —she was breaking up.

Avoiding that rigging which now floated with its grim burden face up upon it, Juarez let go his hold and swam to a nearby chimney which stuck up above the water. He climbed upon the chimney and found that his foot had become entangled in the fallen rigging. Fearful that it might pull him down with the ship, which was even now giving signs of foundering, he was about to wrest his foot free when his gaze again passed over the man who had been trapped by it.

Of a sudden Captain Juarez stopped trying to get his foot free and stared wild-eyed at the man before him.

He saw a long body, muscular and well-built, clad in dark gray broadcloth coat and trousers. A strong hawklike countenance, floating face up. That face was darkly tanned, the eyes closed, blood trickling from a head wound somewhere in that heavy shoulder-length black hair.

But it was none of those things that had arrested the captain's attention.

Captain Juarez was staring at the boots, which were fast filling with onrushing water and threatening to drag the fellow down: black jackboots with wide bucket tops made of scarlet leather. He peered forward and saw that one of them had a gold insignia of some kind.

It was enough for Captain Juarez, who was first and last a man of action. At great risk to himself, he began frantically pulling the fallen rigging toward him and finally managed to pull the unconscious man from the water.

When he had him free at last and draped face down over the chimney so that any water he had swallowed might more easily drain from his lungs, Captain Juarez seized one jackbooted leg and hauled it up for closer inspection. There it was, glittering at him from the boot's wet surface: the initials DV intertwined in gold upon the soft red leather of the bucket top with its back scooped out to allow for bending of the knee.

Captain Juarez sat stock-still for a moment and stared at his strange catch. Don Diego Vivar arriving in Port Royal on the deck of a buccaneer vessel?

And of a sudden, being a practical man, it came to him what must have happened:

Don Diego Vivar had sailed from Spain on the *Santo Domingo,* but the ship would never make port in Panama—she had been blasted from the seas by the guns of the *Sea Wolf.* Don Diego himself had been taken prisoner by these accursed buccaneers and was being brought to Port Royal—for ransom, no doubt—when the earthquake had struck. He was not shackled, but then how often did these buccaneers shackle their prisoners? In the confusion of the tidal wave that had sent the *Sea Wolf*'s broken hull crashing into the town, Don Diego, clinging to the rigging, would have been washed overboard with the others save that his boot—one of that pair the King of Spain had sent him—had got caught in the rigging and so probably saved his life.

And identified him as well.

"His boots?" cried Penny, startled. "You mean you identified him by his *boots?*"

Her guest, now aglow with wine, nodded triumphantly. "I tried to rouse him. His heartbeat was strong and his breathing made me believe that it was a blow rather than water that had rendered him unconscious. With those of my men who were still alive, we carried Don Diego and made our way to our pinnace, then sailed back to Havana—and all during the voyage Don Diego slept."

Penny was watching him brightly.

She listened as he recounted how the governor had ordered Don Diego's boots slit open and had read his sealed orders—Don Diego still slept. The governor had ordered surgeons to attend him and leeches to bleed him—Don Diego slept on. Don Ramon del Mundo had come to the governor's palace to stare bitterly at his rival—Don Diego still slept.

And when finally Don Diego Vivar had awakened—with a splitting headache—and looked about him at his world, he could remember nothing of his past. Nothing. And had remembered nothing since.

"By his boots . . ." murmured Penny. She looked up. Marina and her elderly *duena* were just now entering.

Captain Juarez sprang to his feet, sloshing the wine from his glass.

"Doña Marina." He swept her a bow that nearly grazed the courtyard tiles.

Marina looked upon him in vague distaste.

"Captain Juarez," she said in a bored voice. "How nice to see you." And cast a brief smouldering glance at Penny, sitting nearby.

Penny wanted to give the bluff soldier his chance with Marina. She quickly excused herself and went upstairs to her room.

There she walked about, thinking. Then she sat down and thought some more.

By his boots . . . the captain had said.

Her dark sapphire eyes were narrowed.

For Captain Juarez had told her a deal—indeed more than he knew.

THE HOUSE ON THE PLAZA DE ARMAS HAVANA, CUBA

Chapter 23

It was late morning and Penny was racing up the stairway, shaking Carolina into full wakefulness.

"Get up, sleepy head!" she cried. "Come to the window and view your competition!"

Carolina shook her head to clear the sleep from it, leaped from her bed, and accompanied Penny to the window.

"There she is," Penny said triumphantly. "Doña Jimena Menendez. She paid a call on the governor this morning and is just now leaving."

Carolina looked down to see that in the street below a slender dark woman was being handed into a carriage by no less a personage than Governor Corrubedo himself. She moved gracefully but from here it was hard to tell what she looked like. Even at this distance her clothes appeared very rich.

"Black silk," said Penny. "Light and sheer—the best. And fine black lace. And jet jewelry frosted with diamonds and perfectly enormous pearls. I hope she looks up—you must see her eyes. They're huge. No wonder Don Diego is so taken with her!"

Carolina flashed her sister an irritated look. "Perhaps *she* is so taken with *him!*"

"Perhaps it is mutual," Penny said cheerfully. "Ah, there she's looking up to wave at the governor's daughter—the hateful minx refused to come down but she's obviously standing behind the grillwork of her bedroom window. I doubt Doña Jimena can see her, but she guesses Marina is there so she waves! Oh, it is hilarious how jealous Marina is of Doña Jimena!"

Carolina, staring down into that lovely face so suddenly uplifted, seeing the froth of black lace fall back from that pale slender forearm, thought Marina might have cause for jealousy. Old Juana might have exaggerated when she said that Doña Jimena was the most beautiful woman in the world, but she was certainly a great beauty. Her thick shining hair shimmered blue-black in the bright Havana sun, her pale olive complexion was smooth and creamy, her vivid features even from here had a dramatic flare: black winglike brows, lashes so dark they made an ebony frame for eyes that were a dark flash in her expressive face. Small-boned, elegant, aristocratic—no wonder poor little Marina hated her!

"She has a voice like honey," supplied Penny, rubbing salt into the wound. "It fairly drips sweetness. And she sinks into chairs with a languorous air—as if she would much rather be in bed. It is easy to see why she has so many lovers!"

As far as Carolina was concerned, Doña Jimena might have all the lovers in Havana—except one. *She was not to have Don Diego Vivar!* On that one item, at least, she and young Marina agreed!

"The servants say Doña Jimena manages to fit Don Diego into her schedule several times a week," Penny added wickedly, with a slanted look at Carolina.

That will stop as of now! Carolina promised herself. Aloud she said, "I doubt he cares for her much—she is a loose woman, and loose women have a way of attracting unattached men."

"Well, aren't we philosophic?" mocked Penny. "I'm sure she finds him fascinating, for it seems Don Diego is a man of mystery."

"How so?" Carolina asked absently. She was watching the carriage with its elegant occupant disappear down the sunlit street.

Penny went over and plumped herself down on the bed. She was, Carolina noticed, extremely well dressed this morning. Her elegant black lace gown would have delighted any Spanish lady's heart, and her riotous hair was upswept and held in place by a carved tortoiseshell comb.

"I see you've noticed that I look different," Penny remarked.

"Obviously the governor has discovered you," Carolina observed dryly. "Don't tell me he ordered you that new gown!"

"It belonged to his wife," Penny said, smiling. "It seems that Doña Constanza and I are the same size. He has told me that I may make free with her wardrobe—the better to decorate his table!" Her throaty laugh rang out.

"So you are sleeping in his bed," sighed Carolina.

"Well, not yet. The governor is a gallant soul. He is courting me. Marina is furious!"

"You don't mean he intends to marry you?" gasped Carolina.

"Well, *he* may intend to marry *me* but *I* certainly don't intend to marry *him*," Penny said carelessly. "A wife in Spain may be trampled on at her husband's pleasure—it doesn't suit my style!"

"No, it certainly doesn't!"

"So for the moment I am to be called his 'housekeeper' and have taken charge of the house."

"As I have here," Carolina said ironically.

"Precisely."

"But in what way is Don Diego a man of mystery?" Carolina was determined to drag her sister back to the main topic.

"I can hardly wait to tell you! There is a certain Captain Juarez who dangles after Marina. He speaks English, and yesterday when Marina was out he told me all about Don Diego." She outlined swiftly how Captain Juarez had recognized Don Diego by his boots there upon the deck of the *Sea Wolf*.

Carolina hung on her words. Now at last she understood what had happened and how Kells—an injured Kells whose memory had been wiped temporarily clean by a blow received during the earthquake—had turned up in Havana wearing the name Don Diego Vivar.

He had been there—hurt—all the time in Port Royal! And while she was ministering to others aboard the *Swan*, Kells was being carried away by his well-meaning Spanish rescuer who had mistaken him for somebody else.

And all of this put him in deadly danger, for he was living a lie—and he did not know it!

"There is a very strange look on your face, Carol," observed Penny. "One might very well think that you know something I don't!"

Carolina started. She supposed the raw emotions on her face had given her away. In the old days she would have told Penny instantly and counted on Penny to keep her secret. But she did not entirely trust this new, more worldly, more capricious Penny to keep anyone's secrets. And the thought that Kells might be found out here in Havana was terrifying!

"No, I—I was just thinking what a miracle it was that

he should have been saved during the earthquake and in an enemy stronghold," she said hastily.

Penny was studying her; there was a shrewd look on her arresting face. "The governor agrees with you," she laughed. "He muttered yesterday that it is all too pat, that it was almost as if Don Diego had been placed there to be rescued!"

Carolina felt a chill steal over her. Kells was in even more danger than she had thought if the governor had begun to suspect him!

"Fate works in mysterious ways," she said cryptically.

"Yes, doesn't it?" was Penny's cool response. "Look how it brought you and me together after all these years! But now to the main question: What do you intend to do about Doña Jimena?"

I intend to keep Kells away from her! thought Carolina. Aloud she said, "Why should I do anything about her?"

"Because," Penny pointed out with slow deliberation, "it is apparent to one and all that you fancy Don Diego."

"Yes. I fancy him." That much at least she could admit!

"So how do you plan to wrest him from Doña Jimena's arms? By making him jealous of Don Ramon?" And when Carolina turned to her with a gasp, Penny chuckled. "Don't imagine that you can keep secrets here in Havana, Carol. Over at the governor's palace the servants talk of little else. It seems you took the town by storm when you strolled through it yesterday—and Don Ramon squired you about, took you to a tavern, and bought you a new pair of shoes!" She cast her eyes about and saw the high red heels peeking out from under the bed. "And very good-looking they are, too. I must remember to tell the governor that his wife's shoes don't quite fit me." Her throaty laugh bubbled. "Perhaps we will use the same bootmaker, Carol!"

Carolina gave her sister a wan smile. Usually it was a delight to talk to brash, light-hearted Penny—but not today. Today she had more important matters on her mind.

"Do you think you could get me a truly sheer chemise?" she asked. "The governor's wife must have had several in this climate!"

"Oh, I'm sure I can," sparkled Penny. "And if I can't find one in her trunks, I'll filch one from Marina."

"Don't get into trouble," warned Carolina.

Penny shrugged. "I've been in trouble all my life," she said carelessly. "It's really too late to do anything about it now."

Carolina supposed that was true. The Penny she had known at Level Green was gone and in her place was this worldly amusing stranger, this—yes, she might as well face it—this courtesan. Penny had been right when she had described herself. She was not born to faithfulness—she was born to lie in the arms of many men. And love it.

"What will you do, Penny, if you ever find a man you really *want?*" she asked soberly.

Penny's dark blue gaze mocked her, but her voice was suddenly as hard as steel. "Why, then I will take him," she drawled. "And nothing—*nothing* will stand in my way."

So Penny was still searching for that love she had never found—and might never find. Carolina's face was wistful as she watched her sister depart.

That night at dinner she was on her best behavior. She chatted with Don Diego—whom she now was certain was Kells even though he himself did not know it—she showed her pretty teeth winsomely as she smiled, she agreed with everything he said, she urged on him more wine.

She hoped that she was making a good impression, and it seemed to her eerie that she should be thinking such thoughts about her own husband, a man who knew her as well—sometimes, she thought, better—than she knew herself.

She was very careful not to bring up the subject of Spain, to speak only of recent happenings in Havana as reported to her by old Juana, who was a veritable mine of information.

The man across from her was watching her warily. She guessed he was wondering what had transformed this tempestuous wench into so pliable a companion. In truth he was marveling at her beauty, admiring the way she held her spoon as she daintily ate her flan. And he was wondering why there was such an odd tug to his heartstrings at the very sound of her voice. There was something about her that tantalized him, drew him. Something more than sex. Although he remembered no women before Havana—indeed, nothing of his past life—he felt an easiness in women's company that told him that many of them had succumbed to his charms.

So what was different about this girl whose eyes flashed silver and whose hair was gold in the candlelight? She had lain in his arms but once—and that time under a misapprehension that he was somebody else—yet he had felt an almost overpowering flash of jealousy at the thought that she had let Don Ramon buy her a pair of shoes.

How could the wench have got her hooks into him so quickly? he was asking himself—and she a buccaneer's woman at that! For as a *caballero* of Spain, he had only scorn for the buccaneers. They were outside the law, outside the true faith—and this woman had been one of them. He must watch his step with her.

But tonight Carolina was all wiles, all femininity. She sat long at table and finally yawned delicately and said it had been a long day—she must to bed. And graciously she thanked him for the shoes again, stretching out her foot so that he might admire them and showing a length of pretty ankle and calf as she did so.

Up the stairs, past the tinkling fountain she went—there to don the sheer black chemise that Penny had smuggled over to her this afternoon. It was a trifle too large but that did not matter—what mattered was that it was almost transparent, and in the candlelight the pale pink tips of her breasts glowed through it rosily, her slim hips and long slender legs were richly displayed through its rippling length, and the lace around the hem caressed her ankles.

On tiptoe now she stole down to Don Diego's front bedroom and threw back the coverlet. She lay down on the bed, carefully arranging the chemise so that it was pulled up enough to display one gleaming bare leg. She sat up and beat the pillow into submission, then she tossed out her long hair so that it would stream out around her like the radiance of the sun—she did it twice to make sure she had it right. She lay there with outflung arms, one leg drawn up so that a white knee glimmered.

And waited.

Don Diego did not linger downstairs long. Presently she heard his light step ascending the stair and for a moment her stomach muscles tensed. Then she reminded herself sternly that this was her husband who was about to enter the room, and why should she fear him? Certainly he had offered her no hurt!

The door was flung open and Don Diego, entering fast, came to a full stop and stood there staring at her.

Carolina moved slightly, luxuriously, every motion an invitation.

"I am tired of sleeping alone," she pouted.

The dark brows rose, but the gray eyes considering her narrowed. "I have told you, Mistress Lightfoot, that I will not substitute in your arms for another man. Now—"

"But I want only you," she said beseechingly. "I have been thinking about it all through dinner. Surely you find me attractive—your eyes have told me that!"

"I find you damnably attractive," he said reluctantly.

"Well, then?" She shrugged, and that slight motion rippled her breasts deliciously. The sheer chemise seemed a gossamer cloud about her enticing nakedness. Her hips swayed a little in anticipation, her breath came quickly, her eyes had darkened with desire. He could not miss the sincerity of her passion. Her voice had gone husky. "I promise to think of no one but you," she said, and there was a richness in the way she said it that brought a slight flush to his cheeks. God, the wench was inviting, lying there!

In silence, devouring her with his eyes, he took off his clothes. In silence, joined her. In silence, wrapped his arms about her and kissed her lips, her breasts, her silken stomach, the triangle of golden hair at the base of her hips. He kissed her knees, her elbows, her shoulders, her throat.

And then he moved luxuriously and single-mindedly above her, took her soft rounded buttocks in his hands and pressed her body tightly against his—and with his first thrust brought a soft moan of joy from her lips.

He smiled down at her—so young, so willing, so wonderfully responsive to his every move. It was as if they had made love before, sweetly and often, for she fit into his arms as if formed for them alone.

She did not speak. In silence she shared his joy, his wonder as their bodies moved and swayed softly against each other, and the linen sheet rasped lightly against the smooth skin of her back—for her chemise had somehow come down and her breasts were bare to his gaze. Indeed it had ridden up as well so that it lay across her slender waist like a sheer lacy scarf, forgotten by them both.

Her hands caressed him as she moved to his rhythm, her lips moved against his chest, her back arched to bring her closer to him and she seemed to hear singing, impossibly sweet, as all the familiar glory of her love for this man returned to remind her of how it had been between them.

What matter that he did not know who he was or that they had made love before on countless starlit nights? He was here and he was hers again—and he was falling in love with her; that much she had already guessed.

And then passion swept her up on stormy wings and she soared with him to shimmering heights to an explosive world licked by the flames of desire—and fulfillment. And at last she descended reluctantly to the real world of sheets and bedstead and found him smiling down at her.

"You are a wonder," he murmured. "How well you fit into my arms!"

It was on the tip of her tongue to say, *I always did!* But she refrained.

"Do you think it would shock the servants if I stayed here for the night?" she asked with mock innocence.

He laughed. "I think they expect it!"

She studied him through seductive lashes. "And what will the governor think when he hears?"

"I think he will be delighted," her lover said cryptically.

Although his daughter will be less so! Carolina was thinking with satisfaction. She did not voice the thought. "So we are pleasing everybody," she said. "Most of all ourselves."

There was a smile on his face as he turned over and went to sleep.

Chapter 24

The next week was a sort of bittersweet honeymoon for Carolina. No longer did he own her as his wife—but she had become his mistress.

And for her, lying in the scented darkness while he strained above her, it was enough.

She heard him explaining to the governor's daughter that he could not ride with her because his head wound bothered him—and smiled. She heard him give orders to Luz to tell Doña Jimena, if she called, that he was out—and her smile broadened.

Perhaps she had not won him yet, but she was winning him! For he could not seem to get enough of her perfumed body. They made love and then they would lie there companionably in the afterglow, talking about all manner of things. He spoke to her with pride of this handsome New World town of Havana, of the strength of its defenses. It was the pride of Spain speaking, and she never by word nor look let him know that he was not Spanish, that the pride he took was in enemy fortifications, that he would find himself hanging high if others learned about him what she already knew.

And then on Saturday she could stand it no longer. She waited until the house was dark and quiet and all the servants had gone to bed—for no one must hear what she was about to tell him. She let him make love to her and then she sat up and looked at him thoughtfully in the candlelight.

"I have something to tell you," she said. "And you would do well to listen for it is your life I hold in my hands."

He grinned at her. "You may have all of me, *querida.*" And reached out again for her.

But this time she eluded him.

"First," she said, "tell me how Captain Juarez recognized you, for I am told that he found you dangling unconscious, tangled into the rigging of the *Sea Wolf* in Port Royal. He had never seen you before. How did he know it was you?"

"By my boots," he told her with an engaging grin, "since you're so interested. They were made for me especially by the King's bootmaker, and one of them had a message sewn into the side."

"They don't fit you very well," she scoffed, casting a glance at the scarlet-topped jackboots which he had so recently removed.

"Ah, that's because they were made up from an old pair that must not have fit me very well either," he countered. "It seems that I had left them at my bootmakers and their fit was duplicated."

"I'm surprised you didn't have them adjusted," she observed.

"And let the King of Spain know I didn't like his gift?" He laughed. "I'm rumored to be an ambitious man!"

"In Port Royal," she said slowly, "you had just had a

new pair of boots made. We quarreled, and you stalked out in your old ones. I think I know what must have happened. When you took the *Santo Domingo,* the salt air must finally have done in your boots—and you put on the boots of a dead man. Don Diego Vivar."

Her words hung between them like an accusation.

"So we are back to that, are we?" he said grimly.

"Kells, listen to me." Her voice was low and urgent. "I have been married to you, I know you well. There is not a mark on your body that I do not know. I can tell you how you got that scar on your wrist—and that one along your side. They were both in defense of me."

"You have not explained how I speak Spanish so well, nor why the ways of a Spanish *caballero* are second nature to me," he said harshly.

"You lived in Spain for a time. In Salamanca. You told me all about it. It was there you learned to hate the Spaniards. It was really because of what happened to you in Salamanca that you became a buccaneer! Oh, Kells, you must escape from here—you are in deadly danger! At any time one of the Spanish prisoners who had been held on Tortuga—and so many of them must have come back to Havana—could recognize you and you would be lost!"

"And any day a galleon could arrive from Spain with someone who knows me from my days at the Spanish Court," he countered. "And recognize me as my true self—Diego Vivar!"

"No," she said in panic. "That will not happen. It will be a disaster if anyone comes here from Spain who has known you!" In truth she had forgotten about that—he was menaced from *both* sides: Not only those who had known him in Tortuga as Kells could denounce him—those who had known the real Don Diego in Spain could denounce him as well!

He was staring at her, a cold light in his gray eyes. "What would you have me do?" he asked at last.

"I would have you leave here by the fastest way possible," she urged. "Steal a boat, anything—but get away. Anytime you show your face you could be recognized!"

The ghost of a smile passed over his lean features.

"And how do you account for the fact that I have not already been recognized as this Kells?" he demanded.

"It is because your clothes are so very different," she said frankly. "Because you sit beside the governor, you ride with his daughter. But if ever you take off your coat and stand with your shirt open in the sunshine, if ever you wear leathern trousers or sport a cutlass—!" She shuddered.

"So you would have me leave my heritage and seek—what?"

"A new life somewhere else. You have gold in England—let me go and claim it!"

"England," he murmured. "You would take me to England. . . ."

"No, for there you are a wanted man. Let *me* go there for you. Let me—"

She had reached out and grasped his arm as she spoke, and now he brushed her fingers off and stood up. His face was cold but no colder than his voice.

"So all this week you have been planning this, you lying wench! You would snatch me from my heritage and turn me over to the buccaneers! What devil is in you that would make you lie in a man's arms and then try to destroy him?"

"I would never destroy you!" she cried.

"Would you not?" He seemed to tower over her, glowering. "Yet you would deliver me to my enemies on a platter!"

"The buccaneers are not your enemies! They are your friends. Hawks—"

"Bah!" he said. "It is all of a piece with your devious ways. You sought to charm me, to cajole me, to bend me to your desires." He was angry because she had so nearly done it. Listening to her, he could almost trust what the lying wench said!

"Kells, believe me, I would not lie to you! I am trying to save your *life!*"

"I was wrong about you," he said. "I would have given up other women for you—but you are a buccaneer's wench after all!"

Of a sudden he picked her up, and before she guessed his intention he marched down the corridor with her, kicked open the door to her bedroom and tossed her upon the bed.

"Stay out of my way," he said thickly.

He turned and slammed the door behind him.

In fury and exasperation, Carolina began to cry. Through her angry sobs she could hear his own door slam in the distance.

Their short honeymoon had come to an end.

The next day he did not appear for breakfast and later in the morning she saw him driving out with the governor's daughter. But the worst was reserved for later: After he had returned from that jaunt, she saw Doña Jimena's carriage stop before the house. Doña Jimena was not in it, but Carolina had seen the Menendez carriage and its matched team of dancing black horses often enough to recognize it. Kells must have been waiting for it because he promptly went out and got into it and was driven away.

Watching him from the window of his bedroom where she had gone to mope, Carolina felt her eyes sting.

That he was squiring the governor's plump assertive daughter meant little to her, for she knew that Marina meant nothing to him. But that he had gone back to the arms of beautiful lecherous Doña Jimena, ah, that was something else!

Carolina walked about, growing more and more

upset. She would confront him at dinner! She would have it out with him!

But he did not come home for dinner. Indeed he did not come home that night at all.

The next day he passed her in the hall with an impassive nod—no greeting. When she would have spoken to him he brushed by her and closed the door.

She couldn't know what it cost him to do that, for the lure of her white arms was almost overpowering. He had lain with Doña Jimena and she had been her usual intriguing self. But she was not Carolina, and his soul and his body both ached for his lustrous wench. He had spent the night in a tavern drinking—but even that had not helped. *Madre de Dios,* the wench was in his blood. She had bewitched him!

But he would not let her know it. Indeed he would fight this mad infatuation that seemed to have dulled his wits and weakened his resolve! He would spend more time with Doña Jimena, whose interest in sex was as keen as his and who had perfected her own style of lovemaking—a style calculated never to get her pregnant. And if Doña Jimena's eager lips lacked for him the warmth of Carolina's sweet body—for Carolina seemed entirely careless of the chances she took of bearing a child out of wedlock—well, then he would find other hot wenches, the world was full of them!

So he reasoned—and so he suffered.

But Carolina did not know that. She was living in her own private hell, a world of fear for him—and fury with him.

"Men!" she told Penny bitterly.

"Yes. Devils, aren't they?" laughed Penny. "Do you know, I think I almost have the governor lured to my bed? I can't imagine why he's so shy!"

"He's probably afraid of you," sighed Carolina. "You look as if you might eat men alive!"

"Oh, come now! What's so upsetting? I thought you two lovebirds were getting along famously!"

"Not anymore," muttered Carolina.

"Oh, so he's back to his old tricks? Well, men are like that," Penny said philosophically. "There's an answer to that and it's always the same—get a new man!"

Carolina stared at her sister. Perhaps that *was* the answer! Don Ramon del Mundo had called every day and she had always told Luz to say she was out. There was no mistaking the hot light in the lean Spaniard's eyes—she could have a new man any day she wanted. Don Ramon was hers for the taking!

"It isn't the end of the world, you know," chided Penny, "whether Don Diego is faithful to you or not."

"Isn't it?" Carolina asked in a hollow voice.

"Well, I must say this thing has certainly sprung up fast. It seems only yesterday that you were mourning for Kells, and now you fly into bits because Don Diego sees Doña Jimena!"

"Perhaps I *should* stop mourning," muttered Carolina. "Perhaps I should find my own way in the world!"

"My sentiments exactly," was Penny's cool rejoinder.

But Carolina could not quite bring herself to do it. Deep in her heart she was still faithful to her buccaneer.

"I do not know how you can hate me—I have but told you the truth about yourself!" She confronted him squarely the next day, as he was coming through the door, fresh from a rendezvous with Doña Jimena.

He paused and scanned her—and the way he did it brought a flush to her cheeks. "I do not hate you," he said flatly, and it was the truth. Not only did he not hate her, he desired her with a heat that was hard to control.

Her femininity burned like a brand in the back of his consciousness and he carried in his mind a picture of her wherever he went. He would have died rather than let her know it.

"Then why do you avoid me?"

He took a deep breath. He avoided her because he felt that like a storm, she could sweep him from his moorings, dash him to disaster. She was beguiling, this lovely wench, and there was a terrible sincerity in her silver-gray eyes that he found daunting. Looking into those eyes, it was hard not to believe her—and that would be terrible, for all that he knew of himself, this self that he had become acquainted with so recently, was that he had spent his life fighting for God and Spain. To betray either—with this beautiful heretic—would make him a traitor, without honor, cursed in his own country.

"I avoid you," he said coldly, "because your lies would drag me down. I am a Spanish patriot—"

"A patriot, yes—but an *English* patriot," she corrected him angrily. "You were always that!"

"But Kells is known to be an *Irish* buccaneer," he told her, and there was a note of triumph in his voice.

"Kells *pretended* to be Irish in order not to shame his family in England," she retorted hotly. "Kells is in truth Rye Evistock, the eldest surviving son of a viscount—Lord Gayle."

He accepted this information without comment. "I have no doubt you know your man," he said, shrugging. "But I am not Kells. You must give up this bizarre fantasy that I am a buccaneer, somehow spirited to Havana!"

"I will not!" she cried, and her voice was now low and desperate. "I will not give it up because you are in great danger. Every moment that you remain in this city your life is in jeopardy!"

His contemptuous laughter echoed through the hallway. "I cannot believe that your mind is unhinged, so it must be that you seek to hoodwink me. I will have you know, mistress, that it cannot be done—at least not in *this* manner. Before God, I have served no master but the King of Spain—nor ever will!" His voice rang with a sincerity that infuriated Carolina.

She leaned forward with her slender hands on her hips and it was no unfortunate captive who was speaking now but the arrogant Silver Wench whom all Tortuga had held in high esteem.

"You have sunk their galleons and raided their towns," she said between her teeth. "You *married me* aboard the *Sea Wolf* in a buccaneer wedding while all Tortuga cheered! You have fought for me in many lands and against all odds. Would you deny me now?"

He could not but admire her spirit. After all, he told himself, she had found herself cast away among enemies—who could blame her for trying to better her position?

"If you were a man and told me I was Kells," he said slowly, "I would ask you to defend yourself and carve the lie upon your body. But you are a woman and defenseless here. My fingers itch to tame you with the lash but I will not because I recognize in you a fighting heart. Cease these lying accusations and we can become friends again."

She looked at him hopelessly. How could he be so stubborn?

"You are a fool," she said bitterly. "And you are bent on losing your life."

"At least I will lose it in a way of my own choosing and not in the way you have devised for me," was his cool response.

"Kells," she pleaded desperately, "what can I do to make you believe me?"

His tone was without expression. "If you call me Kells again, I will pull up those skirts and thrash your lovely white bottom until it is as pink as your cheeks!"

Her eyes flashed silver. "Oh, you would not!" she cried in exasperation.

"I would."

"Well, I shall call you Kells whenever I like! And I shall certainly call you Kells whenever we are alone!"

She had driven him too far. She realized it the moment the words had left her mouth.

Before she could move—and she was already in the act of drawing back, dismayed by the expression on his face—he pounced upon her like a big cat and swept her up against him. Ignoring the futile flailing of her beating fists against his chest, deaf to her furious screech as she kicked his shins—managing to hurt her toes in their soft slippers against the stout hardened leather of his jackboots—he carried her up the tiled stairway, bounding three steps at a time with his angry squirming burden.

Juana and Luz, alerted by the commotion, had come running out from the kitchen to see what was the matter. With pure delight on their rapt faces they watched Don Diego mount the stairs with a raging Carolina pinioned firmly against his hard body.

"What do you think he will do with her?" wondered Luz, impressed by Carolina's wails.

Old Juana laughed. "He thinks to beat her," she told Luz. "But he will reconsider."

And when Luz looked doubtful, Juana poked her jovially with her elbow. "He is in love with her, Luz. Why else would he—who always came home looking so relaxed and satisfied when he had been visiting Doña Jimena—now come home from the same lady looking tormented?"

"Perhaps he fears Doña Jimena's husband will find out?" suggested Luz.

Juana laughed again. "I think Don Diego fears neither gods nor devils," she said. "And especially I do not think he fears husbands—Doña Jimena's or any other's." An angry scream from upstairs penetrated down to their domain. "Come back to the kitchen, Luz. They will return smiling, and we will not want to be thought spying on them."

That angry scream from upstairs had come when Kells strode into the big front bedroom, sat himself down upon the bed and turned Carolina across his knee.

This devil is going to do it—he is actually going to spank me! Carolina had thought in blind rage as she felt her voile overskirt, her yellow petticoat and her cambric chemise all jerked upward in a single determined gesture that bared her white bottom to Don Diego's view.

The next moment she felt a large hand descend with a smack upon that bottom and she gave a cry of rage and did her utmost to squirm about and bite him.

She was rewarded with a rough cuff that put her back in position, to the sound of ripping of voile, and the large hand descended smartingly upon the reddening flesh of her soft bottom again.

"I am trying to make my point," he said evenly. "Which is that I am in command here. You will not go against my direct orders *and I order you not to call me Kells!*"

A sob of anger caught in her throat as she found herself suddenly righted and standing upon her feet before him. Her hair was a bright tousled halo tumbling wildly about her, and the expression of indignation on her lovely face was almost more than he could stand, but he kept his own countenance impassive as she trembled before him.

"You are *not* Kells!" She bit the words at him. *"You may once have been, but to me you are no longer*—you are not fit to lick his boots!" And in blind rage she drew back a white forearm and struck at his expressionless but determined countenance.

"Ah, now that's better," he said smoothly, and—overwhelmed by his desire for her—drew her abruptly into his arms.

For a moment Carolina swayed dizzily beneath the hot pressure of his lips. Then with a wrench that ripped the thin voile of her gown (indeed she could feel her sleeves part company from her bodice!), she pulled away from him—only a small space, for his arms were still around her. She looked up at him with blazing eyes and he could feel himself kindle to flame before her trembling fury.

"I do *not* desire you!" she gasped angrily. *"Don Diego!"* she added scornfully through clenched teeth.

"Do you not?" His dark brows shot up mockingly and he drew her back to him with perfect aplomb. "Your body tells me otherwise, wench of the Devil!" he told her and bent his head to revel in the sweetness of her flesh, to torment the soft lobe of her ear with his lips, to trail along the white column of her throat with the tip of his tongue.

Now was the moment to resist him—now, while he held her fast. But even as the thought crossed her mind she could feel her senses reeling, for her desire for him was as keen as his for her. Even though she had meant to remain rigid, to keep her knees locked together, she could feel her body relax against his with a sigh of perfect content, feel herself borne to the bed, feel herself falling—no, dissolving—backward upon it with his long body atop her own.

She did not even protest when he reached down and lazily but firmly spread her thighs apart. Indeed Carolina was overcome by a dizzy awareness of fate overtaking her as he thrust within her—not violently as she might have expected, but tenderly, savouring a lover's delight.

She felt the remnants of her defenses melting, crumbling beneath the sweet assault of his flesh. Even through a haze of remembered anger she could feel herself clinging to him. Against her will a little sob formed in her throat.

She thought she heard him chuckle and felt a new surge of fury that drove her to squirm and thrash about in his arms—which only completed the ruin of her sheer gown and increased this blinding overpowering sweetness that was stealing over her as every nerve end came alert and the world seemed a medley of confused responses to his lover's thrusts.

You should fight him! pealed a distant echo from that inward Carolina who still trembled in spent fury.

How can I when I love him so? wailed that other Carolina who had wept for his loss in Port Royal and who even now felt a burning terror that he might be lost to her again—this time past all reclaiming, to a Spanish executioner.

But the wars within her dimmed beneath his expert caresses, the voices stilled and drifted away to be replaced by swift flashes of passion racing through her blood. Through torrents of emotion she seemed to be rising, lifted up toward some far, unreachable goal, unutterably sweet.

She could feel his grip grow stronger now as they moved to their own wild rhythm. The world was far away and there was only this rushing magic, winging them along with it as their bodies touched and melded, as every physical sense drove them onward, straining toward a peak of passion that seemed to glitter above them, like a distant snowfield struck by the sun.

She had forgotten her anger now, forgotten her fear. She moaned against him, delighting in the hard masculinity of him. Her lips moved against him, and she murmured broken endearments, half heard, not noted. She felt his hot breath, felt his heart beat strongly against her own hot body and she seemed to flame to new heights with his every thrust.

Gone from her—at least for now—was every care, every worry, every danger, as the world sped away from them as if in flight to the farthest stars.

No man had ever made love to her like this, with such wild sweet gentle fury—and she gave back to him the very essence of herself, in moaning lost abandon.

It was wonderful, it was exciting, it was triumphant and it ended in a burst of glory before, still tingling and atremble, she felt her spent body relax and she sank down with a contented sigh from those marvelous heights they had just achieved.

She nuzzled against him, warm and safe in his love as he lay beside her, and felt his outflung arm on which she lay tighten briefly about her, felt his free hand rove over her body with affection, stirring to soft flames the embers of the afterglow.

"Oh, Kells," she murmured, still under the spell of his strong masculine appeal. *"I love you so*—I always have."

Beside her his tall form stiffened. He put her away from him and sat up.

"It is Diego Vivar in whose arms you have just lain," he reminded her sternly.

The world came back to Carolina with a crash.

"Oh, don't be a fool, Kells," she cried despairingly. "Do you think I don't know the man I'm married to?"

He was out of the big bed and landed on the floor on both feet with a thump.

"By God, there's no reasoning with you!" he growled. "I will find me a Spanish wench to share my bed!"

The door slammed behind him as he strode down the hall away from her.

Behind him Carolina burst into tears of vexation. She threw the bed pillows across the room. She ripped the sheets from the bed and stamped on them.

Blazing-eyed, she faced her reflection in the mirror that had been sent over from the governor's palace. It gave her back a marvelously rumpled reflection. Her white-gold hair seemed to radiate from her head in great shining tangles. Her face was flushed, the lips parted as she gasped slightly for breath. Her chest heaved, making her soft breasts rise and fall.

I look battered, she thought, her stormy gray gaze surveying the wreck of her thin dress. The petticoat had survived for it was linen and stronger, but the lighter red voile had given way in numerous places—both sleeves were out of the armholes, giving silent testimony to the struggle that had taken place. Two of the darts were ripped. The toe of her slipper had gone through the red voile hem, leaving a long swatch of material trailing her across the floor, and the gathered skirt had been ripped from the bodice at one side, giving the entire gown a lopsided effect.

Down below she heard the front door slam and she ran to the window and saw Kells striding away into the heat, moving fast away from the house. Away from *her.*

He would not be back tonight, she guessed. She would dine alone, wincing beneath Luz's impudent grin as the girl padded about, serving her with studied insolence.

Of a sudden her anger left her and despondency took its place. She went back and sank down upon the bare mattress, trying to blank everything from her mind. She was like a newly trapped bird, she thought, a bird beating its wings helplessly against the wicker of its cage.

For her there was no way out.

Chapter 25

Carolina was still sitting there listlessly on the bed when she heard the sound of Penny's feet tripping up the tiled stair treads.

A moment later Penny herself burst in, a vivid Penny jingling with jet and with a brilliant red scarf tied around her bright hair.

"Well, this room looks like something has struck it," she observed, coming to a halt and looking around her at the sheets lying heaped up on the floor, at the bed pillows flung into corners. She peered at Carolina. "I was just coming out the door when Don Diego dashed by looking as if he were on his way to his execution."

He may be, thought Carolina pessimistically. *He may go to his death one day still maintaining vigorously that he is Diego Vivar!*

Penny looked her up and down. "He was glowering so, I came over to find out if you were in an equally ferocious temper." Her observation of Carolina ended with a sigh. "I take it you had a little discussion of whether you would or you wouldn't?" She cocked her head at her sister. "And I take it from the state of your clothing—I doubt me that dress can be mended—that you didn't exactly win? But of course, with a man as attractive as Don Diego, perhaps you didn't exactly lose, either?" She gave a throaty chuckle.

Carolina gave her a dull look. "We had a difference of opinion," she stated.

Penny's chuckle became a full-fledged laugh. "That's obvious! And might one ask what sent Don Diego off in such a temper?" She was watching Carolina with bright eyes.

"No, one might not," sighed Carolina. "It is a private matter." For something told her she could trust Penny only so far, that Penny might shift her loyalties just as she had so frequently shifted her affections.

"A private matter . . ." Penny thought about that. "Well, at least you'll need some clothes," she said briskly. "That dress you're wearing—or should I say that's still hanging on to your figure—will never bear another such discussion! I'll poke about in the governor's palace and see what I can find for you."

Carolina gave her sister a grateful look. "Thank you, Penny. I don't know what I'd do without you."

"Well, I imagine you'd soon be down to your chemise—and when it was gone, where would that leave you?" Penny laughed heartlessly. "I'll be back soon," she promised, and left, to return in a little while with a black silk petticoat and a black taffeta riding skirt. There was a separate black taffeta bodice with long sleeves, and Penny had brought along a wide-brimmed black riding hat and a burst of white lace for her throat.

"But these are riding clothes," objected Carolina. "And where would I find a horse?"

"Well, perhaps you'll find yourself riding double with Don Diego," Penny suggested brightly, and Carolina gave her a sharp look. Did Penny know something? Had she guessed Don Diego's true identity? Was word already being muttered about the town? It seemed incredible that someone had not already recognized him.

The very thought gave her a headache. "You're right, perhaps I will," she murmured.

She tried on the clothes. The bodice was almost unbearably tight. "Doña Constanza was leaner in her younger days," observed Penny. "Before she bore Marina. And these riding clothes are obviously of that vintage. That's why I thought they might fit you."

"The sleeves are too long," Carolina pointed out.

"That's no trouble, we can tuck them up," Penny said.

But the main barrier was the black taffeta riding skirt. The petticoat was shorter and although it swept the ground, Carolina felt she could wear it without alteration. But the skirt was far too long.

"Do you think I dare ask Luz to shorten this skirt?" wondered Carolina. "She's the only one around here who's good with a needle—"

"Yes, I can't help you there," sighed Penny. "I'm worse with a needle than you are, Carolina!"

"And if Luz carries tales over to the governor's palace that I'm altering clothes that look as if they might have belonged to the governor's wife. . . ."

"Yes, I see your point." Penny frowned. Suddenly she had a flash of inspiration. "Here's your answer!" She tore the red scarf from her head and waved it at Carolina. "We'll tuck the skirt up higher and secure it with pins—and we'll wrap this scarf tightly around and around your waist and there"—she was doing it as she spoke—"no one will ever know these riding clothes weren't made for you!"

Carolina turned slowly before the mirror. Save that her hair was such a vivid blonde, her skin so pink and white, her eyes so light a gray as to seem silver, she might almost have been a Spanish lady. Her wide-brimmed black riding hat with its silver band sat squarely on her head. The tight black bodice made her slim figure seem arrow-straight and narrow. The wide sash that encircled her waist was of shimmering scarlet silk, and it cut a gash of color that—along with the burst of frosty white lace that Penny was just now tying about her white throat—gave her outfit a dramatic flare.

"It's too bad we have no boots to fit you," Penny said. "But neither Marina's nor Constanza's will fit your small feet!"

"No matter." Carolina's chin lifted as she pirouetted before the mirror. "I'll wear these that Don Ramon selected for me at his bootmaker's." She kicked her black skirts aside as she turned and exhibited a flash of red heels.

"Yes, how *is* Don Ramon?" wondered Penny.

"Well, I suppose. He's called several times but I've always sent down word that I was out."

Penny digested that. "He hasn't been near the governor's palace, and I understand he was a frequent visitor before—"

"Before Marina developed her interest in Don Diego," Carolina finished bitterly. She turned to Penny with a burst of honesty. "Oh, Penny, I don't think I can stand much more!"

Penny took that to mean that Carolina was jealous of the governor's plump daughter. "Oh, I've given Marina something new to think about," she said lightly. "She saw me coming out of the governor's bedchamber this morning."

Carolina gave a little start.

"Clad very lightly too." Penny chuckled as she remembered. "In one of her mother's sheer black chemises. You should have seen her face—I thought at first she was going to faint. And then she sort of hissed at me and dashed on by as if devils were after her." She fingered her jet necklace and ear bobs. "I found these lying on the pillow beside me when I woke up—in my own room later today. What do you think of them?"

"They—become you," Carolina forced herself to say.

"Yes, I think so, too," Penny said thoughtfully. "Of course, they aren't really *handsome*—you know what I mean. I'm sure Constanza's jewel box has many things I'd like better—some great sweep of emeralds, for instance. Or deep blue sapphires to match my eyes."

Carolina remembered bitterly a great sweep of emeralds that *she* owned. But they were far away in England. She doubted she would ever see them again.

"What do you think now—of the governor?" she managed.

Penny shrugged. "I was curious, of course, but I wasn't particularly impressed. And he had the bad taste at a most crucial point to actually call me *Constanza!*" There was a look of distaste on her face.

"Perhaps that's why he gave you the jet jewelry," suggested Carolina. "To make up for his lapse."

"Oh, these things?" Penny touched the jet with careless fingers. "They're just the opening gun! I'm sure he left them on my pillow in sheer gratitude because he hasn't had such an exhilarating romp in years! But just you wait and see what he gives me later."

"How can you be sure he'll keep giving you things?" Carolina said in a tired voice.

"Oh, he will," Penny told her confidently. *"He will,* Carol. Wait till I start *withholding* my favors—he'll dig deep into Constanza's jewel box then!"

"Or perhaps he'll just get out his riding whip and suggest you mend your manners," warned Carolina. "Women don't count for much here, you know!"

Penny laughed. "Women like us *will always count,*

Carol, wherever we go. And if the governor doesn't think so, he has much to learn!"

She swept out laughing, and Carolina thought, *That's all right for you to say, for you care nothing for the governor. He's only a pawn to you and could be replaced tomorrow and never missed. But I love Kells—and I will always love him. For me there will never be anyone else.*

She wandered about the room feeling desolate, wounded by life.

How could all this have happened to me? she asked herself in bewilderment. And a hurt voice deep inside asked, *Why can he not believe me? When all I want to do is save his life?*

She picked up the remnants of her torn gown and took it downstairs. Perhaps Luz could mend it after all. . . . But there were some things that could never be mended. And perhaps the human heart was one of those. . . .

Luz took the dress from her sullenly. Luz had hoped to become lady's maid to the governor's daughter and so acquire status in the governor's household—not maid to a mistress who would soon be a castoff, for surely Don Diego would come to his senses and realize that the governor's daughter Marina would come willingly to his bed. Ah, it would be a great marriage, thought Luz. And she herself should have the honor of dressing the bride—and would have, too, had she not been snatched away before she could sufficiently impress Marina with her worth. Snatched away to be scullery maid to this flaunting foreigner!

She gave Carolina a curious look, for she had seen Don Diego depart in haste looking like a thundercloud.

Carolina turned away from that look. She found Luz's constant unfriendly curiosity insupportable today.

She walked to the window and stood looking out.

Somewhere to the north, past Havana harbor, past the Straits of Florida, past the Bahamas, lay the American Colonies . . . and Virginia's Tidewater . . . and Level Green.

She was suddenly terribly homesick.

She wondered if her mother knew about the earthquake.

It would not have comforted Carolina to learn that her mother had heard—brutally and publicly—about the disaster only last week.

Indeed Letitia Lightfoot and her husband Fielding had been dining with friends at the Raleigh Tavern in Williamsburg when the big booming voice of a sea captain, just entering the Tavern's Apollo Room, had announced that Port Royal, Jamaica, had sunk beneath the sea.

"Whole town's gone," he had told his companions gloomily. "Lost with all souls. Earthquake shook it down, water came over the houses—it was built on sand, y'know. And it slid under the waves, it did."

He was unprepared for the effect his words had on the reed-slender woman in lilac satin who suddenly rose from the next table, her face gone white.

"Did you say lost *with all souls,* sir?" she demanded sharply.

The captain, who had been some time at sea, basked in the sudden interest of the loveliest woman in the room. He was but repeating the first wild rumors that had circulated about the earthquake.

"All dead," he told her gravely. "The entire city gone. Fell into the sea, it did, after the first great shock. Fell in layers, I'm told. The waterfront first, then swallowed up street by street."

And Carolina's tall brick house was close upon that "swallowed up" waterfront! Carolina, her favorite daughter. Carolina, too like herself—too rebellious, too reckless, always destined for disaster.

And now she had found it.

Letitia Lightfoot swayed like a flower caught in a strong wind and collapsed into the arms of an alarmed Fielding, who leaped forward to catch his wife.

It was one more story to make the rounds of Williamsburg gossip. The Lightfoots were the talk of the town again!

Back home at Level Green, Letitia Lightfoot put on mourning. But that did not deter her from going into Williamsburg to visit Aunt Pet, and the sight of her in black caused another stir.

"I don't think Carolina would want you to wear black for her," Petula told Letitia even as she dabbed at her eyes, for she had loved reckless Carolina, too. "She loved gaiety and life too much for that."

"You are right," Letitia said calmly. "Mourning does not become me. I am going home to take it right off!"

When next she appeared in Williamsburg she was wearing amethyst silk above a rustling royal-purple petticoat. Again she caused a stir.

"You are making a spectacle of yourself, Letty," complained Fielding. "Mourning on, mourning off."

His wife turned on him, dark blue eyes blazing. "You would do well to wear a black arm band yourself, Field! For it is the diamond and ruby necklace Carolina sent us that has enabled you to pay off all your debts and to commission that new wing for the house!"

Fielding had the grace to look abashed. "Carolina has been a good daughter to you," he mumbled. "I can't fault her."

"To *us!*" Letitia cried in an impassioned voice. "She has been a good daughter to *us,* Field! She has always honored you!"

A dark red flush spread across his strong features. He

gave his wife a look of baffled rage, jammed on his hat and strode for the door.

But the next time he was seen in Williamsburg, seated in an open carriage beside Letitia, he was grimly wearing a black arm band. Heads high, they drove along Duke of Gloucester Street, nodding to friends as they passed.

Letty is parading Field through the town in triumph, thought Petula in alarm. *And for the loss of a daughter not his own!*

Once again the Williamsburg gossips had a field day.

Carolina, lost in homesickness, knew nothing of the turmoil her death had caused in the Tidewater. She started as she heard Luz's faintly taunting voice behind her.

"Juana will want to know, do we set the table for one or for two tonight? Will Don Diego be coming home for dinner?"

"I doubt it," muttered Carolina. Then, "But of course you must set a place for him—after all, it is his table. He should find a place set for him should he return."

Suddenly she could not bear the girl's malicious stare. She turned and went back upstairs.

Slowly the afternoon passed and the golden light deepened as the shadows lengthened and turned to violet. The rooftops of Havana turned from terra cotta to crimson in the last burst of a red sunset. And then it was night, the swift, scented night of the tropics when the palm fronds swayed sensuously beneath a white sliver of moon.

And still he had not come.

Carolina forced herself to go down and eat a lonely dinner. At least she picked at her food and sent compliments out to the kitchen to Juana for preparing it so well.

Afterward she walked restlessly about the courtyard, pausing to lean against the pillars and stare at the tinkling fountain, making its gentle music endlessly. Above her the stars winked from the heavens like scattered diamonds. From somewhere night birds called softly to each other, and from down the street a man's wistful voice wailed a lover's lament to some bright-eyed girl behind the iron grillwork of her bedroom. A serenade to a lady . . .

Carolina could feel the magic, and her heart and her body yearned for her own lover.

And still he did not come.

She walked the empty courtyard until she was tired. All the servants had gone to bed. Around her Havana slept.

And still he did not come.

She went to bed at last, wondering where he was—and if he was alone. Was he carousing in the taverns? Or had he found a woman? Was he toasting her in wine, smiling down into her dark eyes, carrying her off to bed in some upstairs room?

Such thoughts kept her wide-eyed and awake, staring out through the grillwork at an uncaring moon that rode the night sky.

At last, worn out with love and fury and disappointment, she slept.

She was wakened by Luz and opened her eyes to find the morning sun streaming in through her windows.

Luz held out the dress that had been so badly torn yesterday. "It is mended," she said, and Carolina sensed the resentment in her voice and manner.

"Good. I will try it on, Luz." She leaped out of bed, wondering if Kells was already downstairs having breakfast. The thought goaded her. "It must be late," she said. "Here, help me dress, won't you?" She was pulling on her light chemise as she spoke for she had slept naked in the warm tropical night.

Silently Luz held out the mended dress for her to put on.

"Has Don Diego already breakfasted?" asked Carolina as Luz slipped the red voile dress over her head.

Luz shook her head. "Don Diego is still asleep," she said. "And Juana has given us orders to be quiet and not wake him for Miguel came by this morning and said that Don Diego had got very drunk last night and had near wrecked a tavern."

So she had been right! thought Carolina. He had gone out and drowned his anger in wine. Somehow the thought was less wounding than if Luz had said he had near wrecked a brothel.

"Miguel said he had a wench on each arm and was serenading them both when he saw him," added Luz and Carolina winced. "Don Diego is a devil with the wenches," added Luz spitefully.

Carolina managed to ignore the girl by studying her mended gown in the mirror. Luz had done a disastrous job with her needle. The sleeves were now sewn in so tightly she could hardly move her arms, the darts were crooked, and the stitches showed where the torn hem had been mended. Yet Luz was an expert sempstress—Carolina had viewed her work!

"Help me off with the dress, Luz," she told the girl sternly. "And take it apart and stitch it up again. It won't do the way it is."

Luz almost jerked the gown from Carolina's back. She flounced away—but not before Carolina told her to bring her up a bath.

It was a delight to sink into the warm water and bathe her body with scented soap. She lingered long in that bath for she was sure that *he* would be long asleep after his hard night.

In that she was mistaken.

She was still in her tub when she heard the door knocker bang downstairs.

That would be the governor's daughter, she thought irritably, sending in a servant to inquire if Don Diego would not escort her and her *duena* on a drive about the city! She struck the water rather hard with her sponge and felt it splash. Kells would soon set the girl straight!

Still she found herself hurrying with her bath, for someone had probably waked him with Marina's message and he might be downstairs breakfasting even now.

She dressed herself in the clothes Penny had brought her.

I look more ready for riding than for breakfast! she thought as she ran downstairs on her high red heels.

Luz sat in the courtyard where the light was brightest, pulling out stitches from the red voile. She looked up as Carolina's footsteps rang across the tiles.

"I heard the knocker," said Carolina.

"Yes," mumbled Luz.

"Well, who was it, Luz?"

Luz gave her a spiteful look. "It was a carriage come to pick up Don Diego."

Carolina sighed. "And did he go?"

"Oh, yes, at once," Luz said in mock innocence.

Plainly Penny's affair with Marina's father had not distracted the girl enough!

"I will have breakfast now, Luz," said Carolina. And then, just to verify, she added, "It was the governor's carriage, wasn't it?"

"That came to pick up Don Diego?" Luz's heavy dark brows rose in feigned surprise. "Why, no, it was the Menendez carriage that called for him, and he dashed out right away and leaped into it."

The Menendez carriage! Doña Jimena had sent for her Don Diego and her Don Diego had come running! Carolina felt as if a bucket of cold water had just been thrown in her face. Of young Marina she was not at all jealous, for she knew that Kells regarded her as tiresome, but beautiful dark-eyed Doña Jimena was quite another matter. Carolina was wildly jealous of *her!*

She stood with her back very stiff for a moment and outside she heard the sound of horses clip-clopping by decorously. The sound gave her an idea—a wonderful vengeful idea.

"Luz," she said, choosing her words with care, "while I am breakfasting, I want you to go over to El Morro. Tell the commander, Don Ramon del Mundo, that I regret having been absent all those times he has called. Tell him that I find myself free today and that I would be pleased to ride out with him if he so desires. Tell him that, Luz."

Luz leaped up, eyes aglow. There was trouble brewing, she could feel it in the air. Trouble that might bring her back to the governor's palace where she belonged. Oh, she would deliver the message, all right, for it was sure to have repercussions. If Don Ramon was not at El Morro she would follow his trail about the town until she found him! Indeed she could hardly wait!

"Go quickly, Luz," Carolina said in an expressionless voice.

And then after Luz had left, she again studied the tinkling fountain as she had last night. So much had happened, it seemed, in the space of a night and a day. Bitterly she remembered Kells's words to her just before he had stomped out: *I will find me a Spanish wench to share my bed!*

And now he had gone to Doña Jimena. . . . It was a deep wound, with the point well and truly driven home.

But she would stagger up from the sand. She would find herself a new love. She would not live in this limbo! If Kells could not love her, she would find a man who could!

Old Juana, who looked in on her at breakfast, thought she saw a dangerous light gleaming in her mistress's eyes.

Don Ramon del Mundo, found behind the forbidding walls of El Morro, reacted swiftly to the message brought by Luz. Within the hour he cantered up to the house on the Plaza de Armas on a big black stallion. He was leading a white Arabian mare who tossed her mane and tail in the sunlight. Don Ramon had a look of triumph on his swarthy countenance for he had almost given Carolina up, so many times had he been turned away from her door. And now, by heaven, she had sent for him! He carried his shoulders with a slight swagger as he dismounted and banged the big iron knocker.

Carolina herself answered the door. She gave him a winning smile and a curtsy that swept the tiles. "But you are here so quickly, Don Ramon!"

His gaze passed over her in leisurely fashion. "Yet I find you already dressed for riding," he observed.

"Ah, that is true—save for my shoes. These high heels will have to do. No"—she held up her hand, laughing—"I refuse to visit your bootmaker again, Don Ramon. I have a sudden urge to visit the countryside—not a stuffy bootmaker's shop."

So she wished to go out in the country where they would be alone! The tawny eyes lit up. It was what *he* desired, of course, but he had expected her to insist upon riding decorously around Havana.

She snatched up her hat, settled it firmly upon her fair hair. "I will not keep you waiting, Don Ramon." She turned to Luz who lurked nearby. "Should Don Diego return, tell him I have ridden out with Don Ramon," she said carelessly.

She saw Luz's eyes gleam. There was no doubt that Luz would deliver *that* message. The girl hated her! And at that moment Carolina was almost glad.

Don Ramon del Mundo led her proudly through Havana, past the handsome rococo buildings with their red tile roofs, past the iron grillwork balconies that jutted out over the street—and as they rode, he talked. He told her with an arrogant wave of his hand who lived here and who lived there—and regaled her with interesting stories about them. And gradually the white walls disappeared, melted into adobe shacks and noisy wineshops and rubbish heaps and bare ground with the grass worn away. Curious sandaled or barefoot people, sitting in the doorways of thatched huts or carrying huge burdens on their backs, watched them as they passed—the great lord of El Morro and the beautiful lady on the white horse. They wound their way through narrow, dirty, twisting streets crowded with scrambling half-naked children, turbaned prostitutes, dark *mestizos,* past vacant-faced peasants leading donkeys or mules. And then even those faces and those hovels of Havana's outlying *barrios* melted away and they were in the green countryside with the trade winds blowing their horses' manes.

Around them stretched pleasant green valleys and rolling hills dotted with cattle, for they were west of Havana. In the distance as they crested the low hills they could see the glittering blue of the sea.

They rode in silence now, Carolina looking straight ahead and Don Ramon, an easy rider in excellent control of his horse, considering her with an expression that Carolina, whenever she chanced to glance his way, could not fathom.

She could not know that in his mind's eye he was seeing a magnificent future. An impossible future perhaps, but a joyous one—a future with this woman forever beside him. He saw her ordering about the servants of a big new house he would somehow get for her. He saw her leaning back luxuriously, blonde hair shining in the sun, in a handsome new carriage (one he likewise did not possess) as he drove her about Havana so that everyone might envy him this glorious beauty. He saw her, regal in diamonds and pearls, her dainty chin high as he led her out upon the floor at a ball at the governor's house—no, not the governor's house, but a ball at one of the great houses in Seville, in Madrid itself! He saw her presented at Court, the most dazzling woman there—*and himself beside her.*

He saw a life that did not exist, perhaps would never exist. And while he was dreaming mad dreams, he envisioned Carolina as a woman in love with him. Deeply. Passionately. Past all returning. He imagined in her silver eyes an awakening glow, he saw her strolling gracefully to her bed in something sheer and black, saw the clean sweet lines of her figure silhouetted in candlelight as the gauzy material rippled, watched her turn and smile and beckon to him. His blood heated up at the thought! She would love him, by God she *must* love him for he would never meet her like again!

Thinking of it with a lover's desperation, his expression grew so determined that Carolina, now and again gazing at him idly, thought he looked very fierce.

She could not know that in his mind he was swiftly removing the last of her garments, tossing her gauzy black night things away, that his arms had just this moment enfolded her, that she sighed luxuriously and relaxed as he caressed her silken skin, quivered as his hot mouth trailed down her sweet body, moaned as his lips toyed urgently with her breasts, nuzzling their pink crests to hardness, whilst his hands were busily engaged elsewhere, bringing her to quivering delight.

She could not know, nor did she give more than a passing thought to what might be in his mind. She followed the lead of his big horse blindly. Indeed she cared not where they went, for there was a blackness in her soul this day that could have led her anywhere. Still it came to her as they proceeded, not idly but in a definite direction, that Don Ramon had a specific destination in mind.

She was right.

He brought his horse to a halt atop a low hill beneath the shade of a large ceiba tree. Off to her right she could see a great *estancia* with a handsome tree-lined avenue, and tilled land—and the thatched roofs of the Indian *bohios* of the tillers. And in the surrounding pastures clumps of palms waved in the breeze.

"That is the *estancia* of Perez de Cadalso," he explained to her as if the name should mean something to her.

Carolina viewed the handsome holding with enormous disinterest.

Don Ramon tried again. "Perez de Cadalso is the father of Doña Jimena Menendez," he said softly. "She is his only child."

Carolina sat straighter and stared with concentrated interest at the obvious luxury of this sweeping *hacienda.*

"So Doña Jimena grew up here," she murmured.

Her escort nodded. "Here and at their town house. Her father owns two other *estancias* some distance from Havana—and landholdings in the jungles of the Oriente."

"It is easy to see why Doña Jimena might marry the richest man in Havana," Carolina said dryly. "She must have been the town's greatest catch!"

Don Ramon was studying the estate. When first he had come here he had bitterly regretted that Doña Jimena had so recently spoken her wedding vows in the great twin-towered cathedral behind the Plaza de Armas. Like so many others, he had been instantly enamored of the Cadalso beauty. But now, looking down at her father's handsome estate, he felt oddly free and somehow optimistic about his life.

It was, he knew, because of the woman who sat on her horse beside him—a woman whose flashing silver eyes seemed today filled with sadness.

"Doña Jimena fancies Don Diego," he said bluntly in case she did not know, for he wanted it made clear to Carolina that his rival had other interests.

"I am aware of that," Carolina heard herself say in a detached way.

He dismounted and lifted her down.

"We will rest," he said, "and let the horses graze."

Carolina sat down with him upon the grass. It was late afternoon now. A bee buzzed lazily nearby. From somewhere in the distance came the plaintive sound of bells.

Don Ramon leaned against the trunk of the ceiba tree and considered her silently. She could feel the heat of his glance. It was making her nervous.

"I never thought to feel about a woman as I do about you," he said frankly. "I would have stormed Port Royal for you, do you know that?"

"And now both Port Royal and I are swept away," she murmured.

"Port Royal may be gone but *you* are *here,"* he said bluntly.

She had been looking down at her dark skirts and now, at something in his tone, she looked up. He was gazing at her keenly and his tawny eyes said much.

Idly he reached over and took her hand. She did not try to pull it away, but let him caress it, lifting it to his lips, rubbing it against his cheek.

"I desire you as I have never desired a woman," he told her huskily and bent forward to kiss her.

Carolina tensed. Now if ever was the moment to break away. And then she caught sight again of the great *estancia* rising in insolence before her—and for a moment she could see in her mind Doña Jimena strolling its corridors. *With Kells.* Of course Doña Jimena would never dare to take him there—or would she? Were they there right now, making love behind one of those grillwork windows?

A sob caught in her throat and Ramon del Mundo took it for desire.

His strong arms closed around her and he drew her to him, down upon the grass. His lips were on hers and they were tender lips for all that they were so determined.

His every touch revealed something she had not really taken in before—Ramon del Mundo loved her.

It was a shock to realize it and she stiffened.

Don Ramon sensed that withdrawal and he drew back. "Do I go too fast for you?" he asked softly, and she sat up and pushed him away.

"Yes, you do," she said, feeling confused. "I—I am upset today, Don Ramon. Please do not ask me why."

"I do not have to ask—I can guess. The Menendez carriage, with Don Diego in it, was seen on the Plaza de Armas."

"Luz told you that! She is a wicked girl."

He shrugged. "The whole town knows it." His hand gently stroked her shoulder and she felt a heady lightness at his touch.

"I suppose—they do," she said haltingly, and could not entirely keep the misery from her face. For Ramon del Mundo's touch might be enticing, but her heart was with Kells, back in Havana.

He leaned forward until his dark face was very near her own. He took both her shoulders in his hands, kneading them gently. His tawny eyes, looking into her own, were very keen for he wanted Carolina as he had wanted no woman before her and he knew, in a sudden flash of inner vision, that he would want her forever.

"Tell me," he demanded, "what hold is it that Diego Vivar has over you? You have known him but a matter of days! Is he then such a remarkable lover?"

Her guard came up at that and she turned watchful. For Ramon del Mundo must never guess what hold it was that Don Diego had over her. She might leave Kells, but she would never, *never* betray him to the hangman's noose!

"He reminds me of someone," she said, and instantly wished she had not, for his eyes lit up.

"A memory of an old love? Ah, that is romantic—and to be expected. I had not thought of it." He sat back and began to laugh, for it had occurred to him that Doña Jimena reminded him of a girl for whom he had yearned as a callow youth back in Spain. "We are all victims of old memories," he said, smiling at her.

"Yes—that is it, of course," she agreed hurriedly, looking down and plucking nervously at her skirt.

But something in her voice had not rung true, and Don Ramon gazed at her narrowly.

"You are marking time here," he said suddenly, as if he had made a great discovery. "You expect to be rescued by your buccaneer lover!"

She frowned at him. "My buccaneer *husband,*" she corrected him. "And he will not, as you suggest, 'rescue' me. He lies dead in Port Royal." *Perhaps that is true,* she thought bitterly. *Kells is dead and Don Diego has taken his place.*

He pounced on that. "You saw him die?"

"No, but when the city sank—"

"So you are not certain! In the disaster, I am told, there was much confusion. And you cherish the thought that he is not dead, that he will return to you." He leaned upon an elbow and a kind of wry amusement spread over his dark features. "Ah, yes, I see how it is. You expect your buccaneer to reappear, to sail into

Havana harbor, silence the guns of El Morro—and the Punta and La Fuerza—and sail away with you. I can read it in your eyes!"

"No." She sighed. "In truth, that is the last thing I expect."

"Perhaps now that you have seen Havana's superb defenses you realize the folly of such a move? Perhaps it is realizing that you will not be reunited that has made you remember an old love, is that it?"

"Yes," she lied eagerly. "That is it."

He gave a low laugh and seized her by the forearm. "You are lying," he said. "And from you I want only the truth. *You have forgotten your buccaneer! You have fallen in love with Diego Vivar!*"

That much at least she could answer with candor. She looked him full in the face, hopelessly. "I will never forget my buccaneer," she said. "But you are right, Ramon, I have fallen in love with Diego Vivar. And I wish"—her voice was bitter—"I wish I had not."

"Then let me lure you away from him," he said quickly, and drew her toward him by the forearm he had pinioned.

She felt a fluttering in her breast. The lure of this man's masculinity was very strong. Kells was somewhere—perhaps in bed—with Doña Jimena. *I will find me a Spanish wench to share my bed. . . .* His hurtful words still rang through her mind. Around them as they sat there, the shadows had lengthened. The swift night of the tropics was about to fall.

"Ramon . . ." she said in a choked voice.

He sensed her surrender and eased her into his arms, caressing her with his lips. "You should belong to me," he murmured into her ear. "And one day you *will* belong to me. . . ."

Carolina's eyes were closed. She could feel tears sting her eyelids.

"Ramon," she whispered, and he silenced whatever she might have been about to say with his lips.

A kind of stillness seemed to hover over Carolina. She felt suspended between heaven and earth. She had moved into Ramon del Mundo's arms almost without volition. She stayed there like a trapped bird, afraid to move, afraid to breathe.

What she was seeking in those arms was solace, perhaps.

What she found was passion.

BOOK IV

Kells

And so for you I've spun a tale of love that would
not die
(It's in the Caribbean, floating on a perfumed sigh!)
And in the night somewhere the stars flash in a lady's
eyes
And ghostly man and ghostly maid are melded in
their sighs!

THE OUTSKIRTS OF HAVANA

Summer 1692

Chapter 26

The lean Spaniard's arms tightened about her. There was a sense of urgency in him now, and she was swept along with his desires, blown forward like a leaf before a strong wind.

She was hardly aware of how they sank to the grass in the fast-gathering dusk. He was battling the hooks of her bodice now, even as he smothered her with kisses. He was through with the hooks, his determined hand was beneath the bodice, was past her chemise, was gently stroking her breast. As she gasped, his tongue found her parted lips, explored within. She turned her head and the grass tickled her ear. Crickets chirped and from somewhere came the sound of a tree frog.

Her skirts were riding high now, tossed upward by a determined lover. There was a small sound of protest in her throat—instantly hushed. For her soul had been bruised this day and her broken world needed mending. In these moments she needed Ramon del Mundo as much as he needed her. With a little choking cry, her arms twined around him and for long moments they both pushed aside the world they knew—and must deal with on their return to Havana: that he needed a rich wife to keep him going; that she was hopelessly and forever in love with a man who had rejected her. But for them in those moments when they embraced on the grass beneath the old ceiba tree there was no past and no future. Only the shared wonders of the soft tropical night.

To Carolina his touch was balm upon the hurts the day had given her, and in Ramon del Mundo's turbulent soul he cherished the proud hope that she would find his arms irresistible and never wish to leave them. He was wrong of course—but then lovers so often are. Carolina found Don Ramon's embrace exhilarating; with him she was swept along by the thrills of the flesh—with him she even for a few moments found forgetfulness.

But it was all too brief, and even with his kisses still pulsing on her lips, her world was back upon her again. What madness had come over her? she asked herself dizzily. She was Kells's woman, whatever happened, whatever the cost!

"No," she gasped. "No!" And drew away from him, tugging at her skirts.

Ramon del Mundo stared down at her, not comprehending. A moment ago she had been a hot wench, exchanging passionate kiss for passionate kiss. A moment ago he had thought himself on the road to ecstasy. Yet now she flinched back from him, her face averted, a hand raised fluttering as if to ward him off.

"Why do you flinch from me, *querida?*" he asked in a voice rich and sad—because he was afraid he knew.

"I—this is all wrong," she choked. "I should never have let you bring me here, never led you on to believe that I would—" She stopped, hopelessly.

"Why?" he asked reasonably and his hand reached out and gently, yearningly stroked her thigh. "Never did a man more desire to be led!"

She edged away from him, trembling. A pulse beat in her throat. He was terribly attractive. It would be so easy to give in to him. Easy—and wrong.

"You must not fall in love with me, Ramon," she said in sudden panic, abruptly ashamed that this tryst should mean so much more to him than it did to her. "You do not deserve to be hurt. Indeed, I find myself confused. I have been very unhappy of late. I—"

"You want still to make your choice between us?" he divined. The vision of her riding forever beside him was vanishing now, the image of her smiling at him against the blue backdrop of the Guadalupe mountains was fading. He laughed ruefully. "Well, I suppose to choose is a lady's right although"—there was a certain wistfulness in his voice—"I had far rather settle the matter with my sword."

"Oh, no, you must not!" That was to be averted at all costs but she couched her words carefully, in terms that gallantry would understand. "Don Diego still suffers from his head wound," she explained. "He will not admit to it but he has terrible headaches—I have seen him sitting with his head in his hands. It would be murder to challenge him."

What a glib liar I have become! she thought, but his answer surprised her.

"I know." He sighed. "It is what held me back when I tried to buy you from him."

Her head came up. "When you *what?*" she gasped.

"Did Don Diego not tell you?" he asked mockingly. "It was outside La Fuerza before witnesses. I offered him my greatest possession here in Havana—a ruby cross that I had inherited from my father. It has been long in my family so I had never before considered selling it, but in such a cause . . ." His tawny gold eyes caressed her. "I thought Don Diego might covet it. I offered it to him if he would send you along to El Morro to—er—tend my house as you tend his."

Carolina felt her hands clenching. "And what did Don Diego say?" she demanded stormily.

Don Ramon gave an indifferent shrug. "He refused to discuss it. He said you were not for sale. He was very curt about it. Indeed his manner was such that I considered challenging him"—Don Ramon's eyes gleamed—"but I recalled his recent wound and decided the governor would frown upon me if I injured him."

More likely he would injure you! thought Carolina with asperity, for she had solid faith in Kells's skill with a blade. Kells had told her nothing about Ramon del Mundo's offer. *How like him,* she thought with a sudden rush of affection, *to have nearly fought a duel over her and kept it to himself!*

Her joy in that was suddenly tempered by the realization that Kells was probably in bed with Doña Jimena at this very moment.

"When did you make this offer?" she wondered.

"When Don Diego sought me out to pay me for the shoes I bought you."

So he had done that, too! She remembered now how Kells had come home and looked at her cynically and said, "You have found an admirer in Don Ramon del Mundo."

"I must go back," she said. "But I cannot rise—your knee is on my skirt."

Obligingly he moved his knee.

"But why? Why must you go back?" His hand trailed idly over her soft breasts, caressing the nipples. "Why can we not stay where we are till morning's light and ride back with the dawn?"

She pushed his hand away. "But I cannot have a hue and cry raised and ride back to find all Havana searching for me!"

She would have scrambled up then, but his long arm blocked her. "So you are to go back to your life and I to mine? As if nothing has happened?"

"Yes!" She tried again to rise.

"But Carolina, *querida,* something *has* happened. I have fallen in love with you. And I will not be pushed out of your life!"

Oh, she should have foreseen this would happen! She tried to keep her voice calm, to fight the rising panic in her breast.

"You will make of me a scandal," she protested.

His lips twitched. "A scandal? A woman who arrives in Havana by way of New Providence and is snatched from being sold in the marketplace by the governor, who gives her to Don Diego as a plaything? And you think you are likely to *become* a scandal?"

His words brought a flush to Carolina's cheeks. "I was a lady when you dined at my house in Port Royal," she reminded him frostily. "I am no less a lady now!"

He chuckled. "What a beauty you are!" he murmured. "Even in the darkness I can see your eyes shine."

She gave him an affronted look. "I am leaving!"

"Is it marriage you want?" he asked thickly.

"Ramon!" Her voice held a wild appeal. "You have said that I still believe myself married to someone else," she chided him.

"Yes, I have said that." His voice was sad but he released her, let his hand fall to his side. "What is it you wish of me, *querida?*" he asked her softly. "Name it and it is yours."

"I wish—oh, Ramon, I wish—" Tears choked her voice and she leaped up suddenly and sprang upon her horse. Lifting the reins from the ceiba tree where the mare had been tethered, she was off toward the town.

Don Ramon gave a shout—perhaps of warning—and sprang upon his own horse and thundered after her.

The white Arabian mare was fleet and they had covered some distance before the big black stallion caught up with her. As Don Ramon galloped up alongside, he leaned over and said, "Carolina, I am sorry. Slow your mount. I promise I will give you no cause for alarm."

The night wind had dried her tears and Carolina allowed the mare beneath her to find a more decorous pace. She acknowledged to herself guiltily that she had invited his embrace, encouraged it, wanted it. And then rejected him. How bewildered he must be!

"It is Don Diego, is it not?" he was asking her wearily. "You have given him your heart?"

"I—don't know," she said. But she did know. She had given her heart long ago to Kells, whatever name he used.

And if Don Ramon should learn that Don Diego was actually Kells—! The thought froze her blood. Whatever folly her despair had driven her to this night, it must not cost Kells his life! On that point at least she would never falter.

Don Ramon was not looking at her now. He was looking sadly into distant vistas. Proud man that he was, it was a blow to find himself rejected. But—he wanted Carolina to love him and he knew instinctively that he would forever ruin his chances if he sought to take her by force. It was a wrench to let her go when she had seemed so nearly his beneath the ceiba tree, but he could still cherish the thought that she would change her mind. Women did that. He could hope.

Carolina was dimly conscious of this mood of his as they rode through a night magically scented with rosewood and saffron, and the strange exotic scents of lush tropical flowers wafted to them by the trade winds.

Finally she spoke—and what she said was the truth.

"Don Ramon," she sighed. "I have done you a great injustice—and you in no way deserved it. I led you on—and backed away. For that I make no excuses but I offer you my apologies." She flashed him a bittersweet smile. "It is my lot in life to bring my world constantly crashing down upon me."

He did not really understand that last remark but he studied her from shadowed tawny eyes as they rode into Havana.

"Querida," he murmured. "You are all a man could desire. For you I would forgo much, endure much."

Carolina regarded him mistily. She could not bring herself to speak.

They rode silently through the dark streets.

When they reached the house on the Plaza de Armas, Don Ramon leaped to the street and lifted her down before she could dismount. For a moment he held her luxuriously in his arms, savouring her slight weight that rested against his chest, drinking in the faint lemony scent of her shining blonde hair.

"Querida, if you should have need of me, you have only to call," he murmured, then swiftly set her on her feet and went to bang the big iron knocker. It sounded very loud in the quiet street.

Carolina looked up nervously at the windows of the front bedroom above her, wondering if the noise would wake Kells and if he would come down and perhaps confront Don Ramon here in his doorway.

But no candle flared in the darkness above. Indeed it was a long time before old Juana shuffled to the door, unbarred it and let Carolina in.

Almost before the heavy door had closed behind her, Don Ramon had remounted and was gone like a wraith in the darkness.

"Where is Don Diego?" Carolina breathed fearfully.

"He has not come home." Old Juana's voice was stolid. What would be would be.

Carolina took a deep shaky breath. "What are you doing up?" she asked. "Why didn't Luz answer the door?"

"Luz slipped out to spend the night with Miguel. And if Luz does not watch her step, the governor's cook will be pursuing her down the street with a butcher knife!" She chuckled, for the amorous mishaps of those around her did much to brighten her days.

"Go on to bed, Juana. If Don Diego bangs on the door, I will let him in. And one more thing." She turned on the stairs to call to the old woman who was lumbering across the courtyard. "Tell Luz that if she tells Don Diego that I went riding with Don Ramon, I will have her whipped until her back is nothing but stripes." Her eyes narrowed. "No, I will not *have* it done—I will do it myself!"

Old Juana chuckled again. "I will tell her," she promised. And then thoughtfully, "I do not think she will tell him. Luz fears the whip."

"Is Nita awake? I would like a bath."

"I will wake her," said Juana. "She is young, she will not mind—and I will let her sleep late tomorrow."

Carolina, in her black riding clothes, went on upstairs. From the top she called down, "Tell Nita I will be in the front bedroom."

Just on her way to the kitchen, Juana heard that and grinned. Back from her tryst with another man and she would greet Don Diego naked in his bedchamber—ah, there was a wily wench. Juana did not know when she had enjoyed a job more!

Carolina pulled off her clothes thoughtfully. She had made a mistake tonight—made it with a hot-blooded Spaniard who was already half in love with her. And she would pay for that mistake, she had no doubt. A wiser woman would never have done what she did. But then—when had she ever been wise?

Nita brought the water and Carolina sank into the tub gratefully, washing off the dust of Havana's streets, of the outlying *barrios,* of the magnificent countryside. She relaxed in the warm water, feeling it lap about her waist, and she scrounged down in the tub with her knees bent, letting it lap about the white mounds of her young breasts that had aroused such ardor in Don Ramon.

She was beginning to live with regret. Kells did not know his real identity, and as a patriotic Spaniard—for in truth he believed himself to be the genuine article—he mistrusted her as a "buccaneer's wench," and who could blame him?

But she—*she* had been about to betray him, with her eyes wide open. She had been angry and confused and despairing that he had chosen not to believe her, that he had gone off to some other woman's arms.

Her eyes darkened as she thought about it, turned to tarnished silver as she considered the possibility that Doña Jimena had somehow spirited Kells away to her father's house, and that the winking lights she had seen from the *hacienda* had been a candlelit upstairs bedroom where Doña Jimena strained with her lover. . . . It did not bear thinking on, but somehow it eased a little the pain of her own remorse!

THE HOUSE ON THE PLAZA DE ARMAS HAVANA, CUBA

Chapter 27

Carolina awakened in confusion. Somewhere a door had shut. She sat up, putting a hand over her eyes to ward off the brilliant light that streamed in from the windows.

She realized suddenly where she was: in Don Diego's front bedroom, where she had curled up to nap after she had toweled herself dry last night.

Now she lay completely naked upon the coverlet and Don Diego himself stood in the door. A Don Diego who looked haggard and worn, as if he had fought some great battle with himself—and lost.

"Kells . . ." she murmured, not knowing what to say to him.

"You may call me that." He shut the door behind him. "You may call me anything you like. I have tried to fight you off but it seems you are in my blood and the only way to get you out is to stop breathing."

"You—remember?" she asked joyfully.

He shook his head. "I remember nothing. I would swear before God that I have never met you before—

and yet . . . and yet there is something about you . . . and this feeling I have for you." He shook his head.

"That feeling is called love," she told him sadly. "You were in love with me once even though you do not remember it."

"I only know that what was enough for me before you came is not enough for me now. I find myself thinking about you at odd times through the day, no matter where I am." *And through the nights, as well, no matter in whose arms he spent them!* "Try," he pleaded, "to call me Diego."

She sighed. "That will be very hard for me," she said in a voice gone husky. "Because to me you *are* Kells."

"Your lost lover . . ." He looked bemused. "I am to become a shadow of some other man!"

"No," she maintained stubbornly. "Of yourself. You are a victim of what others have told you. They saved your life—so you choose to believe them."

"Carolina," he said, "enough of this. I have come to offer you somewhat more than your other suitors in Havana may offer you." She tensed because she guessed he was speaking of Don Ramon del Mundo. "I have come to offer you marriage. I want you to share my life, Carolina. I will take you away to Spain. You will be happy there."

Her eyes blurred with sudden tears as the declaration he had just made sank in. It was a great deal, coming from a proud gentleman of Spain—which he believed in his heart he was. And to a heretic, the daughter of an enemy country, bride to a buccaneer!

"Kells," she whispered and held out her arms to him, and sank backward down upon the bed.

His gray eyes kindled at the sight of her naked loveliness, so charmingly displayed upon his coverlet.

"Then you will come to Spain with me?" he asked as he divested himself of his clothing.

Her smile was wistful. She would never go to Spain with him—for him to go to Spain, she felt, would be to die. "Perhaps not to Spain . . ." she murmured.

"We will stay here, then," he said eagerly. "I will find a post here. I will write to someone in power there." He frowned suddenly, looking down at his hands. "It is strange," he said, "but I have also lost my ability to read and write."

"You never knew how to read and write Spanish," she told him. "You only *spoke* it. Prove it to yourself. Take up a pen and write something in English—you will find it comes to you very easily!"

Instead he divested himself of the last of his clothing and strode over to the bed, stood looking down at her with yearning.

"Carolina," he said. "Whatever I am or may have been, I love you past all allegiance. And if you will take me as I am, I will defend you against all the world."

Carolina's tears spilled over and the tall naked figure before her blurred.

"That is all I could ever ask," she choked and lifted her arms to enfold him.

Very gently he lowered his big body over hers, very tenderly bent his dark head and pressed a kiss that was a promise upon her trembling mouth.

And although she had lain in his arms many times before and fit to his lean body better than the gauntlet gloves he often wore fit to his strong hands, this joining—here in Havana in the bright light of morning—had a wondrous quality to it. They had found it again—all the breathless magic of new love. And she thrilled to it, knowing from the way he suddenly lifted his head and stared down at her in the golden sunlight, that he must feel the same.

In truth he did. Even as his strong arms had gone round her, even as his lean hips had lowered to caress her feminine softness, he felt that he had known her always. In some other life perhaps? he asked himself whimsically. Or was her incredible story true? He thought not—and at the moment he cared not. It was enough to strain with her there on the big square bed, enough to know that he was carrying her with him to the very heights of passion, the outermost shores of desire.

He had found his woman, and whether she called him Kells or Rye or Diego Vivar mattered not to him. What mattered was that she loved him in return—and her ardent responses to his lightest caress told him that she did, her broken murmurings told him so, the desperate way she clung to him as if afraid that he might leave her told him so.

It was enough.

Eventually they left the big bed, eventually they ate, smiling at each other in the courtyard. Eventually they went back to the big bed and Carolina, lost in love, looked up at her lover in the moonlight with big luminous eyes.

The governor's daughter called the next day and was told that Don Diego was sleeping late and had asked not to be disturbed. She sent word that a mighty galleon, the white and gold *El Dorado*, had cast anchor in Havana harbor, and to ask Don Diego when he woke if he would not care to view such a splendid ship.

"She will not let you alone—you know that?" said Carolina ruefully, when the message was delivered.

"She will. I promise it." Kells left off stroking her hair and went down to leave word with old Juana to tell all who called that he had contracted a slight fever and feared to spread contagion. He would be on his feet again soon; meantime they were not to worry.

Hearing the instructions he had left, Carolina laughed. "Marina will stamp her foot!" she told him. "And break things."

The thought of the governor's spoiled daughter

breaking things because she could not persuade him to drive out with her amused him. "I think she will recover," he said dryly.

"Oh, no doubt," Carolina said. "But I pity the chambermaids when she receives your message for it will be their duty to clean up the broken crockery!"

"Carolina." His voice had grown serious. "I took your advice. I set pen to paper and wrote something in English. You were right, it came to me very easily." He gave her a hunted look.

Her heart leaped. "You see?" she said eagerly. "It is proof of who you are!"

He ran distracted fingers through his dark hair. "No, it is not proof," he corrected her. "It tells me only that the part of me that writes in Spanish is somehow blocked by the blow I received."

She was disappointed but she sank back. "Come and make love to me," she murmured. "We must make the most of your 'fever' for the world will not let us alone for long!"

He was very willing.

And the next day he said, "I have seemed to remember something. It is just a fragment but it seems to come from my past and not my imagination. . . . I seemed to be standing with you on a ship, looking out at a tall dark mountain that rose out of the sea. There was another man there. He spoke to you in English and my hand sought my sword. I think I might have killed him from the way I felt. But . . . that is all I can remember."

Her eyes were wet. "We have been on shipboard so many times," she said. "But that particular time would have been in the Azores. And that black mountain rising out of the sea would have been the Island of Pico. This man you wanted to kill—he looked like you, didn't he?"

He gave a slight start. "Yes, he did in a passing sort of way."

"He was Robin Tyrell, the Marquess of Saltenham," she said bitterly. "And I suppose it is a pity you did *not* kill him for you yearned to do so. He had masqueraded as you and sunk English ships and cost you your king's pardon. It was because of him you went back to buccaneering. It is because of him that you are here today." She moistened her lips. "A disaster *I* brought upon you because I begged you to spare his life." She gave him a sober look. "I have much to answer for where you are concerned, Kells."

He shrugged. She was so believable, was this silver wench who flitted like moonlight through his life. And yet he could not believe it, it was too bizarre. He was under her spell, he told himself. Like a witch, she had cast an enchantment over him, and it would be easy to believe anything she said.

But the next morning he told her of a rambling white house where a great battle with cannon had taken place.

"You have remembered our house on Tortuga," she told him calmly. "And the night El Sangre attacked it. You had a cannon mounted in the garden. You won a great victory."

He stared at her in wonder. "I seem to remember a garden, too," he muttered.

"With a green door," she supplied.

"Yes . . . with a green door." He frowned. "You have bewitched me," he muttered.

She gazed on him fondly—yet with fear, too. For one day soon—very soon—he would come to himself and realize who he really was. But would it be too late? Oh, she must guard against his being recognized, she must keep him off the streets.

And the best way to do that was to keep him in her

bed. She found him most agreeable to all her suggestions that they lie about, dallying through the long hours.

"Do you not wish yourself to be off surveying a great white and gold galleon in the harbor?" she teased him as they lay panting in the heat after a long bout of lovemaking.

"I had rather survey the white-gold of your hair," he responded gallantly.

But in spite of his gallantry, she thought he cast a restless look at the outdoors. He was not a man to be cosseted indoors, she knew; he was a man of action.

"If only we could find some place by the sea for a while." She sighed and moved restlessly in his arms. "Some place where we could be alone." She sounded more wistful than she knew.

He stirred. "I know of such a place," he said suddenly. "Captain Juarez told me of it. It is a great cavern with its mouth opening above a strip of sandy beach. He says it is a romantic spot."

Carolina sat up, all excitement, and surveyed him from a vivid face framed by rumpled fair hair. "Oh, do you think we could go there?" she cried. "I could ask Juana to tell everyone your fever had persisted!"

He laughed. "You will have the governor sending me a doctor!"

"No," insisted Carolina seriously. "Juana can manage it—she loves intrigue. She will frighten the other servants with stories of contagion so they will stay away from our room." She sprang from her bed and began energetically to dress. "I will go downstairs and discuss it with her. I am sure she will be able to ward people off without alarming them too much."

Trusting in old Juana's diplomacy, they rode off just after dusk through the quiet streets. Carolina was sure that no one had seen them go for she had looked carefully about her. They were riding double on Kells's big chestnut horse, who seemed tireless and glad of the exercise.

Kells was an easy rider; he sat loose and relaxed in the saddle and Carolina sat before him, leaning back luxuriously against his chest, feeling the pleasant pressure of her legs against his hard thighs as the horse moved beneath them. Kells kept an indolent arm about her waist that could be tightened should the horse stumble and unseat her. He did not talk much but occasionally nuzzled the softness of her hair and seemed at peace with the world as they left the white city behind them and rode out across the green Cuban countryside. The moon came out as they rode along the broken coastline, shining down on majestic royal palms and waving coconut palms that rustled overhead.

"This cavern is somewhere along the coast not far from the city," Kells told her. "Juarez told me I could not miss it if I look for a great landmark rock that looks like a castle."

They were riding atop seaside cliffs as he spoke and he was peering down at the white beach below where waves were foaming in. "I think I see it—over there."

Carolina pushed back her hair, which was blowing in the sea wind, and peered in the direction in which he waved his arm. There before her, surrounded by a white collar of roiling surf, rose a great dark rock, glistening with sea spray. In the moonlight it really *did* look very like a castle, she decided—a crusaders' castle with a curtain wall.

"The cavern should be just past the castle rock on a little promontory. Juarez said to watch for some natural steps leading down that have been worn into the rock at the top. I think we will walk from here on." He dismounted and lifted Carolina down. She could very well have jumped down, but it was more delightful this way, being held—even though briefly—in his arms.

They strolled along the cliff top, leading the horse,

enjoying the beauty of the wild scene below them with the sea breaking around a pattern of spray-laced rocks.

"Juarez tells me there is a tiny fishing village nearby where vegetables and fruit and fish can be bought. And that the cavern is spacious with a view of the sea." He grinned. "I think he was hopeful that I would take a lady love there so that he could have a freer field with Marina."

Walking along with her arm about his middle, while his was draped lazily over her shoulder, Carolina gave him a swift expressive little hug. She was so relieved to be out of the tense atmosphere of Havana and alone with him in the open countryside at last! Indeed she fervently wished Captain Juarez a free field with Marina!

Soon enough, they found the natural steps carved by nature into the rocks. From them it was an easy climb down the cliff face to the entrance of the big limestone cavern. And Juarez was right—it *was* a romantic spot. The cavern's central chamber, which lay open to the sea, was high-vaulted and smooth-floored and airy although farther back she could see forked and curving passages where tall stalactites and stalagmites almost met—and beyond that, mysterious darkness.

They left the horse atop the cliff contentedly grazing near a little spring that sparkled like a many-pointed star in the grass. Nearby they gathered armloads of the sweet-smelling grasses to make a bed near the cavern entrance, carrying great piles of them down the worn limestone steps to heap up in their seaside lair.

"Is this romantic enough for you?" laughed Kells.

"It is," said Carolina. She dropped her grassy burden and stretched, standing in the cave entrance with the sea wind blowing and tangling her long hair, looking out over a wide expanse of ocean that would by morning be bluer than the bluest blue, and at a white beach where surf frothed lacily upon the moonlit sands.

"I wish we could stay here forever," she murmured and turned to face her tall buccaneer—her buccaneer who sturdily refused to believe himself ever to have been a buccaneer.

Against the moon a broad-winged bird swooped and dipped, and somewhere across the smooth phosphorescent face of the sea there was a silvery flash as a fish leaped out of the water. Aside from that they might have been alone in the world.

"We have bided the night in many wild places," she told Kells softly. "But none more lovely than this."

"Then come to bed," he suggested, divesting himself of his clothes in the warm night but leaving his sword near to his hand in case of need.

Carolina, who had worn her dark formal riding habit, quickly slipped out of it, kicked off her slippers with their high red heels, removed her garters and silk stockings, and pulled the drawstring of her chemise. She did not pause to let it fall in folds about her feet, but caught it as it slid down her bare hips and stepped out of it, folding it neatly and placing it atop her black riding clothes.

She rose from her bent position and stood smiling down at him. He thought she had never looked more beautiful than she did at that moment, naked against the moon, her delicate female body ethereal in silhouette in moonlight that gilded her shoulders and kissed the sweet rounded lines of her hips. He caught his breath at the sight of her, standing there as if to entice him, her long flowing blonde hair cascading over her shoulders to her waist in a bright enchanted halo that dazzled the senses.

"Come to bed," he repeated softly and reached out his arms to her.

In the moonlight she could see a certain well-remembered glimmer in his eyes.

"Oh, Kells," she sighed, falling to her knees upon

the soft piled-up grasses and looking down at him tenderly. "I thought you would never understand."

And maybe he did not understand—maybe he never would. Maybe he would go on stubbornly believing forever that he was Don Diego and she a buccaneer's woman who had bewitched him with outrageous lies. At the moment it did not matter. She *felt* he understood, felt that he knew—as did her own yearning heart—that their love had always endured, that it was older than they were, older than time, that it would outlast them, outlast the stars themselves.

"Kells," she whispered again, vibrantly, and melted downward into his outstretched welcoming arms.

Naked in the warm night, their limbs entwined, they strained together in perfect harmony. They were perfectly matched, these two, and theirs was a silken joining, perfect in every respect. Their bodies moved against each other with the ease of long association and deep understanding. Kells pulled her to him with a masterful gentleness and warmth that told her all unspoken that to him she was a miracle come to share his bed. His hands roved lazily over her smooth body, inciting her to laughing moans and muffled protests as she settled in against him the closer, murmuring incoherent endearments, her warm femininity quivering against his male hardness.

They kissed and caressed, passions steadily mounting, hearts beating as one. Then sanity left them. Bodies locked, every sense alive and surging, they were tumbling fiercely together through a world lit only by desire—and fulfillment.

And spun down slowly, only to catch fire again with sparks lit from the afterglow until again their breath was hot on each other's cheeks, their eyes were closed as they drifted once more into passion's sphere where the blood raced and there were no tomorrows. Tonight, wordlessly, with every tender caress, every responsive ripple of pleasure, they were singing again their love-song, begun so long ago.

But tonight beneath a white moon it all seemed fresh and exhilarating. This wild setting of sea and surf and stars had brought something new and enchanting to the pusating rhapsody of their love, making it seem predestined. Meant to be. It was something both elemental and sublime that had been added, and it gave to their lovemaking this night a wonderful richness and depth that surpassed anything they had found in Havana and left them starry-eyed and exhausted and aglow. And filled with wonder that life, which had so long been harsh, should suddenly be so good to them.

Happier than she had been for a long time, Carolina went to sleep lulled by the soft booming of the sea against the rocks below their romantic cavern lair.

They lingered in this idyllic setting for almost a week. Kells fished, wading out into the surf, and Carolina roasted his catch over a small open fire he built on the sandy beach. Afterward they would lean back in the shadow of the rocks and Carolina would tell him of her life in the old days in Virginia, before she had met him. And sometimes—though not very often—of things they had done together. In Tortuga. In Port Royal.

She knew he did not believe her stories of their wild adventures but at least he was willing to listen to them now without protest—before he took her in his arms and kissed the words from her lips.

They did other things as well:

Together they rode to the tiny fishing hamlet nearby and brought back baskets of fresh fruit, including some ripe coconuts which Kells opened expertly with a rock so that they could drink the sweet milky liquid within.

They swam in the warm blue coastal waters, sometimes diving down through coral castles of pink and white and rose, where colorful blue and green and silver reef fish darted away from them to be lost in the blue depths. Once Kells brought up a great conch and Carolina roasted it in hot embers on the beach and they ate it with their fingers, washing it down with a bottle of the dark local wine which they had brought back from their expedition to the village.

They lazed in their cavern lair on the cliffside, looking out at the glittering expanse of ocean, watching the silver ripple of shoal fish and the occasional white sail that drifted by in the distance. The trade winds caressed them, cooling them on the hottest days. They cavorted like friendly dolphin, looking down through the unbelievably clear crystal waters at beautiful unreal vistas in an enchanted reef world far below. They ran barefoot and laughing down the white beach, they played like children in the shallows, and made love with the white surf sometimes breaking over their heads and making them laugh as they gasped for breath. They even built, one day, a castle on the sand and from the heights at twilight watched the tide inexorably wash it away. They spent their hours idly, as lovers will, and for a brief space forgot the world that waited for them back in Havana.

Carolina would always remember it as a time of bliss.

THE GOVERNOR'S PALACE
HAVANA, CUBA

Chapter 28

But while Kells and Carolina were rediscovering each other, a great deal had been happening to Penny.

She had made it to the governor's bed, but now he had unobligingly come down with the gout and Penny found herself once again sleeping alone—a situation she liked not at all. Moreover he was not available at meals in the large gloomy dining room with its stiff high-backed chairs. He lay with his painful leg propped up on cushions in the big bed of his second-floor bedchamber and groaned so loudly he kept the household awake.

Marina was as intractable as ever; she looked affronted whenever Penny came near. Everybody else spoke only Spanish, so Penny couldn't even enjoy a conversation with the cook, who looked to be a jovial soul. And Carolina was cloistered next door taking care of Kells, who had reportedly come down with a fever. Every time Penny knocked on their door, old Juana refused to open it, calling out in strangely accented English the words Carolina had taught her:

"No admit. Contagion."

Thus frustrated on every side, Penny had been walking about the upstairs restlessly, wondering if the governor might be up to a game of cards, for Marina had been abominable at breakfast, turning away insultingly whenever Penny spoke to her—indeed there were times when Penny yearned for nothing so much as to box the girl's ears.

The arrival of the white and gold galleon had caused a welcome diversion. Penny had even hoped for some distraction from the boring routine of the house, for the governor had promptly given permission for Marina to go down to the wharf and view it—in Penny's company. This had caused an uproar and Marina's spoiled wail of "If *she* goes, *I* won't!" had echoed through the house. Whereupon the governor had risen up from his bed and roared that no one would go—then fallen back in pain, muttering something to the effect that he knew not what he had done to deserve such a petulant child.

Marina, standing by, had promptly burst into tears, sobbing noisily up and down the halls. And when the Hernandez carriage had arrived outside with an invitation for Marina to go driving with Carlotta Hernandez, the governor had hastily said she might go and returned to his groaning, glad to have rid himself temporarily of his daughter.

Penny was glad, too. It was always more pleasant to have Marina out of the house. She had chatted with the governor until he had fallen asleep and was just hesitating on the top step, wondering if she might not stroll down and view the white and gold galleon for herself, when the knocker sounded, the front door was opened and booted feet were to be heard upon the tiles. Amid a flurry of Spanish an attractive masculine voice said in perfectly good English, "I do hope you'll tell the governor I've come a long way on important business and I'd be most disappointed if he refused to see me."

An English voice! Someone to talk to! Penny sped down the tiled stairway and was arrested midway by the sight of a tall dark Englishman of commanding stance, clad in dove-gray satin. He had looked up alertly at the tap of her high heels on the stair tiles and now he swept her a most elegant bow.

"Gracious lady." He spoke before anyone else could. "Could one hope that *you* are the governor's daughter?"

"One could hope," said Penny humorously. "But one would be doomed to disappointment."

The stranger, whose linens were of the whitest and whose laces were of the most elegant, took a deep breath and his chest expanded. "You speak English, dear lady!" There was delight—and relief—in his richly modulated voice.

"Indeed," agreed Penny, standing at her most regal and staring down upon the newcomer. "And who might you be, sir?"

Her question was as much addressed to the dark Spaniard who stepped out from behind the Englishman as to the man in gray himself.

It was the Spaniard who answered.

"I am Don Ramon del Mundo, señorita." He had no doubt he was addressing the famous Rouge and he looked her over coolly, appraising her as he might appraise good horseflesh or anything else that could be bought. Penny gave him back a look of calm disdain.

"And who is this gentleman with you?" she asked.

Don Ramon favored her with a mocking bow. "This gentleman," he said suavely, "asserts himself to be an emissary of the English King, come to treat with the governor on matters military. Allow me to present the Marquess of Saltenham, señorita."

The Marquess of Saltenham!

Penny froze in her tracks, staring at the tall Englishman with the graceful mien and the empty gray eyes, who smiled back at her. But this was Robin Tyrell, the man who had impersonated Kells, then betrayed him! She felt excitement surge through her and studied Robin Tyrell critically. A fine figure of a man, much like Don Diego in appearance. A masterful manner, pleasing to women. A hard face, a dissolute face, but an attractive face with a very winning smile.

"The governor is down with the gout," she told them with a shrug. "He had a bad night and he has just fallen asleep. He isn't seeing anyone."

"Then I had best take this Englishman back to El Morro," said Don Ramon with decision. "I can quarter him there until the governor is better."

"Is El Morro that cliffside fort we passed on the way into the harbor?" asked the marquess plaintively. It was clear he did not relish being locked up there.

"It is," said Don Ramon firmly. "Now if you will just follow me?"

He gestured toward the door, about to escort the newcomer through it, but Penny intervened.

"I am sure the governor would want the King's emissary to stay here, Don Ramon," she said with just the right amount of frost in her voice. "And will take it amiss if the marquess is dragged back to some gloomy fortress to pass the time."

Don Ramon looked up quickly. It was all over Havana that Rouge was the governor's mistress, and if the governor's mistress wanted something, she would probably get it. One way or another. For his part, if he were an older, rather portly gentleman like the governor, he would not care to see a too handsome countryman of his new mistress take up residence in his house—but who was he to judge?

"You are certain of this?" he asked sternly. "You speak for the governor in this matter?"

"I do, indeed," confirmed Penny with a lofty gesture.

"Set your mind entirely at rest, Don Ramon. The governor will be in complete accord with me."

At that point the door suddenly opened and Marina, accompanied by her elderly *duena* and looking very bright-eyed in her white lace mantilla and ruffled skirts, hurried in out of the sunlight into the cool interior.

"Don Ramon!" she said on a note of pleased surprise, and her whole face lit up.

"Doña Marina." Don Ramon bowed gravely. "I bring with me a gentleman who says he is an emissary to your father from the English King. We are currently trying to decide what to do with him. Does he return to El Morro with me or—"

"Oh, no, he must stay here!" Marina cried impulsively, for she was instantly dazzled by the Englishman's good looks and the appreciative smile he had flashed her.

Penny gave Don Ramon a smile of triumph, secretly amused that she had found an unexpected ally in Marina. Don Ramon returned her a cynical look, bowed deeply to Marina and left them. Leaving Marina —with her few words of English—downstairs to entertain their guest, Penny flew upstairs to have a suitable room prepared for him.

At first she thought she would run next door and have old Juana tell Carolina the name of the new arrival. Then she changed her mind. It would be much more fun to surprise Carolina with the marquess—but later, when she herself had the situation better in hand.

Dinner that night was something less than a success. The governor did not come down but the four of them—Penny, Robin, Marina, and Marina's elderly *duena*—sat in formal splendor in the austere dining room, amid an atmosphere that was redolent of New Spain. Marina had made a half-hearted attempt to block Penny's entrance to the dining room but had stepped aside when Penny, with a black look, had apparently been prepared to run over her. They had brushed by each other and had kept their distance ever since.

Marina had dashed to the head of the table and Penny had made for the foot, with the marquess and the old chaperone marooned on opposite sides of the long table in between. Dressed in her frosty best in silks that had come via Mexico from the Philippines, Marina had done her best to charm the newcomer. Waving her spoon excitedly and trying to make up in gestures what she lacked in vocabulary, she had showed off her command of English such as it was. But the marquess's answering witticisms—in a language foreign to her ears—were too subtle for her to understand, and she almost choked on her food every time Penny's eyes lit up at something clever that he said.

"You must not make an enemy of Marina," breathed Penny in the marquess's ear as they left the table.

"I assure you I will do my best not to!" he responded in an undertone and gallantly offered the excited younger girl his arm.

She strutted out beside him with a disdainful look at Penny, who watched in amusement. Penny left them together and went upstairs to look in on the governor. She found him still sleeping heavily and came back downstairs to observe Marina banging hopefully away at the harpsichord to charm their guest. Since Marina had no ear at all for music, the marquess was beginning to show signs of strain. Penny thought critically that he had a rather hunted expression on his lean face as he smiled absently down at his young hostess.

"Marina," Penny told the governor's daughter in a voice of authority. "It is late and I am sure our guest has had a hard voyage and would like to go to bed."

At this interruption, Marina brought both hands down upon the keyboard in vengeful discord and rose trembling to her feet. She was spitting something in Spanish at Penny which neither she nor the marquess could understand as she flung herself out and ran up the stairs pursued by her distracted *duena*.

"A lovely child, isn't she?" Penny observed scathingly when Marina's skirts had cleared the door.

Left alone with Penny, the Marquess of Saltenham showed no disposition to go to bed. He suggested a walk around the courtyard before retiring.

"It would appear the governor's daughter does not take suggestions too well from you," he remarked whimsically, when they had reached the central stone fountain and had come to a halt beside it.

Penny laughed ruefully. "Marina does not take suggestions well from anyone—least of all from me! She hates me because"—her sapphire eyes flung him a challenge—"I am her father's mistress."

Robin Tyrell looked as if that were very instructive. He lounged gracefully by the fountain. "The governor must be a man of blood," he told her admiringly. "He has excellent taste in women. And to have found an unmarried lady of such beauty—!"

"I am not unmarried." She waved him to a stone bench near the fountain. "Would you care to sit down?"

The curiosity in his eyes showed he yearned to hear more. He seated himself with alacrity on the nearest bench and watched her settle her black taffeta skirts across from him.

"I have various husbands," she said lightly. "Both above and below the sod. But surely we've no need to discuss my marital disasters?"

He was staring at her in fascination. "No—er, of course not, se—do I call you señorita, dear lady?"

"You may call me Rouge," said Penny with a broad smile. "For that is the name by which I am best known.

Or if others are about, you may wish to call me Doña Pennsylvania, which is also my name."

"Pennsylvania?" The dark face looked puzzled. "But is that not the name of an American Colony?"

"It is," agreed Penny demurely. "My parents were peculiar. I was born in Philadelphia and my mother chose to name me for the Colony."

"Mine named me for an uncle in hopes he would leave me his fortune," he told her frankly. "He did not choose to."

She joined him in laughter. "So often things do not work out!" she said merrily. "I ran away to the Marriage Trees—you'll not have heard of them, but they are a handsome stand of oaks situated on a narrow peninsula between the Virginia and Maryland Colonies. Parsons lurk beneath the branches there, hoping to wed runaway couples. I must have looked very young indeed because I had to brandish a pistol beneath my parson's nose so he would marry us!"

His astonishment grew. "*You* brandished—?"

"Oh, yes. The lad I ran away with had no stomach for firearms. He was more devious."

The dark eyebrows shot up. "Devious? How so?"

"When we quarreled in Philadelphia he sold me to a ship's captain and had me dragged away by force. I arrived in Havana in somewhat circuitous fashion—by way of a French-Spanish raid on New Providence."

"Rouge! Of course!" He snapped his fingers in delight. "Now I remember. Rouge! Then you must be—"

"The pirate queen of New Providence, some have called me," Penny admitted. "Others"—her throaty laughter pealed—"have used less complimentary names to describe me!"

"But your fame precedes you, dear lady," Robin Tyrell insisted gallantly. "Indeed I have heard naught but good things about the famous Rouge!"

"Then you haven't been in the Caribbean long," was her cynical response.

"Well, that is true," he admitted, nonplused, and proceeded to tell her a long-winded tale of shipwreck and misfortune that brought a dancing light to her eyes.

"Lord Saltenham," she began.

"Oh, do call me Robin, dear lady," he said warmly. "My name is Robin Tyrell."

"Very well, Robin. I am thinking you have rather overdone the account of your mishaps."

He gave her a wounded look. "But I assure you, dear lady—"

"No, don't assure *me*—assure the governor." She burst out laughing. "'Twas the date," she told him demurely. "The date you say you left England did not allow time for all that to happen!"

Robin Tyrell colored a trifle but he was as cool as she. "Then I must correct the date of my leaving," he murmured. "I will say it was a lapse!"

Penny was convulsed. *It takes one to know one,* she was thinking. "By all means correct your date of leaving England," she chuckled, "*before* your audience with the governor—for otherwise he will be sure to take note of the error."

Recognizing this pirate's wench as a co-conspirator, Robin Tyrell edged a little toward her. "And when do you think I will see him?" he asked in a confidential tone.

"Not until his attack of the gout is over," Penny told him ruefully. "Not even a message from the King of Spain would bring him to receive a caller just now—much less the King of England!"

The gray eyes across from her were a little daunted. They had an interesting emptiness, she thought idly, that was striking in his dissolute face. She had taken an instant liking to him and now that she was certain he was a scoundrel, she liked him even better.

"I do not know what your game is, Robin," she said thoughtfully.

"Shall we call it Survival?" He was smiling.

"Yes, well, we're all playing *that* game."

"Indeed?" The marquess pricked up his ears.

"I would have been sold by the market bell as a slave on arrival in Havana had not the governor decided to pluck me from the sale for his"—she shrugged—"household."

His eyes narrowed in sympathy. "So you had no choice in the matter?"

"None at all," she said serenely.

He frowned. "What a lucky man is the governor!" he said lightly.

"Yes, isn't he?" she quipped. "A daughter who is a demon and a mistress some consider worse!"

Robin Tyrell was not used to women who spoke with such directness as this. Reba never did—not to him. And her mother either bellowed unintelligibly or muttered, depending on how drunk she was at the time—he wasn't sure whether he disliked her more drunk or sober. He warmed to the handsome redhead smiling at him across her wineglass.

Penny was enjoying her evening. She was laughing inwardly that the man who had impersonated Kells should have turned up in such an unlikely place as Havana—and on *her* doorstep!

"Are you by chance a gambling man?" she asked him curiously.

His wry nod answered her. "It is one of my chief failings," he admitted.

"Then let us draw cards. High card gets to ask one question which must be answered truthfully." Penny, who carried a deck of cards stuck in her skirt, was shuffling the cards as she spoke, and she gave them a sweeping riffle which raised Robin Tyrell's eyebrows.

She won the draw.

"Your question, dear lady?" The marquess was curious about what she wanted to know. He was entirely unprepared for the question she flung at him.

"Where is your wife Reba?" she asked him calmly.

Robin Tyrell's shoulders jerked. Penny had startled him out of his complacency. He leaned forward, peering at her in the moonlight. "Do I know you from somewhere?" he demanded.

Penny shook her head and her rich red curls danced. "You have never laid eyes on me before—nor I you. Tell me, is your mother-in-law as bad as ever?"

"You *do* know me!" he insisted.

"No." Penny's dark blue eyes sparkled.

"Put away the cards," he said. "Ask me what you will, but at least satisfy my curiosity first. *Who are you?*"

"I am Carolina Lightfoot's sister," she said, sweeping up the cards with practiced fingers. "And I know a great deal about you, Robin Tyrell."

He stared at her in astonishment. "Carolina Lightfoot!" he exclaimed.

"Wife to Captain Kells," elaborated Penny, smiling. "I believe Carolina had something to do with your marriage?" she added innocently.

"Marriage? It's been worse than a jail sentence!" he burst out. "Faith, I'd rather be in Newgate! My harridan of a mother-in-law has taken over my life. She manages my affairs—and Reba grows more like her every day."

"The truth is you've run away from them," hazarded Penny. "And all the rest is moonbeams!"

He sighed. "That's about it—only not quite. His Majesty did once say—more in jest than anything else—that if I could procure any sign of friendship out of the Spanish in the Caribbean, he'd be beholden to me! But you are right, he gave me no commission. I only claimed to be his emissary in hopes of staying alive in this cursed city. It was Barbados I was heading for!"

"A more likely story," agreed Penny. "But one you'll not tell, I hope. It would probably get you locked up in El Morro along with the rest of the Englishmen who are caught in these waters. I would stick to being the King's emissary if I were you. Am I to understand you are in fact a Court favorite?"

"I suppose you could call me that," he said restlessly. "But it takes a rich wife to keep up appearances at Court."

"Well? You've got one, haven't you?"

"You don't know what it's like, dear lady," he said on a note of desperate appeal. "I was being driven out of my mind in England! Did I make any move either my wife or my mother-in-law objected to, I found my funds cut off instantly—impounded! My life has been a living hell!"

"Carolina would find that amusing, I don't doubt," Penny said with an unfeeling laugh.

"Ah, I know that I have used her ill—and Kells, too," he admitted. "But you would have to understand the circumstances. Where *is* Carolina?" he asked curiously.

"How would I know?" Penny shrugged, for she had decided to keep this interesting fellow to herself for a time. "She was in Port Royal when it sank into the sea. Kells, I heard, was killed there."

"And Carolina?" he asked sharply.

"Probably dead as well," lied Penny. She considered him carefully as this information sank in upon him. There was a certain sadness that leaped to his eyes, she thought—a kind of tribute to her beautiful younger sister.

But the marquess recovered quickly. "What are our chances of departing Havana?" he asked abruptly.

It was Penny's turn to raise her winglike brows. "I can understand why *you* might wish to leave," she mocked. "But what makes you think *I* would desire to leave Havana?"

"What you said about being sold." He was blunt.

"Ah, but I was not sold. I am become mistress instead to a very important man."

"But are you free to come and go?"

She shrugged. "Of course."

"Free to leave the city?" he pursued relentlessly.

Penny smiled crookedly. "I doubt it."

"Then you *will* desire to leave!" he said in triumph.

She sighed. "Yes, you are right. I *do* desire to leave. Most ardently." And it was true. Yesterday it had not been so true. Yesterday she had been inclined to drift. Today, looking into the gray eyes of the Marquess of Saltenham, it was suddenly very true. She wanted to leave Havana. "Indeed, I am tired of the Caribbean altogether," she admitted. "But the opportunity to depart has not yet presented itself."

"Perhaps we can escape together!"

But Penny was too aware of the realities of life in this part of the world to take such a suggestion lightly.

"Perhaps together we can get ourselves killed," she amended briskly. "I will warn you to trust no one in this house save myself. And most especially do not trust the governor's daughter. She obviously fancies you."

He looked pleased.

"Those Marina fancies may or may not end up well," she warned him, and the smile left his face.

He sighed and his hot gaze passed over her breasts. "Then I suppose it is good night, dear lady?"

"Robin," she said abruptly. "You do not look sleepy and neither am I. Would you like to see what entertainment Havana has to offer by night?"

He looked delighted. "But can we—?"

Penny nodded. "We can. If we are careful to slip out quietly. But first I must change my clothes." She indicated her elegant black taffeta gown. "Spanish ladies of fashion do not prowl the taverns by night," she pointed out humorously.

"I will wait for you here," he told her, fascinated.

"No, that will not do. You will pretend to go upstairs to bed—in case Marina is spying on us. Meet me at the end of the corridor just past your bedroom in ten minutes. We will go down the back way."

"But I thought I saw someone locking up the house?" he objected.

"That was old Sancho. But he brings the keys upstairs after he has locked up and hangs them on a peg in the governor's bedchamber. It will take me but a moment to collect the key to the back door."

The marquess did as he was told. He had not long to wait. Penny came down the dim hall on bare feet, carrying with her a pair of black slippers with high red heels. She carried a sword under her arm. She was smiling and waving a key as she swung along.

"You look very different," marveled the marquess, staring from the low-cut black bodice that displayed her elegant breasts to the brilliant red cotton skirt that rippled around her trim ankles. He blinked at the flaunting yellow turban that now concealed her luxuriant red hair.

"That is because I am garbed as a prostitute!" she laughed. "I picked up these clothes in the market yesterday—in case I should choose to wander about the town by night. No one would be surprised to see a woman dressed like this come out of a tavern in the darkness but *everyone* would remark a woman dressed as I was at dinner! And here—" She proffered the sword. "Buckle this on, for who knows what the streets will be like after dark?"

Delighted with their escapade, the marquess tiptoed,

at her direction, past the sleeping cook into the back courtyard and thence to the street.

Penny knew just where to lead him. She had been noticing Havana's night spots ever since her arrival. The tavern she found for them was low-ceilinged with smoke-stained plaster walls, and dimly candlelit. It had a trio with stringed instruments strumming away in one corner. They sat down at a table and ordered wine and talked and watched people come and go. The drinking got heavier, the music and laughter louder. When one particularly catchy tune was struck up, Penny suddenly leaped to her feet, climbed upon the table top and executed a wild stomping dance that swirled her skirts about her hips while the onlookers stamped their feet and applauded.

The marquess, applauding too, watched her appreciatively for a time before pulling her down, laughing, into his lap. He told her he doubted he could stand off the assembled onslaught of the patrons if they chose to tear her from him and thus doubted the wisdom of inflaming them like this.

"But then I was never wise!" she laughed.

Thoroughly enjoying herself, for she had been far too prim lately to suit her, Penny threw the applauding patrons a kiss and slid off Robin's lap.

"It's late," she announced. "And we'd best get back, for Cook rises early and there'll be the Devil to pay if we're seen arriving home in the dawn!"

The very thought of what the governor might be inclined to do if he learned his young mistress had returned in the dawn with a strange Englishman brought Robin Tyrell instantly to his feet.

"I will squire you home, dear lady!"

But Penny's wild dance, the sight of her long beautiful legs, had attracted too much attention.

Three strapping fellows slouched out of the tavern after them.

It was very dark and the street was empty. Robin's boots gave forth a hollow echo. The sandals of those behind gave little sound.

"I think we're being followed," he muttered. They were halfway home by now, and no matter how many circuitous turnings they took, the three still managed to keep the same distance behind Penny's swaying red skirts.

"Yes. Keep moving. We'll want to reach the house just down the street—the one with the big balcony overhead. See it? The one with all those potted plants. When we get there I want you to swoop me up so I can grasp the grillwork of that balcony and swing myself up."

He gave her an astonished look and instead loosened his sword in its scabbard.

"Are you a good swordsman?" she asked sharply.

"Indifferent," he admitted.

"Then listen to me and do what I tell you!" she commanded tersely for they had almost reached her objective.

Thoroughly bewildered, Robin bent and let his lady step onto his crossed hands as if he were boosting her up into a saddle. Instead he gave a mighty heave and tossed her upward. Airborne, Penny caught the lower part of the balcony's iron grillwork.

Behind them came a shout and running feet. Robin staggered back, barely able to clear his sword from its scabbard before two of their pursuers were upon him. The other made a grab for Penny's ankle, intending to pull her back down to the street.

It was a bad mistake.

Penny had anticipated that move and she swung from the balcony in such a way that momentum was behind the high heel she suddenly drove into his chin, sending him tumbling over backward.

Before he could rise, she had scrambled over the

railing onto the balcony. Before her she could see that Robin was being pressed hard by the two who had now pulled out cutlasses and threatened to surround him. She picked up the smallest of the flower pots—no mean feat, for none of them were small—aimed it with care and sent it crashing into the back of one of Robin's assailants. It struck him in the back of the neck and he went down like a stone.

Robin flashed a look upward and smiled.

While the man Penny had kicked in the chin got himself up, Penny managed to get a really large potted plant up onto the railing where it teetered dangerously. Below her the man whose face bore the imprint of her heel was circling the balcony warily. She thought he might leap upward and try to swarm over the balcony and overpower her, and she tensed, her right hand meanwhile working desperately to loosen the plant in its pot.

Now he dodged below her, thinking she would try to drop the pot upon his head, never doubting he could dodge it. He laughed.

Penny regarded him calmly from above. She had gotten the plant worked loose by now. As he passed below her, exhorting her with a mocking wave to drop the pot, she wrested the plant from its pot, roots and all, and shook it over his head. Loose dirt cascaded down over his surprised face and into his eyes. He had not been expecting *that.* He fell back, cursing, clutching his eyes.

But the third man was no mean adversary. Large and tough and agile, he was forcing a desperate Robin Tyrell back and back. They were some distance away by now and Robin was getting the worst of it.

Penny kept a grip on the now empty crockery pot and swung a leg over the balcony. She let herself down with one hand and dropped lightly to the street below it. The man on whom she had showered dirt from the potted plant was now no threat—he was still clawing at his eyes.

With catlike stealth she advanced upon the combatants. Behind her now the household was waking up. There were cries from within and the sound of running feet and someone gave a cry from the balcony. Neither man, intent on slashing and thrusting, took the least notice.

Crouched over, Penny and the pot advanced upon that burly back. But out of the corner of his eye this one had seen what had happened to his fellows. He knew he was being stalked.

As she got almost within range to swing the pot, he gave a great roar, knocked Robin backward with a sudden thrust of his cutlass and whirled about to deal with Penny.

Again it was the wrong move to have made. Penny, graduate of the boisterous night life of New Providence and with reflexes many pirates had envied, left her crouch and leaped sideways. As she did, the heavy crockery pot left her hand—it took all her strength to hurl it—and struck her surprised attacker full in the face, knocking him out.

His big body had not yet hit the street before Penny was leaping forward, picking up her red skirts.

"The alarm's been sounded!" she cried. "Run!"

Skirts flying, she ran like the wind. Having just been fighting for his life with all his might and finding himself somewhat winded, Robin Tyrell was hard pressed to keep up with her.

"Faith," he panted, "but you'd have been a good man in a fight!"

She turned to give him a quelling look. "I *am* a good man in a fight," she stated flatly. "But I'm tired of all that. I've decided I prefer to trail about in low-cut ball gowns while gentlemen pay me extravagant compliments and drink toasts to my eyebrows!"

Robin's chuckle told her that that was not quite what she had chosen to do tonight, and she laughed with him.

They arrived, flushed and winded, at the governor's back courtyard, and Penny let them in with her key. They moved stealthily in through the kitchen to the back stairs.

Cook slept on.

As she undressed for bed—in her own room, no less—Penny stared at her flushed face in the mirror and marveled. It had been an odd evening, punctuated by danger and laughter, but not by sex. No tumble into bed—Robin had not asked it of her. Indeed it was the first really companionable evening she had spent with a man in years.

And yet—she had enjoyed it.

She grinned at her radiant reflection in the mirror.

"New Providence wouldn't know me!" she murmured to herself half-ruefully.

Morning brought Penny and the marquess together at breakfast, smiling a bit conspiratorially into each other's eyes, for both of them had enjoyed last night's rather disreputable episode.

Marina sulked through breakfast, realizing full well that there were undercurrents here that did not include her.

She flounced off to her room, and when Captain Juarez called she came down and—seeing that the Marquess of Saltenham was idling in the courtyard—brought the captain in with a great show of pleasure and hung on his words the entire time he was there.

To her vexation, being ignored by her made no impression at all on the marquess. He was, if anything, relieved.

Marina stared at him, baffled.

And then abruptly she had had enough. It wasn't dignified, she told herself angrily, to pursue men who didn't want her. After she had bade Captain Juarez good-by, she left the courtyard with a very straight back.

Afternoon found her sending various servants out on mysterious errands. Penny, watching, frowned in puzzlement, for Marina seemed to be giving them flowers. Each one left with a rose in his hand. She sighed for she had not the command of Spanish to find out what was going on. She supposed she would find out soon enough.

What Marina had been doing remained a mystery until after dinner when she excused herself even before her favorite dessert—flan—was served.

Marina had hardly had time to reach her bedchamber before there was a torrent of noise outside the house that almost lifted those still in the dining room from their chairs. It was as if several groups of musicians were playing discordantly, accompanied by a wild half-human braying that rose wildly above it.

Marina's *duena,* left behind at the table, threw up her hands and then sank back, holding her heart and fanning herself. Penny and the marquess, who had been brought to their feet by the racket, hurried to the front door and dashed outside to see what was the matter.

What they saw was a sight to make the eyes bulge.

Three groups of musicians were indeed playing loudly on stringed instruments—each group a different tune. And three different swains—all glaring at one another and raising their voices in a vain attempt to drown the others out—were determinedly serenading beneath Marina's window. Each wanted to be heard and was bending his best efforts in that direction.

"I see Marina has been busy," muttered Penny, unheard in all the noise, for each of the singers held a rose in his hand. She looked grimly up at the balcony where Marina leaned against the iron grillwork. In the moonlight the girl flashed down a look of triumph. Marina had had one too many possible admirers taken from her. Plainly she was out to show all and sundry that Havana was *filled* with her admirers. To that end she had tolled them to the house—not singly but in groups! By the simple method of having "a rose from the governor's daughter" delivered to each young man's door.

"What is all this din?" inquired the marquess, bewildered as Penny pulled him back inside.

"They call it serenading," Penny informed him. "Marina has brought it on. And the governor has too much laudanum in him tonight to know or care."

They went back to the dining room where they met the old *duena,* hand still over her heart, stumbling out.

"Marina will be the death of her," muttered Penny, staring after the old woman.

"What did you say?" asked the marquess, for Penny's voice had slurred into the throbbing noise that had followed them inside and was almost making the wineglasses dance upon the table.

"I said Marina will be the death of her!" shouted Penny and closed the door.

That helped some, but not enough.

"I wish my bedchamber were not so close to the front of the house!" she sighed. "There is no telling how long it will last—if they do not fall to fighting, which may well happen!"

"Mine is farther back," he murmured, half heard. He leaned forward. "Not that we will be able to hear ourselves speak, but would you care to stay downstairs and have a game of cards with me?" he finished gracefully. "By the time we have finished, so may these suitors."

"Or perhaps they will have grown so hoarse they will

simply give up and march away!" laughed Penny. "But it does seem that we will have the evening to ourselves, Robin. Is that what you think we should do with it? Play cards?"

The marquess, who was beginning to find this spirited beauty irresistible, leaned over and toyed with a lock of her hair. "I can tell you what I would *like* to do with it," he murmured. "I would like to walk with you upon some deserted beach—"

"I have had enough of deserted beaches," interrupted Penny, laughing. "From now on I am going to prefer handsome halls and soft beds."

At the mention of "beds" his eyes lit up.

"A far better thought, dear lady!" he applauded. "Tell me," he added quickly. "How did you say the governor fared tonight?"

"Worse," she said promptly. "At least, groaning louder—until he was filled full of laudanum to make him sleep."

"Heartless wench!" He grinned down at her.

"I suppose I am," she agreed with composure. "Aren't you glad, Robin?" she added pertly.

He nodded, his hot gaze on her challenging face. "Might I ask you to share a glass of wine with me in some more private place than this dining room?"

"Your bedchamber?" she hazarded.

"Or yours, dear lady," was his urbane response.

"Marina must not know," she cautioned. "She would make trouble. Not that she is likely to hear *anything* besides the din below her balcony!"

"I am the soul of discretion," he promised. "Do you think they would miss this bottle of wine if I carried it upstairs?"

"I do not think so. There are wineglasses in my room. I will join you presently." She paused and gave him a droll look. "Shall I bring a pack of cards to entertain us?"

"Why not?" he shrugged. "Since neither of us has any money, what have we to lose?"

"Oh, I don't know!" Penny said irrepressibly. "You could always wager your debts and I could wager my underwear!"

"That," agreed the marquess, unable to keep the eagerness from his voice, "should indeed make for an amusing evening!"

And so the woman who had been through so much and the rake who always took the easy way out found themselves facing each other in a back bedroom filled with stiff Spanish furniture and the windows open onto the tropic night with the trade winds blowing the curtains.

And found themselves, their playing cards forgotten, falling together upon the big square bed and clinging to each other with all the fervor of the damned. They were both skillful lovers, well matched. Together they reached heights of passion, plunged down lovely luxurious valleys, rose again to soar together.

They both had handsome bodies, they were both proud of them. Somehow their clothes had slipped away, they had admired each other's nakedness and now, with bodies gleaming damp in the moonlight, they were trying new delights, goading each other onward. Again and yet again.

Penny had slipped into Robin Tyrell's arms languorously, half out of boredom, half out of a restless seeking for something new. But she left those arms in wonder, knowing she had met her match, while Robin thought he had never before seen such a wench.

And now as they rested on their elbows, lazily touching in the afterglow, she knew she had never felt such kinship with a man before. She had *sympathy* for Robin Tyrell—that was it. In the world's eyes he was a rakehell and always would be—but then wasn't she an adventuress herself?

She had sympathy for Robin's plight, too. Caught between a harridan of a mother-in-law and a wife who was turning into one!

Well—she would rescue him from that! Just how, she wasn't quite sure but she was suddenly certain that she was going to try.

Because . . . just possibly . . . she had found tonight what she had so long been seeking, that *something more* than sex to share with a man.

She just might have found the love of her life.

The next day the governor was better—not well enough for making love but wide awake enough to require caution on the part of the lovers.

Suitors continued to wail love songs nightly beneath Marina's balcony.

Downstairs Penny and Robin ignored the caterwauling. They played whist and gazed smiling into each other's eyes.

They didn't know it, but they were falling in love.

THE HOUSE ON THE PLAZA DE ARMAS HAVANA, CUBA

Chapter 29

The arrival of the white and gold galleon had brought a flurry of social life to Havana. Not to be outdone, the governor—whose gout had improved—was giving a ball the next night in honor of the *El Dorado*'s officers. The entire household was excited about it—even Marina had turned tractable.

Carolina had arrived back in Havana only the day before Penny, having been refused entrance to the house and wrangling with old Juana at the door, had made so much noise that Carolina called out to ask who was there. Upon learning it was Penny, she told Juana to let her in.

Penny brushed past the old woman and found Don Diego and Carolina sipping tall drinks in the courtyard by the tinkling fountain.

"Come join us," Carolina said graciously.

Penny's keen gaze took in the pair of them, lounging at table—Don Diego coatless with his flowing white shirt open at the front above his dark trousers, Carolina clad only in her light chemise and with her fair hair cascading down over her slim shoulders. To Penny, they both looked as though they had just risen from making love.

"Well, so much for fever!" laughed Penny. "I came over to deliver an invitation to Don Diego to attend the governor's ball tomorrow night—but I see now that you'd much rather stay home with 'fever.' Don't worry, I'll make your excuses—and I'll find my own way out."

"Penny, I never meant for Juana to keep *you* out!" Carolina protested in a stricken voice. "It was just that the governor's daughter bothered us so much." She didn't mention that they hadn't been home, anyway!

Penny's sapphire eyes considered her younger sister. She had discovered in herself a reluctance for Robin and Carolina to meet. She had sensed that Carolina had stirred something deep and forgotten in the dissolute marquess—and might again.

But now that she saw how things were, now that Don Diego and Carolina were holed up in the house and apparently reluctant to leave it, there was no problem!

"Oh, Marina is bothering someone else now," she told them in a blithe voice. "An Englishman who arrived aboard the *El Dorado*. It seems he was picked up at sea from a foundering vessel and he tells a wild tale about lost papers, and being shipwrecked twice! Anyway, Marina was suddenly mad for him—she gets these wild infatuations. And when he didn't respond she must have sent a rose to every young man in Havana! All that noise under her window—"

"We heard it last night!"

"—was her swains serenading. She's busy showing our house guest what a popular girl she is!"

"You mean this man is actually *staying* at the governor's house?" exclaimed Carolina. "I had rather thought an Englishman, arriving willy-nilly on these shores, might end up in El Morro!"

"Oh, he has a glib tongue, has this one!"

Don Diego had been listening to this conversation. Now he entered it. "Tell the governor I will be well enough to attend his ball—and with a lady."

Carolina whirled. "Oh, you can't—we can't! I mean—"

"With a lady?" Penny caught her breath. That meant Robin and Carolina were sure to meet! "Don't tell me he means *you,* Carolina!" she said warily.

"I am afraid he does," Carolina said unhappily. "But it would cause a great stir and—"

Penny drew a deep breath. If Robin still cared for Carolina, better to know it now! Quickly she joined in on Don Diego's side. "Let it cause a great stir," she said with a shrug. "I am going myself."

"You *are?*" Carolina stared.

"Yes, I am to be the governor's official hostess—since he is a widower."

And social Havana might accept her as such because—even though tongues would undoubtedly wag—there were those who would see that Marina was still too young and hoydenish to assume that duty. Some of the women would insist, of course, on regarding Penny as merely an upper servant, allowed too much leeway.

But for Don Diego to bring his mistress to the governor's ball? Surely the roof would fall in if he did!

"Of course you must do it," urged Penny, who, if she was in for a penny, was always in for a pound. "The governor will be amused. But have you anything to wear?"

Carolina admitted she did not. "Which is another reason why I must not consider going. I can hardly appear in *riding clothes!*"

"Well, if there was anything Constanza had in quantity, it was ball gowns," Penny said cheerfully. "I will certainly be able to find you something."

And she did. She was back that afternoon with an armload of clothing that Carolina could hardly believe. Great billows of white were spread out across the bed: a glamorous gown of heavy white lace over thin white satin and a marvel of a white silk petticoat, and a tall carved tortoiseshell comb to hold up a floating white mantilla so sheer and lovely—

"It looks fit for a bride!" gasped Carolina. "Wherever did you get it?"

"Oh, it was one of those many gowns packed away," Penny said with a shrug. "Constanza must have worn it as a young girl, so it should fit you, although Luz will have to adjust the hem. Try it on, Carolina."

These lovely things were impossible to resist. Carolina tried it on and whirled delightedly before the mirror in the big front bedroom.

"But—I cannot wear it," she protested to Penny. "This white mantilla. It stands for virginity and I—"

"Of course you can wear it," said a voice from the door, and the two girls turned to see Don Diego lounging there. He gave Carolina a stern look. "You *will* wear it because you are soon to become my bride. I intend to announce it at the ball tomorrow night."

"What?" cried Penny. "Oh, this is wonderful! You can wear the gown tomorrow night and later you can be married in it! Consider it a wedding gift from me," she added, laughing.

Carolina's chiding look reproved her. "You must certainly *not* announce it," she told Don Diego. She sought for a reason. "My—my past will be looked into. Word has not been spread about Havana that I am the Silver Wench. If that were known, with the price Kells has on his head"— she gave "Don Diego" a warning look—"someone might decide that the way to lure Kells to his death in Spain would be to spirit *me* away there, and so collect fifty thousand pieces of eight!"

She saw she had not won her argument.

"Don Diego," she said desperately. "I am afraid to attract so much notice."

"You will accompany me to the ball," he said in a mulish tone. "And you will wear that dress and that mantilla."

"Very well." Carolina sighed, capitulating to the lesser evil. "I will go to the ball and I will wear this dress. But promise me—*promise me* that you will make no announcement!"

He frowned down upon her. "I will make no public announcement as yet," was all the promise she could wring from him. He whirled about and left them.

"I had *no idea* things had progressed so far," laughed Penny, helping Carolina strip off the lovely gown. "I'll drop these things by Luz and tell her how much hem to take up. She'll do it very swiftly, I promise, for I think she's afraid of me now that I'm the governor's mistress!"

"Do you think you will marry the governor?" asked Carolina, feeling that in some crazy way it might all come to pass—*she* who had been the Silver Wench might marry Don Diego and become a lady of Spain, and Penny, who had been the infamous Rouge of New Providence, might marry the governor and have all Havana at her feet. Could such things really happen? she asked herself wonderingly.

"Marry the governor? Not likely! Marina would expire at the very thought and I think the governor is too fond a father to ask her to accept *me* as a stepmother! But I am not so set on marriage as you are, Carolina—and anyway, I much prefer the Englishman. Which reminds me"—she began to make for the door—"he has promised to slip away from Marina and meet me by the quay. No less a personage than Don Ramon del Mundo has invited him to view El Morro—I think because he wants to impress this Englishman, who claims to be an envoy of the English King, with Spanish might—and I am to tag along. Isn't that nice? Care to go with me?"

Carolina shook her head at Penny's impudence. She could be recognized by prisoners in the dark recesses of El Morro—recognized and denounced.

And would that bring her, too, within searing distance of the fire?

THE GOVERNOR'S PALACE
HAVANA, CUBA

Chapter 30

The governor's palace was a blaze of light. All of aristocratic Havana seemed to have descended upon it. The carriages, coming and going by torchlight, discharged elegant dons and their mantillaed ladies at the big handsome house on the Plaza de Armas.

From next door Carolina and Don Diego had just arrived at the door—Carolina had tried to be very late, had kept making excuses, but Don Diego had finally told her impatiently that he would drag her along half-dressed if she did not hurry. With a sigh she had finished combing her hair into a fashionably high coiffure, stuck the high-backed tortoiseshell comb into it at the back and bent her head and let old Juana spread the fragile white mantilla across her blonde hair.

When she lifted her head again, old Juana had clapped her hands joyfully at the sight.

"A bride!" she had cried. "A very bride!"

"Not yet," sighed Carolina, who felt it would never come to pass, despite Don Diego's determination.

She had walked down the tiled stairs regally on Don

Diego's arm and now they were being welcomed in the house next door by the governor himself, a pouting Marina, and beside them, a sparkling-eyed Penny. Tonight Penny was an astonishing vision in her tight-fitting black taffeta bodice, her wide matching skirt embroidered in jet, and her sheer black lace mantilla that drifted down over the tall Spanish comb set into the back of her elegantly coiffed red hair.

Carolina lifted her chin when she saw Marina. She tensed, half expecting a scene. But Marina only bowed stiffly, accepting Carolina's presence as one more insult, and cast a baleful glance at Penny, whom she regarded as being the undoubted cause of Carolina's presence.

The governor looked startled when he saw her, but he was instantly in control of himself and greeted Don Diego courteously. It was obvious that neither he nor his daughter recognized Carolina's white gown and mantilla as having belonged to Doña Constanza, and Carolina felt a wave of relief sweep over her.

Perhaps they would be able to get through the evening after all.

But her feeling of confidence was short-lived.

They had barely entered the big candlelit room, where the milling guests were sipping glasses of wine and the musicians were warming up for the dancing, when Carolina looked across the room and met the gaze of a tall dark man in elegant gray satin. A man who registered shock at the sight of her.

Carolina had the dizzy feeling of being transported back in time to other shores, other days. For a moment she swayed against the tall dark figure of Kells beside her, elegant and Spanish-looking in his dark Spanish clothing. She did not think the man across the room could have seen Kells because his gray eyes were fixed on her in thunderstruck astonishment.

"Don Diego," she said hastily, "I will be back presently. I see someone I want to speak to."

Don Diego had been looking over her shoulder at Doña Jimena Menendez, who was waving her black lace fan rather faster at sight of him and considering the beautiful blonde with him in some alarm. Doña Jimena's messages were among those he had chosen not to answer these days past. He felt it would be best to speak to her before she could say something outrageous to Carolina—for she was quite likely to do just that.

They parted, going their separate ways—Don Diego to wend a circuitous way to his left where Doña Jimena now sought to detach herself from a lively crowd of gentlemen who pressed around her; Carolina to make her way across the room and with the barest nod of her head cause the tall gentleman in gray to follow her into the next room where a table was laid with refreshments for the guests to eat later. The servants had just finished and it was temporarily empty.

Carolina was waiting for him, tapping her fingernails against the side of the long heaped-up table. She was furious to discover that she was trembling as he lounged in, and it was only with an effort that she managed to keep her voice low.

"Robin Tyrell!" she said bitterly. "Can it be that *you* are the Englishman who arrived here with some wild tale about being shipwrecked twice?"

The Marquess of Saltenham grinned at the accusation in her voice. "The very same! An envoy from the King, no less, to the governor of Havana!" At the expression on her face, he added with lifted brows, "Well, what would you expect me to say, Carolina? The truth? That I had run away from Reba and her confounded mother and was escaping across the seas to Barbados?"

"Is that true, Robin?" she demanded, hating him for

being so damnably attractive, lounging there in his elegant gray satins with his lazy gaze traveling appreciatively up and down her slender figure.

"It is true, Carolina." He swept her a rakish bow and placed his hand dramatically over his heart. "Or should I call you 'Christabel' now?" he wondered. "Tell me, does anyone here besides Rouge and myself know you to be the Silver Wench?"

She shook her head, but her lips compressed at the casual way he referred to Penny as "Rouge."

"Well, they won't know it from me," he said. "Your sister told me Kells was dead and that you were most probably dead, too—sunk along with Port Royal." His empty gray eyes narrowed. "Now why do you think she told me that?" he asked softly.

Carolina was thinking fast. At first glance Robin Tyrell looked very like Kells—until one looked closer and saw the difference. And he was a danger to them because he knew Kells. At first sight in this unlikely place Robin might not recognize Don Diego as Kells—but if he saw Don Diego with *her,* he was sure to recognize him! She must get Kells away from here before they met!

"My sister is protecting me," she improvised swiftly. "Now that Kells is dead . . ." She lingered over the words.

"I am indeed sorry to hear that you have become a widow," Robin said promptly—but he sounded his usual blithe self, she noted with irritation. "And especially sorry for *you,* Carolina, since I heard just before I left England that elderly Lord Gayle had died. Had Kells lived, you would have been a viscountess. But what brings you to Havana? I could have imagined you storming some European capital with your beauty—*but a Spanish stronghold in the Caribbean?* It passes belief!" He gave her a droll look.

"I am here because I am Penny's sister," Carolina said blandly. "After I lost my home in Port Royal, I sought out Penny, but when Nassau was raided we were both swept up in the net and brought here."

"And what a haul it was!" he said admiringly. "Faith, what enterprising wenches you are! Are there any more sisters at home?"

"Two," admitted Carolina, glad of the diversion from talk of Kells. "And they will neither of them have you, Robin, so don't come beating at their door!"

He laughed. "Ah, you were ever hard on me," he said lightly.

He was abominably cheerful, she thought, nettled that he should greet her so calmly when he was, after all, the cause of all their troubles! "Robin, how could you have done it?" she reproached him. "How *could* you have let Reba's mother bring false witnesses against Kells?"

He grimaced. "You have not been in the toils of such as my mother-in-law," he said with feeling. "She got me so embroiled that I hardly knew what I was doing. I ended up afraid *not* to let her proceed for I could see my head rolling from the block if I did not go along with her plans!"

Yes, Reba's mother was like that, Carolina knew, remembering how the woman had once had her seized and set upon a ship by force. She had been unwilling even to hear what Carolina had to say! Still, she told herself, Robin should have *done something*. It was shabby of him not to!

"But Reba should have—" she began combatively.

He interrupted to say, with a bitter note in his voice, "Reba has become just like her. I think in time they will even look alike!"

Carolina regarded him steadily. She little doubted it was true. She should have seen it for herself.

His gray eyes narrowed. "I cannot but think that you forced the marriage upon me to punish me for impersonating Kells!"

"Well, you deserved punishment," she murmured, but there was sympathy in her eyes. She could very well understand why Robin might run away from the pair of them! "And Reba loved you," she added mildly.

"Love!" He snorted. "She doesn't know the meaning of the word. And her mother thinks to run me about at her pleasure, like a puppet on a string."

Carolina fell silent. She could have heaped recriminations upon him but what good would it do? Robin was what he was; he would never change. He was, as always, looking for an easy way out. And he had found it—by running away.

One of the servants came through the room and looked at them curiously.

Robin stirred. "Your escort will wonder what has happened to you. We had best get back to the party!"

"Oh, I really have no escort," lied Carolina. "Penny asked someone to bring me and he has melted into the crowd by now."

"Then *I* will escort you," he said gallantly.

"Best not," she warned. "The governor's daughter has set her glittering eyes on you and whenever she is crossed she breaks things. We would not want her to advance upon all this food"—she indicated the groaning table—"in a sudden rage!"

The marquess gave her an amused look. There had been a time when he would have changed his life for this bewitching blonde beauty, he remembered ruefully. Ah, well, changing his life would not have suited him—he preferred his rakish ways.

"For Marina's sake"—*and mine as well,* she could not help thinking—"let us go back separately," said Carolina. "I will go first. Give me a little time to mingle among the guests before you follow me." *Time to find Kells and somehow get him hidden from your view!*

She moved back in among the laughing crowd and looked about for Kells. He was nowhere in sight—indeed he was at that moment being harangued in an alcove by Doña Jimena, who had promptly charged him with neglect!

Behind her Robin Tyrell moved inconspicuously into the room, and the music struck up.

Carolina jumped as the first chord struck, for her nerves were honed to a fine point tonight; she was tense as a drawn bowstring.

But the second chord was never struck—the musicians came to a jangling, discordant halt.

For across the room near the entrance had appeared the tall arrow-straight figure of Don Ramon del Mundo. He seemed to be dragging a ragged sailor sporting a heavy growth of beard. Silken skirts had been hastily pulled away from this scruffy interloper, and the governor himself had stepped forward to protest—how they had gotten past him at the entrance, Carolina could only wonder—when Don Ramon's stern voice rang out.

"This man"—he shook the sailor's ragged arm—"was taken but last week from an English ship by one of our galleons, but four years ago he claims he was on another English ship which was sunk by the buccaneer Kells. I have reason to believe that this man Kells is here tonight."

About to seize Don Ramon by the arm and ask him what was the meaning of this invasion of his party, the governor came to an abrupt halt. Kells? *Here?* He looked around him in dismay.

Among the guests there was a sudden murmur and everybody fell silent, turning expectantly toward the bearded sailor. The musicians let their instruments hang limp in their hands. The servants, moving about, were agape.

"Look about you!" cried Don Ramon, his tawny eyes flashing as he spoke. "Do you see Kells among this company?"

"Yes," came the growling response. "I do see him!"

Carolina felt the world whirl dizzily about her. Her knees buckled and she fell to the floor in a dead faint.

THE HOUSE ON THE PLAZA DE ARMAS HAVANA, CUBA

Chapter 31

When Carolina came to, she was being deposited on her own bed in Don Diego's house on the Plaza de Armas.

"I brought you home," he was saying solicitously. "I liked not the way you fainted. It was indeed oppressively hot but still . . ." He let the words die away as he looked at her keenly.

Carolina saw that they were alone in the bedchamber. "I heard a man cry out that he saw the buccaneer Kells among the company," she said faintly. "I thought"—she was still quivering with fright—"I thought they had discovered you."

"Can you not take it in," he asked impatiently, "that I am not this fellow Kells? I am in truth Don Diego Vivar. And since you will soon become my wife, Doña Carolina, I think you might begin getting used to it!"

Carolina had no faith that she would ever become "Doña Carolina." "Who—who did they identify as Kells?" she questioned but she had a sense of fatalism even as she asked it.

"I was some distance away and heard only the commotion," admitted Don Diego. (In truth he had been almost at the opposite end of the house, closeted with a scolding Doña Jimena, who had sought to know in strident whispers why he was so cruelly neglecting her.) "I saw no one taken. But when I came back, you were lying on the floor, surrounded by ladies fanning you, and I heard someone say that the guest of honor had been accused of being a buccaneer and that Don Ramon del Mundo and the governor and the guest and someone else had gone into the governor's private office to sort things out."

The guest of honor. . . . That would no doubt be Robin Tyrell, Marquess of Saltenham. She had not known the ball was being given in his honor. Perhaps it was not. What Don Diego had heard might have been a garbled version.

She had a sense of doom. Robin had been taken; he would tell all within the sound of his voice that Kells was dead, and his source for knowing that would be herself. She wondered when they would come for her.

Luz and old Juana, evidently sent downstairs for water and wine, appeared in the doorway and she fell silent, letting them minister to her.

She was seeking for some excuse to send one of them back to the governor's palace—and she found it when she realized she did not have her mantilla.

"I seem to have lost my mantilla, Luz," she told the serving girl. "Would you run over and get it for me? And while you are there, inquire what happened. There was some kind of commotion and in the heat I fainted."

Luz brightened. She loved to be in the thick of things. She came back to report that the guest of honor had been accused of being a buccaneer but the governor had taken both him and his accuser aside, and the

Englishman had retorted with such heat that the man was a liar that the governor believed him and the accuser had been taken away by Don Ramon del Mundo, back to El Morro, whence he had come.

"Thank you, Luz," said Carolina, sipping her wine and feeling suddenly much stronger. "You did an excellent job of hemming my gown," she added graciously. "I will recommend your work to my sister for I know that you would like to return to the governor's household."

Luz looked pleased. Carolina watched her go. She felt she was standing on an unprotected beach in the way of a storm spreading out on a long front and about to reach her. There was nothing for it but to wait and try to ride it out.

Don Diego was watching her searchingly. He, of course, could have no idea that the governor's guest would instantly recognize him if they were seen together.

She could only hope that the Marquess of Saltenham would be leaving soon—and that she could hold Kells at home until he went.

Kells was studying her, she saw, as she looked up. "I think you have been under too much strain," he said, frowning, and she realized that he was referring not only to her sudden fainting spell but to her constant references to him as Kells.

"Yes, I have," she told him, for she had a feeling that it was all out of her hands, that fate was going to decide the issue for her one way or another.

"You should rest," he decided, and with his own hands helped her undress. But although her nakedness tempted him—she saw that heat in his gray eyes—he did not try to stir her to desire. He cradled her in his arms and gave her an affectionate kiss on the forehead, then lifted her up lightly and settled her on the big square bed. She might have been a child, she thought, whom he held in affection, for tonight there was nothing of the lover in his manner—only the friend.

She lay beside him, wakeful and watchful, through the long night, and at last, just before dawn, fell into an exhausted sleep.

She insisted upon getting up early to breakfast with Don Diego. He looked every inch the Spaniard, she thought, so relaxed and easy in his dark Spanish silks, his bronzed face as swarthy as that of any Spanish *caballero*.

He conversed easily in Spanish with Luz, who brought their breakfast and looked more kindly upon Carolina than she had at any time since she had been plucked from the governor's household and sent against her will to serve next door.

He fits well here in Havana, Carolina admitted to herself reluctantly. *He must have fit very well back in Salamanca, where he learned his Castilian Spanish and his ease with Spanish ways.* Of course, he was an easy adapter. He had carried off the part of an Irish buccaneer in Tortuga with aplomb—and never been challenged. She had asked him questions about what he knew of what he believed to be his "old life" back in Spain, and she had learned that he was a bachelor, that his family were all dead, that he came from a small town and had by an act of heroism saved the life of a prominent member of the King's council—a gentleman who had since died. He had never been at Court; few knew him. If she had not come along, he could perhaps have settled down happily in Havana—perhaps have eventually married the governor's daughter although, knowing his restless nature and taste in women, she doubted it. But pondering now, she thought that perhaps her fears for him if he went back to Spain were unreasonable. It was her own presence here that endangered him. No one had guessed this dark Spanish gentleman to be the notorious Kells—it was the English marquess in his gray suit, that color of which Kells was so fond, who had been denounced.

I am disturbing him, she thought sadly. *I am trying to make him reconstruct from his shattered memory a life he once had and does not now desire. I am trying to bring him back to me as he was—not as he is now. It could pull him apart.*

Luz was pouring their strong black coffee. Its aroma mingled with the scent of bougainvillaea in the courtyard. The sun streamed down near their table, shaded beneath the gallery behind the pillars.

"They have arrested the governor's guest of honor," she told Carolina importantly.

Carolina, poised with her cup in midair, set it down very carefully upon the table. Her world seemed to spin out, and time stood still. Nearby the fountain tinkled, but she felt for the moment as if she had left the world of Havana and journeyed back in time to the events that had brought her here. She felt as if it had all been predestined long ago.

"That's interesting, Luz," she heard herself say.

"You aren't eating," remarked Don Diego suddenly, a few minutes later.

"I am never hungry this early," she remarked vaguely. "But I have just remembered—I promised Penny I would go over there this morning after breakfast. She is having a new dress made and wants my advice." She rose. "I hope you will excuse me if I am not back for lunch—Penny is such a stickler about these things. Every quarter inch of hem becomes a crisis!"

Don Diego looked at her in some surprise; he seemed to recall a woman called Rouge who slouched about in men's clothing, looking seductive but hardly fashionable. "You look a little pale," he observed. "Do not stay out too long in the sun."

"Oh, I will not," she promised. *For little sunlight filters into the depths of El Morro. . . .*

She turned to take a last wistful look at him as she went out, for this might be the last time she ever saw him. Those who sought El Morro had sometimes looked their last upon the world. He was so handsome sitting there, watching her with a worried look on his dark face. So handsome, so virile—and so *Spanish.* And now that the Marquess of Saltenham had been arrested, it was unlikely that anyone—even marking the resemblance—would give the matter a thought.

He was . . . not safe, he would never be safe while she was around to conjure up thoughts of buccaneers . . . but *safer.*

She left the house and went as fast as she could to El Morro. It took an effort of courage to enter there, for so many of those who entered this grim fortress upon the rock never left it—at least never left it alive. Frightening stories had circulated in Tortuga about what happened to Englishmen unfortunate enough to end up there.

She told herself firmly that that was before Ramon del Mundo had commanded the fort. Squaring her slim shoulders, she walked resolutely up to the nearest guard and asked to see the commandant.

"Who seeks him, señorita?" asked the guard politely, for this slender imperious lady in black riding clothes was evidently an aristocrat.

"Tell him it is Doña Carolina," she said, tossing back her fair hair, and found herself led down tortuous, echoing corridors into what indeed must be the "heart" of this stark abode.

The guard left her and she felt tense, keyed up, as she waited. For she must be a consummate actress this day if she was to convince a man as clever as Ramon del Mundo.

She had not long to wait. Don Ramon bounded into

the small room, looking dramatically alive against the grayness of the old stone walls.

"Doña Carolina!" He bowed gracefully, but his tawny eyes when he looked up were full of curiosity. "What brings you here to my fortress?"

"I would speak with you alone," said Carolina.

He ushered her into a plain room whose grim gray walls were alleviated by velvet hangings. The furnishings were sparse and heavy. He beckoned her to a seat at a sturdy table and poured for her a glass of fine Malaga.

Carolina sipped her wine. She found it hard to begin. *Perhaps it is always hard,* she thought, *to begin a conversation that will surely end in one's own death.*

"I think I have been unkind to you, Don Ramon," she said suddenly. "I led you on—and then I hurt your pride."

He winced. "Why did you lead me on?" he asked curiously.

"Because I found you attractive." There was no point in not admitting the truth.

He sat straighter. "So you found me attractive. . . ." he murmured.

"Yes. In Port Royal and again here. My spirit needed solace. I was wrong to seek it in your arms."

"No," he said gently. "You were not wrong there. I am afraid I did not give you much solace."

"You—helped," she said. "But—I had another life before I met you, and I am still swept forward by that life. We are all of us swept along—I think you understand that."

He nodded. "Yes, I understand that very well. But what is it that brings you to El Morro?"

"You have a prisoner here," she said steadily, and took another long sip of wine. "You took him at the governor's palace. Last night."

"You wish to see him?"

"No, I have no need to see him. I know very well who he is."

"Ah-h-h . . ." He said it on a long sigh. He leaned back suddenly in his chair, toyed with his glass as he watched her with those tawny eyes. "And who is he?"

"He is Captain Kells," she said.

He was still toying with his glass, still watching her. "He swears that he is not. He swears that he is Robin Tyrell, Marquess of Saltenham, an English peer."

"He is very persuasive," she said. "I understand that last night he had the governor believing him."

"That is true." He leaned forward, a hunter on the scent. "But why would *you* wish to denounce him, Doña Carolina?"

She was ready for his question, ready with her lies. "Because word is already circulating about the town that I am the Silver Wench."

He frowned. "Such word has not come from me."

"No, I am certain it did not. But Captain Avila knew it."

"He had hardly stepped ashore before he was back at sea. He cannot accuse you."

"All those aboard the *Ordeal* knew it."

"And they are in El Morro—under *my* command. You need have no fear from that quarter."

She sighed. "Some of Captain Avila's officers knew."

He was silent, for this was bad news indeed. The Silver Wench was too famous a figure not to be implicated with Kells. It was different with Rouge—she was merely a notorious woman from New Providence who had consorted with pirates, a colorful figure but of no real importance to the Spanish authorities. But Kells had been so long a thorn in the side of Spain. He had sunk their galleons, raided their coasts—his name rang like steel throughout the Caribbean. Taking him at last was a triumph that would be toasted all the way to

Madrid. But the Silver Wench was alleged to have sailed with him aboard the *Sea Wolf,* to have assisted Kells in his plans against Spain. She would have to be arrested. Ramon del Mundo drummed his fingers upon the table top that served him as a desk. He was thinking. He looked up suddenly.

"Did you tell the guard who you were?"

"Only that I was Doña Carolina."

His face cleared. "Then there is no need to condemn yourself alongside this buccaneer. These walls have no ears, and I will deny that we ever had this conversation. Be gone from here and no one will be the wiser."

"Many are already the wiser. Word of who I am is spreading about the city. I heard it today being whispered among the servants. It is only a matter of time until the governor hears."

He flashed her a grim smile and she was reminded how young and wild he had looked in the tropical night outside Havana—and how attractive. "If you are arrested, Doña Carolina, you will be brought here to me. And"—he spread out his hands—"you will contrive a miraculous escape, perhaps the first, from El Morro. It will add to your fame!" he promised sardonically.

"I do not wish to bring you to your death, Don Ramon," she chided him.

"You will not do that," he told her with some amusement.

This conversation was not proceeding quite the way she had intended. Carolina moved restively.

He saw her hesitation and leaned forward. "Do you wish to flee the city?" he asked bluntly. "Is that why you have come to me?"

"No—oh, no." She spoke quickly, perhaps too quickly.

He sat back, considering her through narrowed eyes. "What, then?"

She swallowed. "I was not even sure that I would

make it here before being arrested. One of the servant girls hates me, and I think that even now she may be whispering in the ear of the governor." She tried to make her voice quaver. "I was seen by many coming here, and I doubt not that when I step forth from the fort I will be dragged before the governor and accused."

The dark face before her seemed devoid of expression now. "So what is it you wish from me?" he asked silkily.

Carolina made a slight appealing gesture. She looked very feminine sitting there, very vulnerable. She was well aware of it. "I wish you to intercede for me with the governor, Don Ramon. There is no doubt I will be arrested once they know that I am the Silver Wench. I am certain to be brought in to identify your prisoner. I thought that if I came forward now, perhaps I could avoid the fire."

He sat back thoughtfully. Self-preservation was indeed a mighty goad. He had seen men denounce their wives, mothers their sons, daughters their fathers.

"I am surprised you do not wish to see him," he murmured.

"I saw him last night," she countered. "Do you not remember that I fainted when that sailor said he recognized Kells?"

"I remember that you fainted. I was not sure then that that was the reason. You did not seem to be near the fellow at the time."

"I had just been talking to him in the dining room, which was empty and gave us privacy."

"And Don Diego allowed this tête-à-tête?" he asked curiously.

"Don Diego was occupied elsewhere. Someone had claimed his attention. I saw Kells and slipped away." She thought she had it all down very pat.

"There is great danger in your coming forward to

admit you are the Silver Wench," he warned. "And if this man is truly Kells, he must love you and he would not wish you to endanger yourself."

"No, no," she said impatiently. "I thought you understood. I cannot face a future of running and hiding, so I am doing this to preserve my life. By coming forward now, I can hope for clemency."

He rose with decision. "I will take you to him."

Ah, that was no part of her plan! She lifted a trembling hand as if to ward him off. "I—I could not face him now," she said in a stumbling voice. "I could not bear the look on his face—knowing that I have denounced him."

"You will have to denounce him in person," he insisted in a steely voice. "Face to face."

"I will do it," she said faintly. "But not today—please not today."

He stood staring down at her. "Say tomorrow morning before witnesses? Before the governor?"

She nodded. There would be an outburst from Robin Tyrell, but she would carry it off somehow. And he was a wily fellow. He would manage somehow to bribe his way out and make his escape—she had complete faith in the marquess's ability to maneuver. Not that he didn't deserve to hang in Kells's place for had he not masqueraded as Kells some four years ago, she and Kells would be living in Essex now, bringing up their children!

"You look very tired," he murmured, and there was compassion in his eyes. "I would not put you through it now."

"That is good of you," she said. And rose to go.

"I have heard a rumor," he said suddenly, "that you are to marry Don Diego Vivar. And certainly you looked like a bride last night."

The slight quiver of her shoulders gave her away.

"Well, is the rumor true?" he pressed.

"No," she said unhappily. "The rumor is *not* true." The moment she had dreaded was upon her. And now for the big lie, the one she must make Ramon del Mundo believe. She dropped her head. "Oh, I must tell you the truth, Ramon," she whispered. "You were right about me. I do love Don Diego. I had thought Kells was dead, but now he is back and if he were to go free, he would find a way to come for me, to seize me—not all the guns of El Morro would keep him from me!"

"*I* would keep him from you," he said mockingly.

"Ramon, you could not! You do not know him!" She twisted her hands together, hoping he would believe her.

"Perhaps I should keep you here," he challenged. "For your safety!"

"Oh, Ramon, I know you could hold me here," she said on a note of soft appeal. "But I hope you will allow me to return home and call upon the governor in my behalf. There might not be clemency . . ."

She knew there would not be. He knew it, too. But neither of them spoke of that.

Instead she said pleadingly, "I may have no future, but by your charity I would spend this last night with Don Diego." Her eyes were misty. "Good-by, Ramon."

She turned to go but his light laugh shocked her. She stiffened, turned back to face him.

"What an actress you are!" he said admiringly. He reached out, caught her hand, and held it lazily. "*Querida,*" he said softly. "I had already guessed your secret. The resemblance did not escape me, even though I chose to arrest the wrong man. I know who the real Kells is."

A great stillness fell over the room. Carolina's head lifted and her eyes were calm. There was no longer any need to dissemble. Now at last was the time for truth.

"Yes," she said. *"You* know and *I* know. *But Kells does not know.* He is a man of fierce loyalties. When he was an Englishman his loyalty to England was unshakable. Now that he believes himself to be a Spaniard he is just as loyal to Spain. I told him who he really is—and he forbade me to speak of it. Oh, Ramon." Her voice was wistful. "All I wanted was to give him back his world, the life he once knew. But it seems that all I can ever give him is unhappiness. To him I am a heretic and a buccaneer's woman."

To a godless buccaneer, she was a heretic! And a buccaneer's woman indeed—*his* woman, that very buccaneer's! At another time Ramon del Mundo, man of the world, could have found humor in her recital. But today, looking into that beautiful lost face, he could find no laughter in his heart—only tears.

"He has done me the honor to fall in love with me twice—once as Kells and once as Don Diego." She tried to smile and almost succeeded. "But I wrecked his life once *and I will not wreck it again!"* Her voice had gone fierce. "So tomorrow morning I am going to swear before all the world that the Marquess of Saltenham is really Kells, and who will not believe it? When the accusation comes from the Silver Wench of Port Royal! And Kells goes free and the marquess, who brought him to this pass, can take his chances."

"They will hang you together," he said softly. "Unless of course they save you for the fire."

She winced. "Perhaps I deserve the fire," she muttered, "for what I have done to Kells."

He caught both her hands, as if to make her his prisoner here in this gloomy fortress of El Morro, where he alone commanded. His dark face was intense, his voice held an urgent appeal.

"Carolina, forget all this—run away with me! There is a galleon in the harbor—the *El Dorado."* Carolina looked at him thoughtfully, for she had seen that great white and gold ship on her way here. "Her captain and her crew will be drunk tonight, for there are festivities in the town. The captain and his officers will be attending a party given in his honor—there will be only a skeleton watch to guard the ship. Here in the dungeons of El Morro are the captain and crew of the ship that brought you here—the *Ordeal.* I could release them, I could find them a longboat. It would be an easy matter to overpower the watch on the *El Dorado.* We could sail away on that white and gold vessel, Carolina. We—"

"Sail where?" she cut in sadly. "To Spain where I would be found out, for I am, as you say, conspicuous? To England where you would doubtless be turned over along with your ship to the Spanish ambassador, who would get in touch with Spain and have us both burned by the Inquisition? To the Dutch who would not have us? To the French with whom my people are at war? Oh, no, Ramon, there is no place in this world for us." She studied him wistfully. "If I had met you before I knew Kells, loved Kells . . . but I did not. And in any case, it is too late. For the Marquess of Saltenham will not go to his death easily—he will fight for his life. He will ask questions and it will dawn on him why I have done this, why I have accused him falsely."

"Yes," he agreed. "That *would* occur to a man."

"And he is most marvelous persuasive."

"You seem to know him very well," he said sadly.

She caught her breath. She had not expected that question. "I am sorry, Ramon. But I do know Robin—*very* well. He is not to be trusted and you should not feel sorry for him. He masqueraded as Kells and sank English ships. It is because of Robin that we are here instead of living in comfort in Kells's country seat in Essex." Her voice was bitter. "Were it not for Robin Tyrell and his cursed mother-in-law, Kells would be a viscount and I would be a viscountess. But because of their lies, Kells could not return to England to take his rightful place and was driven back to buccaneering!"

Ramon del Mundo's tawny eyes widened. It had simply not occurred to him that the dauntingly lovely lady before him might be wife to an English peer.

He frowned. "But surely there must be some other way than for you to—"

"Robin Tyrell is eloquent," she cut in with a sigh. "He will persuade everyone within the sound of his voice that Don Diego is the real Kells. And with what can Don Diego refute him? With a past he cannot remember because it never existed? And so the trap would close on him, Ramon. He would be in its jaws without ever knowing who he really was—or why I loved him so much!" No need for Don Ramon to know what she had told Kells! "He would go to his death crying honor to God and Spain. I cannot let it happen, Ramon. Surely you can understand that."

His grip on her hands tightened.

"I understand that you are my captive here in El Morro," he said evenly. "I understand that if you disappear tonight, no one will know where you have gone. I understand that much!"

"If you think to carry me away against my will," she said slowly, "I promise you this: I would hate you forever." Her silver eyes flashed him a challenge. "Is that what you want?"

He winced. She had struck on the one flaw of his whole scheme. He would have given up everything for her—position, honor, his future, but—he wanted her regard, he wanted her to love him.

"We are all of us trapped," she said soberly. "And we cannot get out. Mine is the only way, Ramon. I will denounce the marquess."

You will die beside him, he thought unhappily.

The thought was unspoken but it must have shown on his face for when she next spoke it was on a note of sadness. "And when I am gone, Kells will forget me. He will—with your help, Ramon—become that true *caballero* of Spain that he seems today. And you, too, will forget me, *querido.*"

The soft sound of that caressing word *"querido"* went through him on a long tremor. "*I* will not forget you," he said huskily. "I will never forget you."

A bittersweet smile passed over her lovely mobile features. "You think that now," she said gently. "But time heals much. I wanted to die when I thought Kells was dead in Port Royal, but I think that in time I would have wanted to live again. And if I had met you—say a year or two hence, who knows? It will be the same with you, Ramon. You will find some pretty lady who cares for you as I care for Kells and you will forget all about me."

He wished it could be so, but he knew in his bones that it was not. He would never forget her. He would carry her memory with him always.

Still holding her wrists, he sat and looked at her. He could see her as she would look tomorrow, fragile and determined, standing before the governor and pointing a finger at the Marquess of Saltenham and denouncing him as Kells. Pounding nails into the marquess's coffin with every word.

He could see her as she would look later, when they had hanged the marquess and consigned her to a fiery death. He could see her high on a stake above the moaning, praying crowds at the *auto-da-fé,* with the orange flames licking her body and sending her fair hair up in a bright pyre.

His hold on her hands loosened.

"Go, then," he said dully.

She paused. She bent and pressed a gentle kiss upon his forehead. He closed his eyes and fought against the desire to seize her, to hold her here, to shut her up like a bright bird in this fortress and fight the world for her.

But she had spoken truly—she would hate him forever if he did. And he would not be able to bear the sight of her mourning Kells. Even the knowledge that she was mourning him would be a rowel to his heart.

Don Ramon del Mundo, gentleman of Spain, turned away from her and closed his eyes that she might not see the bright tears that shone in them.

"Good-by, Carolina." He said it softly and was never sure later that he had said it at all. Had he really said it, or was he only saying good-by to her silently in his heart?

She was gone when he opened his eyes. He could see the hem of her black riding skirt just disappearing through the open doorway.

When he sank back to his seat at the heavy wooden table, he felt old. It was as if his youth had gone blithely through that door into the corridor, following the beautiful reckless woman to whom he had given his heart.

And then with a great sob he dropped his head to his hands and his lean body rocked in silent misery.

He loved the woman who had just departed. And he knew that by letting her pursue her present course he had just consigned her to the flames.

After a while he sat up and poured himself another glass of wine. As he drank it, the story of the jaguar and the woman came back to haunt him. Carolina's own words rang through his head, danced behind his eyes. *Because she was beautiful and brave—and she was only protecting her own. . . . I could not let her die for it.*

The jaguar had been ready to die for her cubs. Just as Carolina was now ready to die for the man she loved. Or die beside him.

If only *he* could have been that man! Don Ramon's

heavy sigh was brought up from the depths of him. This splendrous woman of light had entered into his blood.

A few minutes later he set the glass down hard and stood up. His expression was very resolute.

Carolina was only protecting her own. *He could not let her die for it.*

Chapter 32

Carolina returned to the house on the Plaza de Armas with a sense of destiny. She would hurl her life away. She would not let Kells die for her—going against everything he now believed in. Because of her folly he had lost his king's pardon. Because of her he had been forced back into buccaneering. Because of her caprice in sending away the necklace he had lost his chance to become a planter and so had nearly died in Port Royal, a circumstance that had resurrected him a Spaniard. *She* was the instigator of the long chain of events that had brought him to this place and to this desperate pass.

And tomorrow she would pay for it—she and the Marquess of Saltenham.

She must explain it all to Penny, she must make her understand. After all, someday Penny might be reconciled with the family again. In any event, Penny could explain everything to Virgie—no, Carolina would write a letter to Virgie and she would ask Penny to guard it with her life and to somehow get it sent to Essex. Penny was very resourceful—she would find a way.

She sat down and swiftly penned a letter.

"Dear Virgie," the letter began. *"I must make you understand what has happened to Rye and why it is probable that you will never see him again."* She went on to explain, adding, *"I am sorry to do this to Robin Tyrell, for I think he once loved me in his way, but it is the only way I can save Kells."* She scratched that out and wrote *"Rye"* firmly over the name *"Kells." "I think it best that Mother not know of this—or Sandy Randolph. Fielding would not care. But I would prefer Mother to think of me safe and rich and happy in some far place—just let her go on believing that, Virgie. And I wanted you to know all this for another reason, too. Robin—the Marquess of Saltenham—has told us that Rye's father is dead and that Rye is now Lord Gayle. But in effect Rye has died, too, for he is now another person, and I hope and pray that as Don Diego Vivar he can find happiness and the safe peaceful home that I—with all my mistakes—have prevented him from having for so long. So Andrew can safely claim the title and you will be Lady Gayle. My conscience tells me that what I am doing to Robin is wrong, but my love for Rye tells me that what I am doing is right. I will never see you again and it may be that I will not live past tomorrow, but I hope you will find it in your heart to forgive me for bringing another man to his death to save Kells."* Again she scratched out the name and substituted *"Rye."* The parchment was blurred with tears. She signed it hastily, *"Carolina,"* and sealed it with red sealing wax.

Then she went to find Penny.

She found her in the governor's courtyard, well concealed by palms, sitting thoughtfully with head in her cupped hands and her elbows resting on her knees.

"I want you to see that Virgie gets this," Carolina said solemnly.

"Well, how am I to give it to her?" demanded Penny.

"You will eventually escape from this place. Or at least gain some neutral territory where a letter could be given to a reliable sea captain whose voyage touched England."

"That is probably true," sighed Penny. "But if I escape, so will you. Did you know they have arrested Robin Tyrell?"

"I know they have arrested the Marquess of Saltenham," Carolina said through stiff lips.

"Oh, don't be so formal," mocked Penny. "After all, you and Robin were *quite close* for a time!"

That was one thing she *hadn't* told Penny! Carolina felt her color rising. "Anything Robin told you about me he probably made up out of whole cloth!" she said airily.

"Oh, I do hope not!" laughed Penny. "The story is too delicious not to be true. Making love there on the black sands beneath that great volcano in the Azores!"

Carolina gave her a worried look. "Now about the letter—" she began hastily.

"Oh, stop going on about the letter. Anyone would think you were making your will! Hang on to the letter and take it to Virgie yourself."

"I—won't be able to," said Carolina.

"Carol." Penny peered at her. "Are you ill? Are you coming down with a fever?" She felt her sister's forehead. It was quite cool. "What is wrong?"

"Nothing. I just see things clearly—at last." She paused and moistened her lips. "I'm sorry about Robin—I could see you liked him."

"Oh, nothing will happen to him."

Carolina's silver-gray eyes widened. "Why not?"

Penny shrugged. "Oh, because he'll manage to get a stay of execution until proof can be brought from England. And it won't be slow in coming. After all, he has a wife there."

"*And* a vicious mother-in-law," said Carolina. "They should bring *her* to Havana. Perhaps she'd be shipwrecked along the way!" Her voice was bitter.

Penny looked up sharply. "I can see you're upset," she said. "Very well, give me the letter. I promise to guard it well. I'll sew it into my bodice."

"Use careful stitches," advised Carolina.

Penny laughed. That throaty laugh that so intrigued men.

And Carolina went back to walk through the rooms of this last of the houses that she and Kells had shared together and contemplate the last of her life.

It was there that Penny found her, in the big front bedroom.

"I won't let you do it, you know," she said.

"You read the letter," gasped Carolina. Somehow she had not expected Penny to do that.

"Of course I read the letter," Penny said scornfully. "When you come to me babbling that you won't be able to deliver it yourself and all that rot? *Of course* I read it!"

Carolina moistened her lips. "Then you know what I am going to do."

"I know what you're *planning* to do, but of course I'm not going to let it happen."

"Penny," said Carolina soberly, "once I have admitted before all the world that I am the Silver Wench, nothing can save me. And Robin Tyrell goes with me."

"Oh, you can go to your death if you're fool enough to want to." Penny's voice was contemptuous. *"But you're not taking Robin Tyrell with you!"*

That set Carolina back on her heels. "You mean you're in love with Robin?" she gasped. *Oh God, that complicated things! She had never once thought . . .*

"I don't know whether you would call it love exactly, but *I want Robin*—and I intend to have him." Penny was glaring at her.

Carolina passed a hand over her forehead. At the moment she felt torn and confused. "Penny, if I *don't* do it—"

"Then the trail leads back to Don Diego," Penny said ruthlessly. "And the truth!"

"It's because Robin impersonated Kells when he sank English ships that we're in this mess!" defended Carolina. "Kells let Robin live because I begged him to, and *then* Robin turned on him with lies—"

"That was his awful mother-in-law!"

"I don't care *who* it was! Robin went along with it. It's because of him Kells couldn't return to England, it's because of him Kells was hurt, for if Robin had stood by his confession we'd neither of us have been in Port Royal for the earthquake. If anyone deserves to die, it's Robin!"

"Oh, come along, be your age!" Penny's voice was impatient. "I wouldn't mind if Robin confessed again to what he'd done—but back in England. Not here, not where he'd die for it. They might kill him just for lying about being the King's emissary. And you seem to forget, no one has accused Don Diego of anything!"

"But they will!" cried Carolina desperately. "Robin will accuse him—the moment he sees him."

Penny thought about that. She gave a fatalistic shrug.

Carolina could see that her sister was shucking off the problem. Perhaps because she was in love. She made a last attempt to make Penny understand. "Penny," she wailed. "I don't want to *hurt* Robin, I just—"

Penny's malicious smile flashed. "Hurt Robin?" she echoed scornfully. "I doubt you could bring yourself to do so, you're so squeamish! *I* might, but not you. Have you thought what it would be like to stand there, watching them hang him? For I have no doubt they'd insist on treating your tender eyes to that spectacle!"

Carolina shivered and closed her eyes. She had not

got that far yet in her mind. Indeed she had not reached past the accusation stage. Now silently she asked herself if she could do it. *Really do it.*

"But I must do it, Penny!" she burst out. "Can't you understand? Kells is hurt, his memory is gone, he may never recover. I can't let him be led blindly to his death, believing he's somebody else! Oh, Penny!" Suddenly she saw a way out—for Robin at least. "After I denounce Robin, *you* can sway the governor. After all, you're sleeping in his bed!"

"Not while he has an attack of the gout!" Penny said cynically.

"But *afterward,* you can talk to the governor, you can persuade him that killing Robin might precipitate an English attack on Havana itself, you can get him to arrange an escape!"

"For Robin and you?" Penny asked slowly.

"Not for me, I don't ask it!" cried Carolina, for she could see that Penny was considering the possibility. Across from her those sapphire eyes were narrowing in thought.

"An escape, not for you—just for Robin. . . ." mused Penny. Suddenly the corners of her mouth curled in wry amusement. "You really are the little martyr, aren't you, Carol? And what do you think your precious Don Diego will be doing meanwhile? Do you think for a moment he'll let you perish upon the gallows or at the stake?"

Oh, God, there was that! Carolina's face went a shade paler. *She had forgotten that Kells would try to save her. And if they spirited her away to Spain, he would undoubtedly follow—and die for it.*

"But it's all a wild dream," Penny mocked. "Because I won't let you do it—any of it." She turned to look out the window, and took a step toward it. "I think I see Don Diego coming now." She flung the words over her shoulder at Carolina. *"Or should I call him Kells?"*

Carolina swallowed. She had tried to enlist Penny's support—and failed. Now she must put her original plan into execution. She would make one last appeal to Don Ramon. She would ask him to put Don Diego under house arrest on some trumped-up charge, to keep him from knowing . . . until it was too late. And once the supposed "Kells" and his real Silver Wench were gone, a grieving Don Diego would recover, he would come to believe he had been briefly bewitched by a scheming beauty, he would forget the rest, forget *her.* Indeed in time he might marry the governor's daughter, or perhaps Jimena if her rich husband should conveniently die, and live out his life as a Spanish grandee!

A little sob escaped Carolina's lips. Penny, intent on what was going on outside, did not notice. She stood at the window, staring out.

Feeling as if all this was happening to somebody else, Carolina moved toward the window. Toward Penny. On the way she picked up a heavy iron candlestick. She brought it down in a glancing blow against the side of Penny's head. In horror, she watched Penny's tall handsome frame crumple, then she bent over her—thank God she was still alive, the force of the blow had only stunned her!

Swiftly she stuffed a gag in Penny's mouth and tied her hands and feet together with a piece of hemp. She could hear the clatter of Kells's boots on the stairs and she made haste to drag Penny under the big square bed and to pull the coverlet down so that Penny's body would remain concealed.

She had just straightened up when Kells came into the room.

"A strange thing happened today," he said, and she could see he looked disturbed. "I *remembered* something. It was just a flash but I seemed to see *you.* You were wearing a dress I'd never seen before, some kind of red silk trimmed in black lace and we were *quarreling.* We were standing in a second-floor room for I could look out through the grillwork at the masts of ships in the harbor."

Carolina felt a long quiver of pain go through her. He had remembered their quarrel that last evening before he went away. She *had* worn the red dress. And they had been standing in their bedroom in the house on Queen's Street a block from Port Royal's waterfront.

"Did you—remember anything else?" she asked tensely.

"Well, bits and flashes," he said. "The strange thing was that I seemed to be wearing English clothes. I remember I had on gray trousers. And we were speaking English, too." He ran his long fingers through his hair. "There was something else. I seem to remember a boy, too. It must have been a long time ago for I was shorter. I remember he ran toward me and he was calling, 'Rye, Rye!'" He shook his head as if to clear it. "There seemed to be no one else around and certainly no rye fields. It was forest country and there was a stream. I called to the boy. I called him 'Drew.'"

"Andrew," she murmured. He had remembered his brother when they were boys in Essex. She said, "I must see to something downstairs," and ran from the room. In the courtyard below she leaned dizzily against one of the round pillars, hanging on to it for support.

Rye was remembering. Soon he would remember that he was Kells the buccaneer.

Oh, God, what was going to happen now?

"Carolina." Kells's voice was calling her.

Reluctantly she went back upstairs, her mind in turmoil. He must *not* remember in bits and pieces, not now—it would only increase the dangers threatening him.

"You look pale," he commented.

"I—it must be the heat." Her legs seemed to give way under her and she sat down abruptly in a chair by the bed.

Kells was looking at her intently. He remembered it now—it was coming to him by bits and flashes but he remembered it all. He remembered sailing from Port Royal, leaving an angry, discontented Carolina behind him. He remembered the seemingly endless voyage, the frustrations, wanting to get back to her. He remembered the battle with the *Santo Domingo* and the other galleon, remembered cursing as his boots ripped apart at a crucial moment in the battle and nearly cost him a sword thrust in the body—the leather came apart and caught on something on the slanted slippery deck. He remembered his ship's doctor coming to him with a dead Spaniard's boots, tossing them down before him with a laconic, "Best change to these or I'll have you in my surgery!"

He remembered tugging the boots on, surprised that they fit. *And it was those boots that had brought him here!* He remembered bringing the damaged *Sea Wolf* into port under oars. He remembered how Port Royal's waterfront had seemed to disintegrate before his eyes, the forts at both ends crumbling and sliding into the sea.

He remembered thinking, *Dear God, what of Carolina?* And then his ship had been snatched up as if by giant hands and hurled into the town, riding over the rooftops, shearing off chimneys as it went. He remembered being suddenly airborne and seeing something—perhaps a piece of falling timber from one of the other ships that were riding the wave, crashing into the town with him. He remembered flying into it, and then his world had splintered into a thousand pieces.

He had waked up in a comfortable bed in the governor's palace in Havana and he had remembered nothing—his past was a blank page with nothing written on it. He might have been born in that bed, looking up at the quiet servants who scuttled in and out bringing broth and tall lime drinks.

And they had told him he was Don Diego Vivar, sent to the New World by the King of Spain. *They had divined all that from his boots!* From the boots he had inherited from a dead Spaniard after winning the battle with the *Santa Domingo!* For the boots were so unique as to be the means of recognizing the wearer in a foreign place—as indeed Captain Juarez had recognized him! And the orders sewn into the lining were meant for Don Diego's eyes alone.

He felt awed as he thought about it. Some special Providence must be watching out for him to let him live through such a shattering chain of events!

And now that same Providence had brought Carolina to his side and placed her in deadly danger. . . .

"Carolina," he began. "I remember—"

"No," she interrupted unhappily. "You remember nothing. I have lied to you, tricked you. You are exactly who you told me you were—Don Diego Vivar. Soon you will remember *that,* Diego, and you will forget all the rest."

"Well," he said, marveling. "This *is* a change of tune!"

"It is true," she said. "I have bewitched you."

He stared down at her. "Why do you tell me this?"

"Because Kells—the real Kells—has returned," she answered him simply. "And he has been caught, arrested. I will die beside him."

She kept her voice steady but, oh, how deep the cut, that in these last hours of her life she must renounce this man before her—renounce him to save his life!

"To die beside him?" His frown deepened and he seized her shoulders. "I will not allow it!"

She gave him a wistful tormented look. "There is nothing you can do to prevent it," she said softly. "Buccaneers are hanged in Havana and I am a buccaneer's woman—I freely admit it."

"You are *my* woman," he growled. "And I would have you remember it."

There was a faint groan from beneath the bed.

Kells swooped down and lifted the coverlet. "But this is your sister!" he cried, amazed.

"I know," said Carolina calmly. "Leave her there until I can think what to do with her. There must be some way to get her off this cursed island!"

"But what—"

"I struck her down with this candlestick when she told me that she was going to save Robin Tyrell at all costs. I could not allow her to interfere."

He stared at her. "Are you then so set on death?"

She gave a short laugh. "It would seem that death is set on *me*. But I would die beside the man I love—you cannot deny me that, Diego. I would never forgive you."

"And the man you love is Kells?"

"Yes." It hurt her in her soul that practically her last words with this man she loved must be to renounce him, but there was no other way. "Yes. I love Kells. I have always loved Kells. I sought to find him in you—it was all a trick. You must learn to think of it as a bad dream and of me as a wicked woman who almost dragged you down with her."

"And all this so that I can—"

"Live on in Havana and take your rightful place here. You will be happy here, Diego, if you will forget all that I ever told you. Forget me and be happy."

"First let us take this gag from your sister's mouth," he said, skillfully removing it.

Having been dragged from beneath the bed, Penny

looked up at Carolina with baleful eyes. "What did you hit me with?" she demanded, wincing as she put her hand to her head.

"With this." Carolina indicated the candlestick. "And I would do it again for the same reason, so have the good sense to be quiet."

Penny subsided, looking amazed.

"I am trying to decide how to get you safely off the island," Carolina told her.

"Safely off the—faith, you take a great deal upon yourself, little sister!"

Carolina gave her a bleak look. "Do not cross me in this, Penny. Your loves are light loves—you have said so yourself. And I love but one man: *Kells, who even now is masquerading as Robin Tyrell, Marquess of Saltenham.* Yes, that is the truth, Penny, regardless of anything I may have told you."

"But—" began Penny. "The letter—"

"It is the truth and I would have you believe it!" said Carolina warningly. She had reached out and was caressing the iron candlestick as she spoke.

Penny was familiar with what caressing a weapon was likely to mean. She edged away from Carolina.

Kells was watching this charade. He knew nothing about any letter but even without knowing, it was all perfectly clear to him. Carolina—his own dear Carolina—was out to save his neck at all costs. Even at the cost of her own. It brought a lump to his throat to realize it. And a grim determination to save her, whatever the odds.

"Rouge," he said in a voice of authority—and he was addressing the wench of Nassau now and not the aristocratic long-lost Lightfoot daughter. "I am going to untie your feet now. Try to resist your obvious urge to kick me to perdition!"

"No, don't untie her!" cried Carolina. "She will bring ruin upon you!"

"So that we will understand each other, Rouge," he added pleasantly, "my name is Kells. I saw you once upon the beach in Nassau." He reached down and untied her bonds.

"Yes, Carolina told me about that." Penny sat up, kneading her ankles. She gave Kells a curious look. "Tell me, have you known all the time? If so, you should be appearing upon the stage for you have fooled everyone!"

"No, my memory has just come back to me," he told her vigorously. "In time, I hope to get us all out of here."

"It is perhaps a bit late for that," said a cool masculine voice from the doorway.

Carolina and Kells both whirled. Kells's hand fell to the hilt of his sword.

Don Ramon del Mundo stood there framed in the doorway. He had come up the stairs with catlike silence. Now he stood jauntily, in perfect possession of himself, surveying the scene through faintly mocking tawny eyes.

"I found your front door standing open," he observed by way of explanation of his sudden appearance.

"Yes, I suppose I must have left it open," said Penny, rising in a lithe gesture. She touched the side of her head gingerly and turned to give Carolina a reproving look.

"Don Diego—" began Don Ramon in a courtly tone.

"Let us understand one another," said the lean buccaneer silkily. "My name is Kells. And from the look in your eyes as you came in, I think you already know that."

"You are right, I do," was Don Ramon's cheerful rejoinder. He was remarkably debonair, thought Carolina in amazement. A very different fellow from the man she had left brooding in El Morro.

"And I suppose that you will now say that you have

come to escort me to El Morro to replace a certain Englishman?" Kells's voice was ironic.

"No, I have come to deliver a gift to a lady." Don Ramon's gaze played over Carolina.

"Indeed? And what gift is that?" came the cold voice of her buccaneer, who was even now figuring that with his sword out, a single spring could bring down the commander of El Morro.

"Her life," said Don Ramon simply. He held up his hand at the sudden stillness in the buccaneer's face. "Do not ask me why I do it." He sounded suddenly weary. "I think I do not know myself. But I cannot let the lady burn at the next *auto-da-fé*. And she would surely burn if I allow her to carry out her foolhardy but"—his eyes softened—"selfless plan."

"If you seek to send me away," said Carolina, divining what he would most likely say next, "I warn you that I will not go without Kells."

"No, I did not imagine that you would." Don Ramon sighed. "But I would be rid of all of you. Faith, I will clear the English out of El Morro and out of Havana at a single blow!" He gave a wry laugh.

"The marquess, too?" cried Penny. "You would free Robin, too?"

Don Ramon nodded. "I would free him as well. It is not my usual style to send a man to his death for what another has done."

"But he—" began Carolina, and Penny shushed her.

"Let good enough alone, Carol," she warned. "Remember, Robin is a king's favorite. If his life is spared—and if you let him believe that it was Kells here who saved him—why would he not ask for a pardon from a grateful king for the man who saved his life?"

"He would not do it," Carolina said bitterly. "He buckled before. When Reba and her mother get at him, he will buckle again!"

"Not if *I* take charge of him!" Penny said lightly but

there was a look in her dark blue eyes that Carolina had not seen there before. "If Robin lacks backbone, he can use mine. I assure you that *I* will not be put off by his wife or his mother-in-law!"

The two men were listening in some amazement to this frank interchange between the two women.

"Penny, you could do it!" Carolina cried joyfully. "*You* could make Robin keep his word! But"—she gave her sister a troubled look—"you can only be his mistress, you will never be his wife. Reba and her mother will see to that!"

Penny shrugged her handsome shoulders. "Who knows?" she said philosophically. "I want Robin now, but I may not want him forever!" Her wicked grin flashed. "Perhaps I will find me a royal duke. Or even"—those shoulders moved in a slight swagger that accentuated the generous curve of her breasts—"a king!"

"I little doubt she might," murmured Kells, and Don Ramon raised his eloquent brows.

"So are we managed by the ladies," he said mockingly. "I will take warning."

"And well you might," Carolina said warmly. "But I thank you from the bottom of my heart for giving me—for giving all of us our lives back again. May you not suffer for it!"

He shrugged. "The *El Dorado* lies waiting in the harbor. Tonight she will have but a skeleton crew. Tonight there will be an unfortunate fire in El Morro which will command the attention of everyone. Many prisoners will be released—and some among them"—he gave Kells a mocking look—"might at one time or another have been buccaneers. I little doubt that you will know how to take the ship, how to ease her out of the harbor, how to sail away in her!"

Kells gave him back a grim look. He little doubted it either.

"Ramon." Carolina stepped nearer to him. "Ramon, I—" Her throat seemed to close with emotion.

"There is no need to speak, Doña Carolina." Don Ramon del Mundo's gaze upon the blonde beauty was caressing. "I do this of my own free will—and I think that I will like myself the better for it."

Silent, but with gray eyes glinting, Kells the buccaneer strode forward and gripped his erstwhile enemy by the hand.

At that moment he could find no words to express his feelings either.

In Havana harbor by starlight a great white and gold ship was moving, easing along, manned by desperate men who had taken her in darkness and wanted to see home again. The *El Dorado* was moving out to sea on the strangest mission she would ever undertake—the returning to England of a motley crew of English and American sailors and buccaneers, and a little group of aristocrats who stood on deck, watching silently as the ship moved under the guns of frowning El Morro, and then slid by, unchallenged.

They moved on into the velvet blackness of the night.

Kells looked back at the silent guns of El Morro, a mighty fortress atop the cliffs flung up in dim silhouette against the sky.

"I have made my peace with Spain," he murmured. "I do not think I could bring myself to go against the dons again."

Beside him Carolina, who *knew* why those guns were silent, felt her eyes grow misty. She had brought him peace at last, her turbulent lover. She turned and looked back, too. And of a sudden she blew a kiss to old Havana and to the man who stood frowning over the guns of El Morro, keeping them silent while the *El Dorado* safely carried the woman he loved from Havana harbor. She hoped he would find happiness, and joy—and arms as warm as hers to comfort him. She wished him long life and strong sons who would grow up to be men as good as he; that was her wish for that "man of the world" who—had there been no Kells—she knew she could have loved with all her heart.

Rye's thoughtful gaze scanned El Morro's uprearing bulk, grown hazy in the distance.

"Carolina," he said. "If aught should happen to me, there is a man who loves you back there in Havana."

"I know," Carolina said softly. "I know that, Rye." She dashed a tear from her eye. "I must start calling you Rye again and not Kells for you have left that life behind you."

"Yes." He still looked back toward that dark fortress, fast fading from sight, and saw there a gallant enemy with whom he would never cross swords. "It is over, Carolina. All of it."

"Not quite all," she murmured, moving closer against him so that her warm hip touched his thigh. "We have brought something away from it—from that world."

He looked down at her tenderly, this miracle of a woman he had found, and knew that it was true. Their love had come through it, untarnished and bright. That slender thread of love had endured so much—it had crossed the wild seas yet it had suffered no sea change; it had endured near-death and violence and jealousy, all the woes of the world had sought to wrest it from them and yet it held them still together by its gossamer unseen strands.

He stroked her hair tenderly, loving every strand.

"Carolina, Carolina," he murmured huskily. "What have I ever done to deserve you?"

It was a golden moment, a moment to remember. But Carolina, after all the fear and strain that had besieged her in Havana—yes, and the doubt, too—was suddenly in a playful mood.

"Oh, come now," she rallied him teasingly. "We have enemies who would say that we deserve each other!"

"No man could deserve you," he said softly against her ear. "But you have my promise—given as we slip away from death—that *I* will endeavor to do so."

His words had moved her, but still she mocked him.

"All this for a woman who was so recently your slave in Havana?" she asked flippantly.

His voice was rueful. "Well, I am now *your* slave," he said. "And will prove it every day of my life."

A wonderful warmth flooded over her. They had been through so much—together and separately. And they had come through it all—together.

She cast a look behind her. The great fortress of El Morro had vanished, and from just above where it had been, a single star winked in the velvet night. A guiding star that would lead them through this night and across this trackless ocean . . . together.

Always.

Nearby Robin Tyrell, Marquess of Saltenham, studied Carolina and her sister. Two spirited women so alike in many ways—and yet so very different. And his feeling for them was different, too. Carolina was a bright star—but she shone in someone else's heaven. Carolina had made him wistful to be what he was not.

But Rouge—and that was the way he thought of her, as "Rouge," not "Penny," as Carolina called her—Rouge set him aflame. He desired her in an aching physical way that ground in his groin. For Carolina his heart had ached, but Rouge he must have—whatever the cost.

And she knew it. It was in the warm beckoning smile she now turned upon him, in the silky luxuriousness of her movements as she stretched slightly and then leaned upon the ship's rail, presenting her eloquent woman's body to best advantage.

He groaned.

It seemed to him that women had always ruled his life—and now here was another! Worse, another destined to play a role in it that no one else ever had, a dominant role. God, he knew that he would follow after her like a dog, panting for her favors. He, Robin Tyrell, Marquess of Saltenham! It was degrading. It was—

"Come along, Robin," said Penny, noting his steady regard. "There must be some place more private on this ship than the deck!"

The light in her eyes was unmistakable, her smile promised everything.

"We'll find a place," he assured her hoarsely—and hurried forward, following her.

Carolina turned to watch them as they went. A woman like Penny, she mused, could hold even a rake like Robin in line!

"I rather think that Robin's the slave!" she laughed.

"As I am yours," chuckled Kells, sweeping her up in his arms as he spoke. "Command me as you will!"

The silver eyes looking up into his sparkled. She was very like to do it!

"Oh, Rye," she whispered, snuggling down into his arms as if to remain there forever. "We are safe. We will make it home this time. All the way to Essex."

Rye Evistock, gentleman of Essex, who never again would be called Kells, looked down at her tenderly. She was so lovely, this vivid girl of his, so touchingly trusting and yet so brave and wise. It made him humble to realize how gallantly she had fought to save him these past weeks and how willing she had been to throw her life away for his sake. It told him more than any words how very much she must love him. Carolina would always tempt other men—that he knew. But—she would always find her way home.

To his arms.

The buccaneer and his lady were on their way home at last.

And so I end my saga
Of those who loved and sinned
And left their footprints on the sand,
Their lovesongs on the wind!

EPILOGUE

An Essex lady now she rides along the Essex ways
And turns her radiant face away from other stormier days
When as the Silver Wench her fame was every buccaneer's pride
And made the fair wench Christabel a wild sea rover's bride!

It was late spring and a sultry air hung over northern Cuba. Cane rats gnawed the young cane in the sugarcane fields that would someday make good Cuban rum. The cathedral bells, clanging all over the country, were calling dark smiling dons and mantillaed ladies to mass.

But at the entrance to Havana harbor a miracle had happened. That great white and gold ship, the *El Dorado,* had sailed in from out of nowhere, flying the red and gold banner of Spain.

The guns of El Morro boomed a welcome and were quickly followed by a salute from the Punta and—a little slower—by the guns of La Fuerza.

It was Spain's ambassador to England who came ashore—came ashore beaming, for had he not returned that greatest of galleons, the *El Dorado,* at last to Havana?

In the white city that day, with the sun gleaming upon the white coral limestone and glinting upon the red tile roofs and the black wrought iron of balconies and grilles of the rococo buildings, all was wonder and excitement.

The ambassador was received in state in the governor's offices in the frowning fortress of La Fuerza—and then, when the governor learned of the ambassador's mission here, he was carried away almost at once to the governor's "palace," that big attractive house that fronted the Plaza de Armas, for wine and discussion.

"But such a thing has never happened before!" cried the governor, urging excellent Malaga upon his guest.

His guest, tired of shipboard life after his long voyage from London, looked around the pleasant courtyard in which they sat.

"I know," laughed the Spanish ambassador ruefully. "But, then, I think that we have never had a buccaneer such as Captain Kells before! He has a certain style, this buccaneer! He flaunts our laws, he seizes our ships at his pleasure—and now at the end of his career, he sails one to England and graciously sends it to Havana—bearing gifts."

"Bearing gifts?" The governor could not believe his ears. He poured more wine into his guest's swiftly drained goblet.

"Near half a shipload of French wine for your excellency," said the ambassador. "I am given to understand—France and England being still at war then—that the wine was captured by happenstance on the journey to England." His lips twisted in a wry smile. "This particular buccaneer distributes his largesse as he sees fit. He sends word that not only did you offer him and his lady your kind hospitality in Havana"—here the governor choked and had to be patted on the back; the ambassador's eyes gleamed wickedly for he was a worldly man—"but you, by the 'lending' of this great ship, gave him a comfortable journey back to England to redeem his lost honor—and not only that, but a chance to strike a blow for his country against the French, who were harassing English shores!"

"I never *lent* him a ship!" gasped the governor.

"No, I am sure you did not, but the impudent fellow chose to put it that way. Your wine cellar," he added meditatively, "will be none the worse for all this good Bordeaux."

Indeed it would not! The governor, a fancier of fine wines, felt himself brightening. "The ship is undamaged?" he asked nervously, for he felt he could be called to account if she were not.

"Undamaged indeed," affirmed the ambassador, who after the coolness of London was feeling the heat of tropical Havana. His host recognized that and signaled for a servant to fan him. With cool air from the swaying palm-leaf fan blowing over him at last, the ambassador sighed and relaxed. "I bring other gifts as well."

"Other gifts?" exclaimed the governor. *"Madre de Dios,* this buccaneer must consider himself a king!"

"It would seem he was an unofficial king in the islands, this Lord Admiral of the Buccaneers," agreed the ambassador dryly. "But these gifts are in the most part from his lady."

"The Silver Wench," murmured the governor, shaking his head.

"Lady Gayle," corrected the ambassador. "It would seem that Kells was but a name Rye Evistock used for buccaneering ventures, and now that his father is dead he has inherited the title of Lord Gayle. He is a viscount. Lives in Essex."

The ambassador's head swam. How they did things in England was beyond him! "You mentioned gifts from his lady?" he inquired weakly.

"Yes, they are being carried ashore now. And I was to deliver messages with each. One is for your daughter —a rose jar, and I was to say that it is hoped this rose jar finds her in better temper and that she will hurl it at no one—that she is far luckier than she knows."

The governor gasped. "Impudent wench!" he muttered.

"You will ask me what the message means." The ambassador spread his hands. "I do not know.

"There is a handsome black mantilla and high-backed comb for someone called Juana, who is, I believe, in your service—with the wish that she wear it in church and be as elegant to look at as any great lady of Spain. Oh, and another half shipload of fine French wine for one Captain Juarez for saving Kells's life in Port Royal and bringing him here."

The governor shook his head dizzily.

"And there are gifts for one Don Ramon del Mundo. Kells—Lord Gayle—sends him a sword with the hope that it may never be crossed with his in battle. And Lady Gayle sends him the finest white lace mantilla I have ever beheld, which she says was found on the ship and belonged to no one. She wishes him to know that she wore it on the voyage home to England and expresses the hope that he will give it to his bride on her wedding day—and that he will find the lady of his heart."

"Yes, yes." The governor collected himself. At first he had thought that this buccaneer had bribed del Mundo to keep the guns of the fort silent while he slipped away in the *El Dorado*, for the fire that night in El Morro combined with the escape of all the English prisoners had been, to say the least, suspicious, but in the light of *these* gifts—so trifling by comparison to his own rich haul—he was now of a different opinion. For he now remembered that del Mundo had shown an interest in the Wench—indeed he and Don Diego had nearly crossed swords over it. A peace offering merely. His opinion of del Mundo went up—he might choose to bestow his daughter on the man after all!

Don Ramon, receiving his gifts in silence from the hand of the ambassador later that day, was of a different opinion.

"A fine blade," he commented, studying the sword, which was a miracle of Spanish workmanship.

"The finest workmanship I have seen," agreed the ambassador. "I believe he said he 'liberated' it in the raid on Cartagena."

Don Ramon del Mundo fingered the sword. A handsome gift, indeed, and in its way symbolic. For Don Ramon knew that he could never cross swords with the man who had sent it—not that he would not kill him willingly enough, but he could not do it because it would bring *her* sorrow. And he thought that the erstwhile Don Diego had sent him this sword because he felt the same way. *She* loved Kells—but perhaps a small part of her heart belonged to Don Ramon as well, and in this way she had made peace between them. It was Kells's way of saying, *You saved my life, but I know it was because of her.*

He looked up at the ambassador, his face inscrutable.

"He sent a further message, but it is a letter, under seal. You will see that I have not opened it."

Frowning, Don Ramon took the parchment and broke the red wax seal that secured it. What he read was scrawled in a careless hand across the single sheet of paper.

"If ever you find yourself in an English jail anywhere, let me know and I will get you out."

It was signed with a flourish, *"Kells."*

It was a buccaneer's way of saying thank you. Don Ramon laughed.

The ambassador's curiosity was piqued. "Might one know what was in the letter to cause mirth?" he wondered.

"Just an exchange of friendly insults," shrugged Don Ramon—but he set the corner of the letter into a candle flame and watched it burn nonetheless.

"And his lady sends you this." The ambassador spread out the mantilla before Don Ramon, sheer and white in the candlelight. "She said she wore it on the voyage home to England."

Don Ramon del Mundo—that man of the world—fingered the lovely mantilla. So she had sent him something she had worn, something she had touched—it was a bond between them, saying something more than mere words could express, sending him an unspoken message across the sea: *I might have loved you. . . . In other times I* would *have loved you. . . .*

He held it up, studying it. Sheer—but not so sheer as her silken skin. White—but not so white as the gleaming brilliance of her blonde hair in the sun, its pale glow by moonlight. Intricate in pattern—but not so intricate as the web of thoughts he had spun about her, lost in a maze of desire. . . .

"She says she sends it to you in the hope that you will bestow it on the lady of your heart to wear on her wedding day," explained the ambassador.

Del Mundo looked up. For a moment there was a lump in his throat and he could not speak. He had found the lady of his heart—but he could never claim her for she belonged to someone else. But he would wish her well, far away across the sea.

"She was a most wondrous lady, who sends me this," he said huskily.

"I know for I have met her," the ambassador said softly. For he noted that del Mundo had spoken in the past tense—it was in its way a renouncement.

Don Ramon did not hesitate. He sat with the mantilla across his knees for half a night while he drank himself insensible on Bordeaux wine from the new shipment which the governor had been pleased to give him. For the governor had decided that it would be best to pass Marina into strong hands that could take care of her rather than give her into the keeping of some foppish son of a merchant prince—and besides, she *fancied* Don Ramon, had ever since Don Diego and the marquess had left the scene.

Don Ramon had come to Havana a fortune hunter, intending to win in this New World fame and glory and with it go back to Spain and make a great marriage. He had found instead true love—and the governor's daughter.

And now, staring moodily at that mantilla—lovely reminder of the beauty who had worn it—he resolved to seek Marina out.

He found her next day sitting bored in the courtyard of the governor's palace on the Plaza de Armas, her *duena* snoring nearby.

He ignored her arch look.

"Querida mia," he said whimsically, for he was still slightly drunk. "You deserve a better man than myself—you deserve someone who will truly love you."

"But I do not want a better man!" Marina wailed, for she had already made her choice. "And if you do not love me now," she added stubbornly, "you will *learn* to love me!"

"No." Don Ramon smiled his regretful refusal. "You deserve someone who will not need to *learn* to love you, Marina. You deserve a dashing *caballero* whose heart you will enchant at first sight."

"No!" Marina, who was not used to refusals, leaped up and stamped her foot. She had shouted so loudly that her *duena* woke up with a start, crying, "What? What?"

And Marina won the day, for after a month or two of languishing, Don Ramon del Mundo—that man of the world—remembered his original purpose in coming to Havana.

He returned to the courtyard and proposed on bended knee to a beaming Marina.

And so it was that the governor's daughter, a little older now and much more slender (having lost what her father had been pleased to call her "baby fat"), wore the white mantilla, gift of the Silver Wench, when she married the valiant Don Diego del Mundo in the lofty echoing interior of the great twin-towered cathedral behind the Plaza de Armas.

All the bells in Havana rang that day in uncontrolled joy.

But on nights when the moon rode pale across Havana's skies, nights when the fleecy clouds shimmered fair as Carolina's long light hair, nights when the stars shone as silvery and as beckoning as Carolina's eyes, Don Ramon del Mundo, possessed at last of a wealthy bride, sat quaffing his wine in the courtyard of his fine new home in Havana and remembered a woman of moonlight who had swept across his life like a bright wind.

He would always remember her. . . .

Port Royal, struck first by hurricane and then by the new more awful disaster that dropped the city into the sea, was never really rebuilt.*

---

*A fragment of the old town survives upon the sandspit that once provided a haven to the buccaneers, but Kingston, a white city against a backdrop of blue hills, now has taken the place once occupied by the old port. The olive-green waters where the ruins lie at ocean bottom only grudgingly give up their secrets, but underwater explorations almost three hundred years later would prove the exact time of the first great shock to strike the doomed city—for divers brought up a watch, and when the coral encrustation was cleaned away, the watch was found to have been made by one Paul Blondel of Amsterdam, a Huguenot refugee, and X-ray showed it to have stopped at seventeen minutes before noon on the fateful day.

But to Carolina, safe at last in England, riding out in velvet riding habit and plumed hat to call upon her Essex neighbors, it was of little consequence that she had been witness to—indeed a part of—one of the great catastrophes to strike the Western World. She heard with a shudder that what was left of Port Royal was still sinking, and heard, too, a year after the disaster, that the new town of Kingston was being built on what was considered a safer location on the nearby mainland. But she never cared to return to Jamaica. The world she had known there was gone—swallowed up by the blue-green waters of the Caribbean.

There were reminders, of course—and Hawks was one of them.

The pardon Kells had won from the King included a pardon for his men. And so it was that he sent to Kingston, for Hawks to come and join him in Essex.

Hawks arrived in England looking as laconic as ever, and with his rolling sailor's gait unchanged. He brought with him a large hoop to which clung a perpetually astonished looking red and green talking parrot he had affectionately christened Poll—and a surprise gift for Carolina:

Moonbeam.

"Oh, Hawks, where did you find her?" Carolina gasped, opening the wicker basket in which Moonbeam had cowered during most of her voyage—for she still hated the sea.

"I found her clinging to a branch in the mangrove swamp," Hawks told her. "I went there with some men who were looking for somebody's sister who was washed away the day of the quake and they wouldn't give up looking for her. And I could hear a cat crying. I floundered about for a while and then I found her—I don't know how she got there but there she was!"

"Oh, Moonbeam!" Smiling and damp-eyed, Carolina gently drew the cat out from the wicker basket in which she had remained during the rolling voyage. She held her up in the air joyfully. "Welcome to Essex, Moonbeam!"

The cat, grown thin from her misadventures, began to purr, and when Carolina set her down, after a couple of token rubbings against her ankles by way of greeting, she set off determinedly to explore the gardens and hedges of her new domain.

She settled down happily to make her nighttime trysts in boxwood hedges instead of streets made up of coral sand—and Virginia was later to claim proudly that there wasn't an estate in Essex that didn't boast of having one of Moonbeam's kittens!

The fluffy white cat of the adventurous life was to become even more famous, for it amused Carolina to train Moonbeam—who was nothing loath—to sit primly on a chair at the long dining table at dinner, being served a small portion of each course along with the family. Moonbeam thoroughly enjoyed the whole ritual—although she steadfastly turned up her dainty nose at the *salades* and took only halfhearted laps of dessert. She would sit in queenly fashion meeting the amazed gaze of Carolina's dinner guests with a level look from her glowing green eyes. "It is a look," Virginia was heard to whisper irrepressibly, "that says 'I am a buccaneer's darling—I have even survived Port Royal's sinking into the sea!'"

"As has her mistress," murmured Virginia's brother-in-law fondly, eyeing his beautiful wife down the long table as she merrily engaged the rapt attention of both a duke and a belted earl. As he watched, Carolina threw back her lovely fair head and her laughter rippled. Her heavy emerald necklace flashed against the pale smooth skin of her bosom and her white satin gown was the most elegant in the room. She was every inch the viscountess tonight, he thought—and after dinner not a man but would vie to propose a toast to her eyelashes. He who had so long been known as Captain Kells had been proud of her when she had dazzled first Tortuga and then Jamaica—he was even more proud of her tonight.

Carolina had indeed melted effortlessly into the easy ways of the Essex gentry. To a marveling Virginia, she seemed to have forgotten the old days in Port Royal.

There were nights when she dreamed about it of course—restless nights when she found herself back again, strolling sandy tavern-lined streets full of swashbuckling men, listening to the squawk of brilliant macaws and red and green parrots like Poll, hearing the clash of cutlasses and women's strident laughter. Nights when she tossed on her handsome English bed and felt again the seductive lure of the tropics and worried that Kells was off on some dangerous mission from which he might never return.

It was wonderful at those times to wake with a start and turn over in bed and see Kells's dark hair gleaming in the moonlight beside her on the elegant goose-down pillow, his strong features relaxed in sleep . . . wonderful to touch reassuringly that long lean masculine body and feel a sudden rush of joy that after all their harsh experiences they had at last won through.

In time she bore him a son, a wild youth who became a swashbuckling adventurer like his father and ended up marrying the greatest heiress in England—for love alone. And a daughter who grew up to be—almost—as beautiful as Carolina, and who broke half the hearts in Essex.

Just as the news of Carolina's miraculous escape from Port Royal had been reported the moment she heard it, the news of each of those births was hastily reported by letter, penned by Carolina's older sister Virginia to Level Green, and caused Letitia Lightfoot —on the birth of Carolina's second child—to take ship for England alone, Fielding having no desire to accompany her despite her pleading. She would travel via Philadelphia, visit briefly with old friends, then on to England to spend the summer there visiting her daughters and her grandchildren. That summer found Sandy Randolph gone from Tower Oaks. His leaving preceded Letitia's by all of two weeks—indeed he left rather ostentatiously from Yorktown on a ship bound for New York. But there were those who whispered that Sandy's ship made an unscheduled stop at Philadelphia, that he met Letitia there and that they voyaged to England together across the windswept seas.

However that was, nobody was ever able to prove anything, and no word reached Fielding Lightfoot, engrossed in improving his handsome plantation.

That summer when her mother visited Essex was a summer when Carolina sent word to all that she was "indisposed" and never entertained. But there were reports of a handsome pair seen galloping through her stone gateposts to ride the leafy Essex lanes—a woman with flashing dark blue eyes and a man whose hair was as white-gold as Carolina's own. Both of them voyaged back to Virginia—again by way of Philadelphia—and arrived in Yorktown on separate ships, so no one was ever the wiser. But Aunt Pet thought that Sandy Randolph's handsome face had lost a little of its melancholy after that long sojourn away from the James, and that Letitia returned looking very satisfied. Indeed there was a hint of springtime laughter in her voice that brought a glint to Fielding Lightfoot's eyes when she greeted him at Yorktown after a voyage over wintry seas.

"Two of our daughters have found safe harbor,

Field," she told him contentedly, brushing snowflakes from his handsome bronze greatcoat after he had swept her up in a bear hug.

"And you, Letty," he said with a wry look at her wind-whipped, fur-lined violet velvet cloak and matching fur-trimmed hat, "have found as usual all the latest fashions."

Letitia laughed, that light confident reckless laugh that he had found so bewitching in the days of his courtship. "I'm *laden* with them, Field!" She nodded gaily at the big trunks straining men were carrying after her through the lightly falling snow.

"Then we're for home, Letty!" Fielding nodded toward his waiting river barge.

Anyone watching them that gray winter day (and many sharp eyes in Yorktown were doing just that) would have testified that Letitia's homecoming was—amazingly—a triumph.

Publicly and often, Letitia, looking her imperious best in her new London gowns so hastily bought, stated that her daughters Virginia and Carolina were both well and happy. Of her eldest daughter Penny, reported to be unrepentantly roaming the Continent with her married lover, the notorious Marquess of Saltenham, Letitia forbore to speak—and even the brashest of Williamsburg gossips were too intimidated by those challenging blue eyes to question Letty Lightfoot about the young "hussy" she had bred!

But when news reached Williamsburg that, amid a wild scandal, the Marquess of Saltenham had divorced his wife and married his mistress—in London no less!—there was more excitement at Aunt Pet's brick house on Duke of Gloucester Street than either of Letitia Lightfoot's younger daughters could remember.

"Penny got him—at last!" marveled Della, her eyes round with envy, for both young girls knew the story by now of how Penny had led a wild life in the Bahamas and then had capped that by living in sin with a married marquess in London—and practically everywhere else!

"Of course! *I* always knew Penny would win out anywhere!" declared Flo, who was growing up to be almost as beautiful as her older sisters. "And I certainly don't believe that wild tale that Penny actually won enough money gambling at whist with the King of Naples so that the marquess could pay off his debts and cast off his rich wife!" she added with spirit. And then more cautiously, "Do you?"

"Oh, no, of course not!" was Della's hasty rejoinder. "Although . . ."—she dimpled—"I *do* remember that Penny could always beat everyone we knew at cards! Do you really think it happened, Flo? I'm not even sure there *is* a King of Naples, are you?"

The blue eyes across from her sparkled. "Well, if there is one, I'm sure Penny found him."

"And left him the lighter in the region of his purse!" crowed Della, tossing a big pink cabbage rose into the air and catching it expertly.

Among a shower of flying rose petals both girls regarded each other with glee, for Penny's wild adventures had been a source of great delight to them, trapped as they felt they were in the more demure world of the Tidewater.

"And you know what this means?" demanded Flo, her voice quickening. "It means we'll not only be visiting London and Essex, we'll be visiting Hampshire too, for isn't Hampshire where the Marquess of Saltenham has his seat?"

Della nodded dreamily and set her teeth into one of the drifting rose petals. "And we'll be invited everywhere since we'll be related to viscounts and marquesses, so you and I should both end up with dukes!"

"Oh, at the very least." Flo shrugged, shaking out her long hair, which she had just washed, to dry it in the sun. "And we'll both live in great castles and command large staffs and"—she giggled—"we'll tell absolutely everyone awful lies about life in the Colonies and how we all run around exclusively in moccasins"—she glanced down merrily at her smart red heels—"and they'll believe every word!"

Both girls collapsed with laughter. They were sitting on the grass in Aunt Pet's side garden, shielded from passersby on the street by a white paling fence and some boxwood that managed almost to shut out the view. Their light skirts lifted with the breeze to display their pretty knees, but neither of them seemed to notice or care. After gloomy mutterings about financial ruin, their father had one day become—mysteriously it seemed to them—wealthy again. It had happened very suddenly after a certain sea captain had visited Level Green, bringing with him a pair of cheap pattens, a gift from Carolina. Almost immediately their father had paid off all his debts, their mother had gone about smiling fondly—even upon her enemies—and they had all begun to spend money as blithely as if there were no tomorrow.

Now their mother, a year after her summer spent in England, spoke with open affection of Carolina, and Fielding, hearing her, no longer seemed to mind. His only glowering was reserved for Sandy Randolph, whenever that gentleman rode up with aplomb, elegantly attired, to pay a cousinly call on the Lightfoots of Level Green.

"It's too bad," sighed Flo humorously. "I had really hoped to elope to the Marriage Trees just to uphold the family tradition, hadn't you? But now that our older sisters have married into the nobility, we may have to give that up!"

Della again collapsed with mirth, rolling on the grass. "We'll just have to be content with dukes!" she gasped when she could speak again.

From inside Aunt Pet's checkerboard brick house, Letitia Lightfoot peered out in disapproval at her hoydenish daughters.

"They are too much like Penny and Carolina," she sighed. "I don't know what will become of them, Petula!"

"Say rather that they are too much like you, Letty!" was Aunt Pet's tart rejoinder. "For we both know where your daughters get their wildness!"

Letitia did not demur.

They *were* both rather like her, those wild ones, she mused with secret pride: Penny and Carolina—oh, especially Carolina! And being like her must have been rather a cross to bear! But they had both won through—indeed they had more than won through, they had triumphed!

And so I end my saga of a love that would not die
But fought its way across the seas 'neath many a
stormy sky,
And in a toast to Christabel and her wild love,
I quench
My dust-dry throat that yearns to tell
More Tales of the Silver Wench!

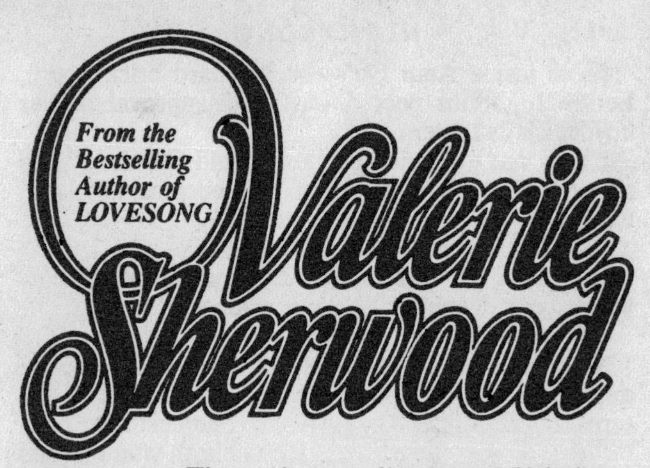

The excitement lives on as Valerie Sherwood brings you a breathless love story in her new tantalizing trilogy. Sherwood first captured the hearts of millions with LOVESONG a sweeping tale of love and betrayal.

And the saga continues in WINDSONG as you are swept into exotic locations full of intrigue,. danger, treachery and reckless desire.

____ LOVESONG 49837/$3.95
____ WINDSONG 49838/$3.95
____ NIGHTSONG 49839/$3.95

POCKET BOOKS

POCKET BOOKS, Department VSA
1230 Avenue of the Americas, New York, N.Y. 10020

Please send me the books I have checked above. I am enclosing $________ (please add 75¢ to cover postage and handling for each order. N.Y.S. and N.Y.C. residents please add appropriate sales tax). Send check or money order—no cash or C.O.D.'s please. Allow up to six weeks for delivery. For purchases over $10.00, you may use VISA: card number, expiration date and customer signature must be included.

NAME ______________________________

ADDRESS ______________________________

CITY ________________ STATE/ZIP __________

947